Praise for *New York Times* bestselling author Maisey Yates

"Fans of Robyn Carr and RaeAnne Thayne will enjoy [Yates's] small-town romance."
—*Booklist* on *Part Time Cowboy*

"Passionate, energetic and jam-packed with personality."
—*USATODAY.com*'s *Happy Ever After* blog on *Part Time Cowboy*

"Yates writes a story with emotional depth, intense heartache and love that is hard fought for and eventually won In the second Copper Ridge installment... This is a book readers will be telling their friends about."
—*RT Book Reviews* on *Brokedown Cowboy*

"Wraps up nicely, leaving readers with a desire to read more about the feisty duo."
—*Publishers Weekly* on *Bad News Cowboy*

"The setting is vivid, the secondary characters charming, and the plot has depth and interesting twists. But it is the hero and heroine who truly drive this story."
—*BookPage* on *Bad News Cowboy*

"Yates's characters are masterfully written with a keen eye for establishing emotional depth...each book [is] like a mini vacation."
—*RT Book Reviews* on *Last Chance Rebel*

In Copper Ridge, Oregon, lasting love
with a cowboy is only a happily-ever-after away.
Don't miss any of Maisey Yates's
Copper Ridge tales, available now!

From HQN Books

Shoulda Been a Cowboy (prequel novella)
Part Time Cowboy
Brokedown Cowboy
Bad News Cowboy
A Copper Ridge Christmas (ebook novella)
The Cowboy Way
Hometown Heartbreaker (ebook novella)
One Night Charmer
Tough Luck Hero
Last Chance Rebel
Slow Burn Cowboy

From Harlequin Desire

Take Me, Cowboy
Hold Me, Cowboy
Seduce Me, Cowboy

Look for more Copper Ridge

Down Home Cowboy
Wild Ride Cowboy
Christmastime Cowboy
Claim Me, Cowboy

For more books by Maisey Yates,
visit www.maiseyyates.com.

MAISEY YATES

Slow Burn
Cowboy

HQN™

HQN™

Recycling programs
for this product may
not exist in your area.

ISBN-13: 978-0-373-80194-7

Slow Burn Cowboy

Copyright © 2017 by Maisey Yates

The publisher acknowledges the copyright holder of the additional work:

Take Me, Cowboy
Copyright © 2016 by Maisey Yates

CONTENTS

SLOW BURN COWBOY   7

TAKE ME, COWBOY   379

Slow Burn
Cowboy

CHAPTER ONE

"ANOTHER CASSEROLE?"

"You're welcome," Lane said, crossing the threshold into Finn Donnelly's house carrying a disposable tin pan that looked like it was full of enough food to feed a small army.

"I can't eat all of this, Lane," he said, watching his best friend's petite form disappear as she made her way from the expansive entry into the kitchen.

"But your brothers can," she shot back.

He followed her path, his footsteps echoing on the stone floor as he entered the kitchen behind her.

"I don't know how long they'll be staying."

His brothers. The entire Donnelly clan was theoretically showing up any day now. To collect an inheritance none of them deserved. Who knew that his grandfather—possibly the most difficult old bastard on the planet—possessed such a sense of fairness from the great beyond?

Finn had dedicated the last twenty years to working on the Laughing Irish Ranch while his brothers had gone off and made their own way. Which was fine by him. At least, it always had been. It was much less fine now that the old man was dead and his three brothers had been left with equal share in a property they had no blood, sweat or tears invested in.

But Finn figured they would come to pay their respects, and then he could offer them monetary compensation and send them on their way.

They'd never been interested in the ranch before. He didn't see why they were acting like they wanted to be involved now.

"I imagine they'll be staying long enough to eat a meal," Lane said, her tone dry. She flipped her dark hair over her shoulder as she opened the fridge and bent down, examining the available space. "I have brought you a lot of food," she said, looking back over her shoulder.

"Yes. A lot."

"Well, most of these dishes you shouldn't have to cook while you're dealing with all of this. But some of them are also the result of my testing various sauces and spices that get sent to me. So I can figure out what I want to stock in the Mercantile."

"Lane of Copper Ridge," he said drily, "the patron saint of self-serving charity."

She made a scoffing sound as she straightened and closed the fridge, then set the pan on the counter before turning away from him again. "No one else is cooking for you, Finn. Because you're a cranky asshole. So maybe you should show a little more appreciation."

She jerked the fridge open again, bending back down and starting to rearrange the contents. She made a little humming sound, her back arching as she reached deeper inside.

He looked at her ass. He didn't even bother to try and stop himself. He had accepted the fact that he was attracted to Lane a long time ago. And around the same time he had accepted that he was never going to do anything about it.

He had a host of reasons for that, all of which he'd spent the past several years reinforcing. She was younger. Her older brother would kill him. But more than that, it just wasn't worth messing with their friendship, no matter how fine her ass was.

Lane was special to him. Important. There was also something fragile about her that he'd sensed from the first, when she'd turned up in Copper Ridge to live with her brother. Finn was the wrong man for fragile.

The first time he'd ever felt attracted to her had come as a shock. Like getting hit in the chest with a bolt of lightning. She'd been eighteen to his twenty-four and he'd been at her and her brother Mark's house for dinner. Mark had gone to bed, citing an early morning, and he and Lane had ended up staying up to watch a movie.

It was a comedy, and Finn could barely remember what it was. But he remembered Lane laughing. It had been the sweetest sound, and it had done something to him. Then she'd leaned up against him and placed her hand on his thigh to brace herself, and that *something* had become abundantly clear.

He'd been so disgusted with himself he'd made a thousand excuses and gone straight home. It had never gone away. Not after that. Not once he'd seen her as a woman.

But it had dulled to a vague ache now, instead of that sharp shock of heat. And that was how it had to stay. Repressed. Controlled.

Given that he'd made his decision early on, normally, he made a show of controlling his desire to check her out. Right now, he didn't see the point. Right now, his grandfather was dead and he was going to be invaded by family that he hadn't seen in longer than he cared to admit.

Right now, his focus was dedicated to dealing with that.

Amid a host of unenjoyable things, he was going to go ahead and enjoy the sight of Lane's ass in those jeans.

"I'm sorry, Lane," he said. "I will try to be more appreciative of the fact that I'm going to die buried beneath a pile of bereavement foods."

"At least you won't die of starvation," she said, straightening and turning to face him, her smile brilliant, her brown eyes glittering. She picked up the casserole pan and put it in the newly cleared space in the fridge, then closed the door.

"Well, that's a small comfort." He crossed the kitchen, making his way over to the sink, pressing his palms flat on the countertop and gazing out the window. The house—which was a giant monstrosity that Finn had never understood, given the fact that for as long as he'd known his grandfather the old man had lived here alone—was nestled into a hillside, overlooking interlocking mountains covered in pine trees that stretched on into the distance until they faded from deep green to a misted blue.

The back of the house faced the ranching operation. The fields, containing herds of dairy cows, and the barns.

His blood, sweat and tears were there. Soaked into the ground, the wood and basically every other damn surface in the place. Like the rest of his brothers he had spent summers here as a kid. Unlike them, when he was sixteen he had decided that he was here to stay.

Finn had never felt anything quite like the peace that came from working his body boneless out in the field. And after a life spent with his volatile mother and completely unreliable father, he had liked finding something that he could control.

If he did the work, he got a result. If he spent the day fixing a fence, at the end of the day he had a functioning fence. It was tangible. It was real.

It completely boggled his mind that his grandfather had decided to give any of the property to the grandsons who had never showed an interest. But there was no arguing with a dead man. Hell, there had been no point arguing with the old man when he was alive.

"Do you want to stay and eat?" Finn asked, now that Lane had put the food away.

"Don't mind if I do," she said. "Of course, I spent most of the day tasting different products that came into the store. I got some pistachio cream from Italy. You have no idea. It was amazing."

He frowned. "What do you do with pistachio cream?"

"Eat it with a spoon? Bathe in it?"

"As long as the food you made me is normal."

She waved a hand. "Normal. Dull. Your palate needs work."

"If loving chicken nuggets is wrong I don't want to be right."

"You'll be pleased to know that the casserole I brought tonight is mostly pasta-based, and is in no way in violation of your steak and potatoes philosophy on food."

"Pasta-based *and* steak and potatoes? That sounds weird."

"I meant that in the metaphorical sense. The metaphor being that you like boring food and it grieves me."

"I think you're adventurous enough for the both of us, Lane."

"Well, tonight I think we're going to have a combination of potpie and pot roast. There's a theme." She took two containers out of the fridge and set them on the counter. "I shall commence warming them."

"Why don't you let me take care of that?" he asked.

Lane arched a brow. "Oooh. You mean I don't have

to microwave my own dinner? And they say chivalry is dead."

"I am a chivalrous bastard, Lane Jensen." Something about the way the corner of her mouth turned up just then caused a tug low and deep in his stomach.

"You're a study in contradictions, Finn Donnelly," Lane said as she continued to assemble the dinner as though he hadn't offered to be the one to do so.

But this was how things went. He took care of everything in her house that she considered to be *man's work*. Any kind of plumbing or wiring issue, arachnid-related concerns and the extermination of the odd errant vole in her yard.

In return, she often took care of things like feeding him, or buying him clothes when she went into Portland or Eugene. He never even had to ask. She just appeared with things. Usually after noticing that he had worn a hole through his boots or something like that.

Basically, Lane was his wife. But with virtually none of the perks a man actually wanted from a marriage.

But, considering he didn't ever want a wife, that was fine by him.

A blow job. Sometimes he would like a blow job. But a friendship was hardly worth detonating over that.

"That's me, a walking contradiction. Complicated and shit," he returned, his voice a little harder than he'd intended it to be.

Due in large part to the fact that he had just been thinking about Lane's lips on his body. Always a mistake. One he didn't usually make.

"Yes, a man of deep complexity. And steak and potatoes," she said, a laugh hovering on the edges of her words.

The sounds of domesticity settled around them, and

he let them wash over him just for a moment. There was something nice about watching her bustle around the kitchen.

Probably because he had never really experienced that growing up. His father had taken off when he'd been little, making a new life with another woman, and for a while with the two kids that had come from that union—Liam and Alex.

After his father had left, his mother had been more concerned with the drama in her love life than dealing with her son.

Finn had learned early on to make peanut butter sandwiches and hot dogs.

Cain, the oldest Donnelly, was from their father's first serious relationship, Finn from his second. His brother Alex had been part of an affair that had occurred around the same time as the marriage to Finn's mother, which put the two of them close in age.

Then Finn's father had left and married Alex's mother and produced one more child, Liam. Making the youngest two the only full-blood brothers in the crew.

Which left Finn with his mother. Until she'd left him too.

Family fun with the Donnelly's was rarely all that fun, for all of those reasons.

He had never really been close to his brothers, for very obvious reasons. And now, they were all going to descend.

"How long has it been since you've seen your brothers?"

"Well, Alex was deployed for eighteen months, and then he went back to base rather than Copper Ridge when he got out. So it's been a couple of years. Probably about the same for the rest of them." He was pretty sure. He didn't keep track. "Hell, I think I talk to your brother more than I talk to any of mine. And I don't even talk to him that much."

She let out a short, one-note laugh. "When you do, can you get more than a one-word conversation out of him?"

"Not really," Finn said, not seeing the issue.

Lane laughed. "He's so cranky."

"That's probably why the two of us get along."

Mark Jensen was one of his oldest friends, and even though he'd moved down to California a few years ago he and Finn still kept in touch.

The two of them had gotten acquainted after high school, both of them young and away from their parents. Mark had moved to Copper Ridge at a young age and taken work on a fishing boat. And Finn had been working the ranch.

Eventually, Mark had moved away and gone to college for a while, but then he had come back and taken on engineering work on the same fishing boats he had started on as a grunt laborer. Finn was still a laborer. In fact, that was what he intended to be for the rest of his life. That was what he liked. There was honesty in it, working the land.

You couldn't bullshit the earth. He liked that. You had to work, and the rewards were merit-based. Sometimes the weather swept in and messed things up, but living on the coast in the relatively temperate Oregon climate and with modern conveniences, that was not the biggest concern for a dairy farmer.

He had good contracts with one of the major dairies in the state, and additionally had been working on developing some other avenues for selling their products. Yeah, he was a laborer, but he had always been proud of it. Better to be like that than like his father. Running around the country screwing anything that moved and trying to get out of having to work for a damn thing. He had never understood how his grandfather's only son had managed to turn out that way.

The old man was a hard-ass. Possibly because he was compensating for what had happened with Finn's father. But either way, he had taught Finn the value of an honest day's work. And he was grateful.

It had also shown him the value of staying. Investing. Which neither of his parents had managed to do.

And it had given him a way to have some control in his life. After spending his childhood being jerked around by the whims of adults, figuring out he could actively affect the world around him had been a revelation. That he could work at something, cultivate the land. Build up something that no one could take from him.

Except, apparently, when his grandfather died and left the land to his brothers. That felt much closer to losing his foundation than he would have liked.

"I don't know about that," Lane was saying, pulling their food out of the microwave. "I don't actually think you're as grumpy as Mark is."

Lane turned around and nearly ran into him. Finn reached out to steady her, gripping her shoulders and holding her there. Her shirt was soft, and so was she, and it made it hard to pull away as quickly as he should.

He cleared his throat, releasing his hold on her. "Maybe I'm just not as grumpy with you."

The moment extended, her blue eyes locked with his, then slowly, a tight smile curved her lips, slackening as the air between them seem to clear. Some of the tension loosening. Then her expression turned amused.

"If that's the case, I really would hate to see you with

other people. You might not be as cranky as Mark, but you're not exactly rainbows and sunshine."

"If I were rainbows and sunshine you wouldn't like me. Anyway, without a thunderstorm you wouldn't have a rainbow."

"You are my very favorite thunderstorm, Finn."

He ground his teeth together, still feeling the effects of his earlier lapse in self-control. Still feeling the impression of her warmth beneath his fingers. She did not seem similarly affected. "Happy to be the dark cloud in your life."

"Stop scowling at me. I'm making you dinner."

He did his best to relax the muscles in his face and to give her something that looked a little bit less surly. He would only ever do that for Lane.

Right when Lane took his plate out of the microwave, there was a knock on the door. He let out a heavy sigh. "If it's another casserole…"

"Who else is bringing you casserole?" Lane asked, her tone full of mock offense. "I'm just kidding," she said, smiling. "I know that no one else is bringing you casserole. At least, no one under the age of eighty."

"Maybe I like older women," he said, lifting a shoulder.

She arched her brow. "To each his own, I guess."

His scowl returned and he walked out of the kitchen, heading toward the front door. He jerked it open without bothering to look and see who was on the other side. And when he saw, he froze.

"Hi, little brother. It's been a while."

As Finn stared at his older brother, Cain, he had to concede that it had probably been more than a couple of years since they had seen each other. Cain's dark hair was longer than the last time he'd seen him, his face a little more lined. Around his eyes. Around his mouth.

When a girl who could only be Cain's daughter started to make her way toward the door from the car, her expression sulky in that way that only teenage girls could accomplish, Finn amended that timeline to *way* more than a couple of years.

The last time he'd seen Violet, she had been a little girl. This half-grown young woman in front of him was definitely not the child he remembered.

Her hands were stuffed into her sweatshirt pockets, the hood pulled up over her head, her shoulders hunched forward. She came to stand beside her dad, looking incensed.

"It was a long drive," Cain said.

Finn looked past his two relatives to the beat-up truck with the Texas license plates that was parked in the driveway. He hadn't realized Cain was going to drive. The very thought of driving halfway across the country with only a teen girl for company made Finn want to crawl out of his own skin.

Though, actually, the idea of driving halfway across the country with his brother made him feel that way too.

But more concerning than any of that was the trailer hitched to the back of the old truck. Suspicion lodged itself in Finn's chest.

"Why didn't you fly?" he asked.

"Wanted to have the truck." Which didn't answer the unspoken question about the trailer. Cain looked past him. "Aren't you going to invite us in?"

As if it were an option to leave him out there on the porch. A large part of Finn wished it were.

Finn fought against the desire to say something confrontational, and focused on the reality of the situation. No matter how he felt, Cain had a right to be here.

But that didn't mean he had to like it.

"You own exactly as much of this house as I do, Cain," Finn said, the words sticking in his throat on the way out. "You don't really have to ask my permission."

"That's how it is then," Cain said, walking past Finn and into the house.

Violet remained stubbornly rooted to the porch.

"Violet," Cain said, his tone full of warning. "I thought you were going to *like, freeze to death.* Maybe you should come inside so you don't die of exposure."

Violet rolled her eyes and crossed the threshold into the house. She pulled the phone out of her pocket and immediately busied herself by tapping her thumbs on the touch screen.

"Say hi to your uncle Finn."

Finn had never gotten fully used to the idea that he was somebody's uncle. But then, it was difficult for him to believe that his brother was a father. Actually, it was even stranger now that Violet wasn't in diapers.

The last time Finn had seen her she had been maybe seven or eight, looking at Cain and at all of her uncles like they were gods. And Cain had still been married. Maybe that was another reason this was so strange. Seeing Violet as something other than the bright-eyed imp who worshipped the ground her dad walked on.

And being treated to her total and complete ambivalence when before his very existence had made him as unto a god.

He supposed he didn't really have a right to feel much about that either way. It wasn't like he had been very involved in her life.

Though in fairness to Finn, Cain hadn't made much of an effort to involve him.

"Hi, Uncle Finn," Violet said, not looking up from her phone. "My, how you've grown."

Her response stopped him short. "I wasn't going to say that," he said.

"Sure."

"I wasn't," he returned.

Finally, Violet looked up, a long-suffering expression on her face. "They all do."

Not him. He was thirty-four years old. He wasn't somebody's elderly relative.

"Do I have a room or something?" Violet asked, directing the question at her dad.

Finn could tell that Cain was about to lecture her for being rude, but as far as Finn was concerned getting rid of the teenager as quickly as possible was optimal. "Up the stairs. First room on the left," he said.

It had always struck Finn as odd that his grandfather had designed the house to hold so many people, when the old man had few friends and little contact with his family in the broad sense. But the place was big enough to house a small army.

Most of the bedrooms had gone unused since the house had been built five years ago. And when Finn had gotten a look at the will after the old man had died, he'd wondered if they'd been put there for this purpose.

Which had made him feel like a damned idiot. Thinking any of this was for him. Was for a job well done. Hell no.

He'd busted his ass, worked his fingers to the bone—literally in some cases—and they would reap the rewards.

"Thanks." She shoved her phone back in her pocket

and tried to force something that looked vaguely like a smile before walking up the stairs. It was strange to see somebody come into the house for the first time and not be completely awed by the sheer scope of it.

The custom-built cabin, with its high beam-crossed ceilings and breathtaking views of the misty green wilderness, was usually enough to stop people in their tracks.

Apparently, that reaction did not extend to surly teenagers.

After Violet disappeared, Finn turned to his brother. "Well," he said, "she's gotten—"

"Impossible?"

"Not what I was going to say. But, you're the expert."

Cain pinched the bridge of his nose. "I'm not an expert on anything, just ask Violet. But that's not really relevant to why we're here."

"Okay," Finn said, shoving his hands into his pockets. "You're here because?"

"Why do you think? It's not like this is some random appearance you weren't expecting. Our grandfather died."

"And per his wishes there was no service. He wanted his money to go back into the ranch, and his body to go back to the mountains. I spread his ashes and didn't make a deal out of it, just like he said to do."

Cain set his jaw. "Grandpa left part of the ranch to me, and I'm here because I want it."

Tension crept up Finn's spine. He'd known his brothers would come for their inheritance. Hell, who wouldn't? But he'd imagined they would be discussing money. Finn had been prepared to issue payouts—or make arrangements for them anyway.

What he hadn't thought was that anyone might want their share of the ranch itself.

"In what capacity, Cain? Because you've never paid much attention to the ranch or what goes on here before. In fact, you never even came to visit in the past eight years. It has to have been that long. The last time I saw Violet she was a kid, now she's...*that*."

"I'd apologize to you about that, Finn, but I was kind of in the middle of dealing with my life, which hasn't been easy for the past few years."

Finn knew that his brother had been going through a hard time. With the divorce and all of that, but he'd also figured if Cain was having trouble handling it, he would have said something.

He wasn't sure why he'd figured that, since he would rather die than go to one of his half brothers for help.

Which made him feel like a jackass. He resented that something fierce. Feeling like a jackass in his own damn living room when he was the one being invaded.

"Right," Finn said, unable to make his tone anything other than hard.

It wasn't that he didn't care about Cain's issues. It wasn't that he didn't have some sympathy. It was just that it was all buried beneath the mountain of resentment he felt over this situation.

Cain shrugged. "Now I figure I'm going to deal with it here."

The sound of a feminine throat clearing caused both men to turn. "Hi," Lane said, a sheepish smile on her face. She was standing in the doorway to the kitchen, her hands clasped behind her back.

"Cain," Finn said, doing his best to school his voice into an even tone, "this is Lane."

"Is she your..."

"Oh, no," Lane said, a note of incredulity running through the denial. "I'm just his friend. I came to bring casserole, because I knew that you would be coming. At least, I assume you're the person that I thought would be coming. You're his brother, right? You do look like him," she said, rambling now at that full-tilt pace that he had only ever seen Lane accomplish.

Cain looked slightly surprised by the avalanche of words he had just been subjected to, but then he seemed to recover quickly enough. "Hi," he said, "I'm Cain."

Lane looked at Finn as if she was waiting for additional information. Well, Finn didn't have any. At least any he felt like giving. The silence stretched on, and he could sense Lane getting increasingly twitchy, since silence was an enemy she typically made it her mission to defeat.

"Cain and Lane," she burst out. "That's funny. And you probably won't forget my name."

She stood there, looking no less uncomfortable. As uncomfortable as Finn was starting to feel.

"How long are you staying for?" Finn asked.

Cain glanced around the room, studying the surroundings intently. And then his blue eyes fell back to Finn, looking far too serious for Finn's liking.

"Well," he said slowly, "I figured we would be staying for good."

CHAPTER TWO

MAYBE SHE HAD demonstrated a little bit of cowardice in leaving Finn alone with his invading family. But Lane hadn't really seen what she could contribute to the scene. She loved Finn to pieces, and he was her best friend in the world. But he was gruff and he didn't share his feelings easily. He was the kind of guy who led with angry, then made up for it with grand gestures, like the time he'd come to her house and built a deer-proof fence for her new garden. Or the time he'd spent an entire day clearing away all the thick brush around the cabin, and forging a path for her that led into the woods so she could more easily access the berry bushes that grew around her property. Or when he'd rebuilt the dock at the lake by her home so that it was larger and didn't have any soft, damaged boards.

Yeah, Finn was more hammer and nails than hearts and flowers. He had a soul of gold beneath his general cranky exterior.

That didn't mean she wanted to hang out and witness the ensuing crankiness, though.

And anyway, she had standing plans to meet up with her friends Rebecca Bear and Alison Davis.

She was just going a little earlier than necessary. And if they could make it at the new time, all the better. If not, she would just sit there and eat French fries while she waited. Since she hadn't stayed for dinner at Finn's, she was officially starving to death.

And here she had given him a hard time about his palate. But she, Lane Jensen, known foodie, also had a soft spot for really greasy food. And when she wanted that, Ace's bar was the place to go.

"Hi, Lane," Ace Thompson said from his position behind the bar. "French fries?"

Ace had made women swoon across town for years. And he still did, but the wedding ring on his left hand put a damper on things. He was lumbersexual hot. But he was also a one-woman man since marrying Sierra West and starting a family with her.

"You're like my dealer. And yes. Regular, not sweet potato. I'm not in the market to pretend that there's any nutritional value involved in this."

She breezed through the dining room and took her place at the counter-height table that she and her friends typically occupied on their nights at the bar.

She sighed, picking up a menu and examining the dinner column, even though she knew exactly what was served at Ace's. Just in case he'd added something new.

Ultimately, she decided that she was going to order a hamburger. And when the server came with her basket of fries, she did just that.

"I was able to get one of the girls to close up for me." Lane looked up and saw her friend Alison approaching the table. Her red hair was disheveled, dark shadows beneath her eyes. "I think I might need a vacation."

"You definitely do. I think you've been working more than overtime getting the bakery stable over the past couple of years."

Alison took her seat across from Lane and immediately stuck her hand in the basket of fries. "True. And I also lost two of my long-term employees last week, so I've been scrambling to try and fill holes in the schedule. I haven't had anybody approach me for a while about a job. Which is good, I guess. Since I have a reputation of hiring people in dire circumstances, I can only suppose that there isn't anybody hanging out in a dire circumstance. But I'd be more grateful if I wasn't working my fingers to the bone."

"That's not a very appealing visual. Considering that your fingers touch baked goods."

Alison made a scoffing sound. "Why did you order those pale, anemic fries?" she asked, as she took another one.

"Oh, you mean real fries instead of your imposter sweet potato nonsense?"

"They're better. That's just a fact," Alison said, reaching into her purse and pulling out her phone, checking it quickly.

"What? Who are you? What is our friendship?"

"Rebecca said she's almost here."

As if on cue, Rebecca walked into the bar and crossed the room, heading straight for the table. "Sorry. I tried to get here sooner but Gage was at the store helping me close."

"I imagine that's relationship code for doing something that is absolutely *not* helping you close your store," Alison said.

Rebecca turned bright red. "Possibly."

Lane tried to ignore the stab of jealousy in her stomach. She had been single going on way too long now. It was getting old.

It was incredibly petty to have any sort of jealousy regarding Rebecca's relationship with Gage West. It had been hard-won, the obstacles between them seemingly impossible to overcome given the fact that Gage had been at fault for an accident that had caused Rebecca serious scarring—inside and out. If anyone deserved happiness, it was Rebecca.

However, her friend's happiness certainly highlighted Lane's own aloneness. Granted, to a degree it was a choice. She didn't exactly have the time or energy to devote to a relationship right now.

Too bad her discontentment had nothing to do with rationality. She knew that she didn't want a man in her life at the moment—not in a romantic capacity—it was just that her bed felt very empty sometimes.

And looking at Rebecca, who fairly glowed with satisfaction, it felt very, very empty indeed.

"Gross," Lane said, not thinking it was gross at all. In fact, she thought it was downright enviable. "Do you need to order? Because Alison and I didn't wait for you."

"I called it in," Rebecca said, "mostly because I knew neither of you would wait."

Rebecca's hamburger ended up arriving before Alison's or Lane's, which seemed unfair on top of everything else. Not only had she very recently had some sex, she was also indulging in a hamburger a full five minutes before her friends. Her single, *celibate* friends.

When Lane's food did show up, she attacked it with gusto. She had the vague thought that she was very likely using her hamburger to help soothe some of the unsettled feelings that were left behind after witnessing Finn's confrontation with his brother. But it was no big news to her that she used food to deal with her feelings.

There was a reason that she had opened a specialty food store, and it was only partly because the old business had been established but needed to change hands right around the time she had been financially able to make that step.

She had always loved the Mercantile on Copper Ridge's Main Street, ever since she had moved to the small town on the Oregon coast when she was seventeen. She loved the exposed brick on the walls, the warm, homey feeling and the easily accessible samples of bread and different types of infused olive oils.

The fact that she got to work there all day almost every day was one of her favorite things about her life. So what if she had a serious emotional crutch in the form of food? She had managed to find a way to continually keep herself surrounded by said crutch.

"I thought you were eating dinner with Finn?" Alison asked, eyeing Lane as she continued to feast on her burger.

She swallowed her bite, and then took a slow drink of her Diet Coke. For some reason, she was hesitant to bring discussions of Finn into the group. But then, that wasn't unusual. Her friendship with Finn was specific. Its own thing.

It wasn't easy or completely open the way her relationships with Alison and Rebecca were. But how could it be? He was a man, and she wasn't blind to that fact. Not only that, he was older than her. And he'd been friends with her brother, Mark, before he was her friend. But as the years had progressed, and Mark moved away, the gap had seemed to close between the two of them.

He was kind of like an older brother. Except a little more equal. She supposed the exact definition didn't really matter. But she still often felt the need to put up a wall between that relationship and her relationship with her girlfriends. She told them everything, but telling them everything about Finn bordered on being a violation of him, and that was what she tried to avoid.

"Well, I was. But… He had a visitor?"

"Please don't tell me he forgot that you were coming over and hooked up with some girl," Alison said, her nose wrinkling. Alison was always prepared to think the worst of men. She tried to keep the negativity to a minimum, and Lane knew that. But she also knew that the other woman had ample reason to have a low opinion of the species.

Lane hesitated. "No. He didn't do that. He wouldn't do that. You know Finn, he's… Well, he's a little bit nicer than that. It's just he has kind of an infusion of family right now. Because of his grandfather."

Alison looked contrite. "Right. I forgot about that. How is he?"

Lane shrugged. "As good as can be expected. He knew that Callum was going to go soon. I just think even when you expect it there's nothing easy about it. Plus, he has to deal with his brothers now. And that's just a whole thing."

"Family invariably is," Rebecca said.

"Speaking of family," Alison said. "How is Jonathan warming up to Gage?"

Lane's attention was momentarily pulled away from the conversation by something flickering on the TV screen above the bar. And then everything faded into the background.

Because there he was.

Cord McCaffrey, newly a senator, darling of the media, instant internet sensation and Lane's personal trial by fire. How was any of this fair? Here he was, in her bar, disturbing her French fry time.

The man was like an incredibly charismatic cockroach. He could not be killed. Not that she wanted him killed; it was just she wanted him a little less successful and a little less in her face. Also, a little less beloved by all.

Seeing him on the screen, in a power suit with a power tie, giving a speech so well constructed it could make angels weep, she felt tiny. Tiny and insignificant. She hated that. She had achieved a lot in her life. Without help from her family.

And mostly, she didn't miss them. Mostly, she didn't ever think about the big house she had once lived in in Massachusetts with her old money blue blood parents. Mostly, she was very happy living in a tiny, seaside town on the Oregon coast, as far away from them and their judgment as it was possible to get without crossing the ocean.

But seeing Cord dredged up memories. And God knew she had been seeing him way more often than usual lately.

"Lane?"

She blinked, looking across the table at Rebecca, whose expression was one of concern. Suddenly, she remembered where she was. She had been outside of herself for a moment. Outside of her body, possibly outside of Oregon. Somewhere else entirely.

Twelve years in the past maybe.

"What? Sorry, I spaced out."

"You seemed distracted by Senator Good Hair."

"Oh," she said, trying to figure out how she was going to spin that. Because she didn't exactly want to have a conversation about the fact that she *knew* Cord McCaffrey. She was never going to have a discussion with anyone about the particulars of that knowledge—

that was for sure. But she was trying to decide on the most believable and innocuous lie.

"I get it," Alison said. "He's compelling. I mean, I think being a politician's wife would be horrible. All I can picture is how controlled it would be. How owned you would feel. But I get why some women go for it."

Lane had a feeling that Alison would find a long-term relationship with any man stifling at this point. Her ex-husband was to blame for that.

"It's just weird," Lane said, going for the closest version of the truth that she could manage. "He lived in my parents' neighborhood. We grew up next to each other. It's always kind of strange to see somebody that you knew in a different context becoming famous."

Saying something so innocuous about him nearly killed her. The fact that she had occasion to talk about him at all—with people who had no idea of their connection—just made her angrier.

At the same time, if Cord had never achieved his political ambition she might have been even angrier. Because then what would the point have been of any of the pain that he put her through?

"I can see that being weird," Rebecca said. "I really can't imagine any of the jackasses I went to school with ascending to political office. It's a terrifying prospect, actually."

Rebecca truly had no idea. "Yeah. Weird." She shoved another fry in her mouth to keep from making further comment.

She felt weird the whole rest of the evening, which she hated. Because Cord wasn't rattling around his giant-ass mansion feeling weird right now. No, he was likely sitting in a wingback chair with a snifter of brandy, letting his Stepford wife rub his feet while his two perfect children slept upstairs. When she walked back to her car later, Rebecca intercepted her. "Are you okay?"

"Fine," Lane said, breaking away quickly, tromping across the parking lot with more forceful steps than necessary, loose rocks and gravel crunching under her feet.

"You were very quiet tonight. You're never quiet."

She let out an exasperated sigh that bloomed in the cold night air, joining the low-hanging fog that was creeping in off the sea. "Just tired. I stayed up late making dinners for Finn last night, and then had to work most of the day. And then I had to deliver the food, so…"

"You do a lot for him."

Lane bristled. Mostly because whenever anyone made comments about her relationship with Finn, those comments contained undercurrents. Undercurrents she didn't like. "He's done a lot for me. Plus, his grandfather just died, and he might have been a surly old coot, but he was pretty much all Finn had to call family."

"Except all those brothers," Rebecca pointed out.

"Half brothers. And he didn't grow up with them."

She didn't know why she was being defensive. About Finn, about anything in his life. She was crossing the velvet Finn rope she tended to put up around her conversations with other people, and hell if she knew how she'd gotten dragged over it.

"Sorry," Rebecca said, letting out a long sigh. "I'm just worried about you and I'm trying to drag out a reason why you might have been upset and I tend to come back to him."

"Well, Finn is not ever part of my upset. Finn is one of the only truly good men on planet Earth."

Rebecca looked at her, long and hard, her dark eyes glittering in the lamplight. "Okay."

Damn her. She still wasn't taking Lane's placating lies at face value. But she was also wrong about the source of her issues. And if her Finn stuff was cordoned off by a velvet rope, her Cord issues were kept in a very difficult to access attic, beneath a really heavy box with a blanket over it, so no one would ever look and she'd have a hard time ever pulling it out herself.

"I'm fine," she said, singsong now, walking to her car with a small bounce in her step. "Fine, fine, fine."

"Keep saying it," Rebecca said, her tone dry. "That will make it seem more believable."

Lane cheerfully flung her middle finger into the air, directing it at Rebecca along with a smile. Rebecca lifted her own hand and made a catching motion, as though Lane had blown her a kiss. Then she put the imagined item in her pocket. "In case I need a good Screw You later."

"I think you had a good screw earlier," Lane shot back.

"Don't hate the player," Rebecca said, her tone completely serious.

Lane rolled her eyes and got into her car. Sometimes she thought it would be more practical to get a big truck. For garden soil, wood chips and anything else she might need for her garden. But she liked the fuel economy of her little car. Plus, Finn had a truck and he could always do that stuff for her.

Her house was a quick trip from Ace's, which sat on the edge of town. In about five minutes, she was at the dirt driveway that led back into the hills to where her little homestead was. Four potholes and three curves later, she was pulling into her driveway.

The house was modest, but it was cozy and perfect for one person. Nestled in the pine trees, the little cabin looked like it might be growing straight out of the earth.

But the value of this place wasn't in the house, it was in the property.

She had spent the past couple of years taming it, getting herself a decent-sized garden plot prepared and revamping an old outbuilding set way back in the trees that was designed to store things like jam and root vegetables.

Well, Finn had helped with a lot of that.

But, like she had told Rebecca earlier, Finn did a lot for her. It was one reason she happily did a lot for him. Anything. She would do anything for Finn.

She walked across the soft ground, bark and pine needles muting her footsteps until she reached the wooden porch steps. She shoved her key into the lock— even out here she kept her doors locked out of an abundance of caution. She wasn't particularly concerned with anyone stealing her things, not in Copper Ridge. Really, she wasn't legitimately concerned with much considering that Copper Ridge was a very safe place to live, but she was a woman who lived alone in the middle of nowhere, so her anxieties tended to center on some deranged drifter lying in wait in her living room when she returned from town after a long day.

That she could live without.

She sighed heavily, dumping her purse and her keys over the back of the armchair that sat adjacent to the entryway. She felt unsettled and restless, which wasn't how she usually felt when she walked into her snug little house.

It was so different to that expansive stone monstrosity her parents had lived in, heaving with dashed expectations and the scent of disappointment. It had always felt so cold. So vast and empty.

Because there was nothing even close to love in the

hallowed walls of the Jensen family home. And no matter what her parents said, she could feel it. And it made that massive manor feel claustrophobic.

She surrounded herself with warmth here. And in this tiny place with its rough-hewn furniture, with the lake on one side and the endless woods on the other, she felt free.

Usually, she felt a sense of relief as the rustic wood walls offered sanctuary from the day.

Not today. Today required more eating.

She flicked on the light and walked into the kitchen. Except those actions blended into one, and it took a moment for her to realize that the light had not turned on. She stopped, letting out a hard breath. She tested the light switch again. Nothing. The kitchen remained resolutely dark. Then she looked and noticed that the lights were off on the microwave and the coffeemaker.

She let out a short curse. Then she raced to the fridge.

When she opened the door the light was off, but cool air emanated from the appliance. She let out a sigh of relief. At least the power outage was recent.

That was all she needed. For everything in her fridge to go rancid. Which it would do if she didn't get this fixed.

There was a lamp on in the living room, so clearly the lights were fine there. It was probably some weird fuse situation because everything in the cabin was old, including the wiring. She wandered over to the fuse box and flipped a few switches. Nothing. She lifted her cell phone up in the darkness and shined it onto the box, attacking the suspect switch with even more intensity, and still, she was bathed in darkness.

She growled. And before she was fully conscious of what she was doing, she turned her phone back toward herself and dialed Finn.

CHAPTER THREE

It had been a long ass day. And it was fixing to be an even longer ass night. Mostly because Finn was so very aware of the fact that his brother and his niece were asleep in his house. And that the rest of them would be coming tomorrow.

Alex, with his easy grin and smart-ass comments. Liam and the chip on his shoulder that he seemed so committed to.

Cain said he wanted to stay. That he wanted to work the ranch. Give Violet a fresh start. And Finn had no legal recourse to stop him. His grandfather had left equal shares of the ranch to all of them, and that meant that Finn was up a creek.

He jerked the fridge open, grabbing a bottle of beer, then changing direction. He put the beer back and closed the fridge, making his way over to the bar on the other side of the room. His grandfather had been a good Irishman who believed in keeping his liquor supply healthy.

Finn reached out, closing his hand around a bottle of whiskey. "God bless you, old man."

Then his cell phone vibrated in his pocket. He bit back a curse, lifting the device to his ear. "Hello."

"It's me," came the sound of Lane's familiar voice.

"Hi," he said, barely managing more than a grunt.

"I need you," Lane said, her voice breathy.

Those words were like a slug straight to his gut. And it didn't matter that he knew full well this was in regards to something that had absolutely nothing to do with his body—his body reacted strongly.

"Do you?" he asked, keeping his eyes pinned on the bottle of liquid salvation in his hand.

"Yes," she said, the word coming out in a long whine.

"It can't wait till morning?"

"No," she said, her voice emphatic. "The power is out in my kitchen. I flipped the switches and they won't work."

"Which switches did you flip?"

"All the switches. They won't work! All of my food is going to go bad. I don't have cheap food, Finn. My cheese. Think of my cheese. Donnelly cheese."

He closed his eyes, letting out a long slow breath as he released his hold on the liquor bottle. "I'll be right over."

If nothing else, it gave him a chance to get out of the house. This house that was a constant reminder of his grandfather, the old bastard. An old bastard he missed, about as much as he wanted to punch him.

He was going to take the chance to get out of this house that now contained two members of his family who seemed determined to stay.

He pinched the bridge of his nose, then reached out, grabbing hold of his truck keys. The metal scraped against the granite countertop, the noise loud in the relative silence of the expansive room.

By the time he pulled up to Lane's house he wasn't entirely sure how he'd gotten there. The entire drive over was a blank space. He had been too busy having imaginary, angry conversations in his head. With his brother. With a dead man.

Good thing he knew the road and the route better than he knew just about any other.

He walked up the porch steps, noticing that one of them wiggled beneath his boot. He would have to fix that for her. Then he looked at the porch light, at the excess of cobwebs hanging around it, made much more obvious with the direct glow of the porch light and the darkness behind it.

She hated messing with things like that too, so he should probably clear them when he came to do the step. He sighed, lifting his hand and knocking firmly on the wooden door.

It jerked open half a second later, revealing a nervous-looking Lane. "I hope it's easy to fix," she said, moving out of the way and allowing him entry. "I have deep concerns about my food." She lifted her hand to her mouth, chewing idly on the side of her thumbnail.

"I can take some back with me if we can't get it fixed—assuming there's room in my fridge after all that casserole. Also, you can put some of it out in your cold room. Not perfect, but overnight it's not going to be any warmer than your fridge out there."

"There you go being all measured and logical." She waved her hands, looking anything but measured and logical.

He hadn't felt like either of those things earlier today. No, dealing with Cain he had felt decidedly un-calm and illogical. He could almost see himself standing in his house, being an ass to the brother who had driven halfway across the country to be there, the brother who had been through a whole hell of a lot in his adult life, and who was trying to do something good for his kid.

But he hadn't been able to be any nicer. He just hadn't had it in him. The ranch felt like his. He'd invested blood and sweat in that land. Probably even a few bone chips from the time he had busted his shin in a dirt bike accident when he'd been thirteen.

Yes, they had all spent summers there up to a point. But Finn was the one who had stayed. He was the one who worked it. The one who had gotten it into the state it was in, and now Cain just wanted to move in and use it as therapy.

"It's a gift," he said, rather than dumping any of those dark thoughts on Lane. "It's probably just a fuse, and it's probably just going to take me a minute."

"I told you I flipped the switches," she said, sounding grumpy.

"I know you did," he said.

"You think I flipped the switches wrong," she said, accusatory.

"I'm sure you're a great switch flipper," he responded, deadpan, as he continued to the fuse box.

He knew that the old cabin was a bit of a mess when it came to wiring. He had a rudimentary knowledge of those things, but he wasn't an electrician. So while he was tempted to offer to sort everything out for her, it would probably be better if she got a professional. Which he'd told her before, but she never hired anyone to help out.

He had fiddled with her fuse box a couple of times before, so he already knew that the labels next to each switch were wrong. The one that claimed to be linked to the bathroom, in fact wasn't. If he remembered right that one went to a back bedroom.

He knew for certain the one that was labeled *living room* went to the bathroom. But he wasn't exactly certain which one went to the kitchen, since there had never been a fuse issue with it before. He turned off one that claimed to be the master bedroom, and heard Lane shout from down the hall.

"Now it's just completely dark in here!"

He flipped it back on. "Sorry," he said.

His hand hovered over the switch for the outdoor power, and then he decided to test it. Off, and then on.

"Nothing!"

"Nothing?" he asked.

"Nothing!" she shouted back.

He walked back to where she was, frowning. "Wasn't the original part of this place built in the twenties?" he asked.

"Yes," she replied, looking confused.

"I need to get up in your crawl space."

"Wow, Finn. Buy a girl dinner first."

He sighed wearily. "Lane…"

"Fine. But I don't know what you're going to find up there."

"Knob and tube wiring, I hope."

He went back out to the truck and grabbed his toolbox, then opened up the attic access in her hallway, lowering the built-in ladder down and climbing into the tight space. It didn't take long after that to find a wire that had been chewed until it had lost its connection.

He fused it back together with his soldering iron and heard a triumphant hoot from down below.

"I take it that did it?" he called.

"Success," she called up. "Now get down here before you get eaten by spiders."

"I don't think you have man-eating spiders," he said, making his way back down the ladder. "I think you had wire-chewing raccoons."

"Raccoons?" she called back.

"Possibly possums." He made his way from the hall into the kitchen.

Lane was standing in the middle of the room and both of them were all lit up. A wide smile stretched across her face and when she spun around in a circle, he couldn't help but notice the way the light caught her dark hair. For some reason, it put him in mind of what it might feel like if he reached out and let those glossy curls sift through his fingers.

"Possibly possums," she said. "Great. Attic possums."

"Better than man-eating spiders, all in all."

"Sure. Thank you," she said, sighing happily. "I don't know what I would do without you."

He shoved his hand in his pocket. "You're welcome. Anyway, now your food won't go bad, and I won't have to listen to you cry about it for the next two weeks."

She scowled. "Is that an implication that I am dramatic? That I perhaps don't let go of things as quickly as I should?"

"Take it however you want to take it, Lane. I'm just saying."

"I take it with umbrage."

"Well, that's a quick change of heart. Turning on your food savior already."

"Hey, buddy. It doesn't benefit you to have my food go bad either. Who would feed you?"

"Damn straight. And I'm going to need more food than usual, apparently."

"Why is that?" she asked, looking concerned now.

Without waiting for an invitation—because he didn't need it, not in her house—he moved to the fridge and took out a beer. If he was going to stay and talk, he would allow himself one beer.

He popped the top off using the edge of the counter,

then made his way across the small space and into the living room, where he sat down on the couch. "Cain is staying."

"I kind of heard some of that," Lane said, grabbing her own beer before joining him in the living room.

She didn't sit next to him, and that didn't really surprise him. They were friends. Platonic friends, and always had been. But there was a definite line of reserve when it came to physical contact.

She settled into the armchair, lifting her beer to her lips. He looked down at his. "Well, that's basically it. He wants to stay. He wants Violet to go to school here. He wants to get involved with ranching. Basically, I think my brother is having a midlife crisis at the age of thirty-seven."

"He's divorced?"

"Yeah. It's been a couple of years, but it was ugly. I mean, from what I understand."

"I see why he'd want a change, then."

He frowned. "Don't you dare take his side."

"I'm not taking sides. I'm saying it's understandable. When you go through something like that… You just want a clean slate sometimes. And it sounds to me like he muddled through where he was for as long as he could. But eventually, it gets obvious that the problems aren't going to be fixed if you stay where you are."

"I will turn your lights off again." He wouldn't. "I will leave you in the darkness."

"The ranch is big. The house is big." She continued as if he hadn't spoken. "Will it kill you to have them living there?"

He set the beer bottle down on the table by his couch without any delicacy. "The ranch is mine. That's the point."

"I get that you feel that way, but you sound like a jackass."

"What the hell kind of friendship is this? You're supposed to tell me what I want to hear."

Lane rolled her eyes. "I'm sorry. If that's the kind of conversation you want, you need to tell me before we actually start talking. Otherwise, I'll assume you want some honesty. And if you want honesty, then this is what you get."

"I don't want honesty. I want you to tell me that it's egregious that somebody who never gave a damn about the ranch before now considers himself entitled to it."

"But he is entitled to it," Lane said, her tone gentle, which was more annoying than her previous harshness. "It's his ranch. Legally. Your grandfather wanted him to have part of it, and it isn't really up to you to say that he can't."

He shook his head. "It never occurred to me that he would want it. He has a life in Texas."

"Apparently, a life he doesn't like."

That made him pause. The whole situation with his brothers was difficult. It always had been. They had a bond—that was undeniable. When he looked at them, it was like looking at himself, with features and coloring rearranged and slightly different. There was no denying they were brothers. Same dark hair, all over six feet tall. Though the youngest brothers had green eyes instead of blue. Still, there was no mistaking they were related. Because that damn Donnelly blood was just so strong.

Finn looked like his grandfather. They all did. They also looked like their terrible jackass of a father who'd had children he didn't particularly care about with women he cared even less about.

That was the bond, though. And that was it. Other

than Liam and Alex, they had only spent snatches of time together growing up. Cain had mostly been raised in Texas and had a little bit of a drawl as a result, while the rest of them had grown up on the West Coast.

They were as much different as they were alike, and while there was no denying they had a connection, Finn liked it best when the connection was distant.

"And that sucks for him," Finn said, knowing he just sounded petulant now.

"You don't have to like it," Lane said. "I mean, you might want to get over yourself eventually. But I understand why it makes you mad."

"Why is that, Dr. Jensen?" he said, his tone dry.

"You don't like anyone else to have control. You like to have all of it. And if you actually have to share space with your brothers, you're going to have to give up some of your control."

He shrugged. "Well, who doesn't want control?"

"Hell if I know." She took another drink of her beer, and his gaze dropped to her lips. To where her mouth wrapped around the bottle.

Dammit.

He might *want* control, but he was beginning to wonder if he had it.

Silence stretched between them, long and tense. He felt it creeping up his spine, up his shoulders, his muscles growing tight. He was very aware just then of the fact that they were all alone. Of the fact that it was late, and that he was a man and she was very much a woman.

This kind of thing was always worse when his life was thrown off. That awareness. Those moments when he would look at her and instead of seeing her very familiar face, he would be jarred by some new angle of her beauty.

It was more than just features, though on their own they were pretty enough. It was the glitter in her eyes when she was about to say something she thought was hilarious. The way she struggled to hold back a laugh at her own jokes. The insane things that came out of her mouth when she was rambling because she was nervous or excited, or just hopped up on caffeine.

Those moments when she was more than a pretty face or a damned fine figure. The moments when he saw a woman who was beautiful all the way down. The kind of beauty years couldn't fade.

Those moments were a big damn problem. Normally, he had a better handle on this.

But then, normally, he had a better handle on his life.

"You know," she said, breaking him out of his thoughts, "with the extra help from Cain you could afford to do more of your own product. I would really, really like to offer some milk that isn't ultra pasteurized in my store. We could sell it in a glass bottle. People would love it."

He groaned. "We've been through this already. I don't have the time. My grandfather wasn't interested and that was for a reason. We're better off just taking the contracts from bigger dairies."

"Not necessarily. The demand for this kind of thing is huge, and I love carrying local products in the store. I want more cheese. More of your cheese."

He snorted. "Now there's a sentence you don't hear every day."

"Maybe if you didn't make cheese." She let out an exasperated breath. "Just think about it. Think about the opportunity that having extra help would present you with. Instead of being a stubborn ass."

With her poking and prodding him he forgot why just

a moment ago he had been feeling tense and like he was a little too big for his skin. Why he had been so captivated with her. Because now, he was less captivated by her beauty and more irritated by that stubborn set of her chin that let him know she wasn't going to back down.

"I'll think about it," he said, mostly to get her off his back. He took another sip of beer, then decided to leave the rest. "I need to go."

"Fine," she said.

He stood, and so did she. Then he moved away from the couch, heading toward the door and she reached out, breaking that unspoken wall between them as her fingertips touched his shoulder.

He jerked back as though he'd been burned. There was something strange in her expression then, like she was a baby deer that had been startled. Then the air changed, and it all just felt weird.

"Thank you," she said, the words coming out of her mouth in a hurry.

"You're welcome," he returned, his voice sounding rough even to his own ears.

For a moment, he just stood there. And so did she. It all settled around them, the weirdness, the tension, and he had a feeling that if he didn't hurry up and get out the door it might wrap itself around them, and then they might find themselves being inexplicably drawn toward each other.

It was either that, or she felt nothing at all while he was standing there gasping for breath. And he did not need to make a move to try and confirm which it was.

So he did exactly what was expected, exactly what was needed. And he moved his ass toward the door.

Once he got outside, the cool night air did a lot to break up the leaden feeling that had settled in his lungs.

It had been a day of weird stuff. And tonight had just been the cherry on that terrible sundae.

Tomorrow morning would come, sure and constant as anything. And he would see to his routine. He would get the cows set up for milking, get the milk prepared for processing. He would ride the fence line making sure that everything was shored up.

He would survey the land that had been his whole life since he was sixteen years old. And even if everything wasn't settled, he would at least have some clarity.

He just had to make it through the night.

Good thing there was a bottle of whiskey waiting at home.

CHAPTER FOUR

HER STORE WAS TINY. It was just *so* tiny. Lane loved it. She really did. But for some reason when she walked in that morning and turned the closed sign, signaling to the citizens of Copper Ridge that it was time for them to come and get their specialty food items, she was incredibly aware of the fact that the empire she had built was most definitely a miniature one.

Cord was still in her head. She hated that. Him and all of his achievements.

Shaking off the mood, she crossed her arms, surveying her surroundings. If she rearranged the things in the corner, mounted some crates and baskets to the wall, she could most definitely fit in more stock. She didn't mind the slightly crowded feeling to the place. It was quaint, if she said so herself. Particularly when combined with the red brick and the dark metal decor she had incorporated.

Yes, right over there in the corner would be where she fit the new fridge that she could keep Finn's dairy products in if he wasn't such a stubborn cuss.

She wondered idly how Alison would feel about making jam. She worked with fruit when she made her pies. Maybe the addition would be a welcome one. Lane would happily sell them in her store.

She already provided some of the berries for Alison's bakery, Pie in the Sky; she could always get more intense about her berry collection and provide her with more. Blackberries, marionberries and raspberries grew wild on her property. *She* could always make jam, she supposed.

She was still musing about various forms of product expansion when her first customers came in. They were tourists, visiting the Oregon coast for the first time all the way from Denver. Lane chatted with them for a while, helping them select products that she considered to be quintessential Copper Ridge items.

Then she referred them to The Grind, her friend Cassie's coffee shop across the street, for a caffeine fix before ringing up all of their items.

"It sure would be nice if there were a way to order these from home," the woman said, examining a can of wild caught salmon that had been provided to Lane's store by local fisherman Ryan Masters.

"Yes," Lane said, the idea turning over in her mind. "It would be."

She was still musing on that when the door opened again and Finn came in. "The power in your house okay?" he said, by way of greeting.

"Everything was fine when I left this morning. Nary an attic possum." She paused. "Thank you again for coming out."

It had occurred to her last night that she didn't thank him enough. She just kind of assumed that he would take care of things for her. Probably because he always had.

"Sure," he said, clearly as uncomfortable with the thanks as he'd been the previous evening.

He meandered through the narrow aisles, divided by wooden shelves. It made her even more conscious of how small the shop was to watch Finn's broad-shouldered frame moving through the tight space. For some reason, she just stood and watched him for a second. Watched as his blunt, masculine fingers drifted over the merchandise, as he paused over a small jar of caviar. "Do you actually sell any of this?"

"Yes," she said, shifting her weight from foot to foot. "Not a lot. But some."

She considered it for a moment. The caviar. She really didn't sell that much. But right now, her store seemed to be straddling the line between tourist trap and specialty store for the few people in Copper Ridge who had a lot of excess time to shop for specific ingredients and cook with them too.

"Focus," she said. "That's what I need."

"To… Finish your crossword? Or…?"

"For the store," she said, ruminating while she spoke. "I need to do something to focus its offerings."

"Okay."

"I mean, I kept a lot of stock simply because it's what the old owner carried. But I've had the business now for going on five years, and I think it's time I started taking it more firmly in the direction I want to see it go."

The need, the burning sensation in her chest, was suddenly manic. Because images of her once-beloved ex parading himself all over national television, reaching levels of success that she would never, ever achieve, had made all of this feel small. It wasn't, and she knew that. She had never had political aspirations. She wouldn't be happy being a public figure. So it was pointless to compare herself and her level of accomplishment to Cord, or to anyone else for that matter.

But she was.

Logic had no place here. There was no logic. There

was only need. The need to do more. To be more. To make everything that had happened worth it. Okay.

"Yes," she said, growing yet more determined. "That's what I'm going to do."

Finn dropped his hand back down to his side. "What?"

"Focus!"

"I would, but I'm not following you."

"No. I meant that I need to focus. My stock. The aim of the store. More and more, I'm interested in supporting specifically local products from Copper Ridge. And possibly Oregon in general, but I don't just want to have general specialty stuff."

"Didn't we have a recent argument about cheese and how you felt it was essential to acquire it from Europe?"

"Yes, but that was before. There are plenty of small businesses in this state that make award-winning dairy products. There's a place down south and off the coast that won an award for its blue cheese on a worldwide level. I should just be carrying things like that. But I would definitely want the focus to be on products that are locally sourced."

"Is there enough of a pool for you to draw from?"

"Beef from the Garretts, seafood from Ryan Masters, microbrews from Ace, wine from Grassroots... And dairy from you."

"Is this your way of trying to push me into changing the business?"

She sputtered. "Yes. No. I mean, it wasn't an idea designed to manipulate you. But I am right. I am. When you don't have to pay the shipping costs your profit margins are going to be higher. If you keep the milk local and sell it as a specialty product—local, hormone free and minimal pasteurization—it's going to be beneficial for you."

"I can't imagine there's a significant market for it."

"Then you haven't been paying attention. Hipsters from Portland would pay through the nose piercing for that."

"I mean, I know that it's a thing. I just mean… Around here…"

"Trust me," she said. "You can keep your contracts with the bigger dairy and still do this. Just to test it out. Especially with the extra help your brothers are going to provide."

"My brothers are only going to be here on a temporary basis. If they plan otherwise, they won't be in Oregon long, because I'll send them straight to hell."

Lane rolled her eyes. "You will not."

"I might," he said, moving on to the next aisle.

"You're all talk. But what do you think about my idea?"

"I'm underwhelmed. You already know that."

She scoffed. "I don't mean about your business. I mean about mine. Do you think the focus would be helpful?"

"Are you having financial trouble?"

"No. Not really. But I'm definitely not making the kind of profits I would like to see. And I just want… I want more. I want to make this mine. I want to make a mark. I love Copper Ridge. I want to put a Lane Jensen stamp on it."

He regarded her for a moment. "You're really serious about this."

"I am. And one of my customers said something earlier about being able to order products. I'm thinking maybe I need to set up a website. Or maybe some kind of box full of all the special goodies that are new for the month. Like a subscription box. A best of Copper Ridge box. It honestly didn't occur to me before, because I've been so focused on getting the place established in the town, and back then all that kind of mail-order-gifts-for-yourself stuff wasn't so big. But now the idea of a subscription box, where you're basically buying yourself a grown-up grab bag, is such a big thing."

"That sounds like a lot of work," he said.

"Says the man with a gigantic ranch that requires he never sleep in or ever take a vacation."

"That's different."

"It isn't different. I want to invest in this business, and build it, and make it mine. You of all people should understand that." She paused, and she knew she was pushing her luck, but she did it anyway. "If you did what I'm talking about with the milk, and if you started offering more kinds of cheese... Well, you could do the same thing with the Laughing Irish. Make it yours. Finn Donnelly would be the one to make the name famous. Instead of just hiding it behind the label of the more well-known dairy."

She knew she had laid it on a little thick, and his irritated expression reflected that. "I'm already getting badgered by my brother, plus I have two more set to show up today. I don't really need you chiming in and pressuring me too. If you want to make your mark on the town, go right ahead. But stop trying to put your Lane stamp on me."

She sighed, feeling exasperated. The man was the most enraging human on the planet sometimes. Stubborn, crabby and resolutely determined to keep his head up his ass. "But I'm right," she insisted.

"My grandfather ran the ranch for forty years. He kept it going through all manner of economic hardship. Why would I act like I know better than him?"

"That isn't what you're doing," she said. "You're not acting like you know better than him. You're just finding a new way to succeed in a new world."

"Expand all you like, Lane, but I've had enough change. I won't tell you where to stack your damned caviar if you don't tell me what to do with my cows."

She sat down on the stool behind the counter, crossing her arms, knowing that she looked like she was pouting, and not really caring. "Fine. Have that control you're so fond of. What are you here for anyway?" She realized that she had bulldozed right over whatever he might have wanted to say when he'd come in.

"Coffee beans," he said, picking up a bag. "Also, I was kind of hoping you could bring something by for dinner tonight. You know, enough for a crowd of people. But since you always have mass amounts of food in that freezer of yours that I spared last night…"

"You don't have to do something for me to get food. Your very presence in my life merits food." She never stayed annoyed with Finn, even when he was annoying. It was impossible.

He had too long a track record of being wonderful for her to take a disagreement seriously. Plus, when he smiled at her, and his blue eyes lit up, she couldn't feel anything but affection for the man.

He treated her to that smile she could never stay mad at. Then he brought the bag of coffee up to the counter.

She set about ringing it up. "You know, you probably have enough food that you don't need anything new. Wasn't it just yesterday that you were trying to turn down the casserole I slaved over?"

"Yeah, but I didn't really want to piece leftovers together. And if I remember right, Liam and Alex are bottomless pits. Of course, my memory of them might be firmly centered on their teens and early twenties. So maybe now that they're both in their thirties they've started eating reasonable portions."

"I'll make something. Pasta, probably. That will be easy to make in the little store kitchen in the back. Don't worry. I won't let you starve."

"Perfect," Finn said, sounding weary. "Could you also figure out a way to handle my brothers for me?"

"Sorry, buddy. Maybe I can sing the 'Song That Never Ends' all night and annoy them out of town. Then again, once they eat my pasta they're going to end up wanting to stay forever. I could put strychnine in it," she offered.

"Maybe don't poison my brothers, Lane."

"Then I guess you're stuck with them."

"Hopefully not for too long," he said, his smile turning rueful.

"How do you plan to get rid of them if not poison?" she asked.

"The way you normally get people to do what you want. Money. Of course…until then, they'll be staying in my house. On second thought…" He looked down at the pound of coffee in his hand. "I better get two of these."

"Just grab the second one on the way out," she told him. "It's on the house."

"Pity caffeine," he said. "But, at this point, I don't have too much pride to take it."

He picked up the bag and lifted it. "See you later?"

"Yes," she said. "I'll bring the food by after I close up here. So it should be around about five thirty."

He grunted.

"Actual human beings with people skills just say thank you, Finn," Lane said.

"Thank you," he said before turning and walking out of the store. She watched him through the window as he adjusted his black Stetson and looked up and down the street.

She caught sight of a table of women sitting out in front of The Grind drinking coffee and admiring the view that was Finn Donnelly.

She turned away, a rush of heat filling her cheeks, and her stomach. She felt weird. Weird that she had been looking at Finn, and that she had been borderline sharing a moment with the women across the street, who were clearly not just looking at him but *checking him out*.

But she had not been checking him out. Not really. She looked up again, and he was gone. She ignored the slight kick in her stomach.

If she noticed the fact that his jaw was square, and that the muscles of his forearms were well-defined, that didn't really mean anything. Not a thing except the fact that she wasn't blind. He was a man. He was a good-looking man.

And she wasn't immune to it. She had just been thinking that his smile and eyes always got him out of trouble with her. It was just—just in a friend way.

She gritted her teeth. That fact had been driven home in kind of a strange way a few months ago when he and Rebecca had nearly hooked up at Ace's one night. Though Rebecca had been adamant that nothing at all had happened, and that really, nothing would have, since she'd only been using him to try and forget about Gage, the man she was determined to stay away from at the time.

But it had all worked out in the end.

Rebecca and Gage had resolved their differences and

Lane didn't have to deal with the weirdness of two of her friends dating each other. Which would have been the worst part of Rebecca and Finn hooking up.

Just the thought made her shudder a little bit. Because weird. It would just be weird. Just like it was weird that someone she knew really well, and had taste she respected, had seen Finn as bangable.

Yes, Finn was an attractive man. She knew that. But all the fantasies about his hands that she'd had centered on things he could fix in her house.

The door opened again and she jumped when the women who had just been ogling Finn walked in off the street.

"What can I help you find today?" She put on her brightest smile. And she did her very best to cast all thoughts of Cord, the eventual expansion, Finn and Finn's stubbornness out of her mind.

HIS BROTHER ALEX showed up looking like a military cliché. He was wearing dog tags and a tan shirt, covered mostly by a dark jacket. What looked to be all of his earthly possessions were shoved in a giant bag he had slung over one shoulder, held like a backpack.

The only indicator he hadn't been in the military for the past few months was that his dark hair was no longer high and tight, but was hanging down into his eyes.

He walked through the entryway and into the kitchen, slamming the pack down on the countertop. "Is Liam here yet?"

"No. And good to see you too."

Alex smiled in that easy way the rest of them could never seem to manage. "You didn't seem particularly thrilled to see me, Finn. Don't try to act like I'm the cranky ass in the group."

"There," Finn said, forcing a smile. "I'm glad to see you." He realized, as soon as he said it, that it was strangely true.

"You're only saying that because if I wasn't here it would be because I was dead or incapacitated in some way."

"No, I'm glad to see you because you're about the only one of us that knows how to defuse tension rather than adding to it."

Alex shrugged. "We all have our gifts." He looked around the room, the slow and thorough evaluation offering a slight glimpse of the intensity that lurked beneath Alex's easygoing surface.

For all that he was the laid-back brother in the Donnelly clan, he was still a soldier.

"Is Cain around?" Alex asked.

"Somewhere. Look for the storm cloud and you'll find him somewhere underneath it. Unless of course you find Violet underneath it."

He'd had limited interaction with his teenage niece since her arrival, since her face had mostly been glued to her phone. But the better part of it had consisted of single-word sentences. Mostly, she'd been holed up in her room.

"What does she have to be stormy about? She's just a kid."

"A teenager."

Alex swore. "I have been out of touch for too long. So, what's happening? Are you having a lawyer read us the will, or...?"

"Not necessary. You all have a copy of the will. We just need to discuss what's going to happen. We all inherited an equal share of the ranch. But I'm willing to offer a monetary payout." He stared at his brother with purpose behind his gaze. "You don't have to stay here."

"I don't have anywhere else to be," Alex said.

There was something slightly haunted in his eyes then, but Finn wasn't going to ask about it. That just wasn't the Donnelly way.

There was another knock on the door and Finn knew exactly who that would be. "I guess the gang's all here," he said drily.

He walked back to the entry, jerking it open. Sure enough, there stood Liam, looking a whole lot like Alex. But where Alex smiled easily, Liam did not. His bags were down at his feet, his tattooed forearms crossed over his chest, his mouth pressed into a grim line. "Hey," he said.

"Come in," Finn returned.

Liam picked up his bags and walked inside before dumping them on the floor again. Alex came out of the kitchen and the two brothers acknowledged each other with a single head nod.

"Well," came a gruff voice from the top of the stairs, "this is a helluva reunion."

Cain chose that moment to walk in, his footsteps heavy.

"We're all here," Liam said, "I guess we can get down to business."

Finn was never more conscious of the dysfunction of the Donnelly clan than when they were all standing in one room. There was—at any given moment—both a disconnect and a connection between all of them.

Brothers. Strangers. Both of those descriptions were true.

By the time the brothers had settled in the expansive seating area it was dark outside, the interior lights reflecting off of the floor-to-ceiling windows. Liam and Alex were sitting on the couch, at opposite ends. Cain was seated in a chair, one leg flung out in front of him and his hands in his lap.

Finn remained standing, taking the folded-up will out of his pocket and holding it out. "Was anybody confused about these terms?"

"Seems straightforward to me," Liam said.

"We're all beneficiaries. And I'm the executor. That means it's my job to make sure that everybody gets what they're supposed to. And of course, if you have any objections to the way I'm handling it, you're welcome to talk to Grandpa's lawyer."

"Does Copper Ridge have a lawyer?" Cain asked.

"Sure, but I'm pretty sure he works at the local general store and also does weddings, funerals and burials," Finn said.

"I can't tell if you're joking," Liam said.

Finn just shrugged. "I'll give you his number if you have a problem. That's all you need to know. Anyway. After I received the will I got the property evaluated. I'm willing to buy all of you out. With projected appreciation up to five years. It's a good offer."

"You have that kind of money?" Alex asked. "I have my doubts about that."

"I'll have to get a loan for some of it, but that's not really your problem. I can't imagine you guys want to be here. I give you the money and you can go do whatever you want."

"We're all here," Cain said, looking around the room. "Do you think the issue is I don't have my own money? I do. I don't get why you think you get to pull rank here."

"Really?" Finn asked. "You don't get it at all?"

"We're all blood, Finn," Cain responded. "We want what's ours. So what is it you want?"

"I want control of the ranch. The Laughing Irish is mine. I've spent the past eighteen years working my knuckles bloody on this place. And where were you?"

"Serving my country," Alex said, crossing his arms.

"Raising a kid," Cain said, shifting his position.

"Pissing into the wind," Liam added, because he was never going to give a sincere answer.

Finn gripped his elbows, then realized they were all glaring and crossing their arms. He lowered them quickly to his sides. "Well, you're all welcome to keep doing that."

"I'm out," Alex said. "Of the military. And I'm not planning on reenlisting. I don't have anything else, anywhere else."

"You aren't reenlisting? Is there a reason for that?" Finn asked. His brother had been in the army for more than a decade. Finn could hardly imagine him doing anything else.

"Nothing I want to talk about right now. Right now, we're talking about the ranch. I don't want money. I don't need money. I've got pay from the army for my service as a veteran of a foreign war. But I need something to do. And this ranch is something to do."

Something to do? His life's work was something for Alex to do.

He had honestly never considered his brothers would want to stay in Oregon and work on a dairy farm when there was money on offer. This wasn't a glamorous life. And as far as Finn was concerned, teamwork wasn't the road to happiness. Space was. Control.

How the hell they could think any different was beyond him.

"I don't see the point of dragging me into your career crisis," Finn said, not particularly caring if he sounded insensitive. "If you want to try your hand at something new, by all means, take what I give you and invest in something new."

"Maybe I want to get back to my roots, Finn," Alex said. "Did you think of that?"

"No," Finn returned. "I didn't. I honestly thought that between a stack of cash and a life spent getting up at the ass crack of dawn, you'd choose cash."

"I'm ex-military, Finn. This doesn't feel like a hardship to me. And anyway…we're family."

"Bull. That's not why you're here."

"My reasons don't matter," Alex said. "Not even a little bit. What matters is the will and Grandpa's express wishes. We all have equal share of the ranch if we want it. And I, for one, want it."

Finn looked around the room, daring the others to turn down his offer. "And the rest of you?"

"I already told you," Cain responded. "I'm staying. We're staying. I've been working my ass off trying to give Violet a normal life in Texas. But everybody there knows that her mom walked out. As if it wasn't enough for her to have to deal with Kathleen abandoning her."

"You mean she doesn't see her own daughter?" Alex asked.

"No," Cain said. "She walked out the door one day and neither of us have seen her since."

An uneasy silence fell over the room. Probably because none of them knew whether they were supposed to express sympathy or not. Another thing they had in common, aside from physical mannerisms. They were deeply uncomfortable with emotions.

"I'm staying too," Liam said.

Finn looked at Liam. "Because you love this place so damn much?" He could remember Liam coming to work on the ranch when he'd been a teenager. A surly, jackass teenager who had never seemed particularly interested in the goings-on at the Laughing Irish. No, he was much more interested in the goings-on of Jennifer Hassellbeck's panties.

"Maybe I've grown an interest in animal husbandry." Liam shrugged.

His brother, who Finn knew was actually something of an entrepreneurial genius, most definitely did not have a sudden interest in animal husbandry.

"Right. And I just started a vegan diet," Finn said. "What does this place mean to you? Why do you want it? I know why I want it. I've bled for it, and that's not a metaphor. So you tell me what reasoning you have for thinking you all having equal ownership with me is fair."

"Our reasons are irrelevant, as Alex already pointed out. Grandpa left a quarter of the ranch to each of us. Sorry if that puts a burr under your saddle, Finn," Liam said, "but that's kind of the least of my concerns."

"I just want to know what you bastards think you're getting out of this."

This time, it was Cain who spoke. "Come on now, little brother. Liam and Alex are legitimate. Only you and I are bastards."

"Legitimate or not, once they were adults they never came back here. And neither did you," Finn said. "You can see why I don't much feel like I owe any of you anything. I'm not sure why Grandpa did."

"Maybe the old codger was sentimental," Alex said.

"No," Finn said, "that is definitely not it."

He had been hard, but loyal. Protective. Of the land.

Of his grandson. Finn had never felt much like anyone loved him. Until the day he'd gotten into a mishap with a barbed wire fence and sliced through his thigh. He'd come back home pale and bleeding, and the old man had nearly lost his mind. Worried, he'd said, that it was serious. That he'd *need his damned leg cut off*.

That was the only love Finn knew. And it had been everything to him.

"This is all speculation," Liam said, "and speculation doesn't mean a damn thing. The fact is we are each entitled to our share of the ranch, no matter how much that pisses you off. But here's the deal for you. If you can't handle it why don't you let me buy *you* out. You don't have to stay here. Go start something that belongs to you."

"This place does belong to me, asshole."

"Not legally. It belongs to all of us. I guess you could say it's a Donnelly operation now."

Finn was pretty sure his head was going to blow clean off, right there in his grandpa's living room. Then these three jackasses would get the place all to themselves.

"If I walked," Finn said through gritted teeth, "you couldn't run this place. I am the only one of us here who could do it. You're all dependent on me. I do not need any of you. Remember that."

There was a knock on the door and Alex raised a brow, then his finger, pretending to count all of the people in the room.

"It's dinner," Finn growled.

"Hello." Lane's voice floated in from the entry.

"In the living room," Finn called.

"Great," came the response. "I'm bringing the food

into the kitchen because there is a metric ton of this nonsense."

All of his brothers were looking at him now. "My friend said she would bring dinner," he said. "Though why I'm feeding you is beyond me." He wished he hadn't thought to feed them now, although, rage aside, there was nothing he could do about any of this.

It wasn't like he could withhold food and walk around the house ignoring them. Well, he supposed he could. But if he knew anything about Donnellys, that would only make them dig their heels in deeper.

Alex arched a brow. "Your *friend*?"

"Yes," he said, nearly snarling. "My friend. Because women have brains and personalities, not just breasts, you jackass."

"I usually just consider the brains and personalities obstacles to navigate on my way to the breasts," Liam said.

Cain nearly growled. "Watch your mouth. Boys talk like that, not men. As I've often told my teenage daughter. Who lives in this house now. And I won't have you saying shit like that around her."

"It's just talk," Liam said.

"It's never just talk, little brother. Man up."

"Dinner," Finn barked, turning out of the living area and making his way into the kitchen. Lane was already setting up, a giant bowl of green salad with tongs sticking out the top sitting on the counter. Next to it was a silver pan covered in foil.

Lane was nowhere to be seen.

She appeared a minute later with two more tin pans. One that was filled with meatballs and sauce, another that had pasta.

"Did I go overboard?" she asked.

"Yes," he said, trying to correct his tone.

Lane didn't deserve his mood.

She clapped. "Good. I would rather have you over-fed than underfed."

"Judging by how good that smells, I don't think you have to worry about us not eating," Alex said, walking into the room. Liam and Cain weren't far behind.

"Lane," Finn said, noticing that his tone was more than a little bit surly, but not able to correct it, "this is my brother Alex, and my brother Liam. You met Cain yesterday. Kind of."

Lane waved. "Hi. I hope you don't mind, but I'm going to eat with you. Because this really is enough to feed a small army."

"You cook," Cain said with a crooked smile, "you make the rules. And based on the meal I ate last night, let me just add that you can cook for us anytime."

"I am fairly amazing," she said, putting her hand on her chest, her expression turning overly sincere. "Just don't fall in love with me." She threw a stack of paper plates next to the food. "And dig in."

"I'm going to go see if Violet wants dinner," Cain said. "Though I'd probably have better luck if I texted her." But he turned and walked out of the room anyway.

They began to fill their plates in silence, and a few minutes later Cain reappeared with Violet, who hung back against the wall. Finn studied her for a moment. She was petite. Short and narrow. But her face was pure Donnelly. From the brown hair that hung into her blue eyes, to the firm set of her jaw and mouth. It almost made Finn feel sorry for his brother. Because Donnellys were not easy people to deal with.

"You remember your uncle Alex," Cain said, gesturing. "And your uncle Liam." He said Liam's name with a slight edge.

"Hey," Violet said, barely nodding her head.

"That's teenager for I love you and miss you and thought about you every day since I last saw you," Cain supplied.

That earned a snort from Alex. Neither of them moved to hug Violet, and Finn had a feeling the teenager was only relieved by the lack of forced contact.

Suddenly, Finn was feeling a little bit embarrassed. That Lane was witnessing all of this. The strange, brittle family dynamic. He felt like he was walking across a lake that had frozen over. The ground cracking beneath his feet, and he was never sure which footstep would send him straight through and down to his freezing watery death.

The rest of them were at least all living the same hell. But Lane… Well, to her they must look like a bunch of dysfunctional idiots.

"So," Lane said, her tone a little too bright, which confirmed Finn's suspicions, "Violet, what grade are you going to be in?"

"A junior," she said. "Unless I end up having to repeat a grade because I'm not prepared for advanced tractor mechanics and cow-tipping."

"I doubt you'll have to take those classes. They probably fill up early," Lane said, keeping her tone chipper. "Then again, I can't speak from experience. I didn't actually go to school at Copper Ridge High."

"How much has the town changed in the past ten years?" Alex asked. "I figure that's relevant since we are going to be living here now."

Finn knew that Alex was just poking him now. It didn't make the sinking in his gut any less real.

"Oh," Lane said, shooting Finn a look of surprise.

"He was our grandfather too," Liam said. "And this matters. It means something. God knows we'll never get anything from our father. But we got this, and not him. For that reason alone, I want to stay."

That hit Finn somewhere vulnerable. Somewhere he didn't want to examine too closely. It made Liam's reasoning seem almost justified. And that wasn't what Finn wanted at all.

"Well, things actually have changed quite a bit here," Lane began. "Just in the past few years we've been really revitalizing Old Town. For my part, I bought the old Mercantile, and I sell specialty foods."

"Oh, that boutique food stuff is doing well right now," Liam said. "If I was still doing start-ups, that would be something I'd look to invest in."

Lane sent Finn a triumphant look. "Interesting." She turned her focus to his brothers, and he had a feeling he wasn't going to like what she had to say next, "I've been trying to talk Finn into expanding the ranch's dairy products so that I can sell them in my store."

"Lane," Finn said, his tone full of warning.

"Sorry," she said, licking some sauce off of her thumb, which momentarily distracted him from his irritation. And that was even more irritating. "The business is just on my mind and it slipped out. Especially because I'm going to be starting those subscription boxes soon."

"Smart," Liam said. "I think it's always a good idea to branch out beyond the local economy if you can."

"See?" Finn asked. "Beyond the local economy. That's why I have contracts with a larger dairy."

"I didn't mean it's not good to be part of the local economy," Liam said. "In fact, there's such a big movement for local food, it's a great area to invest in."

"You don't want to work on a ranch," Finn said, pointing at his brother.

"Maybe I want to bring what I already do to the ranch. Did you ever think of that? I'm good at building businesses, Finn."

No, he had not thought of that. Because that would mean giving Liam some credit, which he realized in that moment he never really did. Stupid, since he knew that Liam was successful in his own right, and that he wasn't the sullen teenage boy that Finn had always known him best as.

"I think you should see how things actually run before you start trying to make changes," Finn said, looking at his brother hard. Then he looked at the rest of them. There was no point arguing this out, he knew it. But, truth be told, he thought—no, he believed deep in his gut that a few weeks, maybe months, of the ranch life grind, and they'd be gone.

"All of you. My offer to buy you out is going to stand from here on out. This isn't fun work. I know that you all spent some summers here, and I know you have a vague idea of how it all goes. But to do it year in year out, day in day out, spending your life up to your elbows in literal bullshit is not something any of you know about. So, if at any point it proves to be too much for you, I'll buy you out. But, hell. Don't let your pride stop you if after a couple of weeks your bones ache and you just want to sleep in and it proves to be too much for you. But don't think you can stay then either."

Violet made a face and glared at her father. "Just so we're clear, I'm not doing any of that. Just because you've gone country and dragged me along with you doesn't mean I'm getting involved in this."

Cain looked at his daughter. "I'm sorry. I missed the

memo that you were calling the shots now. If I give you chores, you're going to damn well do them."

"There are child labor laws, you know," she said, taking a bite of pasta and shooting her dad an evil glare.

"Do you think anyone cares much about that out here in the country?"

"You're the literal worst," she said, putting her plate down on the counter and stalking out of the room.

Cain took another bite of his dinner. And he made no move to follow her.

"Should you talk to her?" Of course, it was Lane who questioned him, because the woman never could leave well enough alone.

Cain shrugged. "Maybe. But, trust me, my talking to her doesn't ever smooth anything over." Then Cain looked at Finn. "You think you're going to scare me off with tales of early mornings? I'm already elbows deep in bullshit. At least here, it will be for a reason."

CHAPTER FIVE

LANE KNEW THAT Finn was mad at her. The rest of dinner was tense—not that it had been extraordinarily calm in the beginning, but it certainly didn't get better.

There was no easy conversation between the brothers either. Finn had told her that things were difficult between them, but until she had witnessed it, she hadn't fully understood. She should have believed him. After all, she knew all about difficult families. She hadn't spoken to her parents in years.

By the time she was finished eating and ready to head out the door, her sense of unease had only grown. She hated feeling like he was angry at her. It happened. They had known each other for a long time, and initially in the capacity of her being Mark's irritating younger sister. Who lingered around in the shadows when they were trying to watch an action movie in peace, or who forced them to be guinea pigs for her latest cooking experiment.

But as they'd eased into adulthood, and into a real friendship in their own right, rarely had Finn ever looked at her like he wanted to drown her in the ocean. About now, he was looking vaguely murderous.

When she said her goodbyes to everyone and headed for the door, she wasn't surprised when Finn followed her outside. He closed the door hard behind them, crossing his arms over his chest, then dropping them almost immediately. He let out a long, slow breath. "Are you going to apologize for that?"

"Me?" she all but squeaked. "You were being a jerk."

"I'm sorry if you don't understand my family dynamic, which consists mainly of us calling each other names while we try not to punch each other in the face. But that has nothing to do with you, and it's definitely not for you to lecture me about. What was that stunt you pulled?"

She threw her arms wide, the cool night air washing over her bare limbs. "Oh, do you mean cooking you a delicious dinner? How dare I?"

"I mean bringing up the dairy stuff. I know it's what you want me to do, but if you think you're going to railroad me by going through my brothers—"

"Are you serious right now?" Anger spiked inside of her. "You honestly think that I was trying to manipulate you?"

"Can you *honestly* say on any level that you weren't?"

She almost exploded with denial, then stopped herself, chewing on the words for a moment. Being honest with herself—really honest—she supposed there was part of her that maybe brought it up in front of other people to get a more positive consensus. Because she knew it was a good idea, and she figured that if someone besides stubborn Finn heard it, she would find an ally.

"I thought so," he said, rocking back on his heels.

"You know me," she said, instead of denying it outright. "I was just carried away by my own enthusiasm. That's all it was—I promise."

"The situation with them… I cannot believe that they think they're going to stay here and take ownership of this ranch. It's mine."

She wanted to reach out and touch him, but she remembered what had happened when she'd done that the night before. It had been strange. It had left her fingertips feeling tingly. And she didn't want to do it again.

Instead, she did her best to make her face sympathetic. "I don't know what to tell you. Except that life changes and people suck."

"Thank you," he said, his tone deadpan.

"Hey, I don't make the rules. If I did, unicorns would be real and we would definitely have figured out teleportation by now."

"I'd vote for you."

Something about that made her stomach curdle. Mostly because it made her think of Cord again. She had been thinking of him way too much over the past few days. She felt wrung out. And watching Finn go through this too… She wanted to curl into a ball and lick her own wounds, not deal with his.

Typically, he was the steady rock of the two of them. He was a cowboy, for heaven's sake. Riding around his property on a horse with a big hat. Doing all the work, day in day out. Finn was like the tide. Dependable. And always where he was supposed to be when he was supposed to be there.

But right now, he seemed on the verge of cracking, and when she had looked at someone and seen a stalwart for so long it was a little bit jarring.

And completely unfair. She was having a thing. She needed him to not have a thing right now.

"Thanks," she said, feeling like a jerk, because of course he was having a hard time. He'd lost his grandfather, and now he was expected to share the ranch he'd invested his entire life in. Finn didn't share well. And he didn't unclench easily.

She had a feeling his real resistance to considering her plan had to do with the fact that he didn't like being told what to do, even if he was being told to do the right thing.

"I'm sorry," she said finally, because she probably did owe him an apology. Maybe she hadn't meant to be manipulative, but she couldn't argue that there was a little of that underneath the surface. Even if it was well-intentioned and deeply buried manipulation. "I meant to bring pasta, not an agenda. And you know that I would never ask you to do something I thought was a bad idea. I'm not going to tell you to do something that benefits me but not you."

"I know that. But too many things are changing, and I can't consider another one right now." He took a deep breath and moved to the edge of the porch, grabbing hold of the railing and wrapping his fingers around the top. "I was twelve the first time I came here. My father was consumed with Liam and Alex, who were younger, so they needed him more. My mom was involved in her own stuff. When I came here… I felt like my days had a purpose. I could change the earth with my hands. That's pretty intense for a kid whose entire life was made hell by selfish adults. Who didn't have control over one damn thing up until that point."

He turned to look at her, his expression deadly serious. There was something in his face just then, the intensity and the glint of his dark eyes, the set of his square jaw and the firm press of his lips that made something respond inside her. An answering tension that began in the pit of her stomach and worked its way down her limbs, leaving something restless and edgy in its wake.

He continued, "I know that the rest of them all spent some time here. But nobody connected with the place like I did. And when I was sixteen I left my mom's house for good. I came here, and my grandfather treated me like a man. He gave me work to do. He gave me a purpose. This place is my purpose."

Her throat was dry, and so was her mouth. She wanted to do something. To close the distance between them.

Put her arms around him, maybe.

She could only imagine how he would react if she tried to hug him after he shared his feelings. He would probably have a straight-up allergic reaction.

So she just stayed where she was, curling her fingers into fists, trying to do something to stem that flow of restless energy that was coursing through her. This was where their friendship was strange. Because if it were Rebecca, Alison or Cassie, she wouldn't hesitate to offer them some kind of physical comfort.

Here she was. Made of hesitation.

"I understand that," she said, her voice sounding scratchy. "I mean, I know what it's like to find hope in a place." She bit her lip. She really didn't like talking about the circumstances that had brought her to Copper Ridge. She was good at dancing around them. But Finn had been there from the beginning. So while he didn't know the details—her brother didn't even know—he had a sense of what it had been like in her childhood home.

"When I came here," she said, "I felt lost. And scared. And yes, I had Mark, but leaving my parents like I did was... Terrifying. You don't even know. Louise and Philip Jensen do not allow for dissent in the ranks. And I...dissented. Leaving like I did made it very clear, and I could never go back. As soon as I got to town it was like finding a safe haven. A harbor that sheltered me from the storm. I know that's total hyperbole, but it's the truth. My heart is here. So when you say that this ranch gave you focus, when you say that it matters—bone deep—I get it. I do. I'm not your enemy. But I might just play devil's advocate. Maybe your brothers need this place right now too."

He let out a long, heavy sigh. "I mean, I guess it could be worse."

"How? Sneaker waves? An anvil falling from the sky?"

"No," he said, his tone sounding impatient.

"Oh! Plague of locusts."

"Lane," he said, his tone a warning. "No. It could be worse because I could be the one stuck with a teenager."

Lane wrinkled her nose. "Poor Cain."

Though, in some ways, her heart went out to that girl. At sixteen, Lane's life had changed forever. She'd been forced to grow up too quickly. She had a feeling that Violet had been too, though in a different way.

It was clear her mother wasn't around, and Lane knew that no matter how messy your relationship with your parents was, it hurt when you finally pulled the plug on it.

"They won't stay," Finn said, and she had a feeling he was saying it more for his benefit than for hers.

"Maybe they won't."

"You don't believe that."

She closed her eyes for a moment, let the sounds of the night sink into her skin, all the way down to her bones. There was a faint dampness to the air, a tinge of salt and pine on the breeze. It was a cold night, but it was getting to be summer and she could hear the chirp of a few crickets. The faint croak of tiny tree frogs, likely hiding in the dampness beneath the porch.

"No," she said eventually. "I don't. Mostly because

I don't see why anybody would ever want to leave this place."

"The ranch, or town in general?"

"I meant Copper Ridge in general. But I have to admit that this house has a leg up on my rather rustic little cabin. You'd better be careful, or I'm going to want to move in too."

"I'm much more likely to move in with you," he said after a pause. "I mean, if my house gets any more crowded."

She laughed, and for some reason it sounded a little more nervous than she felt. "There may be fewer people in my house, but it's small. Tiny. We would have to share a bed."

For some reason, that comment seemed to land in an odd spot. It just kind of hit heavy between them, like a sad, popped balloon that had fallen back down to earth.

And they both just stood there, staring at it. "I mean," she said, making a last-ditch effort to redeem it. "You would sleep on the floor. In my room. Like a slumber party. But don't laugh at my headgear." He still wasn't saying anything. "We could braid each other's hair, talk about boys..." Why wasn't he saying anything? She really needed him to stop her. She was making it weird, and there was nothing to make weird. And yet, frequently over the past few days things had felt exactly that.

Something hard was in his gaze now, and she didn't like it.

"Eat cookie dough," she said finally. And then she was done. She really was done. "Okay." She took a deep breath and started to step away from him. "I have to go. I'll see you tomorrow. Maybe. I mean, you don't have to see me tomorrow. But, actually at least call me, because I want to know what's going on with everybody. Your brothers. That's what I mean. Okay."

She took a step away and he surprised her by reaching out, grabbing hold of her arm and stopping her from taking another step. She froze, her gaze meeting his. Her heart kicked into a higher gear, and she couldn't for the life of her figure out what was going on. But breathing was suddenly very difficult.

It was related to the awkwardness. To this whole strange path she had started to walk down earlier in the day, and had continued on into that never-ending ramble. And now it had led to this. Except, her mouth had stopped so her heart was now moving at a near-impossible pace.

"When I spend the night with a woman I don't do any of those things." His voice was rough, and it skimmed over her frazzled nerves in a way that sent a strange electric current through her. "Just so you know."

Then he released his hold on her and she stumbled back, her skin burning where his fingers had just been.

He was holding on to the porch rail again, looking out into the darkness. "See you tomorrow."

Lane got in her car and started to drive, and it wasn't until she saw the lights on Main Street that her heart rate returned to normal.

CHAPTER SIX

THERE WERE FEW things more satisfying than looking across the breakfast table at his brothers at five in the morning and seeing just how miserable they were.

Cain was leaning back in his chair, his arm slung over the back like it was a brace that was keeping him from sliding right to the floor. Liam was scowling, one hand curved around a travel mug full of coffee, the other pushed into his dark hair, his elbow resting on the table, like it was propping his head up.

Alex was the only one who was upright, his cup held tightly in both hands, and placed down in his lap. Finn imagined the military ran on ranching time.

But the other two—they thought they wanted to be ranchers? They thought they wanted to live this life, this punishing, rewarding life that made you both master of and slave to the land around you? Yeah, he had a feeling that about now they were questioning that decision.

Their misery was balm for his soul.

And a much-needed distraction from all the tension that had wrapped itself around his spine and tied him up in knots over the past few days.

His grandfather. His family.

Lane.

Damned if he knew why he'd said what he had to her last night. Why he'd given in to that snarling, hot beast that was ravaging his gut and demanding he make her as uncomfortable as he was.

She had looked at him like—well, like he'd grown another head. Which should be all the reminder he needed as to why he didn't go there with her. Ever.

He blamed his grandfather for dying. Blamed his brothers for being here. His whole damn life for being out of whack.

He needed to find his control again.

The ranch.

Once he got his brothers out there working, they would see how in over their heads they were. And how on top of things *he* was.

He took a sip of his coffee. "I get up this early every morning," he commented. "Rain or shine. Can't skip a day. Animals are needy like that."

"You sound like Grandpa," Liam said, his tone gravelly and terse.

"You hated it when you were sixteen, Liam. I don't know what made you think you might like it now. Five o'clock is still very early in the morning."

"Things change," Liam returned.

"Not getting up before sunrise," Finn said.

He turned and headed back toward the coffeepot, frowning when he saw that it was empty. That was going to take some adjusting. He was going to need to get an industrial-sized coffeemaker. He might be an early rising convert, but he didn't do it without caffeine.

"Let's go," he said, turning back to face his brothers.

He led the way through the house, grabbing his Stetson off the shelf on his way out and positioning it firmly on his head. He didn't bother with the jacket, though mornings were cold, even at the end of June.

It would warm up soon enough and he didn't need to be encumbered.

The rest of them—he noticed—were wearing coats and sweatshirts. Only Alex had a hat on.

"You think it's cold?" he asked, smiling. An evil smile filled with more than a little enjoyment for their suffering.

"I've been living in Texas for almost twenty years," Cain responded. "This coastal air is mean."

"Are you admitting that Texas made you soft? Because I think I hear the sound of an entire state challenging you to a duel."

Cain grumbled something about Texans preferring a bar brawl to a duel while zipping his jacket up all the way as they made their way down the stairs and headed toward the barn.

Finn made quick introductions to the facility, and set to getting the cows into their positions. He made quick work of explaining prep and milking—since none of them were completely unfamiliar with it—and then he put every single one of them to work.

He had to admit, it was nice to have extra hands.

Morning milking went quick, and from there it was time to deal with the other animals. Then they had to move the cows from one pasture to another.

"Saddle up," Finn said, smiling as he presented his brothers with the horses they would be riding today.

"I didn't know you still went in for this cowboy bullshit," Liam said.

"Without the cowboy bullshit I wouldn't bother," Finn said, swinging himself up easily onto his horse. "Besides, at the end of the day, it's much easier to do it this way. At least by my way of thinking. Don't need half as many access roads."

"I don't remember Grandpa moving the cows around. From pasture to pasture I mean," Cain said. "We had to bring them in to eat."

"Well, that's something else that's changing," Finn said. "Mostly we're not doing grain anymore. Or corn. We've been working to get them on a primarily grass diet. A lot of people think it improves the flavor of the milk. Of course, now everything needs to be hormone free. And the more asterisks you can put on the label the better. Hormone free, antibiotic free, grass fed, vegetarian fed… Whatever. It doesn't necessarily make a huge difference with the bigger dairies, but we were transitioning in order to keep our options open."

While he made his grand explanation, the others had finished with their tack and had gotten on their horses.

"Does that mean you're considering that thing your friend was talking about?" Liam asked.

"No," he said, "it doesn't. Just hedging our bets is all. Because you never know when some health guru is going to get pulled off the internet and onto a morning show, telling people about the supposed dangers of something everyone has eaten forever. It's nice to be ahead." He was being stubborn. Maybe he was even lying a little bit. "What I do," he continued, urging his horse to go a little bit faster, "I do because I want to do it. And I'll do it in my own time."

"Yeah," Alex said, and without even turning to look, Finn could tell his younger brother had a smart-ass grin on his face, "you have definitely turned into Grandpa."

There were worse things, Finn thought privately as he maneuvered the horse closer to the cows that were happily grazing in the field. Callum Donnelly might've been a cranky son of a gun, but he had been constant. Steady. Nothing like that worthless son of his that had fathered four sons with three different women and hadn't stuck around to raise a blessed one of them.

Their father had died because of hard living. And he'd left them absolutely nothing.

Yeah, he would much rather turn into his grandfather than his father. No doubt about that.

"Follow my lead," Finn said. "You may remember something about this from your time here. Cain, Liam, I want you on the sides. Alex, bring up the rear. I'll be with you."

They brought the horses into formation, and after that, Finn turned everything else off. All he did was focus on the mountains that surrounded them, covered with evergreen trees and reaching toward the sky. The clouds were burning away, the summer sun pouring out onto the field, spilling drops of gold on the grass, making it look like the ends of each and every blade were glowing.

Yellow flowers mixed in with the green, joining in with the sunlight to make it look like a bit of that warm magic had touched the earth right here.

Finn wasn't a man given to poetry, but out here, it was easy to veer that way.

Easier still when his brothers were quiet.

This place was his sanity. His soul. And he let that sunshine burn away as much of the tension inside of him as it possibly could.

He could think more clearly out here, on the back of his horse. The world was reduced to the hoofbeats all around him, to the mountains, to the trees.

And he didn't think about what might happen to the ranch if all four Donnellys ended up living here and fighting over their piece of it. Didn't think about that dumbass stuff he'd pulled with Lane last night.

If there was a perfect moment in his life, he knew it was going to happen on horseback, riding on his own property.

So whenever he saddled up he took care to live in the moment. Took care not to miss it.

By the time they finished driving the cattle from one place to the next and rode back again it was nearly lunchtime. They were all sweaty and dirty, and he could tell that they were all regretting their choice of outer-wear and their lack of a hat to keep the sun off their faces.

"I may have a farmer tan," Finn said, unable to resist the urge to needle them, "but at least I'm comfortable."

"Beer," Alex grunted when they walked into the house.

Liam went to the fridge and pulled out two bottles, handing one to Alex before taking a seat at the table. A very slow seat. "Fuuuuuuuck." The word extended through the entire motion, until he was settled in the chair. "That is not like riding a bike," he said.

"No," Finn said, leaning against the wall and survey-ing the group. "Not even a little bit. And if you think it hurts now…just wait until tomorrow. I went easy on you guys today."

"I don't think my daughter is even awake yet," Cain grumbled, getting his own beer out of the fridge and popping the top violently on the counter.

"Yeah, I'm going to leave the designation of chores for the teenager to you," Finn said. "I'm her uncle. Not her dad. And I don't particularly want to play the part of bad guy."

He was feeling cheerful for the first time in days.

"You got fat in the off-season, Liam," Alex said.

Liam shot him a deadly look. "Tell you what. I invite you to start a fight with me and see just how out of shape I am. I just haven't ridden a horse in... Well, since I was last here."

Alex shrugged, crossing his arms and lifting his beer to his lips. "I don't need to fight you to know that twelve years in the army gives me the advantage. I haven't ridden a horse recently either, but I'm fine."

Alex hadn't looked all that fine only a few moments ago, but it seemed as though he was redirecting his stance now that he saw how miserable Cain and Liam were. It was impossible not to like Alex sometimes. Even though he was an obnoxious son of a bitch.

"Yeah," Liam grumbled, "well, some of us haven't lived at boot camp for the past twelve years."

"True. But then, neither have I. Boot camp looks friendly next to Afghanistan," Alex said. "Trust me." He took another sip of beer. "Come to that, cows look friendly next to Afghanistan too."

Alex was going to be the toughest one to scare off, Finn realized. He seemed like the easygoing one. Like the one who would cut and run when things got difficult. But there was an intensity that went beneath the surface, a strength that the rest of them hadn't really been around to witness but that Finn knew was there just the same.

"We're going to have to milk the cows again in a couple of hours. Take a break. Eat. There's food in the fridge from last night, or you can drive down to town if you're in the mood. Just be back by two."

Alex and Liam looked at each other, then left the room. Either to go grab some rest or a burger, Finn didn't know. But he didn't really care. Unless they were going to hightail it back to where they came from.

But that left him alone in the room with Cain. And

he had never really known what kind of things he was supposed to talk about with his older brother. They had a lot in common in some ways. They were the ones that stood alone, isolated. No full-blood brother, and very little in the way of attention from their father.

Though it was a strange thing to have the common ground between yourself and your brother marked by all the things you didn't have in common. Where you were raised. Who you were raised by.

But in his family those strange connections were all you had anyway.

"You don't have to enjoy this so much." Cain leaned back in his seat, resting his head on the back of the chair. "I'm thirty-seven, not seventeen. And I feel every year of it right about now."

"You own a ranch, Cain," Finn said, looking at his older brother. "Why are you acting like you haven't been on the back of a horse since the dawn of time?"

"It's probably been a couple of years," he said. "I paid other people to manage the actual day-to-day stuff. At least, that's how it's been since my wife left."

"So you just turned everything over to other people?" That was unfathomable to Finn. He liked to have his hand in every aspect of the ranch. Sure, he had people who worked at the Laughing Irish other than himself and his grandpa, but he was in charge, unquestionably. And he went out and rode the perimeter of the place almost every day. It was in his heart, in his blood. And he didn't possess the ability to let go of even a piece of it.

"I had too much to hold on to in my personal life." Cain swore, setting his beer down on the table. "I love being a father, but I can't say that I ever thought I was the best one. But now I'm all Violet has. And I felt like… How could I possibly be out working on the ranch when there was more than enough money coming in if I never touched it? Someone had to make sure everything was all right at school. That all of her homework was getting done. And I could let the work go, so I did. Anyway, there was still paperwork. And I basically buried myself in that, plus doing the legal work of making sure I got sole custody. So that Kathleen could never just walk back into our lives and decide she wanted to try and take Violet from me. Not after she left the way she did."

"Why did she leave?" They had never talked about this. But then, they had never talked about much of anything. Finn hadn't even fully realized that Cain's ex-wife had removed herself so completely from the picture.

"Probably for a million stupid reasons. And a couple of really good ones." He paused, looking down at his hands. "But the worst part about somebody leaving you like that is you can't shout it out. I mean, I know enough to know she wasn't kidnapped or anything. Because trust me, that was my first thought. Your wife disappears on you and the first thing you want to do is call the police. Because there's no way she'd leave her thirteen-year-old daughter, right? I mean, sure, maybe she'd leave the husband she could hardly say a civil word to. But Violet? That's the part I don't get."

He stood, pacing the length of the kitchen before he paused at the window over the kitchen sink, just as Finn had done a few days ago. He looked out at the view, taking it all in, and Finn felt a strange mixture of irritation and pride as his older brother surveyed everything Finn had worked to make this ranch over the past nearly two decades.

"It's the part I can't forgive," Cain said heavily. Then he turned back to Finn. "If you think a full day of work, day in day out, scares me, you don't know what I've been through. I'm raising a teenage girl, Finn. I'm not scared of jack shit except all the ways I might fuck that up." He took a weighted breath. "But I need something new. She needs something new. Otherwise, we're just going to sit there mired in old memories and drown. I need your money even less than Alex does. My ranch was big, and when I sold it I got more than I'll ever spend. I can invest it back into the Laughing Irish. I can invest in Violet's future. That's what I want. But this isn't about needing property, or needing to earn a living. Not for me."

Cain didn't have to get into a deeper explanation than that. Mostly because Finn recognized exactly what Cain needed this place to be. It was the same thing Finn had needed when he'd showed up, angry and lost at sixteen.

He didn't need money. He needed salvation.

"I'm warning you," Finn said. "This ranch will drag a whole lot out of you before it starts putting anything back. And then, it'll always be that way. Give and take. You and the land."

"That's all right," Cain said. "I kind of want it to hurt."

Finn didn't want to understand Cain. Because that was perilously close to being on his brother's side. To wanting to help him out in some way. He bristled against his growling conscience.

He should want to help his brother, he supposed. It was much easier to oppose his presence when he imagined that Cain wanted to be here for the wrong reasons. That it didn't matter. That a payout would make things square.

This made it a whole lot more difficult. It made Finn feel a whole lot more petty.

"Violet doesn't seem very happy to be here," he pointed out. Which was maybe the lowest blow he'd tried to land yet.

Cain laughed, but there was no humor in it. "She's not happy anywhere. I don't know what to… I mean… It's like she's a different person now. She used to be this adorable, little bitty thing. And I can remember her with two missing front teeth and a big smile so clearly that half the time that's still what I expect to see when I look at her. Instead she's this sullen creature that will barely make eye contact with me. She was mad at me in Texas. I figure she can be mad at me here. But at least maybe with a little less baggage hanging around." He shook his head. "I could never shake the feeling that she was waiting for her mother to come back. And the longer we stayed at the ranch, the more I felt like that was why. That it was why we were both still there. It had to stop."

All of this, the emotion, the understanding, scraped against Finn like a particularly splintered board on bare skin.

"I don't know what to say," Finn responded finally. "Mostly because there's nothing I can say that won't make me sound like an ass."

Cain lifted a shoulder. "Maybe because you are one."

"Maybe," Finn agreed.

"I'm not the easiest person to get along with," Cain said. "Every woman who has ever passed through my life will attest to that. Particularly, at the moment, my daughter. I'm not one to promise that we are not going to butt heads here. But I can tell you that I'm not here to ruin your life. I'm just trying my damnedest to fix mine."

CHAPTER SEVEN

A DAY OFF was exactly what Lane needed to get her head on straight. She was tired, that was the thing. Overtired and emotionally taxed. It was why she had acted like such a weirdo last night when Finn had touched her.

And why she had been persistently weird about it all the way home, and while she was trying to go to sleep.

What he had said had continued to play over and over in her mind.

When a woman spends the night with me, I don't do any of that.

She was a curious creature by nature, and his saying something like that forced her to try and imagine all the things he might do. Which had ended very quickly because the images she'd conjured had been awkward and strange and had left her stomach feeling tight and flipped inside out all at the same time.

Normally, she did her best to never imagine Finn doing anything remotely sensual. He was a constant in her life. And he was a man, yes, and she wasn't blind. But when she'd met Finn she'd been in such a terrible, vulnerable place, and he'd been the friend she'd needed. She'd spent the ensuing years resolutely keeping him in that category.

It had taken Rebecca's almost hooking up with Finn to jolt Lane into finally acknowledging that he was, indeed, a man.

And then there was what he'd said last night. About what he did and didn't do when a woman spent the night. It left a lot to the imagination. And her imagination was a bright and inquisitive thing.

So today, she was doing her best to keep it dampened by puttering around in the garden. She had kept herself outside, and all forms of media shut off. No internet. No radio. No TV. No chance of upsetting images infiltrating her home.

Being on the ground, up to her elbows in dirt, was much more satisfying than catching a glimpse of the Ghost of Teenage Mistakes Past on the news.

Anyway, she had plenty to do. There was enough lettuce that she was going to have to bring it to the store if she had a hope of using it all. Picking and processing that, separating it out into individual plastic bags so it was ready for people to take home as premade salad mix, had eaten up a good portion of her time.

Then she had gone to wander around in the thicker part of the woods around her property. Her knee-length lace dress kept getting snagged on sticker bushes, but she didn't mind. She minded more when the raspberries and blackberries twined around her legs and left little teeth marks in her skin.

But there were no prizes for timidity when it came to picking blackberries. The good ones were typically on the very top of the bushes, reaching up toward the sun. She hummed as she dropped the plump fruit into milk jugs she had cut the tops off.

They made for handy berry buckets, and they were cheap and disposable so if the juice stained the inside it didn't much matter.

She didn't mind the typically gray weather on the Oregon coast, but she very much prized the summertime. She closed her eyes, allowing the sun to bathe her in gentle warmth as she continued her work.

The mild weather through the winter and slightly earlier warmth of the summer had ensured that the berries ripened a little bit earlier than usual. And she held out hope that even more would ripen between July and August.

Little containers of the berries would fetch a decent price in the Mercantile, and anything extra would go to Alison, for pie and pastries and maybe for that jam she was thinking of asking Alison to supply her.

She wondered if Cassie would want any for The Grind, for a kind of special scone or biscotti. The thought had Lane humming to herself, imagining all of the baked goods she could talk her friends into making for her.

She liked her own baked goods too, of course. But sometimes things just tasted better when they were made *for* you.

She bent, grabbing her half-full container of blackberries by the handle, then scooping up the one she'd managed to fill most of the way up with raspberries, as well. With her free hand, she held on to her dress, trying to keep it away from the sticker bushes as she picked her way back through the thick foliage until she got to the well-worn path that would take her back to her house.

She paused for a moment in a clearing, allowing a shaft of sun to fall over her bare arms. She relaxed, holding the heavy buckets down low at her sides as she closed her eyes and tilted her face up. She listened then. To the birds, and the faint sound of the breeze ruffling through the treetops.

She breathed in, that heady mixture of soil, wood

and pine that was only headier in the damp forest as the temperatures rose.

Then she heard the sound of car tires crunching on the gravel driveway that led to her house. She paused, frowning. She wasn't expecting anybody, and unless they had gone too far and needed to turn around, no one had any reason to be driving up to her place.

She mobilized, walking up to the back door of her cabin and letting herself inside, passing quickly through the small house and peeking through the front window so that she could get a glimpse at the driver, without him seeing her first.

She let out a sigh of relief when she saw that it was Finn. And then for some reason on the heels of that relief came a surge of tension that rested like a ball in her chest.

She breathed in again, just like she had done outside, but this time, it was for fortification. This time, it was to try and do something to get rid of that tightness in her lungs.

Lane waited until he got out of his truck. Until he walked up the steps and stopped in front of the door. Then she waited until he knocked.

Only then did she open the door.

"Hi," he said.

She just stood there, staring at him for a moment, her chest feeling tighter. He looked tired. His hat was pushed back on his head, dirt on his face making the lines around his eyes and mouth look more pronounced. His tight white T-shirt was streaked with even more dirt, and she could see on his battered jeans where he had wiped his hands on his thighs all day.

It was typical for Finn to look this filthy after a day on the ranch. But it was the exhaustion that struck her.

"What's going on?" she asked, stepping back and allowing him entry into the house.

"It's just a little too crowded at my place. So I thought I would come out here for a while."

"Of course," she said, backing into the kitchen, moving behind the counter and for some reason breathing a little easier once she did.

"What do you have there?" he asked, gesturing to the milk jugs.

"Raspberries and blackberries," she said, picking them up and turning to put them in the fridge. "I'll deal with them later."

"I take it this is your version of a day off."

"Some of us don't work outside every day. I find a little bit of time in the garden relaxing. I took a walk through the woods, spent some time picking lettuce."

"Basically, a rabbit's perfect day."

She made a face at him. "And a Lane's perfect day."

He chuckled. "I was actually wondering if you'd mind if I took a swim in the lake."

"Of course not," she said. Suddenly, she felt hot and sticky, and the idea of cooling off at her own piece of Lake Carmichael was more than a little enticing.

"Great. I have all my swim stuff in the truck. I'll strip down out there so I don't get any of my dirty clothes on your floor. Do you want to join me?"

For a full second Lane's brain was hung up on the words *strip down* and *join me*. She knew that they were separate. She did. But there was something about him saying them in such close succession that snagged her brain and just sort of hung there. Like the stickers against her dress.

"In the lake," she said finally.

"Yeah," he returned slowly.

"Sure. Yeah. I'll just… I'll go get ready while you… Strip down." She cleared her throat and scampered her ass out of the room.

She forced her brain into a blank space while she undressed and pulled her bikini on. The idea of walking out in her bathing suit seemed weird somehow. Even though they were only going to swim together, which they had done a million times. She growled and grabbed her dress, tugging it over the top of her swimsuit. There.

But was he done getting dressed? That was the question.

She hemmed and hawed for a minute before finally exiting her bedroom and making her way cautiously back to the front door. She peeked out the curtain again, and saw him standing there in nothing but a pair of shorts.

Well, he was dressed. Sort of.

He had a towel hung over his arm, and that reminded her she needed to grab one. She detoured back to the bathroom and took one off the shelf, then burst outside, not hesitating this time. "I'm ready," she said.

He looked at her, a strange light in his eyes. "Okay," he said.

The gravel was warm beneath her feet, and she kept her eyes down, making sure she didn't step on anything sharp as they walked down the well-worn path to the lake.

There were houses all around the perimeter of the lake, but mostly on the other side, around a slight curve that kept everything from view. Those were larger houses, more desirable.

Lane's friend Rebecca had owned one of the more modest houses on that end of the lake, near to Gage West's extravagant lakeside cabin.

Lane's house wasn't exactly lakeside. Neither was it extravagant. But still she owned a little bit of the shoreline. The first year she'd been financially solvent she had had a dock put in, and then she had commissioned Jonathan Bear, Rebecca's brother, to build her a bench swing that hung from a tree that stretched over the water.

It was her sanctuary.

Finn bent down and picked up a rock, running his fingers over the smooth-looking edges. And she tried not to think about why that made her stomach feel hollow.

He drew his arms back, then flung the rock toward the lake. It skipped three times across the surface before sinking to the bottom. "Want to make a wish?" he asked. "I've got three."

This had been their game for a long time. Skipping rocks and earning wishes. Mostly because she couldn't do it. So he always got to portion out the wishes he earned with his superior skills.

"I will get my own," she said, bending to choose her own rock.

"It's not flat enough," he said.

"It's fine," she countered, moving to the edge of the lake.

She repeated the same motion he'd just done, running her fingers over the cool surface of the stone, ignoring that hers wasn't perfectly smooth.

Then she cocked her arm back and flung the rock forward.

It hit the surface of the water and crashed on through, a splash like a fountain rising up in its wake.

"One wish," she said, holding up her finger. "I get one."

"No," he explained. "It has to skip."

"You got three! If the first one doesn't count you should only get two."

"The first one counts if it's a skip and not sinking," he said.

"You're mean. And I think this game is rigged."

"Do you want a wish or not?"

"I wish you would jump in a lake," she snipped.

He turned and smiled at her, that crooked grin of his making something inside her feel off balance too. "Your wish is my command."

He took two long strides to the dock and then another long one off, diving headfirst into the still, serene water, leaving nothing but a circular ripple behind as he disappeared beneath the surface.

He reappeared a second later, whipping his head back, a stream of water flying from his dark hair. He rubbed his hand over his face, pushing water drops from his skin while he kept himself afloat.

"Come on." He gestured broadly, slapping the surface of the lake.

She rolled her eyes and reach down, grabbing the hem of her dress and shimmying slightly as she pulled it over her head. She could feel him watching her, and for some reason it felt incredibly awkward.

Apparently stripping her dress off in front of him was more awkward than just walking out in her bikini would have been. Even though she knew she had a swimsuit on underneath, she felt somehow strange and insecure. Like maybe she was wrong, and she had forgotten something crucial and she might be getting naked in front of him without realizing it.

She flung the dress to the side, letting it land in a patch of grass. And then she checked quickly to see that she was—in fact—wearing her suit.

She wrapped her arms around herself, clinging to her own midsection as she shuffled across the dock. The wood was warm beneath her feet, but she knew the water was going to be cold.

"How is it, Donnelly?"

"Like a hot tub," he said, smiling in a way that let her know he was lying. And not even very well.

"Somehow, I'm skeptical of that."

"You think I would lie to you?" He swam nearer to the dock.

"Yes," she said.

He gripped the end of the dock, looking up at her, his brows lifted, his forehead slightly wrinkled. He was the picture of boyish innocence. Except for his muscles. For some reason, she found herself drawn to the way the water droplets slid down the ridges of his shoulders, over his chest.

She blinked.

"I'm shocked," he said, doing a very good impression of someone who might be wounded. "How could you not trust me? One of your very oldest friends?"

"That's exactly why, Finn," she said, leaning down slightly. "Because I've known you for far too long. And I think that you want me to jump in and freeze myself. Because you'll think it's funny. You're a child. And I know you well enough to know that."

"Really?"

She bent down lower, hands on her knees. "Really."

And that was the last thing she said before Finn reached up, wrapped his arms around her waist and pulled her up against him, bringing her down beneath the surface of the water with him. He brought her right back up again, still holding on to her.

She sputtered, a hank of dark hair drooping in her

face, lake water streaming down into her mouth. "You brat!" She shrieked, pushing her hair up out of her face, feeling it resting there on top of her head in an inglorious mat. She reached out, holding on to the dock while kicking her legs, the cool lake water swirling around her.

"You were going to get in anyway. I saved us both a bunch of time *and* shrieking."

"I'm still shrieking!"

"But not as much as you would have if you'd worked your way in slowly."

"Oh," she said, "okay, you saved shrieking. But who's going to save you?"

She turned, launching herself away from the dock and at Finn, pressing down on his shoulders and pushing his head beneath the water. He went easily. Easily enough that she knew he hadn't bothered with any real fight. In fact, he had allowed the dunking. It was a pity dunk.

When he came back up, he shook his head and doused her with water. Then he grinned, water rolling down his face, the look in his eye mischievous and maybe even a little bit predatory.

She became very aware, suddenly, of the warmth of his skin beneath her palms, in stark contrast to the chilly water. She kicked her feet, and her legs tangled with his for a moment. She gasped, moving away from him and ducking beneath the water, swimming as hard and fast as she could. Away from him.

When she resurfaced, he was still back by the dock and she had gone out quite a way. She continued to tread water there for a while, keeping an eye on him. As far as she could tell he was just looking at her. Looking at her and doing nothing. For what reason? She had no idea. But she wasn't about to ponder it too deeply.

She shook her head and went face forward into the water again, swimming in a straight but aimless line. When she looked back at the dock, she saw that he was lying out on the wood, his arms thrown up over his head, water pooling around him.

Submerging again, Lane swam back toward where he was, gripping the edge of the dock and levering herself up beside him. She was breathing hard, the exertion of her impromptu lap swim leaving her limbs feeling wrung out and vaguely like spaghetti.

Wind whipped across the surface of the lake, rippling the dark water, and then skimming over her skin, leaving goose bumps behind. The wood was warm, so she lay down too, next to Finn but with a healthy amount of distance between them.

They had done this a thousand times—swimming, dunking each other, relaxing in the sun afterward. And never before had there been this strange undercurrent. It was her. It had to be. The non-thing with Rebecca and Finn nearly hooking up was only part of it. Normally, she would have just brushed that off. But the intensity of how unsettled she'd been recently, the almost-manic energy and drive she had felt to do something—anything—with her business so that she would be as accomplished as she needed to be—it was making her tense even around her oldest friend.

She felt like a fragile, knit creation that had gone through the past ten years with a loose thread hanging free somewhere. Unnoticed. Undisturbed.

Until the past few weeks when Cord McCaffrey had gone national with his whole handsome, charismatic politician shtick.

Now the thread had been pulled. *She* had been pulled. That loose string yanked and yanked until she felt threadbare and dangerously close to unraveling completely.

This edginess was just a symptom of that unraveling. All of those patchy, unprotected places suddenly more vulnerable to…whatever this was.

What she had to do was get their friendship back on typical footing. She should ask him how things were going with his brothers. Why he was so tired. If there was anything she could do.

She rolled over onto her side, and her breath caught in her throat. Anything she'd been about to say died.

Her eyes were held captive by him. By that sharp, angular curve of his jaw that was dusted with a couple days' worth of stubble.

From there, she looked at the strong column of his throat, which was notable somehow. Maybe because it was yet another thing that signified his maleness. And then there was his chest. She had been swimming with him about a million times, give or take. She had seen him without a shirt the moment she had looked out her living room window today. They had walked down to the lake together. But still, she had somehow managed to avoid really seeing.

For years, she had managed to avoid seeing.

Now all she could do was *see*.

That broad expanse of chest covered with dark hair. The ridges of muscle that shifted each time he breathed, running down his abdomen like a perfect, living washboard. Down to the hard cut of muscle at his waist that pointed downward, framing the flat space of his stomach just below that final ridge of ab and drawing her eye down to the waistband of his shorts.

She refused to ponder any farther down.

He sucked in a deep breath, every well-defined line moving as he did, then again as he released the breath on a masculine sigh.

Finn Donnelly was a man. Like, a MAN. In all capital letters. With muscles and chest hair and everything beneath the waistband of his shorts.

She knew that. Of course she did. But she had spent a very long time pretending she didn't. Pushing it to the back of her mind. What did it matter if Finn was a man? Why would she ever think of him that way specifically? He was her friend first. Above all else. Her rock, her comfort and her stalwart in times of need.

The fact that he was a man had only ever been secondary in their relationship. An incidental.

But it was full frontal now. Big and glaring and impossible to ignore.

She didn't know why it was suddenly so obvious. Except for that damn pulled thread. It was the only thing she could think of. That everything felt like it was a little bit off balance, and this was just one of the many symptoms of that.

She felt breathless. Like she had been hollowed out from her chest to her stomach. She was about to look away when Finn turned, opening his eyes.

That electric blue hit her hard. All the way down. To where she felt hollow and for some inexplicable reason it made her feel full again. But not in a good way. In some kind of strange, restless way that made it seem as though her skin was too tight for her body.

She wasn't an idiot. It might've been a while since she'd had a relationship—physical or otherwise—but she knew what attraction felt like.

It *wasn't* this. It couldn't be this. Because this was

Finn. And they weren't that way. She didn't see him that way.

He didn't say anything. But he shifted slightly, his tongue dragging briefly over his lower lip before he swallowed, his Adam's apple bobbing up and down with the motion.

And just as the strange pang hit her stomach, in response she levered herself upward, pushing herself to her feet. "I'm cold," she said, moving quickly off the dock and over to that patch of grass where she'd flung her dress down.

He was still looking at her, and for some reason putting the dress on didn't make her feel any more covered up than she had just a moment ago. Maybe because he had already seen her in her bathing suit, so she knew that he could still see it in his mind.

Not that there was any reason for him to want to. Just because she was having a great unraveling didn't mean *he* was.

But she thought of the way he had looked when he walked up to the house today. There was a slight, unraveled edge to it, she couldn't deny.

"Feel free to stay down here as long as you want," she said, turning on her heel and cursing when a piece of gravel dug into her skin. "Ouch," she muttered, lifting her foot and brushing her hand over the bottom, making sure there were no rocks lingering behind. "See you at the house," she said, flinging her hand in an approximation of a wave.

It took a minute to realize she was literally running away from her best friend. She slowed for a moment, her heart thundering sickly in her throat.

She swept her hand over her forehead and tried to catch her breath. She turned, facing a knotty pine that was just off the side of the trail that led to the lake. She braced herself against it, pressing her hands firmly against the bark. Then she leaned forward, resting her forehead against it too.

For a moment, she just stood there, conscious of the way her heart was beating in her head. She stood there until it slowed. Until her breathing slowed. Until the quivering sensation in her stomach stilled.

"Are you okay?"

She turned and saw Finn coming up the path, dragging his towel over his damp chest. Her mouth dropped open as she watched the motion of the terry cloth over his muscles, as she watched him wick away the drops of water.

She squeezed her eyes shut tight, then opened them again, forcing herself to look away from his chest.

He was carrying her towel in his other hand, and right then she realized that she had left it sitting down there on the dock. And also, that her dress was wet and clinging to her skin because she hadn't thought to dry herself off before she had run away.

Her mouth went dry as he continued to advance on her. And the quivering sensation was back.

"Fine," she said.

His gaze was hot on her, and far too assessing. She didn't know what he was seeing. How could he be seeing anything? She couldn't untangle what was happening inside her, so there was no way he could. And yet, she felt something. Thought she might see something a lot like understanding in his eyes.

That wasn't fair. Not at all. Because there was nothing to understand. Not only that, if there was, she deserved to understand it first. So she could deal with it. Crumple it up in a little ball and throw it away. Or at least stuff it back down deep inside of herself where she didn't have to acknowledge it.

"Then why did you just run away from the lake like there was a rabid varmint after you?"

"I told you, I got cold," she said, gripping her elbows with opposite hands. "It's cold. And you dragged me into the water."

He took a step toward her, and she didn't move. She just kind of stayed there, rooted to the spot, watching him take another step toward her. Then another.

"That's what happened?"

She was mad that he was asking, because she had a feeling that he knew. That he knew this terrible, strange thing that was happening inside of her that she didn't want to put a name to. That he knew exactly why she had jumped up and run in the opposite direction like her very life depended on it.

Or, at the very least, her life as she knew it.

She didn't know why she was still standing there. She should turn around and walk back toward the house. They looked like idiots, her standing there with her dress clinging to her damp skin, and him shirtless in wet swimming shorts, just staring at each other.

He tilted his head back, swallowing, a motion that she was somehow hyperconscious of now. This every-day thing that he did as easily as breathing. *Breathing.* What the hell was wrong with her that she was notic-ing his breathing?

He took another step forward. He was close enough that if she raised her arm and reached out, even with her elbow bent, she would be able to plant her hand on his chest. Not that she would. That would be inappropriate.

Or maybe it wouldn't be. Maybe if she really saw him as just a friend it wouldn't be strange or wrong at all.

She gritted her teeth, rebelling against that thought. Of course he was a *friend*.

A friend who was a man. Something she knew, and always had, but was a little bit more aware of right now. That was it.

He lowered his head then, leveling his gaze with hers. He looked at her. Really looked at her. His eyes searching hers, wandering over the planes and angles of her face. She could feel him looking for the answers that she didn't have.

She balled her hands into fists, keeping them resolutely at her sides.

Tension stretched between them, long and tight. Then, heat rose in his eyes. So blatant and obvious, making such a mockery of all the vague *I don't even know what's happening* assertions that were jumbling around inside of her that she had to turn away.

She walked in front of him, toward the house, taking a deep breath, then letting it out. Doing her best to keep it rhythmic. To keep her pace slow.

So that she didn't look like she was running.

Even though she was. She absolutely was.

He didn't say anything, but she could hear the weight of his footsteps behind her, crunching on the gravel. More than that, she could sense his presence, and that just weirded her out even more.

When they came up to the house, she stopped on the bottom step, flinging her arms to the side and turning to face him, grabbing hold of the railing, forming something of a human blockade. "Thanks for coming by," she said.

He blinked. "Okay."

"It's late," she said. "And I have some work to go

over. Things for tomorrow." She was lying. "Because, you know, the subscription boxes."

"Right," he said.

"And I'm going to go to bed early. And probably, I'm going to wash my hair. I have to do some cuticle thing, with my fingernails. And scrub the dry skin off my feet. I have a pumice stone." She wanted to grab all those words and stuff them back into her mouth. A pumice stone? She had no idea what was wrong with her. Except, if what had just happened down by the tree was actually sexual tension she had probably killed it forever.

She had just mentioned *dead foot skin*. She had a feeling that was in the handbook for how to turn a man off permanently.

Not that Finn had been turned on. Absolutely not.

"Okay. Well, I guess I will leave you to your…pumice stone."

"It's a real thing," she said, immediately wanting to brain herself.

"I don't doubt you. Maybe you should put them in your subscription box."

She took a step back, up onto the next step. "They aren't a local thing. I mean, this is a pretty volcanic region, so I imagine you could probably… But, they aren't specific to Copper Ridge. Which is kind of the whole idea."

"Right," he said. "I'll see you later, Lane. Thanks for the swim. I needed it."

"Sure. Anytime," she said, taking another step away from him. "Later."

He turned away from her and walked to the truck, and she wasted no time scampering back into the house and closing the door behind her. She leaned back against it, pressing her hand to her chest, waiting for her heart rate to go back to normal.

She made her way back toward the kitchen, the silence of the house settling around her. It didn't feel like a refuge right now. It just felt like a big echo chamber of every stupid thing that had gone on in the past hour.

She heaved out a long, vocal breath, going to the fridge to retrieve her berries. Then she stopped and swore. She caught sight of the calendar that was hanging there, and the girl's night she had written down on it. Unlike their casual catch-up dinner the other night, this was their official monthly let's-never-let-life-get-too-busy-for-friends night.

They were all supposed to go to The Grind tonight for their Main Street get-together. She, Alison, Cassie and Rebecca all owned businesses on Copper Ridge's Main Street and as female business owners they had all bonded pretty quickly.

Usually, she didn't take a day off on girl's night, but everything was all jumbled up in her head so her decision-making had suffered.

She could skip tonight. She could legitimately stay home with a pumice stone.

But no, that was a bad idea. If she stayed home alone there would be nothing in the house with her except the memories of today's events, which she would undoubtedly play on an endless loop, combined with that loose thread. Which she would pull out endlessly until she had finished the damage external events had already started.

She didn't want to sit at home alone. She didn't want to feel sad. She didn't want to feel regret. She didn't want to feel at all.

So, the alternative was going out. And that was exactly what she was going to do.

CHAPTER EIGHT

SHE WAS EXCEEDINGLY grateful that she had decided to come into town. Spending time with a group of friends was precisely what she needed to lift the dark cloud that had fallen over her lately. She was being overdramatic. About everything.

Spending time listening to other people talk about their lives had given her some much-needed perspective.

Maybe the real issue was that she was working too much. Not that she needed to work harder. She needed to do something to get out of her head, most likely.

"I know he's going to propose," Rebecca said, talking about her boyfriend, Gage.

"That's great!" Lane said.

"How do you know?" Alison asked, folding her arms and leaning forward on the table.

"You just do," Cassie said pragmatically.

Cassie had been happily married to her husband, Jake, for a little over three years, and of the group, was definitely the expert on relationships.

"Well, that and he's terrible at keeping secrets," Rebecca said. "He left a receipt for the ring in his pants pocket, which I found..."

"When you were doing laundry?" Alison asked.

"No," she said, "when I was going through his pants pockets."

Lane snorted. "Well, then that wasn't too indiscreet of him."

Rebecca shrugged. "He had better never have an affair. He leaves too clear a paper trail."

"You're not actually worried about anything like that, are you?" Cassie asked.

Rebecca shook her head. "No. And I was kidding about going through his pockets. I trust Gage."

She said it so easily, so matter-of-factly. As if there was nothing huge or concerning about a statement like that. About trusting another human being so completely.

Lane didn't even trust herself.

But, instead of pondering that any deeper, she smiled a little wider. "Are you going to say yes?" she asked. She already knew the answer, but she was enjoying the conversation.

"I might make him suffer a little bit," Rebecca said, a smile playing with the edges of her mouth. "But there's no one else for me. He knows that. And I think... I think there's no one else for him. It's kind of an amazing feeling. To find the person that just fits with you. I didn't think that person existed for me."

Cassie was smiling and nodding in a knowing fashion.

Lane shared a glance with Alison. She knew their thoughts on the subject of romance were similar. Although Lane had never known Alison to date at all.

Ever since her marriage had ended in divorce, her abusive husband driven out of town, Alison had sworn off the male species.

Lane couldn't really blame her. She had certainly suffered her own brand of pain at the hands of a man. But it wasn't like what Alison had been through. Lane couldn't even imagine. To love someone, to marry them and to have them betray you like that. To have them turn into this whole different monster.

It was nice that Rebecca had someone now. It was nice that Cassie had someone. But sometimes Lane wondered if she and Alison had just been wounded too deeply to ever take that kind of chance again.

Oh, Lane dated. Casually. She liked men. But she liked them in their own space, and not in hers. She liked them to fill a manageable portion of her life. To fulfill a physical need and that vague emotional craving for romance that she sometimes got, particularly around Valentine's Day or the holidays.

Someone to go to parties with. Someone to go out to dinner with. Someone who might bring her flowers and tell her she was pretty. To kiss her and make her feel good.

She'd had boyfriends since leaving Massachusetts. Some of them had even lasted quite a while. But they had never been serious. Not in the sense of her imagining they would become anything long-term.

The very idea of a husband, of children, made her feel sick inside.

It was a future she couldn't have.

A future she didn't deserve.

Without permission, a vision of Cord McCaffrey and his family flitted in front of her mind's eye. His beautiful wife, his two darling children.

Her throat tightened, bile rising in it. Why did it hurt so much? Why did it still hurt so damn much?

Or rather, why did it hurt again after so many years of lying dormant? It was his fault. For being in the public eye like this. For bringing it all up again.

"Well," Alison said, too brightly. Lane figured she had been traveling down her own dark road just then.

"Congratulations, Rebecca. I can't wait for you to officially accept his proposal."

"Me either," Rebecca said. "I would never have thought... Well, I would never have thought that I would get married. Not in a million years. And I really never thought that I would marry him. For obvious reasons."

The reasons being that Gage had been responsible for a terrible accident that Rebecca had been in when she was a child.

Lane didn't possess that kind of capacity for forgiveness. But she had to admit that theirs was a rare case. Where both of them had been lost in the past, continually punishing themselves for something neither of them was truly at fault for. So in the end it was better they had let it go.

Lane just couldn't quite fathom how they had let it go with each other.

More power to Rebecca, though.

Nothing had proven more clearly to Lane that she still had an iron grip on the past than Cord's recent resurgence.

"Crap," Alison said suddenly. "I was going to bring a couple trays of chocolate croissants that I had left over in the bakery. Can someone help me carry them?" Alison was looking meaningfully at Lane.

"Sure," Lane said.

"Be right back," Alison said, leading the way out of the small coffee shop.

It was dark outside, and the streetlamps—made to look like old-fashioned gas lamps—were lit, casting a bright orange glow on the sidewalk. Most of the cars were gone, and the ones that were parked up against the curb likely belonged to people who had walked down the street to Beaches, Copper Ridge's fanciest restaurant.

Or they had all done a park and ride to Ace's bar or brewery.

Lane tugged on her sweater, pulling it closer to her skin. Once the sun sank into the ocean, nights were cold and invariably a bit damp when the mist rolled in off the sea. "I thought you might need a little bit of reprieve from those who are one half of a happy couple," Alison said, her tone dry.

"Is it that obvious?" Lane asked, keeping step with her friend, then pausing while Alison unlocked the door to the bakery.

"Not really. I just assumed you might feel like I did. Come on in." Lane walked in behind Alison, the room cast in darkness, the tables and chairs inky shadows on the light wood floor. The bakery case was empty, as were all the display cases that were normally full to the brim of pastries and breads.

"I really do have a tray of croissants," Alison said, setting her keys on the table before heading into the back. Lane lingered in the main dining area for a while, and then followed her friend.

"Admittedly I'm a little bit of a relationship Scrooge," Lane said, leaning against the kitchen door.

"I'm *a lot* of one," Alison returned. "Here," she said, handing a wide bakery tray laden with croissants to Lane. Then she turned back into the kitchen and reappeared a moment later holding her own. "See, I'm not a liar. I just have a convenient memory."

They both walked back out into the dining room and Alison set the tray down for a moment so that she could grab her keys.

"Do you think you're ever going to date again?" Lane asked.

She couldn't see Alison's expression, but she had a

feeling it was a frown. "I don't know. I like being by myself," she said finally. "Nobody gets to tell me what to do. Nobody makes decisions about what I'm going to wear or where I'm going to go. I lost myself in Jared. So deeply that I never thought I would find me again. I wasn't even sure who I was. It took so long to resurface. To let go of all that fear, that baggage... I don't know. The idea of sacrificing any of my freedom just seems crazy to me."

Lane chewed on her bottom lip. "I totally understand that. But sex."

Alison laughed. "Yeah, that's a whole separate issue."

"Have you... You know, since?"

Alison shook her head. "No. Like I said, it took a long time to sort out my own stuff. So, for the time being I'm committed to... *Sorting out my own stuff.* In every way that applies."

Lane thought back to all of the tension from earlier. To what had happened with Finn. How she had felt jittery and hollow, and needy in a way that she hadn't really associated with wanting sex before.

She grimaced. "I guess that's why some industrious person created vibrators."

Alison laughed uneasily. "I don't have one of those."

"Seriously?" Lane rocked back on her heels. "Doesn't every woman have one? Every red-blooded single American woman with a career and not enough time for a man?"

"Not this one," Alison returned.

"Me neither," Lane admitted. "Which I always thought was weird. Because according to every romantic comedy I've seen in recent years we should all have them."

"Vibrator hype," Alison said. "I would rather have

the real thing." She shook her head. "Of course, I'm much more likely to get a vibrator than an actual man."

Lane sighed heavily. It had been a long time since she had dated anybody. Which translated to it being even longer since she'd had sex. More than a year. Way more.

"I think that's my problem," she said finally.

"You have a problem?" Alison asked.

"Not a big one."

But for some reason, those words forced every incident that had gotten under her skin in the past few days into the forefront of her mind. From getting a glimpse of Cord on the news to every touch, every flash of strangeness and every lingering look that had occurred between herself and Finn.

Suddenly, they felt insurmountable. Like pebbles that had been stacked on top of each other and turned into a giant mountain.

"Just enough of one?" Alison asked, wrapping her arm around Lane's shoulders and drawing her into a quick hug.

"Yes. Just enough of one."

"If you ever want to talk about it… I'm kind of the master of the unpleasant topic that everyone would rather ignore."

"Is that what you feel like? Like you have something big to deal with that nobody wants to talk about?"

Alison lifted a shoulder, then went and picked up the tray of pastries. "It's complicated. Because sometimes I feel like I can't escape it. Like everyone looks at me and sees someone weak or damaged. Even someone that deserves contempt. Because I stayed for so long. Sometimes I want to pretend it happened to somebody else. I want to pretend that my life started when Pie in the Sky opened. That nothing else happened before then. Other times…"

Her words reached inside Lane and grabbed hold of her stomach, squeezing her tight. She related to that more deeply than Alison could possibly realize. That desire to talk about the horrible thing that defined who you were, and the desire to make it go away, fade into the distance, vanish into nothing.

That big thing that defined everything you were, that was necessary, because you wouldn't be standing on your own two feet without it, but that you despised more than anything else.

"If you ever want to talk," Lane offered, "you can always talk to me. Don't feel like you can't. I know that I don't…that nobody wants to make you talk about something that could be painful. But if you want to you can tell me. You can tell me whatever you need to tell me about him. I don't judge you for staying."

Alison set the tray back down on one of the tables with a clatter, and then, she wrapped both of her arms around Lane and hugged her close in earnest. "Thank you," she whispered finally.

Lane wrapped her arm around Alison, then set her tray down with one arm, freeing up the other. And while she hugged her friend, she felt like a fraud.

Because Alison was being raw, was being vulnerable, and Lane had nothing but mountains of secrets that she didn't share with anybody. Her past had happened outside of this little town, and here she was insulated from her downfall, with Copper Ridge acting as salvation.

For Alison, it was both. The source of her pain and the source of her relief. Everyone had witnessed both.

For Lane, there was escape.

And even though part of her wanted to tell Alison everything, there was another small, selfish part of her that couldn't bear to bring the past any further into Copper Ridge than it had already come in the form of Cord McCaffrey on a TV in Ace's bar.

So, she just let Alison be vulnerable. And when she was done, the two of them picked up their trays and walked back to The Grind with smiles pasted on their faces and not an outward sign to be seen of what had just passed between them.

CHAPTER NINE

FINN HAD A strong suspicion he was hallucinating. The sun wasn't up yet and he could hear voices and the sounds of clattering dishes coming out of the kitchen. That meant there was a strong likelihood his brothers had woken up before him. That was unacceptable.

He looked at the clock and saw that it was after five. Then he swore, grabbing his hat off the top of his dresser and heading down the stairs.

Partway down he met Cain, who had clearly also just woken up.

"What the hell is going on?" Finn muttered.

"I thought this was all normal for you," Cain grumbled.

"Not the noise."

Then he heard feminine laughter. And he was left in absolutely no doubt as to who it belonged to. He frowned.

When he got into the kitchen, he saw Lane standing there at the stove scrambling eggs. She was also talking cheerily to Alex and Liam, who were sitting on bar stools at the big marble-topped island eating pastries.

"Good morning," Lane said, turning around toward him, a bright smile on her face.

"What are you doing in my house?"

She furrowed her brow. "I brought you chocolate croissants, Donnelly. I'm not going to take your guff."

She turned back to the pan, stirring vigorously before shutting the burner off. "And now there's protein to go with your pastries. Coffee is ready. Have a seat."

Cain, clearly not caring about the fact that Finn didn't find this scene to be normal at all, took a seat beside Liam. "Thank you," he said.

"You're welcome," she returned, bringing a plate and the pan over to where Finn's brothers sat. She set the plate in front of Cain then scooped him a helping of eggs. Then she added eggs to Liam's and Alex's plates.

Finn scowled. "I take it you had a relaxing evening at home with the pumice stone?"

She cleared her throat, shooting him a deadly glare. "I am descaled, as a matter of fact."

"Right," he returned, moving across the kitchen, not bothering to lighten his footsteps as he stomped over to the coffeepot.

"I do greatly appreciate this, Lane," Alex said, his voice so smooth it sounded like it was coated with honey. "We have a long day ahead of us, and I can't say that Finn is much of a cook."

"If you have a problem with store-bought doughnuts you can cook your own damn food," Finn said, grabbing the carafe and pouring himself a generous helping of black coffee.

"My friend and his brothers should never stoop to eating store-bought doughnuts," Lane objected. "Not when I can easily get day-old treats from Alison. Or scones from Cassie."

"I don't need your friends' butter-laden castoffs, Lane." He took a sip of coffee, one that was too big, and scalded his mouth and his throat. It burned all the way down. He was being an ass, and he wasn't even really sure why.

Except then images from the day before swirled through his mind, and he had a much better idea. Lane in her bikini, looking like too big a temptation for any man, let alone one who had been doing his best to keep his lust tamped down for a long ass time.

Lane, who had clearly been affected by him in some way and had run the opposite direction. And then had stood there, staring at him like she wasn't sure if she was afraid he was going to bite her, or afraid she was going to bite him.

And now she was in his kitchen. In his kitchen puttering around like she had every right to be here. While his younger brother—who possessed about nine times the charm he did—*flirted* with her.

"Some people appreciate the gift of carbs," she said, her tone brittle. "Sit, Donnelly." She gestured to the stool next to Cain with her spatula.

"I don't want eggs," he said, knowing that he sounded slightly petulant. He took a step toward the tray that contained the croissants and lifted one up. "This will do."

"You need protein," she said.

"I do the hell not. If I want to carbo-load that's nobody's business but mine."

She sniffed. "Fine."

"I'll take some more eggs," Alex said, smiling easily as he looked over at Lane, and looked her over a little too thoroughly. Lane filled his plate. "Thank you," he said, charm dripping from every syllable. The bastard.

Finn's house felt too full. Too full and too different. When he and his grandfather lived here by themselves there was no noise in the morning. They drank their coffee, they went to work. That was it. None of this conversation crap.

And Lane had certainly never let herself in to make breakfast.

Everything was turned on its side, and he didn't like it.

His home, this place that he'd made for himself, had helped his grandfather keep alive after the rest of his family had left him by his damn self, was out of his control now. And this need for Lane, the one he'd ruthlessly tamped down for the better part of a decade, was being tested. God help him, he didn't feel like he was in a space where he could pass those tests.

Not when she looked at him like she had yesterday. With wonder and curiosity, and like she wanted to touch him as much as he wanted to touch her.

It was one thing to push it down, to steer clear, when he thought of her as vulnerable. As someone who needed protecting from his particular brand of passion and possession.

A whole lot harder when she looked at him like a woman looked at a man.

And harder still when she looked at him like a woman looked at a man and was presenting him with croissants.

"I have to say, this is about the grumpiest I have ever seen anybody who was being gifted with pastries," Lane remarked.

"I have a morning routine, dammit," Finn said, taking another sip of coffee and burning himself all over again.

"Yeah," Alex said, "this is better."

"How?"

"She's way better looking than you, for starters."

Lane smiled. "Thank you, Alex. It's nice to know that I'm appreciated. At least by somebody."

"I *appreciate* you," Finn said. "But I think it's weird that you let yourself into my house to deliver food. And now you're cooking."

"First of all, Alex let me in. Second of all, it's awfully convenient that you want food from me on your terms, but when I bring it to you without being asked it's suddenly a problem?"

Liam and Alex exchanged glances. "I don't think you're going to win this one," Alex said. "I would turn back if I were you. And anyway—" he stood up off of the stool " we have work to do." He winked at Lanc. "See you later." He and Liam stood and made their way out of the room.

Cain finished eating, and he didn't seem to notice the fact that Finn was mentally boring holes through the side of his head. Or maybe he did, and he just didn't care, because raising a teenager meant that he was immune to any and all kinds of dirty looks.

"Thank you again," Cain said, standing up and tipping his hat. All that was missing was the *ma'am*.

Obnoxious Texan bastard.

Then it was his turn to walk out.

"I didn't realize you were so grouchy in the morning," Lane said, snatching up the dirty plates that were sitting on the counter.

"Possibly because you don't usually see me in the morning. Because you don't usually invade my house."

"Why is it a problem?" She dumped the plates into the sink with no finesse, the ceramic dishes clattering against each other. If they didn't chip, he would be surprised.

"I…" He honestly didn't know. Except that he was still wound up from yesterday, and it all centered on her. Well, and his brothers. The fact that he felt like his entire house had been commandeered. That nothing was his anymore.

Broken down like that, it made him feel a little less crazy.

"You're mean?" She set about washing the dishes, her movements ferocious.

"Don't wash those," he said.

"Why not?" She threw her sponge down into the sink and it must have knocked one glass down into another, because there was a loud, dangerous-sounding noise. "I made the mess—it seems like I should clean it up."

"First of all, I would rather you didn't do my dishes because it sounds like you're going to break them. Second of all, you made breakfast—you're not cleaning up."

"An unappreciated breakfast," she said, sniffing loudly.

He sighed, grabbing the back of his neck and rubbing it. "I'm tired. I'm still getting used to all of them being in my house, and I did not expect to walk in and see you too."

She frowned. "When did *I* become a problem? When did I become another person who was invading your space?"

He wanted badly to tell her that she wasn't. Except the feeling persisted. That she was just another thing that felt too difficult to handle right now. But he wasn't going to say that. Because introducing the subject was even more impossible than just having her here.

"It's me," he said, gritting his teeth. "It's not you."

She snorted. "Now it just sounds like we're having a bad breakup."

"We aren't," he said, his tone harder than he intended. "It's not like that. Friends don't break up."

That was the bottom line. Friends didn't break up.

And she was a friend. It was one of the biggest reasons she had always been a friend, and nothing more. Why he had never, ever made a move on her. Not just out of his loyalty to her brother, Mark, but also because he valued the connection between them.

Yeah, he wanted her. But there were a lot of women to want. A lot of women to have for temporary moments in time.

There was only one Lane.

He repeated that over and over in his mind while he continued to look at her. She was hurt—he could see that, her dark eyes looking a little too bright in the dim morning light.

"Good," she said. "Because you can't."

"I can't what?"

"Break up with me," she said, a thread of genuine emotion winding around the teasing note in her voice. "I mean, I know how to get into your house. You would never be able to get rid of me. It would make things really uncomfortable. You would be like, 'Lane, I'm not speaking to you, why are you in my house?' And I would be like, 'you're doing a really bad job of not speaking to me, since you're speaking to me.'"

"That's what it would be like?"

"Yes. So, you can see that it's silly."

"Definitely. You have nothing to worry about. I have no desire to break up with you." Using those words to talk about the two of them was weird.

"Good," she said.

She shoved her hands into the back pockets of her jeans, looking around, the air once again thick between them. He had thought that maybe it was just him. Until yesterday. And that made him mad all over again. It was one thing to feel attracted to her knowing that she was completely oblivious.

It was another when he had a feeling she sensed the tension.

"I have to go," he said, using the cows as a convenient excuse.

"Okay," she said. "I'm going to clean."

"I wish you wouldn't."

"And I don't care. I have a while until I have to go open the store. Just let me help." She reached out, like she was going to put her hand on him, and he took a step back. She stared at him, and then lowered her hand back down to her side.

"See you later," he said.

"See you."

CHAPTER TEN

THE MORNING HAD started tense, and she was still annoyed about it. The day was not getting along any better. First, a shipment of jam that had come in from a little farm down the coast had arrived with two broken jars that had left everything a sticky mess.

The deliveryman—the son of the woman who made the jam—was apologetic. But that still saw her wiping jam off each individual jar in the boxes.

Though, things didn't start getting really terrible until later that afternoon when a group of giggling women walked into the store holding smartphones.

Lane couldn't make out words so much as indistinct squeals. "He's holding baby ferrets," one of the women said. "I can't handle it. And then—"

Lane didn't get to hear the rest of the *and then*. Mostly because it was overshadowed by more laughter.

"Hi," Lane said, doing her best to keep her tone bright. "Are you ladies having a good day?"

"Great," one of them said, adjusting a flimsy infinity scarf. "We're on a wine tour."

Well, that explained the squealing. "How fun. I hope someone else is driving."

"Yes," another woman, a blonde, told her. "We have a tour bus."

"Very nice."

"We just came from Grassroots. What a beautiful

place. Set right into the woods, with a lovely private dining space by the river. The view is lovely. And there was an actual rodeo cowboy there. He was a nicer view than the ocean."

Lane wondered if that meant that Dane Parker was back from the Pro-Rodeo circuit. He was definitely the kind of man that caused a county-wide hot flash with his mere presence. Assuming tall, cocky and cowboy was your type.

He was essentially a local celebrity, even though he was from Gold Valley. But when it came to rural areas like this, being from a neighboring town meant every other community in the vicinity claimed you as their own.

"I do like a view with my drinking," Lane said, smiling even more broadly.

"Oh," the woman in the scarf said, "as sexy as he was, he doesn't have anything on that new senator."

Lane just about gagged.

And when she found a phone being shoved in her face, a video already playing, she was pretty sure she did. Because there he was, wearing a suit and a red power tie, clutching an armful of ferrets like a little furry bouquet.

What the actual fuck was a politician doing with an armful of ferrets? More important, why did this man insist on being both across the country and in her face constantly?

"It's at the zoo in DC," the blonde said. "It's a whole montage of him holding baby animals while he hears about the various breeding programs. He is just such a *nice* man. And *handsome*. Not just for a politician either."

Suddenly, the woman lowered the phone, and Lane

knew she must be registering her disgust in her facial expression. Except, she was still smiling. She realized when she tried to widen it, that her mouth was stretched as far as it could go. But she had a feeling there was a murderous light in her eye. She must look terrifying.

Yet she had no idea how to fix it.

"Are you not a fan?" the phone woman asked.

"I'm a Quaker," she lied. "I don't engage in politics. I conscientiously object."

She had no idea if Quakers voted or not, or if she was remembering that wrong. However, she could see that the slightly tipsy women didn't know either. In spite of her near apoplexy—or maybe because of it—they ended up buying several packages of crackers and a pound of Laughing Irish cheese.

But by the time they left, Lane felt spent. Wrung out.

This was her life. Until the internet picked a new golden boy. Until his fame subsided. Unless he decided to run for president.

She spent the rest of the day engaging in busywork around the store. When the steady stream of tourists abated, she went into the back and started to cook some dinner for the night. There would be no harm in cooking for Finn again. She wouldn't have to cross the threshold of his house if he was going to be a weirdo about it. She could just hand a casserole to him and scamper off into the night.

She snorted. What was the deal with that, anyway? Him being cranky with her. She hadn't moved into his house and taken over a quarter of his ranch.

She'd gone over this morning with the idea in mind to establish some kind of normalcy. And okay, her bringing breakfast unannounced wasn't normal. But random gestures of kindness were normal for them, and surely croissants were a gesture of kindness?

Then he'd been cranky with her.

Sure, she was applying a little bit of pressure on him to alter his business plan, but she wasn't wrong. And it came from a place of love. And she hadn't even mentioned it in a couple of days.

She huffed around the back kitchen, coming out periodically to check on the store, just in case someone had managed to walk in without setting off the bell.

The afternoon passed without incident, and by the time she turned the closed sign she was more than done. She sighed, sitting down in her chair behind the counter.

She should do something. Something pertaining to the subscription boxes, probably. She hauled herself up out of the chair for a moment, leaning forward to fetch a notebook and a pen. She wrote a header on top of the page: Box Things.

Then she stood again, wandering slowly from behind the counter and through the narrow aisles of the store. She started to write down various items she thought might make good representations of Copper Ridge goodies.

Suddenly, she saw a muddy brown blur flash across the floor, and over her foot. She screamed, jumping backward and knocking into a shelf, sending a box of scone mix tumbling onto the ground.

"Rodents!" she growled. "I am beset by small mammals."

Between the potential attic possums and *this,* it was getting ridiculous.

Her heart thundering hard, hands shaking, she went back to the counter and, without thinking, dialed Finn. "Where are you?"

"I was just about to head back up to the ranch," he said. "I was in town grabbing some hardware."

"Come over to the store," she said, knowing that she sounded desperate, and not caring. She didn't know how to catch a mouse. And she could not have mice chewing holes in her things and making nests in various corners. She sold food. It wasn't hygienic.

"Is everything okay?"

"No! Just… Agh! Get here now."

"I'm on my way."

The mouse made another mad dash over the floor and she shrieked and hung up the phone. "Gross!" she shouted at the mouse.

She didn't know why. The mouse didn't care that it was gross.

She ran to the door, turning the locks so that Finn would be able to get in. Then she wrapped her arms around herself, pacing back and forth. She muttered under her breath while she waited.

Only a few minutes later Finn burst through the front door, his hat on, his expression intense. "What's going on?"

"A mouse ran across my foot," she said.

The features on his face seemed to lower slowly, the intensity morphing into something else. Anger? "A mouse."

"Yes. A mouse. It was horrifying. I'm emotionally scarred." It had startled her, enough to call him feeling vaguely hysterical, because what the hell was she going to do about a mouse? But she was feeling calmer now, her heart rate returning to normal.

"Dammit, Lane," he said. "You said that everything wasn't okay. I thought maybe there was a knife-wielding maniac in your store."

"You did not. Or you would have called the police."

"I thought the odds were you were probably okay, but it doesn't take much to imagine the worst, Lane. I came as quickly as I could. And it's a mouse. It is not a knife-wielding intruder." He was actually mad at her about this. And she didn't know what to do with that. Didn't know what to do with how off-kilter their every interaction had been for the past few days.

"Okay, yes, but it is a razor-toothed pest. Which is also alarming." She did her best to try and lighten the mood with humor. He didn't take the bait.

"You aren't in danger," he said, clipped. "You let me think you were."

"I did not."

"I was worried about you, Lane. And you're brushing that off."

"I am not! But it wasn't nothing, and you're being ridiculous," she said, some of the initial surprise from her earlier mouse shock beginning to burn away, the quivering in her stomach taking on an entirely different quality. She had to look away from him. From his blue eyes, which were burning with anger and intensity. She ground her teeth together, deciding then and there that she was going to dig in on this. He had been so surly with her lately. He had been treating her like she was one of his invading family members, and she wasn't.

She had made him food. She was taking care of him. And he was treating her like… Like this. Well, she wasn't going to let him get away with it.

"What were you going to do?" she continued. "You burst in here with no weapon. If I was being held at knifepoint you wouldn't have been able to help."

The intensity in his eyes took on a dangerous glint. "Is that what you think?"

"You're bare-handed, Donnelly. There would be no saving me."

He took another step toward her, and for some reason, she shrank back. "Lane, trust me. If you were in any kind of danger, if there had been somebody in here trying to hurt you, I would have torn him limb from limb. I don't need a weapon to protect you."

She realized then that he was…not shaking, but vibrating. With unspent energy. Unused rage. And probably, she really had scared him a little bit.

"Finn," she said, reaching out and putting her hand on his shoulder before she could stop herself.

Whatever she had been about to say burned right out of her head like water on a hot surface. Just sizzled and floated right up into the atmosphere. Away from her. She had no hope of reclaiming it. No hope of doing much of anything but just standing there, her fingertips burning against his hard body.

She knew better than to touch him. They didn't do that. And she had done it twice in the space of just a few days. And here she was, doing it again. Persistently. She was still touching him.

She jerked her hand back down to her side.

"This has to stop," he said, his voice rough.

"What?" Was he talking about her touching him? Because she agreed. She just wished he hadn't said it like that. In a way that acknowledged there was something loaded in the touching. That there was something nonplatonic there. She didn't want to think about it. She didn't want it to be an acknowledged thing.

"This," he said, gesturing around the room. "It's seven o'clock at night. You have a crisis, you call me. From wherever I might be, I come running."

So. Not the touching. Because that was all her, apparently.

"You're my *friend*," she said. "Of course I called you."

"Yes. But you don't call Cassie, do you? You didn't call Alison, or Rebecca. You called *me*."

She scoffed. "Right, it would have done me so much good to call them about a mouse. We would have all ended up standing on chairs screaming." She frowned. "Okay. Rebecca wouldn't have. But the rest of us would be useless."

"So you see my point."

"No," she said, even though she was pretty sure it was obvious and she was missing it on purpose, just because she wanted to push back at him. Even without knowing his bottom line, she wanted to push back.

"You called me because I'm a man."

"Well, yes. Obviously. If I have drama with my electricity, and pest issues, I kind of need a man to handle that. I'm proficient at a lot of things, but I can't be proficient at everything. Nobody is. That's why I cook for you. That's what I'm good at." He continued to glare at her, so she swallowed hard and pressed on. "I guess when you put it like that, it feels a little like I'm labeling certain jobs man jobs and woman jobs, and I get that that's a problem for some people, but it works for us. It's playing to our strengths. That's all I mean."

He still didn't say anything, and she was starting to feel nervous, that hollowed-out feeling in her stomach returning.

"Don't tell me you find that offensive," she said finally, hearing herself start to sound annoyed. He was letting her twist in the wind, and he didn't seem at all bothered by that. "But if you do, if you really want to,

I can come look at your fuse box and you can cook me dinner, but I have a feeling we would both be unsatisfied by that arrangement."

"Stop it, Lane," he said, the words weary. "You know that's not the problem. The problem is we do have an arrangement. Or, it's fallen into one. I'm not your husband."

The words hit her like a slap, and her cheeks stung. "I know. That's a stupid thing to say. Of course I know that."

"I'm not your boyfriend. I'm not even your dial-a-dick. But you treat me like one. In every way except for the benefits."

His words punched straight through her chest, grabbing her heart and twisting it. "That's not fair." She couldn't quite articulate why it wasn't, just that it wasn't.

"Isn't it? You don't treat me like you treat your other friends."

"I know. Because you *are* a man. Do you honestly think I'm blind to that?" It was poorly phrased, because in many ways, until recently, she *had* been blind to it. She had known, in an abstract sense, but she hadn't spent a lot of time dwelling on it. On purpose.

That time he and Rebecca had almost hooked up, it had forced her mind to go there and she had found it completely unsettling. She'd been angry, nearly sick over it, and she hated herself for it. To want to keep her single friends—who had no obligation to her—from being with each other if they wanted to be seemed churlish and petty.

But she hadn't wanted Finn's time occupied by another woman.

That realization made her mouth drop open. She didn't want him occupied by another woman, because she wanted him on hand for her. And that made what he was saying sound a lot like their whole arrangement wasn't fair. A lot like she was, in fact, using him as a boyfriend without giving him any of the benefits of being one.

It was uncomfortable, and she didn't like it. It made her feel like she was the one being hunted, not the mouse. Like she had been backed into a corner and had no other choice but to fight back.

So, she did.

She shoved at his shoulder. The equal and opposite reaction to the ill-advised placating touch, she supposed. "This is a stupid fight," she said.

"Oh, really?"

"Yes. It is a stupid fight because you want me to cook you dinner. You like it. You want me to ask about how you're doing, how you're feeling, because none of the guys that you hang out with will. You get something out of that. And yes, I want you to come trap my pests and change my lightbulbs, but you like doing it. And you've never given any indication that you didn't. That it wasn't what you wanted. Don't come in here and complain to me now and say it's not fair just because you're mad about your family. Just because you want to punch something."

"Is that what you think?"

"It's what I know. You're mad, and you don't know who to lash out at, so you're lashing out at me. You're using our friendship as a punching bag. Complaining about stuff that doesn't even bother you so that you can deal with…all of this," she said, sweeping her hand in an up-and-down motion. "Complaining about not getting something you don't even want."

Those words hit hard between them, and settled

there. And Finn just looked at her for a moment, all rage and hard glitter in his blue eyes.

Before she knew it, he moved, wrapping his arms around her and pulling her up against his chest. She was on fire. Everywhere. From breast to toe. He had never touched her like this before. Had never held her in his arms. Hugs were different. Quick greetings. Goodbyes. She hadn't been *held* by him then. Hadn't been pressed against him. Soft against hard.

Her first instinct was to struggle, like a cat that was being forced into a bath. Except she wasn't struggling. She was frozen. She couldn't move. And she didn't. Not even when he lowered his head.

When his lips touched hers, the world ignited. A bright white light that was something like an explosion. But whether it was happening in the store, or just in her, she didn't know.

It was destructive. Ripping through her and breaking down walls that were essential to her life. To her very survival.

He raised one hand, cupping the back of her head, holding her up against him as he changed the angle of the kiss, taking it deeper.

In spite of herself, she shivered. Arched more deeply into him and just let him kiss her. Let him slide his tongue over hers, let him devour her mouth like he was a starving man and she was the only thing that would give him sustenance to go on.

Her heart was raging in her chest like a trapped bird in a cage, fighting to get out, and her knees were gone. Just completely gone. And if not for his strong arm locked around her waist, she would have fallen to the ground in an undignified heap.

Her eyes were closed, but her lids trembled, fighting against the urge to look. To see what it was like to watch Finn Donnelly kiss. Of course, the other half of her, fighting just as hard, wanted to close out the reality that she was being kissed by him. Wanted to pretend the kiss wasn't happening. Or if it was, that it wasn't him doing the kissing.

Her hands were trapped against his chest, and she found herself curling her fingers around his T-shirt, holding great handfuls of it as she looked for something else to brace her.

There was a storm raging. All around. Inside. The nuclear fallout of the strike that had just been detonated in the center of the two of them. But she didn't know what else to do but hold on to him. Even as her brain was screaming for her to make it stop, her body wanted more. Beyond that, it was natural to hold on to Finn. When things felt like they'd been upended, he was always the one she went to. Her support. Her everything.

That made her feel like she was being torn in two. The need to stop the madness, to put things back to rights, to start reclaiming the debris that had fallen all around them, warred with those other desires. Deeper, darker and long suppressed.

It wasn't a gentle kiss. It was rough. It was destructive. And certainly not by accident.

And when she returned it, she injected her own anger into it, as well. For all of this confusion. Not just the confusion he had caused. With his anger, with his kiss. But the confusion caused by the demons in her past that were tearing at her, taking chunks off her, piece by piece, one shred of sanity at a time.

Then he growled. A deep, feral sound that rumbled in his chest, echoed through her. And it was unmistakably, undeniably Finn.

That was what did it.

Finn. Finn was kissing her. She was kissing him back.

She released her hold on his shirt, planting both palms on his chest and pushing backward, nearly sending them both down to the ground as she separated their mouths. Harshly, roughly.

"What," she said, her voice low and shaking, "are you doing?"

"You said I didn't want it. I figured I would show you differently."

Something inside of her crumbled. Fell. "How… How dare you?" She took a step back toward him. "How could you do that? You're my friend. We just talked about this. Why it's important. Why would you do that?" She felt tears stinging her eyes. She was disgusted with herself. For being so weak, for being so affected. If she had been able to just go on like nothing had happened, maybe the kiss wouldn't feel so important. Maybe things really could just go back to normal.

But she couldn't. She couldn't pretend it hadn't happened. And she couldn't pretend to be okay. Not when she had been shaken to her core. Not when that big, promised Pacific Northwest earthquake had just happened. Inside of her own body.

"We don't do this," she said. "For a reason."

"Is that your story?"

"Yes," she hissed. "I can kiss any guy, Finn. But you are *you*. You're you and our friendship is important to me. And I can't deal with this right now."

"I can't deal with *not* doing it," he said, his voice like gravel. "I have too much going on to practice self-control with you."

She couldn't process what he was saying, and more

than that, she didn't want to. She needed all of this turmoil to just go away. She needed to be able to open her
eyes and find herself at home, in bed, alone. The events
of the past few minutes having been some kind of weird
twist of her subconscious, a response to all of the stress
that was happening inside her.

"I don't need this right now," she said. "My life is
complicated enough."

"Oh, why? Because the idea of subscription boxes is
just so daunting? My grandfather is dead, and my brothers have taken over my home and my life like they have
a right. So don't talk to me about your boutique angst."

He had no idea. And she didn't want him to have
an idea. Didn't want to spill her guts to him about her
tragic past and how it was being shoved in her face.

But she couldn't handle him being condescending
either. Not when she felt so raw.

"Get out," she said, her voice shaking. "I mean it."

He took a step back. "Don't you need me to kill the
mouse?"

"I feel safer with that mouse than I feel with you right
now. I'm going to name the mouse. The mouse is my
new best friend. Until such time as you get your head
out of your ass." She extended a shaking finger, feeling overly dramatic and ridiculous, but unable to stop
herself. "Get. Out."

He nodded once, his mouth pressed into a flat line,
his jaw set, and then he turned away from her, leaving
before she had a chance to ask again. And for all her
rage and bluster, she had kind of hoped she would have
to ask again. That he would insist they talk. That he
would stay. That he would try to help her clean up this
mess, this debris that had been left behind by the kiss
that she had never wanted to consider might happen.

Instead, the door closed behind him, the bell above it jingling slightly. She took officious action, grabbing hold of the dead bolt and latching it with more force than was strictly necessary.

Then she turned, leaning up against the door and burying her face in her hands. She needed him. She needed him to be there for her. She needed him to be her rock. She needed him to keep her from falling apart; she didn't need him to do the demolition.

She took a deep breath. Then another. Then she closed her eyes, and when she opened them, she half expected to see her store in ruins. But everything looked in its place. Everything looked the same.

Maddeningly so. It made her want to mess things up. To throw a couple jars of jam on the floor, because why not, she had already cleaned up spilled jam once today. What was another disaster?

She didn't, though. Instead, she stood there, letting the normalcy soak into her skin. It was easy to believe that she had hallucinated the last half hour. That it hadn't happened at all.

And as she went to collect her things, she decided that that was exactly what she would do. Pretend it hadn't happened at all.

For her, there was no other option.

CHAPTER ELEVEN

IF HIS GOAL was to blow up his life, Finn was doing a damn good job of it. Not that the presence of his brothers was his fault, or anything he could have prevented, but the way he'd behaved with Lane last night certainly didn't match up with the actions of a man who was desperate for the status quo.

She was pissed.

He paused for a moment to ponder that.

He didn't care. Yeah. He didn't.

He maneuvered his horse down toward the fence, riding along the line, making sure everything was shored up. Mostly, it was just an excuse to get out and clear his head. To get away from Cain, Alex and Liam.

To do a little work by himself. To clear his head, even though he had a feeling a brace and bit and a strong breeze wouldn't clear his head.

He was angry. Still. So the fact that Lane was angry too didn't hold all that much weight. It did, in that he didn't exactly want to blow their friendship all to hell, but it didn't because there was no way her rage could take precedence over his.

That was the problem. The damned problem in a nutshell.

Her comfort always took precedence. And forget his.

He gritted his teeth, battling against that part of himself that was saying he was being unfair. Considering he had never, ever made a move on her until yesterday. That the righteous indignation had gone a little bit over-the-top, even if there was no one around to hear it. He wanted to cling to his righteous indignation. To his well-cultivated anger over the fact that he wanted a woman he should never have.

She had kissed him back. There was no denying that.

And in that moment, it had been about the sweetest pang of torture he'd ever experienced. Like a jagged knife cutting down under his skin, the pain so sharp and shocking it had twisted itself into something else.

There were a lot of years of need between them. At least, on his end.

When she had first come into town she'd been seventeen years old, and far too young for him to show an interest in at twenty-three. Plus, she had been Mark's younger sister. But then he'd gotten to know her in her own right. Care about her not based on who she was related to, but who she was.

And while he had never found out exactly what had transpired between Lane and her parents, he knew that it was big. Big enough that she never spoke to them. That she never went back to visit.

Hell, since coming to Copper Ridge the most traveling she'd done was up and down the West Coast. She had never gone back east.

Though, it had never really struck him as overly strange, since he never went back to Washington, to the town he was raised in. He had left it behind when he had come to live with his grandfather, and he had left it behind thoroughly.

Still, no matter that he'd known he should be protective of her, rather than turned on by her, it had been a challenge since she was eighteen years old. Since that

moment that was carved into him like a mark on a
tree. Part of him now, no way to remove it. That moment when she'd looked at him laughing, her fingertips
brushing his thigh...

But he'd pushed it down, even then. Because he had
known she wasn't what he needed. That he couldn't
give her what she deserved. And it had nothing to do
with Mark. He was closer to Lane now than he had ever
been to her brother.

But no matter that he'd decided years ago he couldn't
act on his lust, it was still there. Always beneath the
surface.

It was her obliviousness to it that had finally gotten him. When he had burst into the shop and seen her
standing there, completely fine, afraid of a mouse and
not in any physical danger, he had wanted to shake her.

Because even though most of him had known there
was probably nothing serious going wrong, part of him
had gone completely cold at the *what if.*

He had wanted her to feel even a fraction of what
he did in that moment. And it had hit him with all the
force of a kick from an angry quarter horse that she
simply didn't feel a fraction of what he did when he
was around her.

For him, their friendship mattered, but more than
that, it was all about restraint. All about shoving down
the desire that he felt for her. All about trying to control this deep, needy thing that he had never managed
to master.

He had known that odds were nothing fatal was happening when she had called last night. But it was the
possibility that had struck him. The possibility that
something could be wrong, that she could be in serious danger. And faced with the prospect of losing Lane,

his life had opened up into a yawning void. It had terrified him. And very little terrified him.

But the worst part wasn't the terror. It was how she hadn't understood. Not even a little. That he was shaking, that he was shaken.

He wasn't in love with Lane. Love, to him, was something right next to torture. It was one of the biggest reasons—up to now—he'd never made a move on her.

He wanted her, but couldn't offer much more than what they already had, coupled with a physical relationship. She was vulnerable, and he'd always known that, and he didn't want to push her into something she wasn't comfortable with.

She was important. And she occupied a space inside of him that lovers didn't, that friends didn't. That family didn't. A spot that belonged solely to Lane. He had a feeling he did that for her too, but when he had looked at her last night, he had realized that it was something less, not something more.

Yeah, Lane Jensen was something more than a friend to him. And he was her handyman.

His phone vibrated in his pocket and he sighed, retrieving it. He frowned when he saw the name, but he was hardly going to avoid his friend's call.

"Mark," he said, looking out toward the mountain, bringing his horse to a stop. "What's going on?" For one, wild second, he was afraid that Lane had called him. That she had tattled on him. Told her big brother that mean old Finn Donnelly had grabbed hold of her and kissed her against her will until she had renounced their friendship and taken up an alliance with a rodent.

"I just thought I would check in with you," Mark said. "Your brothers are there, right?" He and Mark weren't the type to have heart-to-heart talks, but of course he knew about Finn's family situation.

"Yes, they are. All of them."

"For how long?"

"Indefinitely."

Mark swore, which was the mark of a good friend in Finn's estimation. "That sucks."

"No kidding," Finn returned. "How's everything on the fishing boat?"

"Fine. But I'm always happy to be back on dry land." Mark hesitated. "You know I don't like to do covert reconnaissance on Lane through you, because it's a little bit awkward." Tension crept up Finn's spine, and he waited for the brick to drop. "But, does she seem okay to you?"

His mind was cast back to last night. To the feeling of her warm body beneath his hands. Her soft lips beneath his. The way she had tasted. The way—just for a moment—she had leaned into it. Into him.

It was possible Lane had told her brother, but the odds weren't high. So Finn was going to go ahead and play dumb. Act like everything was normal. He had no reason not to. Though the fact that Mark was posing the question made Finn frown. Because if there was something going on that wasn't related to the kiss they had shared, he wasn't aware of it.

Considering how uncharitable his line of thinking had just been, about their friendship and his proprietary ownership on *caring the most*, it seemed damned unforgivable.

"I've had trouble getting her to return my calls. And when I get a hold of her she's less chatty than I am. Which is weird."

"She's busy with work things," he said. Which was

true. And, come to think of it, she had been kind of manic about that lately. About trying to get him to move forward with all those plans she had for the dairy. Frantically trying to come up with ideas to expand the business.

"Lane is the first person to accuse me of being impossible to read," Mark said. "She's always going on and on about how difficult I am to talk to. But she's worse. She just pretends to talk. She's my sister, Finn, and I don't know that much about her. Not really. She's always been more comfortable with you. So, just keep an eye on her." There was a pause. "Has she been dating anyone recently, or anything?"

"No," Finn said. *That* he knew definitively. Because he always knew when Lane was dating someone. It never failed to bother him, even if he happened to be with someone himself at the time.

Whenever he and Lane dated other people it threw things into a little bit of a tailspin. Because inevitably the woman he was with hated Lane hanging around, and of course every guy who passed through Lane's life hated the fact that Finn spent evenings at her place.

No matter what either of them said, nobody really believed they were platonic.

But, up until last night, they genuinely had been. At least, externally. His fantasies were another matter.

"I assumed maybe she had gone through a breakup or something."

Finn shook his head, belatedly realizing his friend couldn't see the motion. "Not that I know of. And typically, I know. The town is too small for her to hide it." Unless she was sleeping with somebody secretly. He was thinking of dating, of course. But she might have a hookup he didn't know about.

He didn't like that idea at all.

He gritted his teeth, wondering now if part of her reaction to him last night had been based on the fact that she was with someone else. Or had been recently.

Now he was going over every interaction he'd had with her over the past couple of weeks, looking for signs to connect what Mark was telling him with what he had observed during time spent with her.

"To be honest with you, I've been up to my neck. And Lane has been bringing me food and in general making sure everything's okay." As soon as he said that he felt guilt, yet again, for his earlier uncharitable thoughts. "But I promise to pay closer attention."

"Hey, your grandpa just died. I don't really blame you."

Yes, his grandpa had just died. And he most definitely had grief associated with that. But it wasn't the biggest part of the turmoil in his life right now.

"Still," Finn said, "she is your sister. And my friend." Again, memories of last night crept up on him. Her hands on his body, pressed hard against his chest… The way she'd made him feel made a mockery of that statement. "I'll figure out what's up."

The problem was it was more than likely him.

"Thanks," Mark said. "Appreciate it."

For some reason, Finn reflected, once they'd hung up, that phone call had gotten his head back in the right space. He was being unfair to Lane. Maybe there was something going on in her life, and he had missed it, because he had been so consumed by his own. She had a right to be mad at him about last night.

He gritted his teeth. He didn't like admitting that, even to himself. But she had a point about their friendship. About the importance of it. For both of them. And the fact remained that the reason he had never made a move on her in the first place stood. Yes, denying the attraction between them was hard. But now probably hadn't been the best time for him to make a move toward dealing with it. Especially not the way he had chosen to.

He wasn't thinking clearly. And he sure as hell wasn't feeling clearly.

So, he would go check on her tonight, as a favor to Mark. And he would do what he could to try and set things to rights between them.

He pictured her as she had been last night, enraged, her lips faintly swollen, her cheeks flooded with color. And in spite of himself, he felt his body beginning to harden. Desire rolled through him like dark clouds, signaling a thunderstorm was on its way.

He pushed it down, because he was good at that.

Yeah, he was going to confront her tonight. To deal with the aftermath of what had happened yesterday. Because whatever happened after this, Lane mattered to him. She was one of the pillars of his life here in Copper Ridge. That all-important existence he'd built for himself when he'd finally decided to cut and run from his life in Washington. From a life lived at the mercy of his parents' whims.

One kiss wasn't going to change that.

HE DIDN'T CALL FIRST. He didn't want her to make an excuse not to see him. He was reasonably certain she didn't have any plans tonight—because no matter how unobservant he might be about her mental state, he was pretty damned observant about her schedule—and he knew about what time she would get home after quitting at the store.

He was also armed with dessert. And okay, technically he was kind of regifting dessert, since Alison had
sent over some pies a couple of weeks ago and he had
put them in the freezer. But he knew Lane well enough
to know that she wouldn't look a gift pie in the mouth.

It wasn't only dessert he planned to use to help
soothe her anger. He had also come with a new lightbulb for her porch. He was bringing food and man ser-
vices. She could hardly complain about that.

He shifted the items under his arm, then knocked.

He didn't know what he expected. Maybe some hesi-
tance. Maybe for her to ignore his presence altogether.
Given the way she had acted last night, there really
was no telling. Except he knew he had not expected
her to open the door immediately, a wide grin fixed
on her face.

But that was exactly what happened.

"Hi," she said, the grin stretching impossibly wider.
Any more, and it would crack her face completely. "I
wasn't expecting you. Did we have plans?"

She knew full well they did not have plans. And she
was being weird.

"No," he said, "but I brought pie. And I brought a
lightbulb for your front porch. I thought I would change
it for you."

There was only a slight flicker in her dark eyes that
betrayed the fact that she found this remotely strange.
"That's thoughtful of you. I really appreciate it."

"So," he said, frowning, "I'm going to change the
lightbulb now."

"Great! I'll take the pie." She was all too bright and
sparkly when she grabbed the pastry box from his hand
and disappeared back into the house.

He turned to see to the task at hand, clearing the

cobwebs away from the porch light before taking out the old lightbulb and putting the new one in. He felt like there was a rock in his chest. And then he felt like maybe there was a rock in his head.

She was going to pretend that nothing had happened. She wasn't just mad, she was furious, but she was going to keep on smiling at him, keep on pretending that everything was fine so that they didn't have to talk about this.

Rage trickled through him like wildfire. Burning everywhere it touched. He threw his tools down onto the porch and walked inside, not bothering to keep his footsteps light.

"That was fast," she said, that same near-manic smile fixed on her face.

He crossed his arms over his chest, rocking back on his heels. "Everything okay?"

"Fine," she said, waving a hand. "Just fine. Why wouldn't it be?"

Oh, that did it. He was a strong man. Growing up like he had, that had been a necessity. When his father had left his mother, it had been up to Finn to take care of her. To assume the responsibilities of the household, even though he'd been a boy. And then, when his mother had left... He'd been on his own.

There had been no space for him in his father's life, with his new wife and his sons. He could bear a lot of things. Had done so. Would continue to do so, if his brothers' presence at his ranch was any indicator. But he would be damned if he would bear this. She could be angry about his kiss, but he would not let her ignore it.

It had changed things. Rearranged something in him. Ripped away the excuses he'd been making for years about not touching her. Because she wanted him too, and now he knew it.

And he couldn't unknow it.

"No reason," he said, his anger a dark, flickering thing inside of him, making him reckless. Making him mean. "Mark called."

"Cool. Did you guys talk about girls?"

"We talked about you," he said, appraising her openly, not bothering to hide it. She looked wary, and he didn't love that. But he did love the ski-slope curve of her nose, and the way the corners of her lips twitched when she was trying to hold back a smile.

He felt gratified when he saw color mount in her cheeks. "He wanted to know what was up with you."

"Did you tell him nothing? Because there's nothing up with me."

"Really. Did you talk to him last night sometime by any chance?"

Her mouth dropped open, then snapped shut again. "I did not," she said, her tone flat.

"Okay, because I feel like if you had, that might've been significant."

"Why would it have been significant?" The question sounded as though it had been dipped in sugar.

"No reason," he said, taking a step closer to her. She took a step back. Then, she edged around to the other side of the counter, putting it between them.

He was supposed to be here to make things right. But it didn't seem fair. That making it right meant letting her pretend nothing happened. That making it right meant letting her live in a fiction where he didn't ache to have her with every breath.

If she would just acknowledge the kiss. Maybe that would be enough.

Maybe.

For a moment, just a moment, the voice of sanity screamed inside of him that it was ridiculous to be acting like this with the woman he considered to be his best friend in the entire world. But that voice was drowned out by the roar of testosterone. And so he continued on as he had started.

"So, then what is going on?" he asked, placing his fingertips lightly on the countertop and dragging them over the smooth surface as he moved toward her. "Some guy break your heart?"

"My heart is cast in iron," she said, trying to keep her tone flippant. But he could see that she was on edge. Good. He wanted her over the edge. He was going to keep pushing until she had to admit that there was something going on. Something happening between them. Until she stopped resolutely living in Laneland where everything was rainbows and he was sexless, while he lived in the real world dealing with the aftermath of this explosion between them.

He had been prepared to walk in and have her scream at him, but he could not allow her to ignore him.

"Good to know. Are your panties also made of iron? Or are you sleeping with some guy and it's gone haywire and that's why you're in a mood?"

She scowled, her brows locking together. "You jackass. That's none of your business."

"Sure it is, Lane. We're friends. Don't friends talk about things like that? If some guy is messing you up, don't I have a right to know?"

"You're being ridiculous."

"Am I? Because you're acting strange. And Mark thinks so too. He wanted to know what was up, and so do I."

She snorted. "News flash, Finn, Mark can ask me what he wants, but you're not my brother."

She tried to brush past him, and he reached out, grabbing hold of her arm and stopping her. He lifted it, drawing her toward him. There was something rushing through him that transcended anger. Something reckless and hot, something that had done away with his self-control completely.

He knew exactly what it was. But he didn't want to put a name to it. Not now. Not when there was no point at all in assigning an identity to this roaring need inside of him that would never be satisfied. Not until she was naked. Not until he was buried inside of her and she was crying out his name.

He didn't want that. Even as he needed it with a ferocity that made his whole being ache, he didn't want it. Because it would change everything they were. But at the same time he didn't know if he had the strength to go back to acting like everything was the same. Like being near her when he wanted to reach out and touch her was easy. Like the pull between them was nothing.

His life was slowly being wrenched from his control. Like the fist he'd closed around it years ago was being pried open and he was losing his hold bit by bit.

This was part of it. She was part of it.

"I know perfectly well that I'm not your brother," he said. He could feel her pulse racing in the underside of her wrist, could feel the way he affected her. Maybe it was their closeness, maybe it was the shared memory of the kiss. Maybe he had succeeded in making his best friend fear him.

He had never felt lower than he did at that moment. But he still couldn't bring himself to release his hold on her.

"Then stop meddling," she said, the words sounding like they had come at great cost, each syllable bitten out with purpose.

"Now you're going to pretend that I'm acting brotherly? Come on, Lane. I've seen people pretty committed to their fictions, but you win right now. We both know I'm not your brother. We both know you feel a lot different about me than you do about him."

She shook her head, her eyes wide. "I don't," she said, "so whatever you have in your head, whatever crazy thing possessed you to do what you did last night…"

He released his hold on her and took a step back. "Are you ready to talk about that now?" he asked, knowing he sounded pissed. Not really caring.

Her cheeks were flushed dark red, anger shimmering around her in a wave. "We have to," she bit out, "don't we? You wouldn't let me put our friendship back the way it should be. Why wouldn't you let me fix it? You know that I hate this. You know that I don't want it. I don't want this between us. I need you, Finn. I need you right now, maybe more than I ever have, and you're ruining it."

"You were going to pretend that it didn't happen."

"You know why." she hissed. "I need a friend. I don't need another guy I could date. Those guys are a dime a dozen here. But you're the only Finn I have."

"Yeah," he said, "I know. It's what I told myself about you all this time. Even as I was on my way to your house tonight. What I told myself every time I thought about kissing you, in fact. But I need you. Did you ever think of that? You keep talking about going through a hard time, but I haven't seen any evidence of that. I'm not doubting you, not necessarily, but you know what I'm going through. You can see it. I can't… I can't keep being pulled every which way. I can't be there for you all the time while I push aside what I want."

Her throat worked, angry tears glittering in her eyes. "So you want to throw away what we have because you want sex?"

The words hit hard and twisted inside of him, made him feel guilty when nothing else so far had. "That's not it." It wasn't, but he couldn't figure out quite how to articulate it. "I just can't hold it all anymore," he said simply, finally.

"And our friendship is such a burden?"

"No. Our friendship is one of the best things in my life. You have been one of the best things in my life for more than ten years now, Lane Jensen. But pretending I don't want you? When I fulfill what you want me to… I can't hold on to that while I try and balance all of this other stuff."

She shook her head. "I don't… What does that even mean? I can't even deal with the answer. Never mind. I don't want to know."

"I'll tell you what it means. Right now? If you really want to take care of me I need more than casserole."

He felt like a dick. There were no two ways about it. He *was* a dick. But he wasn't sure if there was anything he could do to stop himself. To stop this. It was ten years in the making.

Hell, at this point he didn't know whose side he was on. Whether or not he wanted her to win, with her logic, her desperate need to protect the friendship at all costs. Or whether he wanted his body to win.

Mostly because he had no idea what he was doing. He had rationalized his way out of taking this step a thousand times before. And the reasons still stood. It was his resolve that had crumbled.

Looking at her hurt. All the way down deep. The desire that he felt for her was a yawning, aching void that he knew couldn't be filled by anyone or anything else, because God knew he had tried.

He had slept with any number of other women since he had met Lane. None of them had taken the edge off. Sure, sometimes it was enough to allow him to ignore his desire for her for a while. But it always came back. And the moment he found himself checking out Lane instead of the woman he was supposed to be sleeping with, he broke things off.

And even if he was in another relationship, he hated every man that passed through Lane's life. Every man she took to her bed. Thinking about it made him rage. Gave everything he did an edge of violence that he had never wanted to explain or deal with.

It didn't make sense. And it wasn't fair. To want his friend physically the way that he did, while knowing it could never be romantic.

While knowing it would never be permanent.

He had always known that Lane needed more than that. More than sex with friendship on the side. And he had always valued her too much to ask for that. But he had reached the end of it. The end of himself.

And if he blew their friendship all to hell, then maybe it was best to deal with it now. While the rest of his life was similarly destroyed. While everything else was basically the worst it had ever been outside of his shitty childhood.

"I don't understand why you're doing this," she said. "Because you're sad that your grandpa died? What do you think Callum would say if he knew that you were propositioning me? He would slap you upside your head. He would tell you that's no way to talk to a lady."

"Yes," Finn said. "You're right. But he's not here. The bastard died. And as his last act, he decided to take everything I worked for and I can't even yell at him about it. He's gone, like everyone else in my life."

"Except for your brothers. And, if you don't push me away, I'm here too. But is that what you're doing? You just want everyone to go away and leave you alone in your misery? And you knew the best way to do that with me would be to kiss me?"

"No, that's not it at all. It might be a good theory, but only if you didn't want me to."

Lane drew back as though she had been slapped. "I don't."

"That's why you were looking at me like you did down by the lake last week?"

Her eyes were shimmering now, anger visible across her cheeks in slashes of red. "I ignore those moments," she said, her voice trembling. "And I was willing to ignore the kiss too. Dammit, Finn."

"If you want it, why is it a bad thing?"

"I want a lot of bad things. And I've had a lot of bad things. For example, I had French fries for lunch. That was a bad thing. It's not good for you. You shouldn't eat them. They're too starchy, and there's too much oil. I'm not getting any younger. I'm close to thirty. I need to order side salads. And I need to say no to this too."

"Are you comparing me to junk food, Lane?"

"I'm comparing you to any bad decision I can make on a given day. That's what separates us from the animals. Sometimes we don't make them. I have to not make this mistake."

"Why is it a mistake?"

She laughed, but there was no humor in the sound. She crossed her arms, shaking her head. "Are you proposing? And if you are, do you think I'm going to say yes?"

"Hell, no."

"Then how could it be a good idea? Unless it's going to end somewhere permanent it's just going to end. And then where does that leave our friendship?"

He was out of words then. He was out of restraint. He was out of everything. Everything but the need that had eaten at him for so long he didn't know who he was without it. Didn't know what it was like to take a breath without wanting Lane Jensen. It had become part of him, and he was so damn tired of it he couldn't take it for one more second.

So he wrapped his arms around her, just like he had done yesterday. His hands were pressed into her back, fingers tangling in her hair. It was like silk, she was like silk. He expected her to push away from him, expected her to fight, after all that verbal sparring she had done.

But she didn't. Instead she went still, frozen. Like prey that had spotted a predator. Or maybe she was just leaving it up to him. Her breathing was shallow, and slowly, very slowly, he felt her soften beneath his touch.

Gradually, her breasts met his chest as she leaned against him. But she didn't move to close the distance between their mouths. He dragged his palm up the line of her back, letting his fingertips drift along her neck. She shivered beneath his touch.

Lane shivered beneath his touch.

Other women had done that, he was sure. When it came to his sexual prowess, he had never had a complaint. But it didn't matter. It didn't matter what other women had done, what other women had felt. What mattered was that Lane felt this now. For him.

But he wasn't going to be the one to close the distance between them. She had to make the move. It had to be her. So that tomorrow she wouldn't be able to pretend it didn't happen. So that she wouldn't be able to get angry at him. So that she wouldn't be able to pin it all on him. And maybe she would turn away. Maybe she would keep denying all of the electricity that arced between them.

But he didn't think she would.

He wove his fingers more deeply into her hair, tightening his hold on her head, and at the same time he moved the hand on her back down lower, then to the side, grabbing hold of her hip. She gasped, that small reaction worth more to him than he could possibly quantify.

"Tell me you don't want me, Lane," he said, moving just a little bit closer. "You're going to have to tell me."

She shook her head. "I don't want you," she said, but she came nearer when she said it.

"Come on," he returned, "you're going to have to do better than that."

"I don't—" she inched closer still "—want you."

"Yes," he affirmed, "I can feel just how bad you don't want me. The way you're all pressed up against me proves that."

"You're holding on to me," she said.

He released his hold on her, dropping his hands back down to his sides. "Then run away."

She swayed slightly, but she didn't move. Her eyes widened, and for the first time she looked downright terrified. Mostly, he imagined, because she didn't move back. Because she didn't run. Because, for whatever reason, she was still standing right there, her breasts pressed tightly against his chest, her mouth only a whisper from his.

"You're my friend," she mumbled. "Running away from you would be almost as stupid as…"

"Kissing me?"

"Nothing would be stupider than that," she said, the words a rushed whisper.

Then her eyes fluttered closed and she leaned forward, the movement so slow, so slight, if he hadn't been tuned into every single thing about her, he might have missed it until her lips pressed up against his.

The sound she made was somewhere between surrender and a wounded animal. Distress and satisfaction reverberating between them as she gave in to the attraction that he had never even bothered to deny. At least to himself.

He wrapped his arms back around her, forking his fingers into her hair and wasting no time taking the kiss deeper. He wanted this. He wanted her. And he wasn't going to pretend otherwise. Not while he had her like this. Not while he was finally holding Lane Jensen the way he had always fantasized about doing.

He knew plenty of guys who would say it was a weakness to want a woman and not claim her. Finn had always seen it as a feat of strength. Which was why this surrender to temptation shamed him in some ways. Why it felt like giving up.

But it also felt like summer rain falling on his face for the first time after a long cold winter. It felt like that very first flower persevering through the frost. Like life after so much nothing.

And that won out over anything else.

He tightened his hold on her, moving back, pressing her up against the edge of the counter as he let her feel the evidence of his desire for her. Let her feel just how hard she made him. Just how much he wanted her.

She was clinging to him, just as she had done last night, her fingers curled around his shirt as she kissed him back. And when he felt her begin to pull away, he stopped her, sliding his tongue across the seam of her lips, growling as her flavor flooded his mouth.

She whimpered, an answering sound, an answering surrender. And then the tip of her tongue touched his, that little returned exploration like a lightning bolt that went straight down to his cock.

He slid his hands down her body, down those curves he had spent so many years pretending not to want, and he moved his hands down to that ass he'd worked for so long not to stare at. And now he was holding it in his palms.

Just the thought made his knees about buckle.

He tightened his hold, drawing her forward, and she rolled her hips, a needy sound rising in her throat. She was trying to satisfy herself, trying to get some relief from this heat that was burning between them.

And then it was Lane who let her fingertips drift down his chest, Lane who rested her hands on his belt buckle for a moment, then pushed her hands up underneath his shirt.

CHAPTER TWELVE

SHE HAD LOST her mind. It was official. When Finn had showed up at her door radiating all the male energy that she was working so hard to pretend he didn't have, she had gone into fright mode. She had done what she did best. She pushed things down; she hid them. She pretended that they weren't happening to her.

That was the way she handled things. The Lane Jensen method of dealing with trauma. Just pretend there was no trauma. Tell no one. Not even yourself.

So, she had plastered a grin on her face and proceeded to act like he hadn't devoured her last night and demolished the walls that she had placed very purposefully between them from the moment they had met.

Unsurprisingly, that hadn't gone over very well.

Surprisingly, she was kissing him.

More surprising was the fact that once his lips had touched hers, common sense and any capacity for thought had flown completely from her mind.

She moved her hands down to his belt, rested them there for a moment, and then let her fingertips inch just beneath his shirt. She gasped when her skin met his. When she felt all of that hard, hot muscle beneath her hands at last.

At last. What a strange way to think of it. A strange way to think of something that she had never really thought about doing until this moment.

She had never touched a stomach like his. So well defined, and covered with just the right amount of hair. She knew what he looked like without a shirt. She had just seen him without one. And—he was right—she had checked him out. Fully and completely. She had memorized each ridge of muscle, and so now as her hands drifted over them, she had a pretty clear visual to go along with it.

Part of her was screaming that this was a mistake. But most of her was just lost in the best kiss she had ever experienced in her entire life.

His hands were so firm and sure on her body, so large and strong. The funny thing was, now that she had accepted they were kissing, she could appreciate the kiss they'd shared yesterday. The fact that he hadn't been tentative. The fact that he hadn't asked permission. The fact it had been a claiming rather than an interview.

No tentative meeting of lips that was tantamount to an awkward handshake. Not for Finn Donnelly. No, he kissed like a master. Like a man who knew exactly what he was doing, and exactly how to make a woman's body do just what he wanted it to do. Feel just what he wanted it to feel.

Never, ever had she kissed a man with this kind of skill. Who knew just how to call this level of arousal up in her body this easily. He wasn't even really touching her intimately. His palms were resting on her denim-covered butt, but that was it.

Meanwhile, she ached. From her breasts down to her toes, and everywhere in between. She could feel herself getting wet for him, wanting him.

Wanting *Finn*.

That thought, much like the growl that had rescued her sanity last night, jerked her into the moment. Into reality. She wrenched her mouth away from his. "No way," she said, wiggling out of his hold. "Stop," she said, more to herself than to him. "This has to stop."

"You want me," he said, the words tortured.

She held her hand up, her entire body trembling. With need, both to keep going and to get as far away from him as she possibly could.

"No," she said. "I was perfectly happy to leave everything the way it was, Finn. You're the one that's having a breakdown, or whatever the hell this is."

"This isn't a breakdown. Trust me. None of this is new to me."

"Don't tell me that," she said, clutching her head. "I trust you. I need you. You're my… Everything. I can't deal with this right now. I can't deal with it ever. I've had you in my house. I've considered you my closest friend, and knowing that you were looking at me, knowing that you wanted to do this… That's a betrayal, Finn."

Maybe she was being a little bit dramatic. Maybe spitting these kinds of invectives at the one person she cared about more than just about anyone else wasn't going to go very far in fixing this broken thing between them. But she couldn't stop herself. This new thing exploding between them hurt her. It scared her. She wanted him to be hurt and scared too.

"I never betrayed you, Lane," he said, his voice rough. "I have done nothing but be there for you. I never asked you for a damn thing you didn't want to give. Not even when I wanted more. Don't talk to me about betrayal. Don't look at me like you're shocked, like you're hurt. You're just in denial. You have been for a decade."

Rage spiked in her, and she forgot for a moment. All

about self-protection, all about hiding. She forgot about everything but her anger. Everything but her hurt.

"I am entitled to my fucking denial!" she shouted, not caring when her voice broke, splintered. "This isn't what I need. You, like this, aren't what I need."

"And what I need doesn't matter?"

"If you want sex go down to Ace's and announce that you're looking to fill the vacancy in your bed. You'll find somebody. But it's not going to be me. It can't be me."

"Why not?"

How could she tell him? How could she describe this feeling? Like she was slowly sliding down a hill, and then the ground beneath had given way. A landslide, carrying her all the way down to God knew where, threatening to swallow her completely. To bury her.

She felt like her rock, her safe place had been stolen from her. By the one person she had trusted more than anyone else.

She wanted to hit him. Wanted to make him pay for this. To hurt him the way he had hurt her. Somewhere, down at the bottom of all this blind rage, she had to admit—at least to herself—that he hadn't done anything to her. Sure, he had kissed her, but a kiss was only a kiss. And if there was no heat between them it wouldn't matter.

It was the heat that scared her.

Because she needed him to be Finn. Finn Donnelly, the man she had always known, the man she had taken emotional shelter with for the past ten years. She needed him to be that dependable, reliable rock he had always been for her.

She was suddenly awash in the unfairness of it. All of it. The fact that she expected him to continue being exactly what she needed and nothing more. Nothing less. The fact that he didn't want to be, and she wanted to be entirely selfish and tell him to just stop being attracted to her then.

She didn't want to care about what he felt. About what he wanted. Because she needed him to be hers. Hers in the way that he had always been.

That way that had allowed her to hide.

"Because it can't be me," she said finally, knowing that she sounded both desperate and scared, and wishing she could sound a little angrier. At least then he might take a step back. Instead of just standing there, maddening and immovable in all the wrong ways.

"I need better than that," he said. "You owe me a real explanation."

"Okay, it never works for friends to just have sex."

"Why not? It's worked for us to not have sex this long. Might as well change it up."

"You're being ridiculous. And obtuse. You know perfectly well that there's just no point to it. That it's going to ruin what we have. You probably already ruined it."

Saying those words terrified her. Made her want to run to her room and close the door, lock it behind her. Hide from him. Hide from her racing heart, the ache that still persisted between her thighs, and from her traitorous hands that still itched to touch his muscles.

"I'm not having this conversation," she said finally, turning away from him.

"If we can't have this conversation, what's the point in us talking at all?"

She turned around again, the finality in his words sending a streak of horror through her. "If you don't get your way you're not going to talk to me anymore?"

"That's not what I'm saying. I'm saying we need to

be able to talk honestly. You don't have to *do* anything, Lane. But you do have to talk to me. What the hell is this friendship if we're just pretending?"

For some reason, an image came to mind. Of her in bed, wrapped tightly in blankets, with Finn trying to take them off her. It would have been funny if it didn't feel quite so desperate. If she didn't feel quite so frantic in her need to cling to them. To that warm, comfortable cocoon that she had wrapped herself in ten years ago when she had first crossed the border into Copper Ridge.

It was all ruined now. All of it. Because of Cord Mc-Caffrey. Because of Finn Donnelly and his new insistence that they kiss. Because of her body really liking the way that he kissed.

"I don't know why you're doing this," she said.

"I've been there for you. And I haven't asked much from you. But I want you, Lane, and I'm tired of pretending that I don't."

When he put it like that, it didn't seem quite so horrible. It seemed almost reasonable. Except no, part of her fought back, it was unreasonable. Because yes, his grandfather had died, and yes, he was fighting to keep control of the ranch, but she was fighting an entirely different kind of pain. A different enemy.

And he didn't even know. Not really. He didn't know why he meant the world to her. Why this place, and the safety that she found in their friendship was so important.

"I can't," she said. "Because I need a friend. You're my friend. You don't know what it was like when I came here. What I was running from. And that isn't by accident. But it's followed me here now."

Finn stiffened. "What's going on? Are you in danger? Is there somebody coming after you?"

She shook her head. "No. It's not like that. It's just… It's complicated. You think you know me. You think you know who I am. I guess maybe you even think we've exhausted everything there is to our friendship. And that's why now you want to kiss me, and sleep with me. Because you think that's the only mystery left. Well, there's more."

"That's not it," he said, his voice rough. "That's not what's happening here. It isn't like I think I've uncovered everything worthwhile and now I figure I might as well move on to your breasts."

Dimly, she realized that had it been any other circumstance she would have laughed. But there was no laughing now. She was going to tell him. The moment she realized it, was the moment she realized she couldn't turn back.

"I can make it so you don't want me," she said, forcing a smile because the alternative was crying.

He did laugh, the sound jagged, cutting into her, deep. "If you could do that, Lane, I would be grateful to you. Because I have spent a hell of a long time trying to make myself not want you. Or lost myself in alcohol, in other women, in the ranch. I reminded myself every time I looked at you that you were Mark's sister. And I've tried to make myself see his face whenever I look at yours. I've reminded myself over and over again that you deserve a man who's going to love you forever, a man who's going to marry you, and I'm not that man. I don't know the first thing about commitment or love, and what I have seen of it, I didn't care for. I'm just a man who wants inside you. And you're a woman who deserves a lot more. None of that works. So, if you have the magic key, I'll take it. Go ahead."

It made her feel a little bit hysterical, borderline giddy. "You think I'm kidding, but I'm not. Not even Mark knows this. If you were wondering why he never told you the reason I don't talk to my parents, it's because he doesn't know either." Terror clutched at her chest, making it feel like there was a stone lodged in her throat. Her body's last-ditch effort to keep her secret, she supposed. She had done it for so long, it felt like part of her survival. Even though that was ridiculous. Even though she knew better. She tilted her head back, closing her eyes. "I had a baby, Finn. And I gave him away."

The silence that followed the admission was almost unbearable. He said nothing; he didn't move. His face seemed frozen, and she was pretty sure her body was frozen right along with it. She didn't know what else to say. She had no idea how to tell the story, because she never had.

There was never a need to have this discussion with any of the men she had dated because she had known those relationships would only last a few months anyway. She had never told her friends because she didn't want them to look at her and think of it every time she walked into a room.

But most of all, she had never told anyone here in Copper Ridge because she had left home for a reason. Because she had wanted to leave the past behind and not bring even one piece of it with her.

It had been nice, to put it away like that. To lock it down deep inside of her and to know that no one around her was ever thinking about it. To know that nobody looked at her and thought: she's that sad girl who got pregnant at sixteen.

She had been given a chance to rewrite her story, and she had taken it.

And with just a few words she had blown all of that to hell.

She waited for him to say something. To ask if she was kidding. To say something judgmental. To say something supportive. Just something. Anything to give her an indication of what he was thinking before she continued on.

He didn't.

He was waiting. Waiting for her to finish.

It enraged her. To know that he wasn't going to fall in line the way she wanted him to. To know that he was just outright refusing to be that stalwart inanimate object she depended on him to be.

Yet again, she was very conscious of Finn's maleness. The way that he stood there, all hard-edged strength. So big and broad and just kind of looming near her. She was very aware of the safety net that had once existed between them, and the fact that it was no longer there.

If the kiss hadn't changed things past the point of no return, then her bombshell certainly had. When his lips had touched hers he had altered the way she saw him forever. She had a feeling this admission had done the same for him.

"I was sixteen," she said, pressing on. "He was my first boyfriend. We weren't planning on having sex. You know, basically I'm an after school special. No condom, no forethought at all. I didn't think… I didn't think it would just happen. That we would go from kissing, to fumbling, to that. But we did." She laughed, which was ridiculous, because nothing about this was funny. "And you can most definitely get pregnant the first time, Finn. If you were wondering. That's why you should always wear a condom."

He still didn't say anything. He was just looking at her, that same granite expression affixed to his face. It made her want to… Something. Punch him. Maybe kiss him. Except she wasn't going to do that again.

"Anyway. He was one of those boys with a future. And it was really important. More important than a baby." She blinked, and her eyes suddenly felt scratchy. She didn't know how she was supposed to feel when she talked about this. About her son.

Suddenly, she couldn't stand up anymore. She braced her hand on the wall and went down on her knees. She couldn't breathe. She didn't think those words. Ever. She didn't talk about this. Ever ever.

Then, the mountain moved.

He was down in front of her all of a sudden, his thumb and forefinger pinching her chin, tipping her face up so that she had to look at him. "Can you breathe?"

She shook her head.

"You're going to have to breathe, Lane," he said. "I need you to. Because you need to."

She didn't want to. She wanted to turn away from him, curl up into a ball, her knees up tight against her neck, and block all of this out. Give in to the building, mounting pressure in her chest. Maybe howl a little bit to try and relieve it.

He wasn't letting her, damn him. He wasn't letting her fold in on herself. What good was he? He wouldn't stand there and be an immovable shelter for her, and he wouldn't let her crumble either.

"I didn't rehearse this," she heard herself mumble. "I wasn't going to tell you. I was never going to tell any-

body. That's the point of adoption, isn't it? You give
them a better life, and you go on with yours. And it isn't
easy, but the point is that it's better for everybody." She
took a sharp breath. "It's supposed to be better."

It was. She knew that it was. At sixteen she had not
been ready to be a mother. Particularly without parental support, or support from Cord. There would've been
nothing she could have done. She would have come to
Copper Ridge with the baby; she would have had to live
with her brother. She would have had to find babysit-
ting while she waited tables. Every difficult thing about
breaking away and making a life for herself would have
only been made that much more difficult.

Even if they hadn't pressured her into doing it. Even
if everyone would've just taken a step back and given
her the opportunity to make her own choice, she was
pretty sure she would have done it the same way.

But it was the *pretty sure* that got her. The *pretty
sure* that was part of the problem.

That would always eat at her. That would always
make her wonder.

She looked up at Finn, at the expression on his face,
and she knew that she had accomplished at least part of
what she had set out to do. She had driven a wedge between them. Except, it was more than she had wanted.
Different than she had wanted. He was looking down
at her like he was seeing her for the first time.

She was angry then. Because she could feel it. The
intense betrayal that was rocketing through him over
this. Over the fact that he didn't know this about her.
This foundational, deep thing that had brought her here
to Copper Ridge and had made her who she was.

It was her life, her secret to tell or not. He didn't have

the right to be mad. And it sucked that she understood why he was.

"I didn't see the point of bringing the story here," she said. "But that's been the problem. He... The boy I was involved with had a future. And he really made the most of it. And here I am, and I own this little shop. And suddenly, it just didn't seem like enough. Because if I gave up my son... *My son,* Finn. Then I should have done something really amazing. I didn't. I'm not. He did. They were right about him. He gets to stand up there with his two perfect kids. And every time I see them I wonder... I wonder if my son looks like those kids. If that's what he looks like now that he's older. He's almost twelve. And I can't forget that. I know it. I know his birthday. And every year I wonder all these things. I wonder what his favorite cake is and if he got a bike." She was rambling. The worst kind of ramble.

Emotional. Teary. It wasn't about French fries or pumice stones, but she still couldn't stop it. It was like all of these words had been stuffed down deep inside of her for years, and now that she had started, she couldn't stop them.

"I hate the father so much sometimes," she said. "But at the same time if he hadn't done well, I'd hate him even more. And if the story about the baby ever came out it would ruin him, and then there really wouldn't have been a point."

"I don't know the whole story," Finn said, his tone gentle. "I don't know what you're talking about."

"Senator Cord McCaffrey," she said, her voice muted.

Finn's brows shot up. "Really?"

She lifted a shoulder. "Yeah, well. He wasn't a senator then. He was a high school senior with a really nice car. And we lived in the same neighborhood, in these ridiculous manor houses that have servants' entrances."

"I mean, I knew your family was rich. From what Mark had said."

"He undersells it. Trust me. Because until you see it firsthand, you don't know. It's all that Mayflower Society blue blood First Family kind of stuff. I hate it. I hate all of it." A tear slid down her cheek and she dashed it away. "I've had an entire life ripped out from under me. And I've lost… I couldn't even begin to tell you what I've lost. Because I gave it up before I had a chance to find out. So I ran. As hard as I could, as far as I could. But now, Cord is on TV everywhere. And I have to look at him. And I have to look at myself, and the life that I have, and I can't feel anything but completely underaccomplished."

"Does this have anything to do with the subscription boxes?"

And just like that, she felt understood again. Just like that, the gulf seemed to be bridged. She felt like maybe she wasn't so much of a stranger to him. Not when he understood that so quickly, so easily.

"It might have everything to do with the subscription boxes," she said, her voice sounding small. "But you know, everyone was obsessed with his promise. Even then, he was being groomed for politics. I suppose they thought that I could have been a decent senator's wife. But there was no way either of us could have fit into those roles if we had a kid when we were teenagers."

She took a deep breath, trying to fill some of the emptiness inside of her. There was no point feeling that way now. No point being full of regret.

It didn't mean that she wasn't either of those things. Empty and full, happy with her life and sometimes unfulfilled. Saddened by thoughts of what could have been, relieved that she hadn't put either herself or her child through the struggle.

A little bit ashamed when she saw other people thriving under the circumstances she had sought to avoid. Relieved sometimes too. Especially when she saw someone with a screaming child and a hollowed-out, exhausted look in her eyes.

But guilt. Always guilt. On both sides of the seemingly opposite feelings.

"I feel like he took that second chance," she said slowly. "That opportunity to try things differently, to start things over and he made everything of himself his parents hoped he would. I didn't."

"You haven't done anything to be ashamed of," Finn said. "You're successful. You have a business. People here in town love you."

She laughed. "Did I go to Harvard, Finn? Am I terribly important, or the wife of somebody who is? I was supposed to get a great education, so I could either move in prestigious circles, or marry someone who did, while I sat at home with my very important degree being smug in its existence. No. I am none of those things. I have none of those things. Dammit. I could have subscription boxes."

She wiped the tears from her cheeks, feeling fortified if not completely stable. She wouldn't crumble in the next few minutes anyway.

"Are you okay?" he asked.

"I…yeah."

"Do you want to get off the floor now?"

He moved his hand to her shoulder, let his fingertips drift down to her elbow. And in spite of all the turmoil inside of her, she felt something else too. Something hot and restless and exactly the sort of thing she was trying to banish with her revelation.

His question felt weighted too. Like there was another level to what he was asking, another layer. As if he was pointing out that she had been on the floor for the past decade, and maybe she should stand up.

That wasn't true, though. She hadn't been on the floor. She had come to Copper Ridge, and she had made a new life for herself. She had separated herself from her past and she had moved forward. And yes, she had kept the details of that to herself, and yes, there was some pain that lingered. But she wasn't on the floor. Not metaphorically, anyway. Physically was another story.

"Okay," she said, and tried not to feel anything momentous when he moved his hand to hers and laced his fingers through her own. Tried not to ascribe any other meaning to the action when he lifted her to her feet, his eyes level with hers.

He was just helping her up off the floor. That was all.

"Are you going to be okay?"

It was a strange question. This was something she had lived with for a long time now. So it wasn't exactly a new pain to her. But it was new to him.

"I'm always okay," she responded, which was about the most disingenuous answer she could have given, all things considered. Clearly, she was something less than okay or she wouldn't have just had an extended meltdown all over him.

"I think," she continued, her words trembling a little bit. "I think I need some time by myself, though."

And she felt… Well, she felt pretty crappy saying that to him. She was the one who had chosen to bring it up, and doing so had been a strange experience. Kind of out-of-body. She had been worried it would drive a wedge between them, and in some ways, in the moment, she'd hoped it might. Then it hadn't. He had just stood there as steady as ever, and then he had offered her his hand.

So now she was pushing him away, since he didn't let her bombshell drive him off. Now she felt like she might be a little bit manipulative.

She didn't like that thought. But she couldn't stop her mind from going there.

"I'll call you tomorrow," he said. "If Mark asks… What do you want me to say to him?"

"Nothing has changed," she said, parroting the thoughts she had earlier. "I mean, not for me. If I seem off it's just because I've been having to think about all of this a whole lot more lately. Usually, it's pretty easy to let it stay in the past." She sucked in a fortifying breath. "It's a lot harder when you have to look at that guy all the time. But I'm fine. It's new news to you. It's not new to me."

Even those words tasted disingenuous on her tongue, and she couldn't quite work out why. Or maybe the truth was she threw a wall in the way of figuring out why the minute she got close.

She had the sense—all of a sudden—that the inside of her was made entirely of a series of walls and locked doors. Designed to keep certain things, certain moments, certain people in different places so that they never touched.

She felt both desperately in need of them and desperately constrained by them all at once.

"You want me to tell him you're fine," Finn said. "You want me to lie to him."

She lifted a shoulder. "Tell him I'm dealing with a

bad breakup. That's true. Even if it is twelve years in the past."

"Fine. If that's what you want." He looked at her again, something strange in his eyes. Something she didn't want to name. "I am going to call you tomorrow."

It felt like a promise, one that she kind of wished he wouldn't keep. She had a feeling he knew that too, which was why he made it with such a grave look in his eye.

"Great," she said. "I'll talk to you tomorrow." She plastered what had to be the world's most brittle smile on her face and took a step back from him. Just in case he was going to touch her again. She really needed him to not touch her again.

"Okay," he said, gripping the end of his hat and tipping it forward—a reflex, one he usually reserved for strangers, and definitely not for her.

That made her want to reach out and grab him by the shoulders. Shake him and ask him why he was being weird. Why he couldn't just be her friend. Why there had to be tension, and analysis of every movement and reaction.

And after that, she wanted to shake herself. For being so contradictory. For trying to widen the space between them, and then being angry when she had accomplished it.

Except, it had seemed for a moment like things weren't different between them. Like he was her rock again. Her stalwart. Her Finn. Like somehow she had reset things between them with her revelation.

But then he'd tipped his hat.

While she was still standing there ruminating, he walked out of her house. On autopilot, she locked the door behind him. Then she turned and went down the hall and fell face-forward onto her bed. She was fully dressed, but she didn't care.

She was still wearing her makeup, but she didn't care about that either.

Instead of getting up and getting ready for bed, she gave in to that urge that had overtaken her earlier. She drew her knees up to her chest and curled into the tightest ball she could manage.

Then, she gave herself fully to her misery.

CHAPTER THIRTEEN

FINN HAD A feeling that Lane was avoiding his calls. But finally, about midday she had answered a text. And, much to his surprise, she had agreed to have dinner with him at Ace's. He had considered asking her to go to the brewery with him instead, but that would be a half step fancier than they usually were together, and he had a feeling given the precarious nature of things the change might send her into a tailspin.

He was sort of surprised she wasn't in one already. After the way things had gone down at her house yesterday he had expected her to commit a little bit harder to avoiding him.

But she had promised to meet him after work, and even though very little about being around Lane was a relief right now, that promise was.

He needed to get away from the ranch. He needed to get away from his brothers. Needed to get away from his sullen niece, who wafted around the house like a specter complaining about her boredom.

After work, he took a quick shower and changed into a fresh T-shirt and jeans. Then he put on his cowboy hat.

He walked out of his room, and met Liam partway down the stairs. "Going out?" his brother asked.

"Yes," Finn said. "There's a surplus of leftovers in the fridge. Help yourselves."

"Are you going on a date?"

"Did you want to come upstairs and help me choose my shoes while you asked me these questions?"

Liam's lips twitched. "No. But I was wondering if I could catch a ride down with you if you weren't going on a date. Because I need to get out."

"You want to hook up—that's what you're saying."

Liam lifted a shoulder. "We've been here for a couple of weeks."

Finn could have laughed at his brother's blatant objection to what he clearly felt was a horrendous dry spell. Finn himself hadn't gotten laid in nearly a year. That was what happened when you were hung up on the one woman you couldn't have.

Or maybe it was why he was feeling so increasingly hung up on her. Because it had been so long since he'd been with somebody else. Chicken or egg, it didn't much matter to him. It was what it was.

"The place I'm going to is crawling with local girls, and it is definitely where people go to hook up. But, local girls. That means they have family here. That means if you do something dumbass, their dads are going to show up at the door with a shotgun. And I don't particularly want to deal with the fallout of that."

"Hey, I get very few complaints," Liam said.

"Stay away from virgins and farmers' daughters," Finn said. "And stay away from my table. It's not a date, but I'm meeting my friend Lane."

Liam's gaze was assessing. "Your friend, huh?"

"Go to hell," Finn said, continuing down the stairs, not able to inject all that much heat into the invective.

Alex chose that moment to walk into the house. "You going out?" he asked both Finn and Liam.

"Yeah," Liam said. "We're going to the bar. You want to come?"

"Did I say this was an open invitation?"

"I need a drink," Alex said. "Give me a minute."

Alex walked back toward the stairs, and took them two at a time. Finn looked after him incredulously. "Let's go find Cain," he said, his tone resigned. "Maybe he wants to go get laid too."

As if on cue, Cain appeared from the kitchen. "Well, as tempting as that sounds," he said, "I have to spend some time with Violet. I can't leave her alone. Not right now. She's acting depressed. Or maybe she's not. Maybe she's just a teenager, but I can't tell and it makes me nervous. I might take her out, though. That would be a good idea. Let her see the town. So that maybe she feels a little more enthusiastic about living here."

Liam snorted. "You don't remember the town very accurately, do you? Because if you did, then you would know that showing a teenager around the place isn't exactly the way to make her excited about it. If your goal is to make her run away, though, by all means give her the grand tour."

Cain scowled. "Thanks for that. I hope someone breaks a beer bottle over your head tonight."

And that was how Finn ended up with a full truck driving down into town. Because he was in a particularly bad mood, he made Alex sit in the bed, rather than having the three of them squeeze into the cab, on his bench seat. If his brothers touched him in addition to crashing his evening, there was going to be bloodshed.

"I remember this place," Liam said when they pulled into the parking lot at Ace's. "It used to be called something else, though. Also, the last time I was here I wasn't quite old enough to drink."

"Lucky for Copper Ridge," Finn commented as he got out of the truck and made his way across the parking lot. "One of you better stay sober," he added. "I'm probably going to get a ride home with my friend."

"I'm hoping to get a ride myself," Liam said.

"Don't worry." Alex clapped his hand on Finn's shoulder, a wide grin on his face. "If anyone asks if we know him, I'll deny everything."

Finn walked in ahead of his brothers, then scanned the room, looking for Lane. He saw her sitting in the corner and forgot about the two jackasses who had come along with him. He forgot everything except last night. Or, more specifically, the way it had felt when her lips met his.

And then she'd told him about the baby and he'd broken inside for her. The thought of her going through that alone like she had. The thought of her being so young and making such a hard choice tore at his guts.

It was no wonder she'd seemed so fragile when she'd come to Copper Ridge all those years ago. No wonder he sensed that same vulnerability inside her now.

But knowing about the baby didn't change the fact that he wanted her. He wanted her more than he could ever remember wanting another woman. And until he had her, it wasn't going to go away. What he'd said to her last night had been the God's honest truth. Nothing and no one had done anything to dim his desire for Lane Jensen. At this point, he doubted anything could.

Except maybe having her. That might do it.

It was about the most pleasurable solution he could think of.

He took his hat off, placing it on the table, before sliding into his chair. "You came."

"I wasn't about to say no to a free dinner." The corner of her mouth quirked upward, but there was no shimmer in her dark eyes. She looked tired.

"Who said I was paying?"

"Hey," she said, frowning, "this was your idea. That means you're paying. I, of course, already took the liberty of ordering for us."

"What am I eating?"

"Fish and chips. Regular French fries."

"Don't tell me you pulled some bullshit like ordering a salad thinking you were going to eat all of my fries."

Her lips twitched. "You don't need all the fries. And I'm in the mood for salad."

"You have never in the entire history of our friendship been in the mood for salad. You get it so you have something green to look at on the table. And so it looks like I'm the one who eats fried crap."

She seemed to be warming to him a little bit now, and some of the exhaustion had faded from her expression. Still, the conversation felt strange and unstable. Like a truck driving on a muddy dirt road. At any moment it could all skid off course, no matter how well it seemed to be going now.

"Oh, I'm sorry. You can have my salad. Then everyone will think you're healthy."

"No. I don't want your salad. I want my French fries. And you don't get any."

She gasped. "I don't even know you anymore."

Her rage was fake, but his resolve not to let her have his French fries was real.

Because he was done with this. With this thing that she did. Wanting something, pretending she didn't. Using him for certain things and not for others. The woman needed to ask for what she wanted. And then maybe she would get it.

When his dinner was placed in front of him, he

pulled it back away from Lane. "I told you, no fries for you," he said, when she extended her hand.

She frowned. "You were kidding."

"I wasn't. If you want something, ask for it."

Her gaze turned stormy. "Are these French fries an object lesson?" she asked, her tone stiff. "Because I didn't come here for a lesson, Finn. I thought we were going to let the weird stuff go."

"Why?" he asked. "Because you want to?"

"Yes," she said, reaching down toward her plate, touching the edge of a lettuce leaf and frowning. Then she slowly picked up one piece of lettuce, dunking it in a blob of ranch on another lettuce piece before sticking it in her mouth. "That is exactly why."

"I know it pains you to hear this, but you aren't in charge, Lane."

"Of what?" she asked, looking at him angrily. "The world? Because I am pretty aware of that."

"Of our friendship. You don't get to be the one that sets the rules and makes sure they never change."

And just like that, the metaphorical truck skidded off the road.

She looked miserable, and for a moment he felt like a villain. It made him want to let it all go. To drop it, and to put things back where they had always been.

Except, it wasn't what he needed. It also wasn't what she needed. Last night had definitely demonstrated that she'd been holding things in for too long. She couldn't hold all this in too.

They lapsed into silence, and Lane continued to crunch angrily on her lettuce. He ate his French fries without remorse.

He looked up and past her and saw Alex sitting at a table surrounded by women. They were leaning in, and he was gesturing broadly, clearly telling a story. Probably one about his deployment that made him sound like a very brave hero. Not that his brother wasn't a very brave hero. Finn had nothing but respect for his brother's choice to serve in the military. That didn't mean Alex wasn't milking that service for all it was worth when it came to impressing women.

Liam was sitting between a couple of Alex's admirers. They couldn't all hook up with Alex, so he had a feeling Liam was going to sit there and brood until one of them decided that the quieter, more intense energy he put off was something she wanted to explore.

Watching them together made Finn feel old. He didn't want to do that. Didn't want to go to a bar and pretend to be interested in what a woman had to say just so he could get into her pants. That had lost its appeal when he was in his twenties. Hell, it had never had all that much appeal to him, but sex had, so he'd done what he needed to do.

It was a damned inconvenient thing. To be a man who didn't care for shallow hookups, but didn't want a long-term relationship.

Suddenly, he saw Liam's expression change. Turn sharp. Turn hard. He followed his brother's gaze to the door of the bar, where he saw Sabrina Leighton. He didn't know Sabrina all that well.

Her sister-in-law, Lindy, owned Grassroots Winery just outside of town, but Finn had always been more of a beer drinker, which kept them pretty far outside his circle.

Still, there was no denying that Sabrina's presence affected Liam.

But it was Sabrina's reaction that really stood out. Because when her eyes locked with Liam's she froze, and then she turned right back around and walked out the door.

Finn half expected his brother to follow her, but he didn't. Instead, he picked up his beer and took a long drink before turning resolutely back to the woman sitting on his left.

And that, Finn supposed, was the aftermath of what happened in small towns when things went wrong.

Sure, Finn was making assumptions about Liam's association with Sabrina, but he didn't think he was wrong.

That, he supposed, was the possible fate of himself and Lane if things went wrong.

But how could they? He and Lane were friends. And maybe for him it all made sense because the sexual feelings were new. He knew that he could be her friend and want her. He knew that he could handle both aspects of their relationship. That desire didn't have to lead to any kind of deeper emotional connection. Hell, for him there wasn't really a deeper emotional connection to be had.

He looked back at Lane, and saw that her gaze was focused elsewhere. Just past his shoulder and aimed up high.

He turned and looked, following her line of sight to the TV mounted on the wall. It was him. Cord Mc-Caffrey. The man who had fathered the baby Lane had given birth to. The man who had given her the legion of issues that Finn had always sensed was there and knew it was best to stay well away from.

Which is why you're stepping all over them now?

He chose to ignore that obnoxious voice. She had shown her hand. She was the one who had kissed him back. She had made it clear that she felt this attraction too. If she hadn't done that, if she had gone stiff in his arms, if she had remained unmoved by what had passed between them, then it would be easy to leave her alone. But she'd responded to him. She put her hands under his shirt. And she'd sure as hell wanted him right back.

That changed things. It changed everything.

At least as far as the physical was concerned. Emotionally... The feelings that he saw playing across her face right now, that wounded light in her eyes, were well above his pay grade. He didn't know the right words.

It struck him then how much their friendship was built on the connection they had in the present. Neither of them talked much about the past. And maybe that was why it worked.

He didn't know what to say to her right now. With her face looking like that.

He might know all about secrets, secrets that you kept from everybody, even your own brothers. He might even know how to fix things. All kinds of things. The lights in Lane's house, a tractor, a milking machine. But hell if he knew how to fix an emotional wound like this. In his experience, they were best left buried.

But hers hadn't stayed buried. Part of that was his fault. It made him feel like he should say something, do something. But he didn't know what.

"I would punch that guy in the face if I ever saw him," he said, in lieu of anything comforting or insightful.

He was fresh out of comfort and insight.

"I have to go," Lane said, pushing back from the table and walking out of the bar.

Finn watched her retreating form, then threw some money on the table, knowing that he had overpaid and not caring, and rushed out after her.

Dammit. He had said the wrong thing. But what the hell was the right thing to say?

"Lane," he said, catching up to her in the parking lot. "What's going on?"

She looked edgy, her eyes wide, her lower lip currently being punished by her teeth. "You know. That's the thing. *You know.*"

"Is that what's bothering you? That I know about the baby."

She pressed her hand to her forehead. "It's weird. Nobody else knows. Nobody." He moved in, brushing his fingertips over her forearm. "Don't," she said. "Don't touch me."

Anger roared through him and he took a step back. Those words cut into him like a knife, and damned if he knew why they landed so deep.

He looked at her face, at the stark fear on it. Fear of him. Of his touch and what it made her feel. And there wasn't a thing he could do. She wouldn't let him. He couldn't even touch her to offer comfort. Couldn't say what he wanted, couldn't do what he wanted.

He wanted to hold her. Wanted to kiss her until she forgot. What the hell did she want? To show him her wounds, and then not let him close? To push him away?

He wouldn't have to be pushed, then.

"Fine, Lane. If that's how it's going to be, then I'm going back inside. Maybe I'll join Liam and Alex— they look like they're having a hell of a lot more fun than I am."

And then, feeling like every inch the asshole he knew she thought he was, Finn turned and walked away from his best friend when she needed him most.

PANIC ROSE UP in Lane's chest as she watched Finn walk away. She didn't know what she was doing. Honest to God, she had no idea. But she'd felt like she was falling apart, and sitting there with Cord on the TV while Finn was right there, knowing everything that had happened, was just too much. It was all too much.

Why had she ever thought she should tell him? Well, that was stupid. She knew why. She had told him to shock him, to make him take a step back. To make him rethink wanting her.

But it was more than that. She had also told him to try and prove to him just how important their friendship was. But it hadn't worked. If anything, she felt more distant from him. And he was walking away from her. He knew she was falling apart and he was walking away. He was making good on what he'd said. That he needed something different than what she was offering and he was tired of hanging around while she continued to ignore that need.

She needed him. What was she going to do if he removed himself from her life? There was nothing she could do. She didn't have anyone else. Nobody else knew what she'd been through. And she frankly didn't want to have that conversation with anyone else.

"Wait!" She jogged after him, her heart thundering in her chest, her entire body shaking.

Maybe this wasn't a new meltdown. Maybe it was just an extended meltdown from yesterday. She should have stayed home. She shouldn't have agreed to meet him. But she had been so desperate to cement their friendship. To prove that the kissing hadn't meant anything, that the revelation about her past wasn't important. That it didn't have to change anything.

That nothing at all had to change.

Finn stopped, his broad shoulders going stiff. He didn't turn. "What?"

"Please don't leave. *Please* don't leave me."

"What is it you want me to say? What do you want me to do? You don't want me to touch you." He shook his head. "I'm not going to tiptoe around you."

"Well," she said, panic giving way to anger, fury rising inside of her, "that's your fault."

Now he turned to face her, more than six feet of enraged male advancing on her now. "*My* fault? So I was the only one doing the kissing?"

"You started it," she said, her voice low and trembling. "I didn't. I never would have started it. Now you know. You know why I have to protect myself like I do. Your friendship is so important to me, and I never wanted to do anything to compromise that. That included touching you. Kissing you. How dare you take that from me? How dare you take away my safe place?"

He moved closer to her and she backed away, pressing her back up against the light post behind her. "I am not your fucking house pet. I'm not some therapy dog you can use to help calm your anxiety. I want things. I don't exist solely to fill a void in your life. That void that you can't fill with a husband or a partner because you don't want a real relationship. So you use some other guy for sex and me to fix your shit. That isn't happening. Not anymore."

Angry tears stung her eyes. "That isn't fair. I don't think you're a pet. I never have. But I did think that we were friends. I thought I could trust you. Good grief, Finn, I had you in my house late at night thinking of you like any of my other friends, and the whole time you were trying to scam your way into my pants?"

That was going too far. And she knew it. She hadn't meant it either. She was just mad, mad and hurt and breaking apart piece by piece, and so she was lashing out at the one person that she wanted to hold on to more than anyone else. It didn't make any sense, but then she wasn't sure her emotions had made sense for the past ten years.

"Is that the game now? Because I admitted that I was attracted to you, are you going to act like I was just lying in wait planning to jump on you when I had the opportunity? Here's some real talk for you, Lane. If I wanted to, I could make you forget all of the issues you have with us getting physical. If I wanted to, I could make you want me. I could make you forget all the reasons it's not a good idea. I wouldn't have to coerce you or talk you into a damn thing. You would beg me."

Suddenly, the reckless heat inside of her changed, melted into something else. Something she couldn't define, or rather didn't want to. "Well, aren't you full of your damn self, Finn Donnelly." She led with that. With the anger that was still simmering there at the surface, and she left whatever was happening beneath it—all of that molten intensity of feeling that she didn't want to name—alone for now. "I have never begged a man in my entire life, and you would hardly be the first."

"Is that right?"

"Yes." Something small and mean dug at her, spurred her on. "But you're right about one thing. I have treated you differently than I've treated my other friends. My other friends have heard more about my sex life."

The expression on his face turned sharp, dangerous. "And you want to talk about it with me now?"

"Sure. Why not? You might as well know, since you're expressing an interest in getting on the ride." She continued to advance on him, heart pounding, stomach clenched tight, feeling something more than reckless now. "When I want a man, I usually make him take me on a few dates first. Mostly because I want to like the guy that I go to bed with. I'm pretty choosy. I can think a man is hotter than the surface of the sun, but if I don't want to talk to him at least a little bit, it isn't going to happen."

"Is that it? The Lane Jensen system?"

She crossed her arms, cocking her hip out to the side. "Yes. My system."

"So, is that the problem? You don't like me enough?"

That landed hard, and it almost made her take a step back. Almost made her call a truce. Defuse the bomb. But only almost. "Usually?" She lifted her brow. "I like you a little too much to take you to bed, but that's another story. But right now, I don't like you enough, no."

"Fair enough," he said. "But since we're sharing, let's have a little talk about my sex life. I have wanted you since you were eighteen and your fingers brushed against my thigh, and you lit me on fire. You were so clearly off-limits. I was too old for you. But then, over the years that gap has shrunk. But I still knew that I couldn't give you what you deserved. But you know what? None of the other men that you've dated have given you what you deserved either. What I think you deserve is something you don't seem to want. I think you deserve all that white picket fence stuff. A dream wedding and a guy who will make vows to you and keep them. In a perfect world that's what you'd have. But the world isn't perfect. Whatever you want later… Right now, I think we want the same thing, and if you're really honest we both want each other."

Her mouth dried as she looked into his face—that angry, beautiful face that could never just be her friend's face ever again. Because she'd kissed his lips. Had felt the slow, luxurious slide of his tongue against hers.

Had felt his arousal, hard and insistent and a mirror of her own.

But she couldn't let him know that.

"You're pretty confident in your appeal," she said, "but my entire point in bringing up my sexual history is that you should know I'm selective. I don't get led around by the lady downstairs. My brain does the leading. And maybe I kissed you back, but that was momentary insanity. Once I was able to think and rationalize I realized it was crazy. And that it was the last thing on earth I wanted."

She knew that it was going to happen. She had known it, probably from the moment she had demanded he wait when he had decided to walk away. And, if she was honest, part of her had been gunning for it. There was no other reason she would have stopped him from leaving, when she damn well should've just let him go.

No reason she should have kept poking and pushing and saying the meanest, most pointed things she could think of.

Still, when Finn wrapped his arm around her waist and hauled her against his chest it was a shock to her system. A shock of heat. A shock of desire.

And most of all, a shock of relief.

She wanted this. This was what she had wanted from the moment she had stormed out of the bar, and that was what had really disturbed her.

That what she wanted was to be as close as possible to the one person who knew about her past. The one person who knew exactly why she felt like every image of Cord that flashed across the news was another strip taken off of her soul.

She waited. Waited for him to close the distance between them. Waited for him to give her what she wanted more than her next breath.

What she feared more than anything else.

But he didn't kiss her. She wished he would. Wished he would crush her mouth with his and drown out all the uncertainty. Do something to fix the restlessness that was eating away at her, that was all his fault.

He should have the decency to do something about this—this horrific desire that he had created inside her. It was his monster. The least he could do was slay it for her.

He didn't.

Instead, he just held her. And looked at her, those blue eyes glittering with an intensity that burned away all of the anger that had been simmering inside of her. And without that, it left nothing but the truth. Nothing but the base reality of the situation.

She wanted him. God help her, she wanted her best friend.

He gripped her chin with his thumb and forefinger, pinching it firmly, his hold tight. Too tight for her to move. To look away. "I am damned confident," he said, his voice rough. "There's nothing logical about this. There's no decision to be made. You want me. I want you." He moved his thumb up, just a bit. Until the rough, calloused pad brushed the edge of her lip. She shivered. All the way down. "The only question right now is when. Not if."

She shivered, and she would have liked to pretend that it was a jolt of anger, that it was good sense and common decency coming to her rescue. But she knew that instead it was anticipation. A little thrill at the promise he had just made.

He tilted his head upward, and for a moment, with

the way the light above them cast his face into stark shadows, the planes and hollows of his angular features made even sharper, he was a stranger. This man who was holding her against that hard body wasn't the Finn Donnelly she had always known.

But how could it be? The Finn she knew was easy to talk to. Quick to smile. Easy to smooth over any perceived insult. He protected her.

This man didn't look like he could smile. And he certainly didn't look like he wanted to protect her.

He looked like he wanted to eat her alive. Heaven help her, she might let him.

This rough, masculine side of him was new to her. This wicked, cocky, sexy cowboy who made her tremble all over wasn't her comfort zone at all. Far from it.

And it made her wonder if this was what Rebecca had felt when she had nearly hooked up with him a few months ago. If this was what every woman felt when he turned that blue gaze onto them, and she had just been so committed to keeping up that facade that she had been blind until this moment.

It was like a switch had been flipped inside of her and now she couldn't put it back.

If she was honest, she couldn't even blame the kiss. It wasn't the kiss, not really. It had started before that. That moment she had brushed her fingertips against his arm on his porch at the ranch that night his brothers had first come.

That moment she had touched him and felt something other than skin beneath her fingers. That moment she had felt possibility, excitement, a crackle of electricity and a need that hit her low and dragged her down even lower until she ached.

He was right. That was the worst part. It was too

late. There was nothing she could do to not feel this. It was between them. Part of them. Right in the middle of their friendship. In the middle of what was usually easy conversation. And then she had gone and heaped her past on top of it. There was no safe space here. Not with him. Not anymore.

And she had to wonder if the only way back was to go forward first.

So that was exactly what she did.

She stretched up on her toes and closed the distance between them, pressing her lips against his.

CHAPTER FOURTEEN

IT WAS FIRE. It was insanity. It was obsession and temptation, satisfaction and a need that ran so deep he thought it just might kill him.

She was the one who'd started this. She was the one who had pressed her lips to his. She was the one who was now pushing her fingers through his hair, angling her head so that she could taste him deeply.

The slow slide of her tongue against his was the most erotic thing he'd ever experienced in his life. The flavor of her. The scent. It was a strange thing, having such a new and unique experience as tasting her go hand in hand with the way that she smelled.

The way she smelled was so familiar. So very unique to her. So specific to this woman who had been his best friend for the past decade.

He didn't take the time to get to know the women he slept with. There was no point. Not when he was going to satisfy himself with them a few times, and then move on. Not when he knew there was no future in the cards. He did the very best he could to prowl on the periphery of town. To conduct his hookups within reasonable proximity.

And if that failed, he tried to make sure that he chose women who were more than up for the kind of thing he had on offer. Women with well-worn reputations who weren't going to surprise him and start hinting around about diamond rings and futures, or even space in his medicine cabinet.

No, familiarity had never been on the menu. So he had vastly underestimated just how erotic that might be.

To *know* the woman he was kissing. To know the way she smiled, the way she laughed, the way her nose turned red when she cried during sad movies.

When all of that knowledge collided with everything he didn't know, it about lit him on fire. About made him embarrass himself then and there. And when she slid her fingertips down his face, traced the line of his jaw, he thought his cock might bust through the front of his jeans.

He knew so much about Lane. He probably knew her better than he knew anyone. But he hadn't known how it would feel to be with her like this. Not until this moment. Hadn't known that she would sound like a little unsatisfied kitten when he slid his tongue along her bottom lip. Hadn't known that she would arch into him and roll her hips forward like a needy, greedy thing when he slid his hand down her back and farther still to cup her ass.

He didn't know what she looked like naked. He'd only seen tantalizing glimpses of pale skin over the years as she wore a bikini, as she wandered around her house in cutoff shorts and ratty T-shirts. He had wondered. The mysteries of her body had kept him up at night. What color her nipples were, how soft that thatch of curls at the apex of her thighs might be.

Yeah, they were friends, but there was a hell of a lot he didn't know.

And he was ready to uncover all those mysteries. To peel her clothes off, spread her legs open, look his fill, taste his fill, bury himself so deep inside of her that he would know every damn inch of her.

And she would feel every damn inch of him.

He slid his hands to her hips, gripped her hard, pulled her up against him so that she could feel just how hard she made him. He wanted her to know. He wanted her to ache the way he did. Wanted her to want him in the same way.

His gut felt hollow with the need he had for her and he wanted her to feel that way too. Wanted her to know that the only person who could ever fill that empty space in her was him.

Maybe it wasn't fair to do this to her when she was vulnerable, but he was past caring. Because she was right. It was done now. They had kissed. And there had been a chance that their lips would meet and nothing would ignite between them; that possibility had always existed, even though he had thought it unlikely. But now he had proven there was plenty between them. That she felt it too. And there was no going back.

He slid his hands upward, pushing his fingers beneath the hem of her shirt, feeling the bare skin of her back between his palms, growling when he felt just how soft she was. It was a helluva thing, to touch her like this after so much thinking about it. After all that fantasizing.

Maybe she was right. Maybe he was a little bit of a jackass. Going to her house late at night, eating dinner with her, playing the part of devoted friend, then going home and imagining her when he got into the shower with a hard-on that wouldn't quit.

He had tried his best not to do that. He always tried his best not to give in to his fantasies about her when he was left aching and unfulfilled. But more often than not it was a losing battle.

But this wasn't a late night spent sleepless, being inundated with erotic images he knew full well he shouldn't indulge. This was real. And it was better than anything his brain had conjured up.

It hit him then that they were standing in the middle of Ace's parking lot about to violate a few public decency laws. And while Finn was on the brink of not giving a damn, he figured that Lane might.

"We should go," he said, his voice low, rough.

She took a step back and froze, her eyes wide, and for a moment he thought she would balk again. But then she slowly nodded, and she took his hand and led him toward her car.

LANE QUESTIONED HERSELF no less than one hundred times as she drove down the highway that would take them to her house. Finn didn't say anything, and neither did she. She wasn't sure she could have. Right now, she was torn in two. Between the desire to turn around and take him back to his truck, and pull over quickly so they could just get all of this over with. On the side of the two-lane highway, for all the town to see.

The sooner that happened, the sooner everything could go back to the way it was. At least, that was what she was telling herself now. As for the rest… The ache between her thighs, the restlessness inside of her, the feeling that she was being squeezed in a vise, pressed in on all sides and about ready to implode from the enormity of the feelings she had at the moment… She was going to ignore it.

Because she couldn't sort through it. Couldn't articulate exactly what it all was.

She just kept driving. In lieu of any revelations, that was what she would do.

They made it all the way to her house without anything happening. Without Finn calling it off, without her losing her nerve. Without a white light shining down from the sky and blinding her, effectively stopping their progress. Any of those things would've been nice.

But they didn't happen. Instead, she parked her car in the driveway and they both got out.

She had walked up her front porch with Finn any number of times, so many that the action was entirely unremarkable.

Except right now. Right now the familiarity was weighted with something else. With this sense of the unknown that she had never associated with him before.

Still, she swallowed hard and unlocked the front door, letting them both in. He followed her inside and rested his hand against the light switch.

"Don't," she said, her heart lurching into her throat.

He paused, turning to look at her. She couldn't see his expression, and that was how she wanted it. How she needed it. This was inevitable—she knew that now. But she wanted… She wanted to keep this moment separate from real life somehow.

To keep Finn, the most important person in her life, separate from Finn, the man she had nearly climbed like a tree in the parking lot at Ace's. The man she was about to take to her bed. Yes, she needed to keep those men separate from each other. And once they got through this, once the sexual tension between them had been resolved, they could go back to the way things were.

She needed that.

More than anything she needed to ease this tension between them, the tension that had begun to build weeks ago, the tension that was not even completely his fault because it had started somewhere before he had taken her in his arms in her shop.

"Don't turn the lights on?" The question was asked softly, but there was an edge of danger to his voice. And she couldn't entirely predict what he might do next. Mostly because he had been committed to being unpredictable for the last couple of days.

"Yes," she said, her voice scratchy. "I haven't… I haven't been with anyone in a while. So I'm a little nervous." She was lying about being nervous for that reason. She hated herself for it, even while she remained committed to the lie. "And I'm not really up to doing the looking-at-each-other-naked thing."

He moved to her, closing the distance between them. Then he brushed his knuckles along her cheek, the touch gentle. She still couldn't see his face, but she could sense that he was looking at her intently. And even though she knew he couldn't see her any better than she could see him, she looked away. Because she was ashamed for doing this again. For using carefully placed truths to try and place a wedge between the two of them.

For taking that trust between them and twisting it to suit her ends.

"You're so beautiful," he said, his voice rough, the words pouring through her like honey. "And such a liar." She didn't get a chance to respond to that because he dipped his head, brushing his lips across hers, the touch as gentle as his voice and carrying that same edge of danger.

It left her feeling dizzy, dazed. But when the fog cleared, she responded. "What do you mean?" It was a stupid thing to ask, because she knew she was lying.

But she wasn't going to admit it unless he hit the nail on the head first.

"You want to pretend it isn't me. You want to pretend so that you don't have to admit that I was right. That I could make you want me." He grabbed hold of her chin, just like he had done earlier. "I'm not going to let you do that, Lane. I'm not going to let you have me while you hold me at a distance. I'm not going to let you pretend that I'm some other man getting you off."

Heat blasted her cheeks. "That isn't what I was doing." And that, at least, was true. She didn't want to imagine he was someone else; she just wanted to blunt the intimacy of it. Just wanted to be able to look back on tonight and not have mental pictures of it. Clear and present images of Finn's hands on her body. Of what he looked like naked. She wanted to be able to look him in the eye again when all of this was said and done.

"I told you I was gonna make you beg for me. And that's exactly what I'm going to do. Make you beg. But it's going to be for me—you're going to say my name. And you're going to look me in the eye while I slide deep inside of you. Do you understand?"

He said it so casually. That was what got her. That it wasn't in a stranger's intense tone, but in that voice she knew so well. The voice of her friend, the man she had been so close to for so many years.

But were you close to him? He didn't know anything about your past, and you didn't know this. That you wanted him like this.

She shut off that pesky inner voice. Pushed it away. She didn't want to think about it. She didn't want to think about any serious implications. All she wanted was for him to kiss her again. For him to touch her again. She wanted to screw her eyes shut tight and block out everything but what she felt.

"You're not just going to get this over with, understand?" he asked.

That simple statement enraged her. That he had read her so well. That he knew what she was doing. That he wouldn't allow her to make him a stranger for this moment.

No one else would have known her ulterior motive. No other man would have called her on her BS. She knew that for a fact, because none of them ever had. There hadn't been many. She'd had just three relationships in the past decade, and all of them had been casual. Because she had kept them that way.

But already her relationship with Finn was anything but casual. He mattered. On some days, he felt like damn near everything. That was what made taking this step so deadly. That was what made all of this so sharp.

And if she wanted to blunt some of that edge, who was he to try and force her to feel at all?

"Why?" she asked, her whisper fierce. "You're getting what you want. Why shouldn't I have a little bit of what I want?"

"That's not how this works. I want it all. Or I walk out the door. But you need to ask me to stay because you want me, Lane. Not because you're trying to keep me from leaving. Not because you're trying to blackmail me into doing what you want. Into being what you want. I already told you, I'm not your pet."

"I know you're not," she said, pain welling up inside her and flooding outward. "I never said you were. I don't know why I want this," she admitted helplessly, the words spilling from her. "I don't know why things couldn't go on the way they were, because it was so much easier. It was so much better. I don't know why I can't seem to put this back away. It feels like things inside of me are cracking open, and all of this stuff that I just don't want is taking over." She hadn't meant to be that honest. Mostly because she didn't see the point. Not when it felt like rambling. Like some kind of verbal approximation of the desperation that was going on inside her.

"Because it's not new," he said, his voice confident. And then he slid his hand back over to the light switch and flicked it up. Light flooded the room, washed over them, revealed that lean hungry look in his eye that made him seem much more like a predator than like her friend.

And she knew it revealed her too. All the uncertainty, all the desire.

They were both still fully clothed, but as it was, she felt like they might as well have been naked. That was when it hit her, how embarrassed she was to let him see that she wanted him. To let her friend see her like this, overcome with sexual desire.

Because whatever else was happening inside her, that was no small part of it. She wanted him. And whatever the deep, complex reasoning, simple need was definitely layered over the top.

Sex was a clear line with friends. She might giggle and talk about it with the girls, but they didn't see each other being sexual. And Finn... Well, she didn't talk about it, and she didn't let him see her as a sexual person.

But that veil had been ripped away. Like everything else, longer ago than she wanted to admit.

Her face felt hot, and she knew that her cheeks were flushed, that he would be able to see just how turned on she was. Her breasts felt heavy, and she had a feeling her nipples were totally visible through her shirt, since she was wearing a bra that didn't have much in the way of padding.

And normally, she wouldn't worry about something like that in front of Finn. But now she did. She was afraid she always would.

He was looking too. And he didn't make a show of acting like he wasn't. His blue gaze was hot as it roamed over her curves, as he slowly examined her. Then he raised his eyes from her breasts and looked right at her. Which was even worse. She felt her cheeks get hotter still.

Even more disturbing than him seeing her as a fully sexual being was her seeing him that way. As a man in every sense of the word. Not just with a vague knowledge, not just checking out his muscles on a dock by the lake, but as a man in every way that counted.

A man she was going to touch. Taste. Have inside of her.

For a moment she considered running into her room and locking the door. Or taking the slightly more grown-up approach of telling him to leave. Telling him this wouldn't work.

But in the back of her mind she kept hearing what he'd said earlier. That it wasn't a matter of if, but when. She knew he was right. If she sent him away, she'd be left with hot coals burning inside of her that would be stoked the moment she saw him again. They would burst right into flame the next time they brushed against each other. And they would be back to this. To the push and pull, to the futile resistance that was just so pointless.

He released his hold on her, letting his fingertips

drift down the line of her neck. She closed her eyes, shivered. And then he grabbed hold of her shoulders, turning her away from him. She gasped as he wrapped one arm around her waist, pressing his palm to her stomach.

He drew her hair back, exposing her neck completely. The gentle tug naturally tilting her head to the side. Then he bent his head, pressed a hot kiss to her delicate skin.

Everything in her went tight. The breath in her lungs, her stomach, her core.

She curled her fingers into fists, held herself steady as he kept his mouth on her, then, after a moment, lightened the pressure, tracing on down to her shoulder with the tip of his tongue. The heat, the chill that he left behind, made her tremble.

"You don't have to be afraid," he whispered. "It's only me."

But that was what made it scary. She didn't have the ability to say that though, because she didn't have the ability to say anything. Right now, all of the words inside of her, all of the language, had evaporated. Her thoughts weren't made of language anymore. She was comprised entirely of feeling.

He put his hand on her stomach, bringing her back into his body, the hard press of him against her a sensual shock that made her internal muscles pulse with need.

He gripped her hips with both hands before bringing them up to her waist, then higher still to cup her breasts. He growled then, a low, feral sound in his throat that spoke of a deep, masculine satisfaction that echoed inside of her. Called to a purely feminine part of her that wanted nothing more than to meet his needs. Those needs that she had created.

Suddenly, she didn't feel quite so weak. Instead, she felt powerful. And as that strength washed over her, she was able to fully appreciate the wonder contained in the fact that Finn Donnelly wanted her.

He was…unquestionably sexy. The kind of man that women made fools of themselves going after. He could sell tickets to his bed, and he would have a line that rivaled any theme park.

And he wanted her. Enough that he had detonated a bomb between the two of them. And now that she felt much more desire than anger, she could appreciate that.

It made her feel… Well, it made her feel something much more than broken.

And that was much rarer than she would like to admit.

Suddenly, he whirled her around to face him, his blue eyes intense. It hit her, square in the chest. The force of his need. His need for her.

It touched a place inside of her that she tried to ignore was there. A raw, needy place that she tried never to fully uncover.

She realized that for them, sex wasn't separate from their friendship. It was actually much closer to it than she had realized. Because for the past ten years he had made her feel like she might be worth something. Like she mattered. And being with him intimately was like that. It just reached deeper.

It was the *deeper* that was terrifying.

But more terrifying right at the moment was walking away. Not finishing this. Disappointing him when he was looking at her like that. Like she was all he needed, even more than air.

Nerves skittered to her stomach like frightened creatures, and for a moment she was tempted to run. And so, instead, she wrapped her arm around his neck, stretched up on her toes and claimed his mouth with a kiss.

His response was immediate. Incendiary. He parted her lips roughly, his tongue delving deep, tasting her like she was the best dessert he'd ever had. She wanted nothing more than to do the same. So she did. She shut everything out. All of the fear, all of the uncertainty as she clung to Finn and gave in to the desire that had existed in her, dormant, but very much there.

It was reckless, terrifying, to let herself go like this. To just let herself kiss him, to admit that she wanted this. That she wanted him. She had kept herself from thinking these words, from imagining this, from fully allowing herself to want it for so long. And now, she was just barreling down the hill, gaining momentum, throwing herself into it with a kind of hedonistic abandon that made her feel giddy and gun-shy all at once.

But giddy was going to win out. Desire was going to win out. Because she had gone too far to go back now.

"I want to see you," he said, wrenching his mouth from hers.

With trembling hands she reached down and grabbed hold of the hem of her shirt. She didn't want to think about this. She didn't want to hesitate. So without pausing she wrenched the fabric over her head, then with unsteady fingers unclasped her bra, throwing it down on the floor.

The fact that she was getting naked in front of her best friend hit her fully about the time her panties hit the ground. And by then, it was too late.

He cursed, but the words sounded more like a prayer than anything else. He stood back from her, his lips pressed into a firm line, his blue eyes glittering. He looked like he was wrestling with something, battling restraint, battling an army inside of him.

Then he reached out, brushed his thumb over her tightened nipple. Her breath left her lungs in a rush, desire piercing her like an arrow.

"Perfect," he said, a muscle in his jaw jumping.

He didn't say anything else after that. Instead, he swept her up in his arms, cradled her against his chest, his hands roaming over her bare body. He kissed her, walked her back down the hall, and before she knew it, the back of her legs hit the edge of the bed.

Her heart thundered hard, slamming recklessly against her breastbone as she tried to capture the enormity of what was about to happen, at the same time as she made a small attempt to minimize it. Yes, she was about to have sex with Finn.

But in so many ways it made sense. Because she knew him. And he knew her. And he meant more to her than any other man. It made sense to be intimate with him.

It also scared the hell out of her. But she didn't resist at all when he pressed her back onto the mattress, his hands braced on either side of her shoulders as he stared down at her.

He didn't move, not for a long moment. Too long. The less kissing there was, the more mindful she was about the moment. The larger everything began to feel.

She reached up, grabbing hold of his head and bringing it down to hers, kissing him deeply, parting her thighs and letting him settle between them. The denim was rough against her skin, his cock hard beneath the fabric. She welcomed it. It was overwhelming. It swamped her senses completely. Made it impossible to think. Suddenly, that's what she was desperate for.

Just a few moments of oblivion. Where she didn't have to worry about what this meant for them.

Where she didn't have to think about the future. And even better, didn't have to think about the past. Just for a while. Just for a little while.

"Tell me you want me," he said, angling his head, kissing her just beneath her jaw.

"I want you."

"My name," he said, his voice a growl.

"I want you, Finn." His name came out in a hushed whisper.

"Not convincing enough." He grabbed hold of her wrist, curling his fingers tightly around it before gathering up her other wrist in the same way, holding them together and drawing her arms up above her head, pinning them against the mattress. "Let's try that again."

He held her there like that, immobilized as he lowered his head down to her breasts. He brushed his lips against one distended bud, moving his head back and forth, the featherlight contact building the tension in her stomach and down lower.

Then he closed his lips over one of the aching peaks, sucking her in deep. It shocked her, caused her hips to bow up from the bed, bringing her into sharp, sweet contact with his hardened length. She let her head fall back, a hoarse cry on her lips.

He kept on tormenting her with his mouth, and she rode the seam of his jeans as he did, torturing herself, ramping up her arousal. She had never felt like this before. Had never felt so outside of herself during sex.

What she had told him earlier had been true. For her, sex was a logical decision based on satisfying a basic set of needs. But she had never been in a situation where she felt like she couldn't walk away. Where she felt like her physical desire had overridden her logic.

But there was no logic to be had here. She was made entirely of sensation and need, wrapped up in lust so tightly that she couldn't escape. She didn't even want to.

She struggled against his hold, but his hand was like an iron manacle, keeping her still as he continued to lavish attention on her. He moved his cheek over one breast, his stubble scraping against the delicate skin. She whimpered, arching into him even harder.

"You seem a little bit restless, Lane," he said, lifting his head for a moment, his eyes clashing with hers. "Do you want something?"

That question, that simple question, opened up an array of illicit fantasies inside her mind. Made her want to ask for things she'd never done before. Made her want anything, everything. And more, so much more than what was happening right now.

"Yes," she said, not intending for the response to be a whisper.

"That's not convincing either. You need to tell me you want me. And then you need to beg to have me." He never took his eyes off hers, his expression deadly serious.

She bit her lip, shaking her head.

"Oh, right," he said, "I forgot you don't beg. You're gonna beg for this. You're going to beg for me. I made you a promise. And I'll be damned if I ever break a promise I make you, Lane Jensen."

Suddenly, he released his hold on her wrists. And then he grabbed hold of her hips. She only had a split second to realize what was going to happen next before he moved down her body, dragging her toward his mouth with that inescapable grip of his.

A short, sharp scream escaped her lips as he pressed his own against the part of her that was wet and aching for him.

"I don't," she said, the words coming out sounding more like a squeak. "I don't do this. Nobody does this for me."

This was something she actively avoided. It was too focused on her. And she wasn't comfortable with that. In fact, the thought had always actively turned her off. Being subjected to so much attention, so much scrutiny. It was extraneous. Peripheral. Just the basics were fine for her.

"I do," he said, nuzzling her, going even deeper. Then his fingers joined in, teasing her, tormenting her, pushing her higher than she'd ever been before. "I always wondered how soft you'd be—" he slid his tongue through her slick folds "—how sweet." He made a low, satisfied sound. "Like honey, baby."

She was hot all over, desperate to get away from him, and also desperate to press herself in closer to him, to take more of what he was giving. She was so unbearably aware of the fact it was him. Because he was talking to her, because all of it was so undeniably Finn.

So pushy, and alpha, and enraging. Doing what he wanted, telling her with confidence that she wanted it too. Being right. Bastard.

He kept right on tormenting her until her breath was coming in short, choked sobs, until she was gasping for air, and grasping for the blankets, trying to find something to anchor her to earth. She flexed her feet, digging her heels deep into the mattress as he brought her to the edge of climax for what had to be the fifth time before pulling her back again.

"Finn," she said, his name sounding desperate now.

"What?" The question was lazy, so cocky, so confident. If she didn't know him so well, well enough that she could hear his own tension, his own desperation beneath the surface, she might have hit him.

"You know," she panted.

"No," he said, "I don't."

She threw her arm over her face, covering up her eyes. "I want you."

"Give me what I want. Give me the words." The edge wasn't beneath the surface anymore, it was evident. His need for this, for her to tell him exactly what he wanted to hear, not at all hidden anymore.

"I need you, Finn. I want you."

"What exactly do you need?"

"You," she said, "inside me."

He started to move away from her and she grabbed hold of his shoulders, pulling him back toward her. "I need a condom," he said.

"I think there are some in the bathroom," she said. "I haven't actually needed them for a while."

"Okay." He went into the bathroom and returned a moment later, tearing a condom packet open as he walked back to her.

"Hurry up," she said. "I need you."

His jaw tensed. "Say that again."

"I want you inside me. Now."

He grabbed ahold of his shirt and dragging it up over his head. Her mouth dried at the sight of him. At his cut abs, broad shoulders, narrow waist. And then his hand went to the snap on his jeans and she lost the capacity for thought at all.

All she could do was watch as he dragged the zipper down slowly, then grabbed hold of his underwear and pushed it and those jeans down his hips.

He was not the first man she had ever seen naked, but she had never seen a man that looked quite like him. He rolled the protection over his length, and she just stared at him. Hard, thick. All for her.

She had done her very best to never wonder about Finn's penis. But of course she had. She had figured a little curiosity was totally normal. He was a large man, over six feet, with big hands, so she had figured he would be proportionally endowed.

She had underestimated him.

Her internal muscles clenched in anticipation, with need.

He moved back to the bed, and a little flip of anxiety turned her stomach. "It really has been a long time since I've been with anybody."

"I can take it slow," he said.

She shivered, the thought of taking it slow, all those hard, thick inches, just about sending her over the edge there and then.

He moved up between her thighs, pressing the head of his cock against her clit, sliding it over her slick folds, up and down, teasing her with near penetration.

"Beg for it," he said, the tendons in his neck standing out, his jaw clenched tight.

There was no point in holding out. She was going to beg. And she wasn't even ashamed.

"Please, Finn, I need you inside me. Please."

He looked right in her eyes, and it was too much. She closed them, looked away as he pressed the head of his arousal to her slick entrance, sliding in slowly, inch by delicious inch. Until she was filled. Filled with him.

When he was buried to the hilt, she looked at him again. He was looking somewhere past her, the expression on his face one of extreme torture.

Everything stopped, just for a moment. She clung to his shoulder with one hand, pressed the other against his hip. And then he began to move. And she felt it all. The flex of his muscles, the strength it was taking him to control himself, to establish a steady, measured rhythm.

The extreme hardness of his length, buried deep inside of her.

She was surrounded by him, above her, inside of her. It was too much, too much intensity to bear, and she was sure she would die of it. With each steady thrust he pressed up against her, white-hot pleasure streaking through her veins each and every time.

She had been poised on the brink for so long she had forgotten what it was like to feel anything else. She was lost in a haze unlike anything she'd ever known. But one thing was clear. As her hands roamed over the muscular body so close above her, she couldn't deny that she knew exactly who it was.

She was touching Finn's shoulder blade, dragging her fingertips down the line of his spine, moving her palm over his well-muscled ass.

It was Finn inside of her. Finn who had her strung out in sexual limbo, suspended somewhere between heaven and hell.

And when the tension inside of her finally fractured, splintered and shattered completely, there was absolutely no doubt that it was Finn's name on her lips as she cried out her release.

CHAPTER FIFTEEN

SUDDENLY, THE LIGHT seemed too bright. He was the one who had insisted it be on. He stood by that. Because he would be damned if he was going to let Lane pretend it was some other man bringing her pleasure. Would be damned if he allowed her to hide from him when he had spent so long fantasizing about her naked body.

Oh yeah, he had wanted to see everything.

But now, in the aftermath of his release, it all felt a little too sharp.

All of his nerve endings were fractured, on fire. His orgasm had nearly blown his head off. Among other things.

This was a new experience for him. Wanting somebody for so long and finally having them. Lane was the only woman he had ever wanted for an extended period of time. Usually, he mostly wanted sex, not one woman in particular.

She was the exception. She always had been.

And now she was pressed against him, her full, soft breasts crushed to his chest, her thighs parted, cradling him inside of her body.

He flexed his hips lightly, the shock of pleasure assaulting him.

He looked down at her face. Her eyes were closed, her chin tilted upward, as though she was resolutely not looking at him. But there was a smile tilting her lips upward.

He lifted his hand, brushing her hair away from her eyes, then let his fingertips drift down her face. He stroked her lower lip, like velvet beneath his touch. Her eyes fluttered open then, a glassy, dazed expression in them.

It hit him with full force, like a horse kicking him in the chest.

He moved away from her, swinging his legs over the side of the bed.

She didn't say anything, but a moment later, he felt a hesitant touch against the center of his back. He didn't react. He was still trying to catch his breath.

For the first time he questioned himself. He wondered what the hell he had been thinking. What he had hoped to accomplish with this. Because one thing was certain, sleeping with her hadn't dealt with his desire for her.

All he wanted to do was kiss her again. Sink into her body again. Again and again and again.

This hadn't even been a Band-Aid to put over the throbbing, insistent desire he felt for her. Nope, it hadn't done a thing to lessen it at all.

And when you slept with your best friend, you kind of had to know the end game. With other women, Finn knew the end game. Sex a few times, and then a mutual parting. He didn't deal with ex-lovers, and if he ever did, it was easy. Done in passing, and without any difficulty because both of them had dealt with their need for each other. Were likely satisfying that generic need with other people.

His need for Lane had never been generic. It had always been specific. It had never been about sex. He could be sleeping with another woman and still be caught off guard by how beautiful Lane was. Occasionally get stabbed, deep and low in the gut when she turned to smile at him in the sunlight filtered through her dark hair, illuminating it like some kind of halo.

Which had always seemed somewhat ironic to him since the thoughts he had about her were anything but angelic.

What was wrong with him? He had finally gotten the one thing he'd wanted for years, and he didn't feel any closer to satisfaction. If anything, it had opened up to a deeper, darker and even more fathomless cavern of need inside of him.

He felt like the world's biggest jackass. Sitting on the edge of the bed, having experienced the most explosive sexual encounter of his life—and brooding, instead of reveling in his physical satisfaction and his conquest.

He didn't feel like Lane was a conquest. Maybe that was a problem. He felt much more conquested than anything else.

He got up and walked into the bathroom on unsteady legs, disposing of the condom. He looked up at his reflection in the mirror and wanted to punch it. He had thought—because hell, he'd wanted Lane long enough—that being with her would be the resolution to something.

Instead he felt like there was something large lodged in his chest keeping him from breathing.

He walked back into the bedroom and looked at her. She was still lying down, naked and sleepy looking. Soft and warm. "You okay?" He didn't know what else to say, but that seemed like a caring angle to take.

He slid back into bed beside her, his gut going tight

as he did. Getting into bed with Lane, bare-ass naked, was not a usual occurrence.

She nodded slowly. "Yes." She put a hand on his shoulder. "Are you?"

There was no good answer to that. So he leaned forward, then wrapped his arm around her waist, shifting his weight and bringing her beneath him again. "That's a complicated question."

Her cheeks turned red. "Is it?"

"Do you mean am I satisfied?"

"No, that's not what I meant. But, are you?"

"Not by a long shot. I have a feeling it will take more than once to accomplish that." For some reason, as soon as he said those words, some of the tension in his chest eased. Maybe that was the problem. He wanted more. And as he sat there on the edge of the bed, he had seen himself plunge right back into the hell he'd been living in for the past decade. Wanting her, but not wanting to push her.

Because once wasn't enough. It wouldn't be. He knew that.

What he didn't know was whether or not she was going to retreat back inside of herself again. Whether or not she was going to try and put distance between them. It was her modus operandi and they both knew it.

But he wasn't having that bullshit.

"We have all night," she said, brushing her fingertips against his face.

A night. Yeah, right. She was trying to control it. Trying to put a limit on it.

Hell no.

He curled his fingers around her wrist, drawing her hand forward and kissing her palm. Not an innocent kiss. The pressure was firm, and he darted his tongue out so that he could taste her skin. It didn't matter that it was only her hand. Every single part of her was a sensual delight. A feast he intended to sate himself on for as long as he could.

"You think tonight is going to do it?"

She wiggled. He was hard again already. All of Lane Jensen, every soft, supple inch was pressed up against his body. Damn, it felt good.

"Something has to," she said, her tone laughably pragmatic given their positions at the moment.

"What if it doesn't?" Might as well ask the question.

"I don't know." She frowned, a wrinkle appearing between her brows. "Can you not be on top of me when we talk about this?"

He moved his hands down to her ass, squeezed her tight and drew her up against his arousal. "Are you sure about that?"

She gasped. "I'll take *What is I can't talk with my best friend's penis pushing against my hip* for five hundred, Alex."

"Is that your final answer?"

"Unless you want delicate appendages to be in jeopardy…"

"Your flawless game show metaphor leads me to believe that your brain is working just fine. Perhaps even too well."

"I need…" She wiggled out from under him, moving up to the top of the bed and sliding beneath the covers. "Just for a second."

"Suit yourself," he said, rolling to the side and getting up from the bed. He moved back against the wall, crossing his arms over his chest.

The color in her cheeks got darker. "I'm also not sure I can talk to you while you're naked."

"You have a lot of rules."

"I'm making them up as I go. Sadly, there is a dearth of rules for how to handle having just had sex with your best friend." She pinched the bridge of her nose. "Dammit. I had sex with my best friend."

"I know. I was there."

"Aren't you going to…get dressed?"

"I'm fine," he said.

She clearly wasn't, but he wasn't interested in making her feel comfortable. He wasn't interested in cutting the tension that stretched between them. He knew it was what she wanted. But she wasn't in control here. He didn't have to give a wide berth to her denial. Not anymore. He had spent long enough doing that. But now? Now he had been inside of her.

He wasn't interested in games now.

"I'm going to tell you some things, and they're kind of personal," she said.

"This is kind of personal," he said, gesturing to his naked body.

"You are such a guy."

"I think that's very evident at the moment."

She laughed, flopping onto her back, covering her face with a pillow. "You are ridiculous right now. Aren't you supposed to be serious and making bedroom eyes and whatever else you normally do after sex?"

He pushed off the wall, moving back toward the bed. "Well, I can't do what I would normally do after sex. Because this wasn't normal sex."

She uncovered half her face, looking at him with one wide brown eye. "It wasn't?"

"You're being ridiculous, Lane. You know it wasn't."

She shrugged one enticing bare shoulder, and he

found himself taking extra time to notice the freckle there. He wanted to lick it.

He wanted to lick her. Again. All over. One taste of that magic between her legs hadn't been enough. He had a feeling if he said that to her now she would disappear beneath the covers, never to return.

"Okay, maybe I know it wasn't."

Without waiting for her permission he joined her on the bed, stretching out beside her. She scooted about half an inch in the other direction, but he didn't take it personally. "This is the part where you tell me I was the best you've ever had," he said, propping his face on his fist.

"Maybe you weren't," she said, tilting her chin up.

He took hold of it, lowered her face so that she was forced to make eye contact with him. "Try again."

Her pupils expanded, the ring of brown in her eyes nearly disappearing. "Okay," she said, her voice trembling. "Maybe you were."

"Good. Because you were definitely the best I've ever had."

"Really? Me? You've been with so many women."

"Not *that* many," he returned.

"Still sounds like an indeterminate figure."

"I'd stop and count for you, but I can't remember anyone else at the moment. All I can think of is you."

She laughed again, but this time she sounded subdued, lowering the pillow completely and wrapping her arms around it, clutching it to her chest. Some of the tension in his own chest eased. But the tension in other parts of his body remained.

"What were you going to tell me?"

"Oh," she said, waving her hand, "it's not that important."

"You thought it was really important a few minutes ago."

"Yeah, well. Your abs are compromising my thought process."

"You're welcome to touch them while you talk." That wasn't the only place he wanted her to touch. But he would start with whatever he could get.

She smiled, mirroring his position, propping her cheek up on her closed fist. "This doesn't feel all that weird."

It didn't feel weird at all to him. But then, this attraction wasn't new for him. He had a feeling it wasn't really new for her either, but acknowledging it was new.

"Why would it be?" he asked, reaching out and tracing her face from her cheekbone down to her chin. "It's you and me."

"It's just always seemed to me… That it's best to keep things separate, you know?"

"Is that another rule from the Lane Jensen guide to life?"

She pushed his shoulder. "I just mean… When I left Massachusetts, when I left my parents, I was broken. I was broken in part by my romantic relationship, but it was more than that. I had the baby when I was sixteen." She closed her eyes. "I don't know if we should talk about this now, after all."

He studied her profile, the way her lashes rested against her pale skin. The slight tension in her forehead. The only indication of just how badly this topic hurt her. He wanted her to tell him everything. He wanted her to open up and pour all her pain out onto him. To give it all to him. To let him carry it. He wanted that so badly it shocked him. It was a physical ache, a need that went beyond logic, beyond sex.

He cared about Lane. He wanted to protect her. From everything. And for a long time, that had included himself. But now, now that he knew even more about her, the need had intensified.

"Tell me," he said.

She kept her eyes closed, but she continued talking. "It was decided right after I found out about the pregnancy that we should give the baby up for adoption. And when I say it was decided, I mean our parents told us exactly how it would be. We were both scared. He was my first boyfriend, and while I definitely had thought about marrying him, it wasn't like I was anywhere close to being ready for that. We both had college to look forward to. We both had our whole lives ahead of us. Cord's parents just wanted it all to go away. Him being a part of the child's life was never an option, as far as they were concerned. If I had the baby, they didn't want him involved. So having my parents say that we would put the child up for adoption was…a relief in a way. I didn't have to make the decision. They made it for me."

She took a deep, shuddering breath, holding even tighter to the pillow. Then she continued. "But all throughout the pregnancy I had my doubts. Still, we went forward with the process. The baby was placed with parents before I had him. And I did my best not to think of him as mine. He was theirs. He was theirs because they were the ones who were going to raise him."

"It wasn't that simple in the end, was it?" Finn prompted, trying to keep his tone gentle.

She shook her head, biting her lip. "Sometimes I can't believe that really happened to me. It's like a scene out of someone else's life. And then other times… It's way too real. Way too close to the present. Sometimes I think I feel a flutter in my stomach. And I think it's the baby kicking. But of course, it isn't. I haven't been pregnant for more than twelve years. But it's just... Those reminders. That experience... I can't just forget it. I can't let go of it. It all seemed so simple. You give the baby up for adoption, and then you move on with your life. But there's more to it."

"Tell me," he said.

The image of Lane, so young, going through something that terrified women twice her age, made his heart clench tight.

"My parents told everybody that I was going to study abroad for a year. That wasn't true. I went to a special school with pregnant unwed mothers. Like it was literally the nineteen fifties. And I kept up with my schooling that way."

"Your parents hid the pregnancy from everybody that way."

She swallowed visibly, nodding. "It was for the best," she said, like she was repeating words she had heard before but had never really internalized. "You know, especially for Cord. Because he had political aspirations, like I said. Like you can see. And really, nobody could know that his girlfriend was pregnant. I mean, it was out of consideration for me too. As my mother told me, over and over again, nobody can respect a girl who gets pregnant."

He swore. "That's awful."

"It was really awful. I was so lonely, and everything was scary. I couldn't even talk to my boyfriend. And, anyway, at a certain point I didn't want to. I just wanted to forget that I'd ever had a relationship with him. We broke up over the phone when I was about five months along. I was the one who ended it. I wanted to forget him. And also to never have sex again." She laughed a little. "Clearly I didn't stick to that. But after I had the baby I only ever talked to him once. We didn't talk about the pregnancy. Or the birth. I didn't tell him we had a boy. He doesn't know. He didn't want to know. I did. Sometimes I wonder if that was a good decision."

She cleared her throat. "Anyway. After I had him I went back home, I went back to school. I was going to finish my senior year." She stopped for a moment, biting her lower lip. She let out a long, hard breath. "I tried. I tried to be normal. I tried to forget that anything had happened. The only person who knew about it was Cord, so it seemed like it should be easy. But I couldn't forget. I couldn't feel normal. I couldn't catch his eye from across the school and not remember. I didn't want him to ask about the baby—his son—and yet I was so angry every time he didn't. I couldn't feel like myself again. I couldn't look at my parents and pretend the last year hadn't happened. I just... I didn't feel like I could move on there."

"That's when you came to live with Mark."

"Yes. He had moved away back when I was in junior high. So we weren't all that close, but he knew how Mom and Dad were. He understood. The minute I told him I was having issues with them... He didn't ask questions. He just bought me a plane ticket. And I think... I think my parents were relieved to have me go. Because at the end of the day I think it was a lot harder for them to deal with the fact that I'd had their grandchild, and that they never met him, than they wanted it to be."

"So you came to Copper Ridge. And that's when we met." No wonder he had found her so vulnerable. She had been wounded. Wounded deep. Much more than he had imagined. Mark had made it sound like it was the typical conflict between parents and a teenager.

"Yes," she said. "And this place was... Everything. It was where I really started healing. Where I put all that distance between myself and my mistakes. All that pain. I couldn't live in it. But here... The air, the ocean, the mountains. It started to heal me. I made friends. I found my independence. Who I was. I learned to make my own choices, and that making my own choices wasn't a burden." She looked at him for a moment, then away just as quickly. "I never even wanted to think about being attracted to you. You are too important to me. And I had already lost too much." The words grew tight, small. "That hasn't really changed. It's just that my ability to deny everything clearly decreased."

"Tell me more about that," he said.

"Big ego much?"

"Yes." He moved closer to her. "There is a little bit of ego involved in this. You spent ten years treating me like a Ken doll."

"What?" she asked.

"Like I had nothing but smooth plastic between my legs."

She guffawed. "Lies."

He wrapped his arm around her waist and pulled her up against him. Sadly, the blanket bunched between them and he was denied what he was after, the press of her skin against his. "Not a lie. That's what started all of this. The fact that I couldn't stand you pretending I wasn't a man. And that I couldn't spend another day pretending I didn't want you. I couldn't pretend there was nothing between us. Not anymore."

She reached out and pinched the blanket between her

thumb and forefinger. "Right now there is a very fuzzy blanket between us."

"Not for long." He leaned in, kissed her. Not a simple kiss either. He took it deep. He made it last. When they parted, they were both breathing hard. "But this is what I meant. Not the blanket."

"Okay, when I met you I thought you were hot. But I was kind of off guys then. Plus, I would have gotten you arrested."

"True."

"And I... Well, when I finally did get back into dating it was because I was lonely. Because I had some needs. You know, like you do. But the further I went down the dating road, the clearer it became to me that I wasn't going to have a normal future. I just... I can't. There's too much stuff. I don't want to get married. I can't...think about having another child. It just feels wrong somehow."

He didn't want those things either. And he had his own set of pretty good reasons. But for some reason hearing Lane say that, so definitively, twisted his stomach. He didn't want that for her. It was a funny thing, to feel so confident in his own decision to avoid entanglements, and yet to hate that she was so affected by her past she was doing the same.

But then, another part of him found immediate pleasure in it. In the fact that this association with him wasn't actually holding her back from anything. That it meant they could share an objective. In fact, part of him found it pretty damn satisfying.

"The way I see it," he said, "there's no reason the two of us can't keep being friends."

"Well, we better be able to stay friends. Otherwise, I'm going to take tonight back."

SLOW BURN COWBOY

232

"You can't."

"I would figure out time travel. That's how important it is to me." Her face was serious, so serious he might have laughed if she wasn't so grave. "You're right. I've been attracted to you for a long time. But it was so important to me that we keep what we have that I buried it as deep as I possibly could. That's why I was so mad at you when you kissed me. Not because I never thought about it before, but because I had deliberately forced myself to never, ever indulge any thoughts about what it might be like. Mark helped me so much when I came to Copper Ridge. But you... You were the one that saved me, Finn. Our friendship. You're the most important person in my life."

Why? The question burned in the back of his throat, but he refused to allow himself to ask it. "Because I fix your stuff?"

"No," she said, "just...because."

"The way I see it, the two of us have been playing pretty elaborate games for the past while. Pretending we don't want this, when both of us do."

"You make it sound silly."

"It's not. Our friendship is important to me too, Lane. And not just that, but you. Your feelings. I'm limited in what I can offer a woman. I don't want to get married either. I don't want to have kids. I don't want to have a family. I don't want love." He reached between them, casting the blanket aside. Then he pulled her up against him. "This," he said, rolling his hips forward, letting her feel his hardness. "This is all I have to offer you. That, and what we have already."

"So, you're proposing an arrangement. With multiple orgasms and steady companionship?"

"Yes."

She blinked, the expression on her face turning ponderous. And everything in him seized up, froze. All of him, every cell in his body, waiting on her response.

"That sounds… Dangerously simple and exceedingly attractive."

"What if it's both?"

"Is it ever?"

He ignored the voice inside of him that said it couldn't be. "Why not? We both want the same things."

"More accurately we both want to avoid the same things," she said, her tone dry.

"Yeah, fair enough." He pressed his forehead against hers. "You're not going to forget this. Don't pretend for one second that me leaving tonight means we can go back to the way things were tomorrow."

She blinked, a sheen of tears in her eyes. He hated himself for that. But not enough to tell her to forget it. Not enough to make this easy. "That was what I was planning. That was why I drove you back here." She laughed, a shaky sound. "I thought that if we could just…do it once we would maybe take care of it."

"I'm afraid not."

"So we do it. Until we don't."

He couldn't imagine a time when he wouldn't want to. But, there was no point in saying that. "Exactly."

"And we're friends first."

"Always."

She let out a sigh of relief and her body melted against his. "I'm so… I don't know. Just relieved. All of this has been hard. Everything. Cord being on TV all the time. Everybody acting like he's a god when I know for a fact he's underwhelming if anything."

Finn laughed, more than a little satisfied by that estimation of her ex.

"It will be nice to... To be with somebody who knows. And to not have to try so hard," she said, putting her hand on his face. "To pretend that I feel normal. And not to pretend that I'm not attracted to you."

That was the biggest source of relief as far as he was concerned. The fact that he didn't have to channel all his restraint into resisting her, and resisting the attraction that had only grown more intense over the past few weeks.

"Yeah," he said. "Now all we have to deal with is a lifetime of emotional scarring and issues."

She laughed, and the sound did a lot to ease the tension still lingering inside him. "Well," she said, "thank God for that."

"But first," he said, looking down at that freckle on her shoulder, "I need to taste your skin again."

CHAPTER SIXTEEN

THE NEXT MORNING saw Finn doing the walk of shame up to his front door. Normally, there would be no one around to witness such an event, but this morning when he walked into his kitchen, hungover from sex and lack of sleep, he had three very attentive witnesses.

It would have been comical if he didn't find it so annoying.

Liam, Alex and Cain were all sitting at the kitchen table, and paused with their coffee halfway between the table and their lips when Finn made his entrance.

"We were about to file a missing persons report," Alex said, leaning back in his chair and slinging his arm across the back.

"We almost called search and rescue," Liam added.

"I just went to sleep," Cain said.

"Leave it to you assholes to be up early today without me to drag you out of bed."

"Assholes are good for that," Alex said. "By which I mean only doing the right thing when it might bother somebody."

"Job well done," Finn growled, walking across the room and making quick work of the remaining coffee in the pot.

"You disappeared last night before things got good," Liam said.

"Somehow," Alex said, "I doubt that. I have a feeling Finn went to a private party."

"Are you guys twelve, or what? I'm a grown ass man. If I stay out all night I'm not going to blush and giggle about what went on." He felt protective of what had happened between himself and Lane. They didn't need to know the details, and they definitely didn't need to know he'd been with her.

"I'd like to ruminate on it for a bit." Alex smiled. "I would like to ruminate in detail. I was distracted when you left, so I didn't get to see you go. But I want to know who you left with."

"Excuse me while I change my earlier question. Are you women?"

Liam lifted his coffee mug. "That's sort of sexist, Finn. I feel sullied by our association."

"Feel free to make a sign and march in the streets then, jackass."

"I think I'll just finish drinking my coffee."

"That's what I thought."

"You might have responded to a text," Liam said. "Just one. So that we knew you weren't lying dead or mortally wounded somewhere."

He hadn't even checked his phone yet today. "And you care about that?"

He had meant the question to sound somewhat skeptical, but it came out legitimately curious.

Liam lifted a shoulder. "Who'd ride us hard during ranch chores and make us wish for death?"

"Great," Cain said. "Finn got laid. That's all we're going to hear about it. Frankly, I don't want to hear any more about it. I want to go milk some cows."

"Do you want to talk about that, Cain?" Alex asked. "Because that's kind of concerning."

"Every so often I'm sorry you weren't named Abel."

"Wow." Alex took another sip of his coffee.

"We really do need to get to work," Cain said, the slight drawl he had that the rest of them didn't a little more pronounced this morning. "I need to figure out what the hell I'm going to do with my teenager at some point today. I need to get her out of the house. She can't just sit around until school starts in the fall. Mostly because neither of us will live through it."

Cain drained his coffee and stood, heading toward the door. "See you out there."

Finn had to admire—with grudging respect—the ease with which Cain had adapted to the ranch life. Granted, his older brother was used to this kind of setup, even if daily work had been a thing of the past.

It made it a lot harder to be bitter about his presence here.

The jury was still out on the other two.

"You were supposed to be our wingman," Liam said.

"Dick move, abandoning us," Alex said.

"That's so strange," Finn said, "because I don't recall needing a wingman to get laid. If you do, maybe you need to up your game."

"Probably easier when you know the woman you picked up," Alex said, his tone overly innocent.

He shot his younger brother a deadly glare. "It's not open for discussion."

"Is anything in your life open for discussion, Finn?"

"That's a very good question, Alex," Finn said. "Which we can talk about after we discuss the details of your life, which you have so kindly laid out with transparency for all of us to see."

"I was in the army. Now I'm not. Is there anything else you want to know?"

"Why aren't you in the army anymore?"

Alex's expression turned stony, serious, much more so than Finn was used to seeing. "I got tired of watching people I love die. How about that? Now you go."

"Alex…" Liam turned to face his brother.

"Shit," Finn said.

"No details necessary," Alex returned. "It is what it is. War is hell, and all that clichéd shit. Dairy cows seem like a hell of a lot more fun than dodging explosions… What can I say. Plus, I have some responsibilities to take care of here."

"What responsibilities? Related to the military stuff?" Finn asked.

"Like not your damn business," Alex said.

"You have your stuff, I have mine," Finn responded, before turning to Liam. "What about you? Do you want to tell me why Sabrina Leighton saw you sitting in Ace's last night, and then turned around and ran out of the bar like she'd seen a ghost?"

Something in Liam's expression shifted. "Not particularly."

"No explanation at all?"

"Maybe I'm a ghost?"

He had a feeling Liam might be a ghost in Sabrina's estimation. But he was less interested in the details of his brothers' lives and hell of a lot more interested in getting them off his back.

"Here's how I see it," Finn said, not quite realizing this was how he saw it until he started talking. "You're all pretty determined to stay here. That means we need to figure out how to exist together. We need to figure out what everyone's function is going to be in the Donnelly Family Fun Time Hour. We're dysfunctional as fuck. Have been for more than thirty years. I don't think a few weeks together is going to fix that. Hell, it may take thirty years to fix that. But it doesn't mean we can't make this work." He gritted his teeth against the instant denial that occurred inside of him.

The Laughing Irish was his. Letting go of that, admitting that maybe his brothers had a right to be here, that maybe he was just going to have to make it work with them here… It wasn't easy. But it was reality.

And maybe it was just being here with them that made it all click into place. Or maybe it was Lane. Maybe having her, the way he'd always wanted, had released some of the tension inside him. Had made things a little clearer.

His grandfather hadn't trusted him. Whatever Finn had given hadn't been enough. Callum had felt the need to include the others in spite of all Finn's work and dedication. And Finn just had to accept that.

Just like he'd accepted the fact that his mother had walked away with no interest at all in coming back. Just like he had accepted that Liam and Alex had made suitable replacements for Finn and his mother where their father was concerned.

Two days ago it would've seemed impossible to make this concession. But last night he had finally been with Lane. And with that weight shifted off his shoulders everything else seemed a little bit easier to carry.

"That's kind of what we've been waiting for," Liam said.

"No you haven't. You've just been hanging around taking orders from me."

Liam snorted. "No. I told you in the beginning that I thought that friend of yours had a good idea. And that I thought we should do it. We have more manpower now than we did before, and I have all the cash you could ever want to inject in this place."

"Thanks. But I don't need your money."

"It's we," Liam said. "Not you. And seriously, I could outfit these cows with diamond-studded milking machines."

"But that's ridiculous, so you won't," Finn said.

"You say that like ridiculousness has ever stopped Liam from doing anything in the past," Alex said.

"I don't know him well enough to comment on that," Finn said. Honest, but the moment the words left his mouth he realized how depressing they were.

"I have a feeling that's all going to change," Liam remarked. "Probably pretty quickly."

And, in another testament to just how good things had been with Lane last night, that comment didn't even make Finn feel angry. It didn't bother him at all. If anything, it made him feel a little bit hopeful.

Later, he would see Lane and he would thank her properly. And he would have another talk with her about those subscription boxes.

FINN HAD TEXTED her earlier and asked her to come over after she closed up shop. She didn't know why, but she felt nervous. Giddy. Well, okay, she knew why.

She sighed and set about taking all of the giant tin pans full of pasta out of the backseat of her car. She had been so worked up that she had spent the day scurrying between the front of the store and the back kitchen.

She had needed something to keep herself busy. Cooking had been it. The Donnelly brothers always seemed grateful for the extra food, and now that all of them lived here they went through it a lot faster than when it had just been Finn.

She liked it. Liked taking care of all of them. When it suited her, and not on a daily basis. That would probably be more than a little bit onerous. Immediately, she was forced to imagine herself as Snow White, except instead of taking care of seven little men, it was four very large men and a cranky teenager.

She steeled herself against the onslaught of tension she was certain was going to hit the moment she came face-to-face with Finn. She was not going to be able to look at him without thinking about his naked body. No, there was no way. In fact, she had spent the entire day with images of Finn's naked body superimposed over whatever she was doing.

That never happened to her. She just wasn't the kind of person who lost her mind over sex. It was fine. But it wasn't all-consuming. Finn was becoming a little bit all-consuming.

That was actually good, she reasoned, as she walked up the stairs to the front door of the Donnelly family home. She could use something that was all-consuming. Something that got her mind off everything that was happening with Cord.

She frowned. Not that anything really was happening with Cord where she was concerned. Cord McCaffrey might be a successful politician with a family and a life, but he wasn't actually parading those facts around to hurt her. It occurred to her then that up until this very moment she had kind of felt that way.

Like he had been senatoring *at* her. Rather than just living his life.

She wasn't sure the realization made her feel all that much better. She wasn't really sure how she felt about him going on with his life. That sobering realization was still sitting in the back of her mind when the front door opened.

It wasn't Finn on the other side, or any of his brothers. Instead, it was Violet. "Hi," the girl said, not quite able to manage a smile.

"Hi," Lane returned, shifting her hold on the food, bracing it up her thigh. "I brought dinner."

Violet's expression remained neutral. "Are you my new mommy?"

Lane laughed, half shocked, half amused. Violet's taciturn father was certainly a good-looking man, but there was only one Donnelly that got her pulse racing. Not that she was going to say any of that to the sixteen-year-old. Who made her feel kind of freaking old seeing as she did think the girl's dad was sexy.

"Violet," came a warning voice from somewhere out of view. "Could you maybe just…not be yourself for a few minutes?"

"No. All childhood propaganda I consumed during my youth insisted that I be true to my inner voice. And my inner voice is feeling sarcastic today."

"That's hardly noteworthy," Cain said, coming into view. "Let me know when your inner voice is feeling human again, and maybe we can talk."

"That might be a while. My human inner voice is on hiatus until it can make its way back to civilization."

Cain grimaced. "Then I guess I have to get used to the gremlin."

Lane was almost sure she saw the ghost of a smile playing at the edges of Violet's mouth. But she couldn't be totally certain because the girl turned and went back up the stairs.

"I brought dinner. She might want to come back down," Lane said.

The older Donnelly forced a smile. "Probably not. She might creep down after everybody else is done. That way she can limit the interaction."

"What's she doing with her time?"

"Texting her old friends. Basically, throwing herself into the life she had, and ignoring the life we have now." Cain rubbed the back of his neck. "I thought bringing her here would help with things. But she seems even unhappier than she did back in Texas."

"She's bored," Lane said simply.

"She assures me her cell phone is all she needs for entertainment."

"Right. But she's lying. Even if it's mostly to herself. Take it from me—an exceedingly well-behaved teen-ager in my day—she needs to stay busy."

"Unfortunately, I kind of see her point about Copper Ridge. There's not much to do here."

Lane smiled. "I guess not. But it was the source of my salvation when I was about seventeen. I came here, got away from my parents, moved in with my brother. And I got my first job."

"That's what Violet needs," Cain said, looking suddenly decisive. "Work."

"It would at least get her out of the house for a while."

"Do you know of anyone who's hiring?"

Lane thought for a moment. "Actually, I probably do. I have a friend who owns a bakery in town, and she was just telling me she's a little bit short-staffed. But I work on Main Street so I can keep my ear to the ground for all kinds of jobs. The bakery might be re-ally fun, though."

"It doesn't really have to be fun," Cain said. "Be-cause right about now it's that or military school."

"Why would you consider military school?" Alex

walked up behind Cain. "As you can see, the military did nothing to calm me down."

"Can I come in?" Lane asked, holding up the massive container of food. "I am laden with carbs."

"Oh," Cain said, reaching out and taking the pasta from her hands. "Sorry about that. Usually I'm a little more considerate."

"He's not," Alex said. "But maybe to women."

"Don't ask my ex-wife."

"We can't," Alex said, "because she left. Because the problem was clearly her."

"That might be the nicest thing you've ever said to me, Alex," Cain said, walking ahead of his younger brother and into the kitchen.

"That means you can expect me to be a dick for the rest of the evening."

"I already did."

Lane flexed her fingers, curling and uncurling them, nerves making her stomach tighten and her palms sweaty. It was kind of crazy. Feeling nervous to see Finn. A man she had seen nearly every day for the past decade. And yet, she was almost vibrating with tension.

She had underestimated how difficult it would be to see him—for the first time since they'd been naked together—with an audience. An audience that was probably a whole lot more observant than she would like.

She heard footsteps on the stairs and looked up. Her throat went dry, tight, and then everything else tightened after. Her lungs, her chest... Her... Everything.

Finn. Suddenly, the whole world seemed to get quieter, seemed to slow down. He was... Well, he was kind of beautiful. She had always known he was good-looking, but she had never known it quite this way. This way that was coupled with intense, sensual pleasure at knowing exactly what it was like to feel those hands on her skin.

To know what it was to have his lips pressed against her.

He was wearing a cowboy hat, a tight black T-shirt and a pair of jeans that hugged his thighs and other parts of him she was now intimately familiar with.

There was a dusting of golden stubble over his square jaw, just enough to lend a gritty edge to all that male beauty he possessed.

"I'm glad you came," he said, a small smile tugging the corner of his lips upward.

Her stomach fluttered in response. Honest-to-goodness fluttered.

"Me too," she responded, her words breathy and completely affected.

She was acting like she was about Violet's age, and had a crush on some new boy. Except the new boy was a man. A man who had been in her life forever. A man she was now seeing in a completely different light.

A naked light.

She ignored that dirty little thought and forced a smile. Tried to look normal.

"I see you brought dinner," he said.

It was kind of a stiff, formal thing to say. And she had to admit she was happy that he was struggling with the right balance too.

"I did."

Silence hung between them, and so did Alex, looking back and forth, a knowing smile on his lips. Lane shot him a deadly glare. If he said something, she would beat him over the head. Sure, Alex was actually older than her, but because he was Finn's younger brother, he felt younger to her.

"Dinner," she said brightly, making a broad hand gesture, which Cain took as a call to action.

He made his way into the kitchen and the rest of them followed. From there, the sounds of domesticity filled the air. Clattering plates, shuffling feet and appreciative sounds as everybody took the first bite of their pasta.

It made her chest feel warm. Gave her a sense of accomplishment. And then came a strange ache. A kind of wistful longing. For something intangible, something she couldn't quite put her finger on.

But it got jumbled up with images of Cord and his family, his children, that normalcy. And then mixed up again with images of Finn from the night before, when they'd been tangled in the sheets.

She felt her face heat, her body growing warm. It was a welcome sensation next to that horrible ache she'd been grappling with only a moment before.

"I need to talk to you about something," Finn said, moving over to where she was standing, watching everybody eat their dinner.

"Yes?" she asked, the question infused with a healthy dose of warning.

She wasn't about to have any kind of discussion about last night with him here, with his brothers standing by. That was nonnegotiable. That was not happening.

"I had a little talk with Alex and Liam today. Though Cain wasn't a part of this." He raised his voice slightly. "You're all committed to staying," he said, directing that at his brothers. It wasn't a question.

"We told you that before," Cain responded.

"I know," Finn said. "I'll be honest. I figured the early mornings and the hard work would chase you off eventually. You all actually have places to go. You have money. You have options to have other lives. I'm crazy enough to choose this life. Crazy enough to love it. I had my doubts that you would do the same thing."

"Who knows," Alex said, "it might all change in the future. I'm not committing to being a dairy rancher for the rest of my life. But the Laughing Irish will always have my support."

"I guess that's all I can ask for," Finn said.

His jaw was tense, his expression difficult to read. But Lane could sense his unease with the entire topic of conversation. His slight dissatisfaction with Alex's answer.

"Where is this going?" Cain asked.

"I want to figure out how to make this workable for us. If we're all going to be here, I don't want us stepping on each other's toes. I want us all to have a function to serve here. And I think that's going to mean changing, expanding."

"Are you actually giving me my way?" Lane asked, feeling slightly dazed.

"Kind of," Finn returned. "But not just because you asked. Because I think it's a good idea."

"So, you're talking about expanding into more specialty dairy products?" Liam asked.

"Yes. And that's going to require marketing and business planning, and all of that stuff that you do," he said to his brother. "And it's going to require some extra manpower," he said, directing that at Cain and Alex.

"Well, you have that," Alex said.

"And Lane has a great idea to help broaden interest in products that are coming out of Copper Ridge. Her store is really popular, and she wants to capitalize on the current interest in subscription boxes." He looked at her, a smile on his face that looked a lot like pride. That made her feel like her heart had expanded in her chest.

Made her feel like maybe she was doing something after all.

"I do," she said. "I'm building a mailing list and I'm going to offer things on my website. But I'm also going to feature special products in the subscription boxes. I know I can ship cheese. The milk isn't going to happen, but that I can stock in my store. I guarantee you, people are going to drive to get this stuff. No doubt, what you guys do isn't easy. But the interest in locally sourced food and healthier products is good. We can capitalize on it."

"I'd also like to invest in the start-up," Finn said.

"Of the specialty dairy?" Lane asked, feeling a little bit confused.

"No," he said, "of your expansion. Because we're going to help each other, and I believe in your idea. It also made me believe in mine."

She swallowed hard, her throat feeling scratchy, her eyes a little bit gritty. She was grateful, more than grateful. But she found it a little bit suspicious that he had agreed to all of this after they'd slept together.

Still, maybe that was looking a gift horse in the mouth. And for someone who had received not a lot in the way of gift horses she wasn't sure she could afford to be suspicious of this one.

"I appreciate that," she said finally, once she was able to force the words out.

"Look at us," Liam said. "We're practically a functional family."

"We better hope it's functional," Alex said. "Otherwise, we're all going to end up leaving here broke."

"Well," Liam said, "maybe you. I have plenty."

"Don't be so smug about that fancy degree," Cain said. "I'll have to give you a noogie or something."

"Really?" Liam asked, his tone dry.

"Hey," Cain said, "I've been an older brother all my life without any younger siblings around. I have some making up for lost time to do."

The sadness of their situation struck Lane again. These brothers who should have had each other all of their lives, but were just now learning to deal with each other.

Of course, if Finn had had his brothers, maybe he wouldn't have been such good friends with Mark. And if that were true, maybe he would never have become such good friends with her either. Maybe he wouldn't have needed her as much.

Maybe he wouldn't need her in the same ways now.

She banished that thought. She didn't know why she was being weird and insecure. Almost... jealous of his brothers. Which was stupid. And ridiculous. Of course he should have a relationship with his brothers. A solid one. A good one.

She was just feeling off-kilter because of the way that things had happened between them last night. Yes, she needed to be alone with him. Needed to see how it would be when it was just the two of them.

The question was how did she want it to go? That, she didn't really have an answer to.

"Lane says she's going to help Violet find a job," Cain told the room.

"That's nice," Finn said, his expression slightly tense.

"Well, I got my first job here. It gave me focus." She wasn't sure why Finn was looking at her all weird. Well, she had only one idea, and it didn't make any sense.

"Where are you thinking?" Finn asked.

She filled him in on what she had told Cain earlier, and did her best to try and choke down her dinner. Finn finished before she did, and once his plate was clear, she set hers down even though she still had a bit left, and even though she was still a little hungry.

"Can I talk to you?" she asked him, her voice rushed. She really hadn't meant to ambush him like that. To be so obvious. She wished that she had been a little cooler. That she had waited until they were kind of naturally alone. Or until he had said something.

But oh well, she hadn't. Finn was the source of a lot of new experiences for her. Multiple orgasms in one evening, begging for what she wanted and an extreme lack of chill being just a few.

"Sure," he said, walking ahead of her out of the kitchen. She could feel his brothers watching them, and she ignored them.

"Did you tell them?" she asked, as soon as they were alone in the living room.

"I don't tell them what I eat for breakfast. Why would I tell them about what happened with us?"

She looked past him, at the floor-to-ceiling windows that were reflective now in the dark. She could only see herself. Herself and her very worried expression. "I don't know."

"Now," he continued, "they might have guessed, because they aren't stupid. And I disappeared last night from the bar without saying anything and came back this morning after they were all awake."

"Oh. Oh… I just…"

Before she could say anything else she found herself being caught in his arms, drawn up against his hard body. And then whatever other words she'd been about to speak were cut off by the press of his lips against hers. "You just what?"

"Well," she said, "I forgot now."

"Excellent."

"Except, why are you being weird about me helping Violet find a job?"

"I'm not."

"Oh my gosh, Finn. Are you jealous?" She could have laughed, it was so ridiculous. "Are you jealous of your brother? After what happened between us do you honestly think I'm just looking to cruise the Donnelly clan?"

"No."

"Yes, you do. And yes, you are. That's ridiculous."

Something in Finn's gaze shifted, sharpened. It made her stomach turn over. Made her feel once again like a stranger was looking out at her from inside of her friend. It was a strange thought, maybe, but it somehow encapsulated the whole situation.

Finn as her friend was about as familiar as it got. Finn as a lover was another story entirely. It occurred to her then that she didn't really know how he was with the women he dated. At least, not beyond casual observation.

She didn't know if he was jealous, possessive. If this behavior was somewhat normal for him. Or if it was somehow unique to her. It surprised her, just how much she hoped this was just about her, and not simply the way he was with women once he'd slept with them.

It shouldn't matter. In fact, she should be a little offended. A little insulted. Though, she imagined as off-kilter as she felt, he didn't feel much better.

He didn't know how she acted with the men that she dated either.

"Look," she said, softening her tone. "I know things are different between us now…"

"Maybe for you," he said, keeping his tone casual. "But for me, not much has changed."

She didn't know how she felt about that. Didn't particularly know how to handle that statement.

"How?"

"You know. I didn't wake up yesterday deciding that I wanted you. It's been that way. For me, it's been that way from the beginning. Which is why, to my thinking, this will work out just fine. I've been your friend while wanting you for a long time. I don't really see the problem with being your friend and having you."

A little thrill raced through her, a shock of heat. It was embarrassing just how strongly she reacted to him. But then, if what he was saying was true, he was more adept at handling everything between them than she was.

Not because she had never felt an attraction to him before, but because hers had gone unacknowledged for so long.

"Right. Well, I guess I'm the one in the weird headspace. But you're being possessive. You know me. Do you honestly think I'm going to make a move on your brother?"

"He's an attractive bastard."

"Sure. He also has baggage."

"I'm not exactly traveling light," Finn returned.

"Okay," she said, "maybe not. But your baggage doesn't come in the form of a sixteen-year-old girl. And anyway, you're the one that I want." It was strange to say. Strange to admit. But it felt right too. "I was telling you the truth when I said I hadn't been with anyone for about a million years."

"How long is a million years?"

"A little longer than a year. That's about a million in

sex years, right?" She looked up at him, and the heat in his gaze made her stomach clench tight.

"Just about." His voice turned husky.

The air between them turned thick again, and he wrapped his arm around her waist, drawing her body up against his once more. She shivered. She didn't think she would ever feel casual about this new intimacy between them.

Not the way that he did. The way that he just sort of assumed he could touch her, even outside of the bedroom. Even with his brothers right in the next room. While they were talking, like they might have done when they were only friends.

Except, really, they were only friends now. It's just that there was another dimension added. Nothing had been taken away.

She drew a small amount of comfort from that.

Truly, she didn't dislike the change between them. But she felt more than a little bit thrown off.

"I want to help Cain," she said, "because it will help you." She reached up, pressing her palm to his face. Experimenting with the casual touching herself.

"You think there's anything that will help me beyond getting my grumpy brother off of my property?"

"It sounds like you're making peace with that too."

"In that way that you make peace with a terminal illness."

"Well, that's a nice way to think of your brother," she scolded.

"I may need an attitude adjustment," he admitted, a half smile curving his lips. "But I imagine you could help with that."

"That depends what kind of help you're looking for." She reached between them, pressing her hand against his hard stomach. She was tempted, very tempted, to slide her fingertips beneath the fabric. Well, why not? They were here after all. They had already crossed the line. Hell, they had replaced the line entirely.

Why bother to pretend otherwise?

She did so, tentatively, the first brush of her fingertips against his skin sending an electric shock up her arm and down to the rest of her body.

"Maybe something like this?" she asked.

"Maybe," he said, dipping his head in closer, so close that she could feel the heat radiating from him, could have darted her tongue out to taste him right now if she wanted to.

"Are you going to kiss me?" she asked, sounding more like a breathy teenage girl than she would have liked.

"I'm definitely thinking about it," he said.

"You're really going to help me with my subscription boxes?"

"Are you holding your kiss hostage?"

She let her fingertips trail a little bit higher beneath his shirt. "No. But I do want to make sure that isn't what you're doing."

"What?"

"Giving in to me because I gave you something you wanted. That isn't why I slept with you. It really isn't. And it wasn't because I just wanted to try and salvage our friendship. It might have started that way. It might have started because I was afraid. But... When I said yes, it's because I wanted you. Really. It wasn't because I wanted your help, it wasn't because I wanted your milk in my store—which right about now sounds like an inescapable euphemism."

"That's disgusting," he said.

"Yeah, you knew what you were getting into." She tried to keep her tone light, but she felt like she couldn't breathe. "Anyway, I want to make sure you're not just placating me. Because of... You know, the physical stuff."

He frowned, a dark light in his eyes. "Give me a little credit, Lane," he said.

"It's not about credit. It's about the fact that all of this is new, and it's strange. I'm able to acknowledge that. It seems like you should be able to do the same."

"No," he said, "and that's the point. The point I was trying to make earlier. I don't think this is weird." He moved his hands up her waist, pulled her in closer. "Feels pretty good to me."

Her throat went dry, her heart pounding even harder. Suddenly, all she wanted was to be alone with him. Just the two of them. She would prefer the buffer of darkness, but she wondered if he would allow that yet. Or if he would still think she was trying to pretend he was somebody else. That wasn't it. Not really. It was just that it was scary, revealing herself to him that way. Because he knew her so well.

Everything felt like it cost more. Like she had much more at risk.

With guys she just dated, she never really worried about looking stupid when it came to sex. They were men. Basically, if she showed up and brought her boobs they were game. She didn't have to try. And if they didn't like what she brought to the table, she was more than happy to let the relationship go.

She had a very casual attitude about dating. It was why she never lost her head over attraction. Why she had never begged a man for sex before. Because the man

himself had never really mattered. It was just a part of
the normal-looking life she had built for herself here.

A house, a business, a circle of friends and on occasion a man she was seeing. Who the man was had never
been all that important.

Blending that in with Finn, with her relationship with
him, and the position he occupied in her life, it felt different. Heavy. Exhilarating and light at the same time.
And above all else so incredibly valuable that she didn't
want to do anything to break it.

And so now, she was focused on that. He had been
candid about the fact that he had been attracted to her
for years. That was a lot of fantasy to live up to. Maybe
he had built her up to something in his head that she
just wasn't.

A sexual vixen she was not.

While she had been in some casual relationships, she
was not into casual sex. She really hadn't had that much
of it. In the grand scheme of things. In fact, she imagined as twenty-eight-year-old women went she wasn't
particularly experienced.

Finn, on the other hand, was. And he tended to as-
sociate with women who were probably better versed
in the carnal arts than she was.

If Finn was imagining she was some kind of sex kitten, he was going to be disappointed. Well, he hadn't
been disappointed last night. But there was still time.

He moved his hands down to her hips, tightening
his hold on her. She could feel just how into all this he
was. Could feel him there, hard and thick and pressed
tightly against her hip.

She lowered her gaze so she didn't have to look at
him. Because she didn't want him to see all of her conflict. Didn't want him to see just how turned on she was

by this simple, over-the-clothes touching. She didn't want to want him more than he wanted her.

She couldn't remember ever worrying about that before.

But there was something about this, something about him that made her feel vulnerable. She didn't like it. She had worked so damn hard to not feel that way. To feel in control. That was what she had done here in Copper Ridge. Struck out on her own, built a life for herself.

Her own business, her own friendships—with only elements of her past revealed so that she could control how all those friends saw her.

To a degree, she had always done that with Finn. And now, that was over. She couldn't control what was between them. He knew everything. He had seen her naked. And her heart just about fluttered out of her chest every time he looked at her now.

She was completely out of control. And unable to insulate herself.

"Yeah," she said, trying to keep her voice casual. She forced herself to look at him. "You're right. It's not weird. I guess it's okay."

"In that way that it's the best you've ever had," he said, a cocky smile tilting his lips upward.

"Finn," she said, a warning in her voice.

"Sorry," came a voice behind them.

They jumped apart like scalded cats, then turned toward the sound. Cain was standing in the door, looking not even a little bit sorry.

"You will be tomorrow when I give you stall mucking duty," Finn said.

"I just wanted to ask Lane if it would be all right if Violet came down to her shop around noon tomorrow.

And if she would be able to arrange a meeting with her friend."

"That should be fine," Lane said, her tone as parched as her throat.

"Great," he said, his gaze sliding back to Finn. "Honestly, it's worth having to muck stalls."

Then he turned and walked out of the room.

"I told you he was a bastard," Finn said.

"Do you want to explain that?"

"His smugness? He's a bastard, like I said."

"I mean his clear interest in what is…happening between us."

Finn lifted her shoulder. "I may have made a big deal out of the fact that you and I were only friends when they first met you. And this morning, when I came back home, they were very interested in where I had been and who I was with. I didn't tell them."

She thought about that for a moment. "And you didn't want to tell them."

"I didn't know if you would want me to. I didn't know what to say either."

She was drawing a blank on her opinion on this. Because it occurred to her that the topic might come up with Alison, Cassie and Rebecca. And she wasn't sure she wanted it to. She, too, wasn't sure what she would say. Part of her wanted to keep this all to herself. Part of her was a little upset that Cain knew now.

But if they were going to be spending the night with each other, she supposed it wasn't really practical for them to keep it a secret. If they were going to be together. Were they together?

Finn had said they would be friends who *had* each other. Kind of like friends with benefits, she supposed. Which was different from being a couple.

Also standing to reason, seeing as neither of them wanted a permanent romantic relationship. Neither of them wanted marriage or a family.

But did that mean keeping this a secret? Did she want to?

"You don't have to make any decisions now," he said.

Well, that was the nice thing about being with someone who knew you so well, she supposed. She hadn't had to voice any of her doubts. He had just known.

"Well," she said, "that's good. Although, I imagine in terms of your brothers knowing, there's no decision to make. Since they just know."

"True. But that frees us up to make all kinds of other decisions." Then he did dip down to kiss her, long and deep. And it went a long way in clearing up that unsettled feeling. When he was kissing her, everything seemed to make perfect sense.

When his mouth was on hers, tasting like Finn and sex and excitement, it all made sense. Not in a way she could put into words, but in a strange, unknowable kind of certainty in her chest.

"What kinds of decisions?" she asked, as soon as they parted.

"Well, to start with…your bed or mine?"

CHAPTER SEVENTEEN

THEY HAD DECIDED on hers. Mostly because Lane hadn't wanted to deal with the various reactions his brothers might have if they discovered she had spent the night. Sure, the cat was a little bit out of the bag, but that didn't mean she wanted to parade around the house with the cat, so to speak.

Day two. It was day two of her new relationship with Finn. After a second night of making love. It had been... Well, it had been no less amazing on the second night than on the first.

Now she was trying to work without drooling in front of the customers as she reflected on everything that had happened between them underneath the covers. Trying to make it through the day without calling him and asking for something stupid and desperate like a quickie in her back room.

She was thinking about him a lot. Which wasn't all that weird. It was the way she was thinking about him that was weird. The quantity of Finn thinking time was about like it always had been. For some reason, she was more aware of it now than she had been before. That she thought about him a lot. Almost all the time, really.

She was still thinking about that when the door opened and Alison walked in. She had asked Alison to meet her at the shop around noon, so that she could get

MAISEY YATES   261

introduced to Violet and consider hiring her on for the
rest of the summer, and maybe even into the school year.

"Hi," she said to her friend, hoping that her illicit
thoughts weren't written all over her face.

"Sorry," Alison said, "I'm early, but I was hoping to
steal some of your pistachio cream. I have evil plans
for it."

"Well," Lane said, grateful for the distraction. "You
know I support that."

"So this is Finn's niece that I'm meeting today?"

"Yes," Lane said, "and I warn you, she is a little bit
prickly. But I'm hoping that she can hold it together and
make this work. If not, you know you're not under any
obligation to hire her."

"Come on, Lane. You're my friend. And it's important to you, obviously. Which means I'm definitely
going to hire her."

"No," Lane said, waving a hand. "I don't want you
to feel obligated."

Alison had made it her mission to not just earn a
living from her bakery, but to use it to help women
who found themselves in dire straits. Women who, like
her, had put their lives on hold for controlling men and
lacked support and job skills when they finally came
out the other side.

Alison laughed. "I do. But in a good way. Anyway,
you know the strays are irresistible to me. You said she
needed this job, and that's a huge part of why my bakery exists. Sure, traditionally it's to help women who
haven't been in the workforce for a long time, but, a
woman making her first foray into the workforce works
for me too."

Lane smiled. "I'm sure this job could work wonders
for her. She's had a rough go of it. And she's not happy

to be living here. Her mom left," she said, figuring it was best to try and explain Violet's moodiness before Alison actually met the teenager.

"That has to be rough. Fortunately, handling tough cases is also my specialty. Seeing as I was one for a while." Lane knew that was true. She also knew that her friend would strike the right balance between being gentle with Violet due to her situation, and encouraging her to suck it up.

Alison didn't allow wallowing.

"I have a feeling you're exactly what she needs," Lane said.

Saying that made her wonder if Alison was what Lane needed too. She was tempted to confide in her friend. About Finn. About Cord. About everything.

But the words stuck in her throat, and a moment later it didn't matter, because the door opened again and Finn and Violet walked in.

"Cain didn't come with you?" she asked.

"No," Violet said, looking horrified at the suggestion. "I told him I didn't need him to hold my hand."

"She did need a ride, though," Finn said. "Mostly because she didn't know where she was going."

"Are you able to get to work?" Alison asked. Skipping right to the practicalities.

"Yeah, my dad said he'd help with that," Violet said. Lane had a feeling Cain had put the fear of God in her, considering she wasn't being her usual dour self. The change looked forced, Lane thought. But it didn't really matter if it was genuine or not. As long as the girl knew how to turn it on. "He's really into me getting out of the house and learning…responsibility and things."

"Well, I am also a fan of responsibility," Alison said. "Do you have any experience baking?"

"Not really," Violet said. "My mom didn't cook. My dad hired someone."

"That's fine," Alison responded. "As long as you don't mind mostly handling the register until I can train you to do the harder stuff. Everybody that works in my bakery learns how to make all of the goodies, so you have to be willing to get up to your elbows in flour. Which I guess is the next question. Any serious food allergies? Because that makes things tricky."

"No," Violet said. "And, while I'm not educated on how to make baked goods, I eat them pretty proficiently."

"That helps. I like some enthusiasm for the product." Alison looked her over thoughtfully. "I think you should have a chance. Can you start next week?"

Violet cracked the closest thing Lane had ever seen to a smile. "Yeah," she said. "I don't have a life here at all. So I don't really have any schedule rearranging to do."

"Even better. I most especially like hiring people who don't have lives. All the better to monopolize their every waking moment."

Violet laughed, somewhat uneasily, clearly uncertain as to whether or not Alison was being sincere.

"She's joking," Lane said, except she had a feeling her friend was only joking a little bit. Alison's bakery was her life. Her lifeline. The representation of the new life she had built for herself.

Another way that she and her friend were very alike.

"Maybe I am. Maybe I'm not. I just have some shopping to do here at Lane's if you want to look around for a second. And then I can take you over to the bakery."

Violet immediately backed away from the three adults, pulling her phone out of her pocket and wandering to a deserted corner of the store.

"That pistachio cream would be good," Alison said. "And if you have anything else you think I should fill a pastry with, let me know."

"I got hazelnut cream from the same company. I think that would be great."

"Definitely. Get that too."

The door to the store opened again, and this time it was Rebecca who walked in. Lane hadn't been expecting her, but it wasn't totally unusual for her friends to come by and pick up ingredients for dinner.

As far as she knew, Rebecca didn't cook, but Gage did.

For some reason, the tension in the room began to ramp up slightly when Rebecca walked closer, and it took Lane a moment to realize why. And to realize that it was coming from her.

That whole thing with Rebecca and Finn—as much nothing as it was—was suddenly at the forefront of her mind. But, more than that was the discussion they'd had after. When Rebecca had grilled her on whether or not she and Finn were just friends and Lane had insisted they were. It made her feel horrifically transparent, and also a little bit like a liar. Even though at the time, even under cruel and unusual forms of torture, she would have sworn that she and Finn were only friends.

She hadn't meant to lie to Rebecca. She really hadn't.

Or maybe she had. Because she had certainly been lying to herself. So all the lies were certainly born of self-protection. And were maybe not entirely unintentional as far as her subconscious went.

"Hi," she said, far too brightly.

"I didn't know there was a meeting," Rebecca said.

"A job interview," Alison said, "I'm hiring Finn's

niece to work at my bakery for the summer. And maybe even for the school year if we can work it out."

Rebecca's gaze slid to Finn. "Great. That's good."

She could sense Rebecca's awkwardness, and that made Lane feel even weirder. Because if Rebecca still felt tension, didn't that mean she was still attracted to Finn? Yes, she knew that Rebecca was happy with Gage, but Finn was sexy. Undeniably so.

A strange heat surge through her veins, and she recognized it as the exact feeling she had felt months ago when Rebecca had confessed to her that she had nearly picked Finn up at Ace's with the intention of going home with him.

She had been jealous then. She was jealous now.

And it occurred to her that she was standing there scowling, and everybody in the room—with the exception of Violet, whose attention was focused solely on her phone—was aware of it.

"Yeah," she said, keeping her tone that same false level of bright, "a job interview. Not a meeting that you were excluded from. What did you need?"

"I wanted to pick up some blackberries. You texted the other day and said you had them. I thought I would get some to take home for shortbread tonight."

"Yes," she said, trying to clear her brain of all the ridiculous, extraneous things that were rattling around in there and focus on the food. "I do. So I'll get that and the creams for Alison, and then everyone will be set."

She turned, running into Finn and scampering backward like a startled animal. Her skin burned where she brushed against him, and she knew that her reaction had been both totally obvious and wholly visible.

She put her head down, walking quickly to the back

of the store, where she had stashed the berries in a mini fridge.

"Is everything okay?"

She lurched backward, hitting her head on the top of the fridge. "Ow," she said, turning to see Rebecca standing right behind her.

"You're acting weird," her friend continued.

"Because I just sustained a head injury," she growled.

"I meant before that."

"I'm not being weird," Lane said, digging in. Even though she was being weird, and knew she was being weird, and felt weird.

"Are we talking about how Lane is being weird?" Alison came up and joined the group.

"Well," Lane said, rolling her eyes. "Now we're all being weird. Because we've left Finn and Violet across the store by themselves."

"You're being weird about Finn," Rebecca said.

"I am not being weird about Finn." She was totally being weird about Finn.

"She is," Alison confirmed. "And she got weirder when you got here. Which I think is because of the thing."

"Alison knows?" Lane asked, shooting Rebecca a deadly glare.

"Well, I talked to her about it at some point," Rebecca said. "But the thing is there isn't anything to know. And you know that. Like six months ago I saw Finn at the bar. We danced. He kissed me. And then I left with Gage."

"I know," Lane said, curling her fingers into fists, her nails digging into her palms. "And it's not a thing."

"Jealous," Alison said.

"No. I'm a relationship Scrooge, as you well know.

I'm not in one right now, I'm perfectly happy to not be in one." She looked over at Finn, unintentionally, and both Rebecca and Alison noticed.

The two of them exchanged conspiratorial glances and Lane frowned. "I am," she insisted. "I'm part of the She Woman Man Haters Club."

"Nothing happened between me and Finn, and nothing will," Rebecca said, her voice overly placating. "You don't have to worry about it."

"I'm not worried."

"I'm getting married to Gage," Rebecca said. "I am in love with him. My heart beats only for him. And we talked about that right after all this happened."

Lane felt irritated. Mostly because she was not going to make a big deal out of this, until everybody started making a big deal out of it. She hadn't said anything. And she hadn't done anything. Except probably look a little bit uncomfortable. Having friends was overrated.

"I'm not worried about it," she said.

Well, she hadn't worried about it, or thought about it much until recently. Until things had started to change between Finn and herself. Until it had forced her to think about the way other women saw him, which had brought that whole incident with Rebecca back into her mind.

"Is something going on with him?" Alison asked.

Everything inside her recoiled, scampered away and hid behind an internal wall that she needed right now. Needed, so that she could use it as insulation while she figured everything out.

"No," she said, "nothing."

"Nothing?"

"No. Nothing is going on with myself and Finn."

Good Lord. If she denied him the full three times she would be in a situation of biblical proportions.

"Well," Alison said. "If you ever want to talk about it…"

"There isn't anything to talk about." She grabbed hold of a carton of blackberries and shoved them at Rebecca. "I'll just get your stuff, and then you and Violet can head over to the bakery."

She stomped back and grabbed the jars of cream and brought them out, aware of the fact that her face was probably red, since it was warm. She didn't know why she was reacting like this. Why it was freaking her out to this degree.

If she couldn't get a handle on herself then it wasn't going to be up to her whether or not the relationship became public. She was going to let everybody know with her completely uncontrolled mannerisms.

She asked herself, yet again, if that would be the worst thing. Right now, it felt a little like it might be.

Just because the whole thing was new. And she still felt a bit raw and fragile because of it. Giving other people permission to weigh in on it, to look at it, sounded like her worst nightmare right about now. She was still examining it all cautiously. She did not want anyone else's opinion.

That made her feel isolated, though. It made her so very aware of the fact that she didn't share anything with these women that she considered her very best friends. And here she was, continuing that pattern.

Well, she was going to sort it out. Except, she had never had any plans to sort that out. She had told Finn about her past as a kind of defense mechanism, not because she wanted to let him in, not because she wanted him to understand anything more about herself.

She took a deep breath. "At least," she said slowly, "there's nothing I want to talk about right now."

Just that simple admission made her feel exposed. She immediately regretted it. She just wanted to hide again.

Understanding softened Rebecca's face. "Well, I can definitely understand that."

"Anyway, here you go. Neither of you pay me for them. Just take them. Alison, you can pay me in pastry if the experiment works out. And you'll owe me double if Violet ends up being a great employee."

"I would very much like to owe you," Alison said.

Alison turned and walked back toward Violet, gesturing for the girl to exit the store with her.

Rebecca held her berries close, then looked at Finn, and back at Lane. "Anytime you want to talk," she muttered. "I'm a judgment-free zone. I mean, look who I ended up with."

Yes, Rebecca had ended up with the most unlikely man imaginable. The thing about Finn was, as far as the entire town was concerned, Lane imagined he seemed like the most likely man for her to end up with.

He fit. They fit. He filled all of these spaces in her life—had for years—and that was its own kind of terrifying.

"I promise if there's ever anything to talk about, we'll talk."

Rebecca nodded, then turned to go. But she stopped right in front of Finn. "Don't give me a reason to come after you, Donnelly," she said, "because I will." Then she smiled and continued on out the door and down the street.

"So," Finn said, his voice breaking some of the

tension in the air. "I think it's safe to say everybody knows."

"I denied pretty heavily." She let out a harsh breath. "I'm sorry. I'm just kind of crazy. I'm trying not to be. I really am. But when Rebecca came in I kept thinking about how you two almost..."

He reached out, wrapping his hand around her wrist and drawing her against him. She was breathing hard and she could feel his heart beating against her palm. "Do you know how long I've been celibate?"

"Like, twelve hours," she said, trying to shift some of the heavy weight in her chest.

"No. I mean before you and me. Do you know how long it had been since I was with another woman?"

"No." She had started turning a very blind eye to all of Finn's exploits with women early on in their friendship. Yes, she was vaguely aware that he hooked up a lot. At least, a whole lot more than she did. But she had done a lot of not thinking about it. Because he was her friend, and she really hadn't wanted to think about him getting it on.

Or, in truth, she hadn't wanted to think about him having sex with anybody because it would force her to think about him as sexual. And at the time, that had been about the most important thing to be avoided.

Right now, feeling so warm, and out of control in his arms, she was having trouble remembering why that had been.

"A year. And when the thing happened with Rebecca, it had been a few months. I just wasn't interested in anyone. Not anyone but you. It was getting worse and worse. And she was there looking for a chance to forget. So was I. It seemed like we could help each other out." Lane shivered, moving closer to him. "It was about you," he continued, his voice rough. "All of it. There's no reason to be jealous, because I never would have asked her to dance if I wasn't trying to forget the woman I wanted. The one I was sure I couldn't have. It was you even then."

She swallowed hard, resting her head against his chest. She just wanted to stand like this, because this felt good. He felt good. She didn't know what was going to happen tomorrow; she didn't know what her jumbled-up heartbeat meant, what that vague shaking in her limbs was. She just knew that being with him like this felt right.

After so many years of wrong, she felt like she was due.

"So," she said finally, "we're both a little bit jealous, I guess."

"We spent a long time being close with each other, but not being this. And in that time we both dated other people. I imagine that…makes it tricky."

"Yes," she said. "Tricky."

She curled her hand into a fist, clutching his T-shirt, burying her face deeper into his chest. It didn't feel tricky right now. Not right in this moment.

"Spend the night again tonight?" she asked, trying not to sound too needy. But she was needy. And that kind of neediness opened up a whole well of questions that she couldn't see the bottom of.

If they slept together every night, would they eventually be better off living together? If they lived together, what did that mean? Or would the intensity of their connection burn off? Would they end up just being convenient sex friends? Sleeping together on the weekends? Would he end up wanting other people instead of her eventually?

That made her feel a little bit dire. So she closed the lid on those questions.

"Sure," he said, lifting his hand and stroking her hair. If she were a cat she would purr. "That sounds good."

"I'll cook," she said, feeling suddenly decisive. One thing she wanted to make sure they didn't do was lose their friendship in the middle of all this sex stuff. And it was normal for him to come for dinner every so often.

If they were going to be friends with benefits, they had to take care of the friendship part, right?

"Okay," he said slowly.

"Steak," she said. "And, if you want to bring some blue cheese from your stores that would be much appreciated. I'll barbecue, and we can eat down by the lake."

A strange smile curved the edge of his lips. "Okay."

"I am offering you my prime steak," she said. "I deserve more than okay."

"Is that a euphemism?"

"It won't be if you don't show some appreciation."

He laughed, dipping his head and kissing her deep, long, not bothering with any kind of teasing. It was full-on from the moment his lips touched hers, his tongue plunging deep, the swirling pattern he traced on the inside of her mouth leaving her dizzy and hollow feeling.

It occurred to her then that they were standing in the middle of her store in broad daylight, and anybody could come in at any moment.

She took a step back, smoothing her hair. "That will do."

"How is the mouse, by the way?"

She blinked, not understanding for a moment. Then she remembered. The last time they had kissed in the store, the first time they had kissed. "Oh. Robert. He's great."

"You named him?"

"I told you I was going to." She hadn't really named the mouse until this exact moment, but she enjoyed the look of surprise and vague disgust on Finn's handsome face.

"I will not be edged out by a mouse," he said. "My friendship is superior."

"I can tell you I'm much more likely to kiss you that I am to kiss the mouse. Though once you get past the fact he's a vile, disgusting rodent, he's pretty great. A very quiet tenant. Then again, he never brings me cheese, he just eats the cheese."

"Unacceptable." He reached out, touching her chin, as if he almost couldn't bear to be out of physical contact with her. That did something to her insides. Made them turn over, shifted them around. "I'll see you tonight."

For the first time in a while, as she watched Finn walk out of the store, she felt like a weight had been lifted. In spite of all the questions that she had, maybe this could all work out.

CHAPTER EIGHTEEN

WHEN FINN GOT to Lane's she immediately ushered him down to the dock and thrust a cold beer into his hand. That wasn't particularly unusual. When it came to food, and feeding people, Lane spread her favors around pretty evenly.

All of this wouldn't have been terribly out of place back before they had started sleeping together. A cold beer, a steak on the grill had always been sweet. The assurance of sex later made it all a little bit sweeter.

"Just sit down," she said as she bustled around, preparing a salad and placing it at the center of the little picnic table that was just by the water's edge. "I've got everything."

He wasn't going to argue. Instead, he lifted his beer to his lips and watched Lane walk, those little cutoff shorts she wore showing off the tanned, toned length of her legs. And now he knew exactly what it was like to have those legs wrapped around him.

Male satisfaction gripped him. Probably inappropriate, and definitely objectifying. But he couldn't bring himself to care.

He had saved up a lot of time wanting. Wanting, longing, desiring and not having. Well, now he had her. He wasn't going to embrace any inhibition now. He'd had a decade of it. He was over it.

She came over to the table, placing a plate in front

of him that had a glorious-looking steak topped with blue cheese on it and some mashed potatoes on the side.

"Salad isn't optional," she said, setting a plate in front of herself and taking a seat across from him. "Because it's so good."

She smiled, the breeze ruffling her hair, the orange glow from the slowly sinking sun making her look like she was an angel. Except what he wanted to do with her was decidedly not angelic.

"For you," he said, grabbing the tongs and dishing himself a portion of salad that seemed to have cheese, fruit and nuts in it. "For you I will eat greens."

"That's the nicest compliment you could have given me. I feel like it's a true show of your devotion that you're willing to eat a vegetable to placate me."

She looked down at her plate, then without lifting her face, she looked back at him, her lashes veiling her eyes slightly, the expression impish and so damn sexy it made him hard. Then she smiled, just a hint of one.

Something in his chest expanded to a painful proportion, making it difficult to breathe. He wanted to capture this moment, capture the smile and hang on to both for as long as possible.

This feeling, this feeling that was taking over his entire body, didn't feel much like friendship. But then, he wasn't sure his feelings for her had ever been that simple.

It didn't matter. It didn't matter what it was called. If it was dinners by the lake and nights spent in bed with each other, what did he care? A label wouldn't help.

They ate in silence, but it wasn't awkward. The breeze was blowing over the top of the water, leaving little ripples in the dark surface, the trees that stood tall and proud around the perimeter rustling slightly, the scent of wood and pine and warm earth riding the top of the wind.

"I've never had a guy out here, just so you know. Actually, I've never had a guy spend the night at my house before."

That simple, bland admission hit him hard in the stomach.

"You haven't?" She had invited him to stay over easily enough. In fact, it hadn't even been a discussion. He had slept in her bed until he'd had to get up at an ungodly hour to be home in time to do the ranch work.

She hadn't indicated that his spending the night was a big deal.

"No," she said, shifting uncomfortably on the bench, her gaze focused on the lake, and very much not on him. "I like my space. And I didn't really feel like I could invite any of them over here. Then I would remember them being here. You... You're in every part of this place already. You came with me and the real estate agent when I bought it. You helped me get everything in livable condition. I don't know this place without you." Her eyes met his then, something shimmering there, something that he reacted to on a visceral level. "This whole place. The house, the town."

"Well," he said, doing his best to defuse the tightness in his throat by taking another bite of steak. "I can't deny that I like the idea of being first in some ways."

"Really?"

"Men are simple creatures, sweetheart. We like what we like. And I think I've proven that I'm more than a little possessive where you're concerned. But it does make me curious," he said, hesitating for a moment before pressing on. "What were those relationships for?"

"I don't know," she said. "What were any of yours for?"

"I'm different. I don't have girlfriends—you know that. I hook up. That's different. What I do, I do for the sex."

She bit her bottom lip. "I kind of do the same thing. It's just that I wrap it all in a low-key relationship to make myself feel better about... I don't know. My choices?"

"Why didn't you invite any of them over? Why did you know they were never going to be anything serious?" He didn't know why he was pressing, except part of him needed to know. Needed to know why he was here with her now, and why no other man had been before.

What she'd already said made some sense. There was no keeping him out of her memories of the house because he was already in them. But he didn't know very many people who started relationships knowing they were never going to go very far.

It was one reason he didn't do them. Oh, he'd tried his hand at relationships a couple of times, but he'd learned pretty quickly that women got involved emotionally, and he had never wanted that kind of attachment.

"I don't... I can't," she said, sounding helpless. She put her fork down, pinched the bridge of her nose. "I just... I start thinking about that kind of thing, about having a real relationship. Marriage. Children. And I just... Can't move on from it. I don't feel like I... I don't deserve it, Finn." Her eyes glittered, and she stood up quickly, moving away from the table and down toward the shore.

He just sat there, watching her for a moment.

Watched as she wrapped her arms around her body, held herself tightly like she was trying to keep from falling apart.

He stood slowly, crossing the space between them and making his way toward her. "Why don't you deserve to move on?"

She shook her head. "I don't know. I don't know how. Everything inside me is all walled off, put in these different sections. So that I can function without… I don't even know how to explain it. But you know what makes me angry? When I see him on TV?"

"What?" She didn't say anything for a moment and he pushed. "What makes you angry, Lane?"

"His family. The fact that he moved on. The fact that he got married, that he has children. That he doesn't… That he probably doesn't even think of me. Of everything that I went through. That he somehow feels like he deserves all of this and I just… I can't."

"Honey," he said, his tone soft, "isn't that the entire point of giving a child up for adoption? So that everybody can have the best life?"

She swallowed visibly. "I gave him away. And what if I could have made it work? What if I could have…"

His chest clenched tight. "Lane, you didn't give him away. You gave him up. You gave him up so that he could have a better future. And so you could too. And take it from somebody who really was abandoned by his mother. Not so he could have a better life, but so she wouldn't have to deal with him anymore… It's not the same thing."

She looked startled, looked like she wanted to ask questions. Well, he didn't want to answer them. He gritted his teeth, ignoring the voice inside him that labeled him a hypocrite. For wanting her to share everything, for wanting to share nothing himself.

But this was different. It was different for her. She thought that she was beyond redemption somehow, thought that she deserved to live defined by her past.

It wasn't too late for her to move forward, and she damn well deserved to.

His situation was completely different.

"I just wish…" She trailed off, looking out at the lake.

He bent down slowly, searching for the smoothest, flattest stone he could find. Then he curled his fingers around it, testing the edges for imperfections. "What do you wish?"

"I wish I could be certain I made the right choice. Or at least, accept the choice I made."

He pulled his arm back, then let the rock fly, watched it skip three times over the surface of the lake. "Okay," he said, "that's wish one. And now you get two more."

She looked at him, her face crumpling slightly, tears sliding down her cheek. She wiped them away, took a deep breath that sounded halfway between a gasp and a sob. "I wish… I don't wish that he would forgive me. I wish he would never think of me at all. That there was never anything for him to forgive. That his life is so full, so full of wonderful people that love him, that he can hardly spare a thought for the teenage girl who gave birth without her family there. Without his father there." She stopped talking for a moment, another tear chasing the first. Her shoulders shook, her whole body shuddering.

He wanted to move closer to her, wanted to wrap his arms around her, but he had a feeling if he did, she would shatter completely. She seemed so fragile right now. Like she was made from spun glass. But she was also strong.

The wind whipped up over the water again, invisible, but changing everything around them. That was Lane, he realized. Soft, sweet. But with the power to move mountains inside of him.

No, she wasn't breakable. No matter how she might seem now. She had been carrying this impossible weight for more than ten years. And for all that time, it had raged inside of her.

Now she was caught up in the last gasp of the storm.

He wanted her to lay every single one of her burdens down here at this lakeshore. Wanted her to give them all to him. Because he could carry them. He wanted to. He had never wanted to be that for somebody, had never wanted to know someone like this. But with her... He wanted everything she had to give.

"I wish that I could be one person," she said, looking over at him. "I wish that I didn't have so many pieces of myself, all kept hidden, kept separate. I wish I wasn't hiding here. I wish I was living."

Then he did close the distance between them, wrapping his arm around her waist and pulling her to him. "You're not hiding with me," he said, taking hold of her chin, brushing his thumb over her lower lip. "You don't have to hide anything from me."

It was a desperate kind of offer more than a generous one. He needed it. Needed her stripped bare in every way. He wanted to possess her, to own her. To know her. He didn't know what the hell made that desire so intense, what the hell made it so necessary; he only knew that it was.

He had been fine with the idea that maybe they

would sleep together until it burned out, but he knew full well that wasn't good enough anymore.

He wanted more than that. He wanted all of her. Possibly forever, because he was never going to be able to accept her being with another man. He would have to kill that man, and he didn't particularly like the idea of spending the rest of his life in prison.

He wanted her in his bed. Maybe even in his house, which he knew was going to take some convincing on her end. But that was what he wanted. In this moment, he wanted it more than his next breath. He didn't know where that fit with his vision for his life, what he'd always thought about himself. He didn't know if it could ever work. He only knew he wanted it. Right now, he couldn't imagine the end of this.

If he could just stay in this moment.

She looked scared, terrified, actually, all the color drained from her cheeks, tears glistening on the ends of her dark lashes. "I don't know how. I only know how to hide."

"I know where we can start." He moved his hands down to the hem of her shirt, pulling her top up over her head, leaving her standing there in the sunshine in her bra and a brief pair of shorts. Then he reached behind her and unclipped her bra, exposing her breasts.

"Leave it to a guy," she said, laughing shakily, "to decide my emotional healing requires showing my boobs."

"No," he said, reaching out, sliding his thumb over her nipples slowly until she shivered beneath his touch, "it's going to take a lot more than that."

He wasn't going to let her joke her way around this, wasn't going to let her ramble about French fries or pumice stones or mice named Robert.

"It isn't that I don't want things," she said, her voice a whisper now. She pressed her breasts against his chest, rested her palms on his shoulders. "I want what every-body wants, I guess. I'm just afraid I shouldn't have it."

He gripped the back of her neck, then slid his hand up to her hair, pressing her face against the curve of his neck. "Stop punishing yourself, honey," he said, his voice almost unrecognizable even to his own ears. "You don't deserve it."

"But what if I…"

"Let me tell you something," he said, the words torn from him. "I know what it's like to watch your mother walk away because she can't cope." He gritted his teeth. The reasons his mother had walked away were entirely different from Lane's. It was him. It was always him. But he didn't need to have that discussion with Lane. He was already fucked-up. And saying that, knowing her, she would try to reassure him. Would rush to tell him it wasn't true, no matter what he'd witnessed in his life.

But he would be damned if he ever threw any of his shit down on her. "That hurts. When you're left behind and there's no one there to take care of you. That's not what you did. And maybe you could have raised him, Lane. Maybe. But that's not the life you chose. It doesn't make you bad. You did the very best you could with the situation you were in at the time. You were alone. You were afraid. You hadn't lived life. Of course you feel now like maybe you could have taken care of him. You're almost thirty years old, you own a business, you own a house. The life you have now, the woman you are now, has nothing to do with the girl you were then. That girl, she could only do what she did. Don't be mad at her."

A sob shook her frame, and she let it all release.

Started to cry right into his shirt, leaving her misery all over him. And he just held her right through it. Not because it was what a friend should do. But because it was what he had to do for Lane. What he had always wanted to be for her. It was clear to him in that moment. Why friendship had never been enough. Because he never wanted only part of her. And part of herself was all she ever gave to her friends. He wanted all of her. All of this.

He made quick work of the rest of her clothes, and then took care of his own. Then, he picked her up, holding her against his bare chest as he walked down into the water. He held her tightly as he went deeper. "Ready?"

She nodded, and he submerged them both up to their shoulders, paddling out farther from shore. She wrapped her legs around him, tangling their bodies together.

She shivered slightly, but didn't ask him to take them back out to land. She lifted her hand up out of the water, touched his face, droplets trailing down his skin. He didn't know why he was doing this. Or maybe, just maybe he did. Maybe he was trying to wash it all away.

He wasn't into all the symbolism stuff. Didn't really buy into trust exercises and all of that. But something had to be done for her. He had to do something for her. He was all out of words, all he had was touch, all he had was this. This demonstration. Skipping rocks, making wishes and hoping it all came clean in the lake.

Slowly, the sadness in her eyes faded and was replaced with something else. Heat, desire, longing. Everything that he felt down deep. Every slick slide of their bodies ramped it up further. Then she pressed her hand between them, curling her fingers around his cock, squeezing him tight before moving her hand up and down, the lack of friction beneath the surface of the water making it a smooth ride.

"That's right," he said, his gaze never leaving hers, "show me everything. Give me everything."

"It felt weird the first time," she said, her voice hushed, but amplified out here in the water, "to be with you. Because you were my friend, and the two things felt like they didn't fit. But it's not weird now. Nothing is funny."

She looked deadly serious. He didn't know if he'd ever seen Lane be so serious for such an extended amount of time. Didn't know if he'd ever seen her exist in a moment quite like this one without trying to make it lighter, make it easier.

He kissed her then, with everything he had in him. Everything he could bear to show her. All that pent-up longing from the past ten years. Every ounce of need he'd carried around for her and done his very best not to show.

And when she kissed him back, there was no reservation. There was nothing but pure need, pure desire. It was as if the floodgates inside her had been opened, and she was suddenly able to pour it all out onto him. He had never been kissed like this. With a desperation that bordered on insanity. But he was more than able to give the same right back. He held on to her tightly, did his best to keep his legs moving, so they didn't sink beneath the surface of the water.

She shifted and slid against him, his cock making contact with that soft cleft at the apex of her thighs, brushing just hard enough against her to make her gasp. To make her roll her hips against him and beg for more with each needy breath on her lips, each soft-moan deep in her throat.

He paddled them back over to the dock, lifted her up out of the water, depositing her carefully on the sun-warmed surface. And then he hauled himself up after her. It reminded him of that last day they'd come down here. When she had looked at him and he could feel, for the first time, her eyes roaming over him with no small measure of interest, no small measure of heat.

He had wanted to do this then. But he hadn't. He'd pushed it down deep, just like he always did.

But that wasn't what he did now. There was no room for that here, no room for restraint at all. Their clothes were on the shore, and her pain was sunk down to the bottom of the lake. There was nothing between them now. Nothing at all.

Lowering her down onto her back, he brushed her damp hair off her face. Her nipples were tight from the cold, and from arousal, water sliding down her pale skin, pooling at the center of her stomach.

He put his hand on her thigh, moved it down behind her knee, spread her thighs apart. He had made her keep the lights on that first time they were together, so he'd seen her naked. But this was different. Seeing her like this outdoors, with the sun shining down on them. Nothing to hide. Nothing at all.

His hand between her thighs, he sucked in a sharp breath as he watched himself pleasure her, watched as he rubbed his thumb over the sensitized bundle of nerves there. She gasped, rocked her hips upward, silently begging for more. So he obliged. He groaned as he slipped two fingers into her wetness, feeling just how much she wanted him, just how much she wanted this.

He just stroked her for a while, watching her face as her desire built. As the color mounted in her cheeks, as her internal muscles began to pulse with her need. And then, it broke over her, broke around him, her release undeniable against his hand.

He withdrew his fingers, drawing them slowly into his mouth, wringing every ounce of evidence of her release out for himself, because it was all his, after all.

Need was roaring through him like a storm, but he realized he didn't have a condom.

"I don't have any protection," he said.

"It's okay," she said, her voice shaking. "I'm on the pill. And I… I trust you. I never do this. But I want to. I want to with you."

He shuddered, the full impact of that statement, of that trust, of this moment, rocking through him.

Then he moved his hands to her breasts, resting his palms there for a moment before sliding them down to her narrow waist, then down farther to her hips. He squeezed her tight, pulled her forward, pressed the head of his cock against the slick entrance to her body. He tested her slowly, flexing his hips, teasing them both with a little taste of what they wanted.

Then he slid into her, slowly, gritting his teeth to keep himself from going off as her sweet, tight heat closed around him.

He forced himself to keep his eyes open, forced himself to watch her face. To take in every aspect of the moment. The way she looked, the scent of her skin— water, woman and something that was sweet, unique to Lane—and the way she sounded as he pushed himself in all the way to the hilt. The way she felt all around him, like he was made especially to be here, inside of her.

He didn't want to miss anything. Because if he knew one thing for certain it was that if there was a perfect moment to be had in his life, it was going to happen when he was inside of Lane Jensen.

Her fingertips fluttered to his shoulders, tracing lines down the front of his chest, over his muscles, down to his stomach. Then she put both hands on his ass, urged him forward, whispered commands in his ear. And he couldn't deny them.

He gave himself over to this. To her. Lost himself in the steady rhythm he established. In her softness, in her heat. Her breath on his neck, her fingernails digging into his skin.

He wanted to hold off. Wanted to make it last. Wanted to make sure that she got to come again before he did. But that was a level of control he didn't have with her. There was no finesse here. There was nothing but need.

Maybe someday he would be able to impress her with his staying power, but this wasn't about that. Wasn't about impressing anyone— least of all himself. All he could do was ride that hot tide of release as it swept through him. He couldn't control it, couldn't delay it. Couldn't do anything but surrender to it. To her.

As he lost himself completely, he was dimly aware of her shuddering around him, his name an unsteady whisper on her lips.

And he knew that, as satisfying as his release had been, as beautiful as she looked naked, as amazing as he felt in the wake of all that pleasure, the one thing he would always remember forever was his name on Lane Jensen's lips like he was an answer to her every prayer.

CHAPTER NINETEEN

LANE COLLECTED ALL of her lists and headed out the door of the Mercantile, making her way down the street to Rebecca's knickknack shop.

The sun was setting into the ocean, somewhere beyond the silhouette of the brick buildings on Main Street. There was a breeze filtering through and the American flag that stood tall and proud at the end of the block was currently being lowered by one of the members of the local Lions Club who volunteered for various jobs around town.

She hurried quickly down the cracked sidewalks, pausing to make sure there were no cars coming before she crossed one of the side streets and made her way into The Trading Post.

Rebecca and Alison were already there.

"Where's Cassie?"

"She couldn't make it," Alison said. "One of her kids has an ear infection." She grimaced. "Children seem slightly overrated to me."

Rebecca smiled. "I don't know. I might like a couple."

Lane's stomach clenched, but the reaction felt somehow different than it usually was. She kept thinking of what Finn had said to her down by the lake. About how she was different now than she had been.

She'd been thinking about it basically nonstop for two days.

He was right. She had been a different person then. And, had she kept her son, she would be a different person now. There was no way to play that scenario out, not with any accuracy. She couldn't take the life she had now as evidence that everything would have been fine if she'd made another choice. And mostly, she just had to accept it. Accept that she couldn't know.

She breathed in deeply, feeling a little bit lighter as she let the breath out slowly.

"What about you?" Alison asked. "Are you ticking biologically?"

The thing about being pregnant at sixteen was that it took care of that biological clock nonsense. She had done it once. There was no mystery left in it. But for the first time in a long time she hungered not for the experience of pregnancy—that had been a lonely, horrible time in her life and no amount of understanding that if she did it again it would be different could change that association—but for the possibility of something new.

Of course, when she thought of that, she thought of Finn.

Her heart squeezed. And she did her very best not to imagine what it might be like to have his baby.

Wow, she was a head case. A few good orgasms and lakeside therapy and she was starting to forget what they had agreed on.

"Not specifically," she said.

"As in, not right at this moment?" Rebecca asked.

"Pretty much." Actually, this moment had triggered the first twinge of any kind of longing she could remember that wasn't related to the child she'd already had.

"Me either," Alison said. "Though, I have to say

that's mostly related to how very little I want to deal with a baby daddy."

"Well," Rebecca said. "That's the difference. Because I don't mind the eventual father of my children at all."

"Okay," Lane said. "Enough with the baby talk. I'm sort of afraid that by talking too much about them we might invoke one. What if they're like Beetlejuice?"

"Well, it wouldn't be me that ended up carrying it," Alison said. "Unless you start seeing suspicious stars in the east."

"You're not a virgin," Rebecca pointed out.

"I may be a born-again one," Alison returned.

Rebecca and Alison looked at Lane. She felt her face getting warm. "Like I said. I'm worried they might be catching. And I don't want to catch one."

"But it's possible that you could."

Lane squinted at Alison. "One never knows. Anyway, moving on. I brought a project."

"The point of girls' night is not to bring work," Rebecca said. "You're not honoring the spirit of the get-together."

"Yes," she said, taking a deep breath. "I am. Because while you help me make a list to figure out what items I want in my Best of Copper Ridge subscription box, I'm going to talk."

She felt a little dizzy the moment the words left her mouth. She didn't know if she wanted to get into all of the minute details about her past, but… She had to stop giving it so much power.

And by making it a giant monster that she shut the door on, that she was working to keep out of this existence, she was also hiding herself from her friends.

Keeping things buried, like she had done with Finn

for so long. All the little separate compartments inside of herself where she kept her secrets, where she kept her desires. Things that kept her distant from everyone around her.

Things that were starting to make her feel like a prisoner inside of herself.

She was done. If there was one thing she knew for certain after that encounter with him by the lake it was that she couldn't go on the way that she had been.

Well, she could. She could keep on stuffing everything down. Keep on lying to everybody about who she was by cleverly concealing all that she'd been through. But she might very well implode.

There was something about being open. About taking that first step to revealing her past. About stripping off her clothes, stripping off her mask, about knocking down all those carefully placed walls she had constructed between the two of them, that made her want to do it in other ways. With other people.

Well, not the naked bit. That was just for him.

Her stomach clenched tight. She was more than a little afraid that it would always be that way when she thought of him. That, from now on, it would only ever be him for her.

"Okay," Alison said. "Then let's get listing."

They broke out the snacks—mini pies from Alison's bakery and wine from Grassroots that Lane had in stock—and began to work on the list.

Which came together with surprising speed. Cheese from Finn she would be able to ship well enough with ice packs. Preserves, wines, and Alison wanted to contribute dry mixes with recipes. There were a few local coffee roasters and including a pound of beans every so often would be good too.

"You should talk to Ryan Masters," Rebecca said around a mouthful of pie. "I know you carry some of his stuff already, but maybe there are more options. Like smoked salmon. Also, I wonder if the Garretts would be interested in doing beef jerky or something."

"Okay," she said, "that's good. I wish there was more in the way of local candy. I mean, I can get some from a few places down south, but it would be nice to have something here."

"With the way things are expanding to accommodate tourism I have a feeling you won't have to wait too long for it," Rebecca said. "Oh," she continued, "if you got Chase and Sam McCormack to make bottle openers or something, that might be cool."

The McCormack brothers had made quite a name for themselves even outside of Copper Ridge through both their practical products and Sam's artistic skill.

"This is great," she said, feeling incredibly self-satisfied. "I mean, there are more things than I even thought of initially."

"You might be a genius," Alison said.

"I might be." She felt... Well, she felt like she was taking steps in new directions. After being stagnant for so long it felt exhilarating. A little bit scary. "Thank you, guys, for helping me with this. For dealing with how obsessive and weird I've been lately."

Rebecca rubbed her hands together. "Oh, are we getting to the talking?"

"Cord McCaffrey is my ex," she said, wincing when the words came out of her mouth.

"What?"

"Senator Good Hair?"

Both questions were asked at exactly the same time,

and Lane wasn't quite sure who had asked what. But it didn't really matter.

"Yes," she said. "From high school. My first boyfriend. My first…"

"Oh," Alison said, "holy crap."

"Yeah," she said. She didn't really think she could get into the baby thing right now. Because that would require… Well, more alcohol. Possibly some crying. They would look at her like they felt sorry for her, and she wasn't in that space right now. What she needed was what Finn had given her.

He had been… Supportive. But also pragmatic. He had been strong, something for her to lean against, but not something for her to dissolve with. Maybe someday she would be ready for that. But not now. It was a little too demanding at the moment.

"Anyway, I guess seeing him and how successful he is kind of messed with my head." That was true. "I felt like… What was I doing with my life? He has all of that. This family, children, the promising career. He's famous. And I just…suddenly wanted to kick-start what I was doing."

"That's understandable," Alison said. "Wow. I can't imagine that. Basically, if my ex-husband is doing well it means he's not currently in prison. So… I won. I won the divorce. I have my own business, I'm happy. I have a little apartment, and it's clean, and it's mine. I feel nothing but extraordinarily happy with what I've made, and when I look at his existence—which I try not to—I only see a million reasons why I left."

"That would be so much better," Lane said. "Not because I want to be with Cord. I don't. I mean, I know that I'm unfairly judging his sexual performance based on what he could pull off as a teenage boy, but let me tell you, I have had better since." She was having the best right now. "I don't want him at all. I don't want to be part of his life. I just want... My family was really rich. And, you know, I lived in the kind of neighborhood that you would expect a future senator to come out of. And when he's old enough, I imagine a future president. Or at least a presidential candidate. But that's what everybody in my hometown is groomed for. I left it all behind. It's not what I wanted. I couldn't handle it. And I guess I feel like I need to make something out of my life here."

Alison wrapped an arm around her and squeezed her tight. "I get what you're saying. But you've already done so freaking much, Lane. You have a business, a home, friends, and the most important thing is that you're happy. And if you're happy it doesn't matter if you're on TV, if you own your own store, or if you collect seashells on the beach and sell them on the roadside. Success, like what you're talking about...it doesn't make you happy. All of that comes from inside you."

"I guess so."

"No, not you guess. I'm right. I spent a long time looking for it in other people. In my husband. He would hit me, Lane, and I would try to tell myself that it didn't matter, because without a husband I wasn't anything. That was success to my family. Getting married, having children. It didn't matter if the marriage sucked. A divorce was a failure. So I thought because they defined success that way that's what it was, no matter the quality of my life. But that's not it. I left him, and I had absolutely nothing. No house, no husband, nothing but my waitressing job at Rona's. But you know what? I was the happiest I've ever been, because I was standing on my own strength."

Lane thought about that. She thought about all the years of general discontent. And she thought about what she talked about with Finn by the river. About how angry she was that Cord had moved on and she didn't feel like she could.

She wasn't standing on her own strength because she was still holding on so tightly to the past. Afraid to let it go. She was looking for answers back there. For some kind of moment where she would find satisfaction in the decisions she had made. Where she would know beyond a shadow of a doubt she had been right. Or maybe even that she'd been wrong.

But she didn't think that moment existed. Not really.

She had done physically what Alison had done. Cut ties. Walked away. But emotionally, she never had. Emotionally, everything she felt was curated, protected. Preserved.

For the first time, she wondered if keeping the baby such a well-protected secret had to do with the fact that she didn't want it touched by anyone else. Hadn't wanted anyone else's opinion. Because she hadn't wanted to be absolved. She had wanted to hang on to the guilt. And with a few insightful words, Finn had pointed out to her why that wasn't right or fair.

That was why she was holding it back from her friends now. Because she didn't want to feel certain things. She wanted to feel only what she was ready to feel. She wanted to retain control over her perception of that moment, that event, that memory.

She took a deep breath. "There's more."

Over the next hour, she told them all about the baby. Getting sent away from her family. The pregnancy. And they did cry. They all ended up sitting on the floor, surrounded by empty pie plates weeping pathetically.

But neither of them asked why she hadn't told them before. Nobody accused her of not trusting them. Nobody condemned her at all.

She wiped her face, her sleeve wet with her tears. "Wow," she said, taking a shaky breath. "That was kind of as hard and sucky as I was afraid it would be."

"I can't imagine," Rebecca said, shaking her head. "Though I do know a little bit about keeping secrets. And I know that they get so gigantic inside of you... I never told anyone that Gage caused my accident until years later. My anger felt so personal. It felt like mine. He was my monster, and I didn't want to share him. I didn't want to make him human by giving that name to anybody." She took a deep breath. "It just makes it more powerful, though. And in the end, I think it's always better to talk about it. Or maybe not always. But, when you're ready, if you can..."

Lane nodded, her throat too tight for her to say anything.

Alison reached out and gripped her shoulder. "Life is hard sometimes. But at least we have pie. And friendship."

Rebecca reached down and lifted her wineglass. "To pie and friendship."

Alison did the same. "Pie and friendship."

Lane repeated the motion. "But don't forget alcohol."

"Hear, hear," Alison said, tipping her glass back.

Lane took a long sip. "Oh," she said. "I'm sleeping with Finn."

The shriek that followed was high-pitched enough that Lane was surprised it didn't shatter her wineglass. "I *knew* it!" Rebecca shouted.

"Well," Lane said, "I wasn't back when you almost picked him up."

"No," she said, "I know. Because he never would have hit on me if he was already sleeping with you. But I knew that you weren't neutral. You were trying to tell me that you were just friends with him all while you practically turned green you were so jealous."

She scoffed. "I wasn't jealous. Much."

"I feel like my world just shattered," Alison said. "So much for believing in platonic male-female friendships."

Lane snorted, then tapped the side of her glass with her fingertip. "I'm not really sure if that's ever what ours was. What I think is that I'm the master of denial."

"Well, that is true."

"And he apparently always wanted me." She lifted a shoulder and took another drink of wine. "I just wasn't ready. But that's why I had to tell you the whole story. About Cord, about the baby. It all kind of leads to Finn. To what's happening now. I guess I'm just… Ready to deal with it. Ready to move on."

Of course, what exactly moving on meant, she wasn't totally sure at this point. It was scary. Scary to think it, let alone say it.

It meant doing things because she wanted to. Or not doing things because she didn't want to. It meant expanding the business because it mattered to her, not because she needed to prove something.

It meant… Well, it meant looking honestly at her feelings for Finn. Not in the context of everything she was afraid of. But in terms of what she actually felt.

"He clearly always wanted you," Alison said.

"Really?" Rebecca asked. "I mean, I always got a little bit of a weird vibe off of both of them, but I didn't know they wanted each other."

"You've known them both for too long," Alison said pragmatically. "When I met them I just assumed they were a couple, or at least that they were sleeping together. Until Lane introduced me to her boyfriend."

Lane squinted and thought back. She had been dating a guy named David back then. The last guy she had dated, actually, before Finn. He had been nice. Very nice. And he had also been separate from her friends, and from her relationship with Finn.

It struck her then, with incredible clarity, the way she had structured her life. Finn had been right. Completely. He played the part of boyfriend, or even husband, without any of the romance. She had always chosen some other guy for that. While she had kept Finn close. While Finn had held her heart.

Oh, good Lord.

She didn't want to ponder the full implication of that. Not right now. She had already been through too much.

"Well, it's nice to know that you were all more in touch with me than I was." She looked around, annoyed by the fact that they were all out of pastry. "I should probably go," she said, "otherwise I'm going to chew my own arm off. Or break into Pie in the Sky and get some more food."

"You just want to go bang your new boyfriend," Alison said, her tone knowing.

"I know I would like to go bang my fiancé," Rebecca returned.

"I'm not jealous," Alison said, not sounding all that convincing. "I'm really not."

"Oh, hey, how did everything go with Violet?"

Alison nodded. "Good. She's going to start at the end of the week. Which is nice, because seeing as I have a lack of men and sex in my life I could really use more work to fill it with."

"I mean, that's what I did for years," Rebecca said.

"Bear in mind, I had never actually been with *anybody* until a few months ago."

"Yeah," Alison said. "That kind of confirms the fact that I should be able to stay busy but celibate. Actually, if I keep hiring cynical teenagers I can just make them all my surrogate children and live my life vicariously through them."

"That's depressing, Alison," Lane said, slinging her arm around her friend as they all walked toward the door.

"Maybe a little," she conceded. "Although, at least I'm standing on my own feet. Whatever happens... Whoever I end up with... Or more likely, don't, I know who I am."

"And I think I might be figuring that out, myself," Lane said.

They all stepped outside onto the darkened street and Rebecca killed the lights to the store, then locked the door.

"Same time next month, ladies," Alison said, stuffing her hands in her pockets and backing away. "Hopefully Cassie will have dipped her kids in antibiotics by then."

"I'm sure we'll see each other before then," Rebecca said, patting Lane on the back before she headed toward her own car. "If Lane can be bothered to come up for air."

"You guys are the worst."

She shook her head and walked back toward the Mercantile, back to where she parked her car. And all she could think of on her way was that her friends weren't the worst at all. They were actually the best.

And moving forward, moving on, didn't feel as scary as she had thought it might.

CHAPTER TWENTY

LANE TEXTED HIM a little after three to let him know that she would be coming with dinner. He wasn't entirely sure how he felt about that. Yes, she had come before while his brothers were there since the two of them had started sleeping together, but something had changed down at the lake. And as protective as he had felt over their relationship then, he felt even more protective now.

He didn't want to answer questions. He didn't want any of his douche bag brothers to have questions. Mostly, he liked it when it was just the two of them. It seemed simple then. At least, as simple as a situation like theirs could be.

But, given their pasts, he wasn't entirely sure there was anything other than this strange antechamber between friendship and love for people like them.

"Are you daydreaming over there?"

Finn turned at the sound of Cain's voice. "Do I look like the kind of person that daydreams?"

"You're doing a damn good impression of one. Thinking about anyone special?"

"You know, Cain, sometimes I'm sad about our childhood. About the fact that the two of us didn't get to be raised as brothers should be raised together. The fact that we know each other about as well as strangers I pass on the street. Right now is not one of those moments. Right now, frankly, I'm more than pleased that I mostly grew up as an only child."

"Well, I grew up mostly as an only child too, so I can only guess, but I think that making you hate my very existence means that I'm really killing this big brother thing."

Finn snorted and wrapped the barbed wire around his hand, his leather work gloves keeping it from piercing his skin.

He had been out repairing fences with Cain all afternoon, and for the most part his brother hadn't made him want to crawl out of his skin. This was the exception.

"Hey," Finn said, "I just decided not to kill all of you in your sleep and tell law enforcement it was an unfortunate accident so that I could claim all parts of the ranch back for myself. You might want to tread lightly."

Cain smiled. "All things considered, I'm not really sure that you're the one who has the monopoly on brother killing jokes."

Finn frowned. "Why did they name you that, anyway?"

Cain shrugged. "Hell if I know. Probably my mom's idea of something different and interesting. Or maybe they figured I was doomed to be an ass from day one. But better Cain than Abel, right?"

"I guess."

"So what's your plan?" Cain asked, resting his foot on the bottom rung of the fence and looking out toward the mountains. He tilted his hat back on his head, letting out a long, slow breath. "I mean for your life."

"Really? Are we having this conversation?"

"I'm curious. My plans go as far as Violet getting into college. And then I'm going to have to work to pay for her to be there, because I don't think she's getting any scholarships. She's a great kid, and I love her, but she's not exactly interested in applying herself in any exceptional way."

"Right," Finn said, "why would she want to? At her age, there's about a million more interesting things to do."

Cain grimaced. "Which I also try not to think about. But… I didn't imagine myself here. On the West Coast. Away from Texas. Raising a kid by myself, who's barely a kid anymore. I feel fucking old and I'm not even forty."

"You are pretty fucking old."

Cain gave him a sideways glance. "Thank you."

"I assume based on that expression that I'm now doing exactly what a younger brother should do."

"I suppose," Cain said, his tone flat. "Anyway, that's my plan. Two more years and my daughter will be out of the house. I can't imagine getting married again. Probably won't be having any more kids. And then what? I think… I think that's the real reason I wanted to come here. Because everything in my life back in Texas was finished. Or at least, close to being finished. And it was also… Not really mine. It was a life that I built with somebody else. I can't have that life back. Also, I don't want it back. But I needed something new. I promise it had nothing to do with ruining your life." Cain paused, then looked over at Finn, a smile playing at the edges of his lips. "That's just a bonus."

"You're an asshole."

"That refrain is getting old." But Cain didn't really sound like he minded.

"Well, I'm not sure I understand why you'd want to link your hopes and dreams to cows, but if you do, if you want to make this your life, I guess I get it. I can't really begrudge you that."

"So what's *your* plan?" Cain asked, bracing his hands around the top of the fence. "Cows?"

"Basically." Finn bent and started collecting his tools, sticking them in the rusted old toolbox his grandfather had probably had since WWII. "Expanding the dairy now. I mean, thanks to Lane."

"I thought that we inspired you to do that, by our very presence. And also to keep us busy so we kept out of your hair. And to give Liam something to do so he wouldn't be such a jackass."

"Liam is past the point of redemption," Finn said, his tone dry. "But, I mean, you were part of it—the reason I said yes to expanding. The added manpower alone makes it more possible than ever. And, yes, getting you out of my hair can't be underestimated. But even if that hadn't been a definite fringe benefit, Lane is pretty damn convincing."

Cain smiled. "You gonna marry that girl? Because I wouldn't mind having her around more. I certainly like eating her food."

Finn shifted uncomfortably. "I'm not really interested in marriage."

"I'd ask why. But I'm pretty sure I already know."

"Hey, Alex and Liam had their mother and our father for a little while. You and I don't even know what a functional relationship looks like."

Cain nodded slowly. "Yeah. I mean, I sure don't know what the hell I'm doing. You can see that, given that I torpedoed the one serious relationship I had."

"You did?"

He spread his hands. "I must have. It was so bad she had to leave her child in order to leave me."

"I'd offer you some vague reassurance, but I don't know your life. Maybe it was your fault."

"I appreciate that." Weirdly, he sounded like he meant it.

For a second, Finn let himself think about it. Marrying Lane. Not just that hazy fantasy of having her in his home, but having her with him as his wife. There was definite appeal to that. He couldn't lie. But he'd seen relationships break down. He'd seen what abandonment looked like. Had felt it too deep. Enough that he couldn't imagine taking a step like that, one that offered some kind of false assurance of permanence when he wasn't sure such a thing could exist for him. "It's not like that," he said. "I mean, between Lane and me."

"It looked plenty like that to me when I walked in on you the other day."

"I'm sleeping with her," he conceded, not seeing the point in being evasive about it anymore. "But, she's got some stuff. She doesn't want to get married. She doesn't want to have kids. I don't either. I have long considered that a personal goal," he said drily, "not fathering any kids out of wedlock. Not leaving a string of abandoned people in my wake. It's just better to… To stay away from that stuff. I don't see why things can't keep going the way that they are with her. We have a good thing."

"*I* need that thing," Cain said, bending down and picking up a hammer. "Because another marriage sounds like an invitation to hell as far as I'm concerned. But damn, I miss women."

"Find one."

"I'm raising a kid," he said. "I barely have time to turn around. Much less find somebody to sleep with. I'm certainly not bringing anybody back to the house."

"If you wanted to spend the night away, there are plenty of people there to take keep an eye on Violet."

Cain let out a ragged sigh and Finn had a feeling that— for some reason—he was being a little too pragmatic for his brother. "Well, she'll be gone in two years anyway." He didn't sound particularly happy about that, though.

He looked at Cain, and he saw even more reasons to avoid that kind of entanglement. Hell, Cain had gotten married. And then it had all blown up. He had a kid, and now that kid was getting ready to leave him too. And Finn saw the way they interacted with each other. Saw how difficult she was.

Finn had already had a lifetime of people walking away. He didn't think he could sign on for a wife and kids, only to watch them do the same.

"Hey," he said, "Lane is bringing food tonight, so if you can't enjoy the other pleasures of having a woman, you can eat my woman's food."

Cain laughed. "That, I will take. Your woman, huh?"

Finn frowned. "Well, yeah. But it's not like that."

"Okay," Cain said, bringing the hammer back down on a nail.

"It's *not*."

"I said okay."

Out of everything Cain had said in that conversation, maybe the truest thing was that Finn mostly wanted to kill him. And that older brothers were supposed to make you crazy.

If there was anything else Finn had learned today, it was that he never wanted to feel the depth of the loneliness that his brother seemed to feel. When he saw that stark, hollow expression on Cain's face, it was way too close to a darkness he'd experienced before and he'd be damned if he tempted it again.

No, what he and Lane had was good. He had always wanted her, and now he had her. She had broken down her walls for him. Had given him some of the burden, and he was damn glad of it.

Sharing with Cain hadn't been so bad either. And maybe, just maybe, dinner would go more smoothly than he'd hoped.

HIS HOME WAS NOISY, and the weird thing was, it didn't even bother him that much. Even Violet had come downstairs for dinner. Alex was giving everyone a hard time, because that's what he did, Liam was nursing a beer and Cain was sitting in easy silence.

Lane, of course, was making conversation. A lot of it ridiculous, because that's what she did when she was full of energy. Nerves or energy and you could pretty much count on strange things coming out of Lane's mouth. He liked that, he realized. It was one of the big things he liked about her.

His grandfather had been steady, but taciturn. He had never been one to waste words. Lane wasted them with a particular sort of glee that he found endearing. Always had. This home, the home that now had noise filtering up to the rafters, had always been quiet. Except when Lane had come over.

Even Callum Donnelly had been powerless to resist her charm. And it turned out she had the same effect on every Donnelly.

Or maybe it was on everyone.

That effortless allure was all the more impressive given what he knew about her past now. He had always thought she was amazing, but he'd had no idea she was carrying around something quite so heavy.

It made her lightness seem like a feat of magic.

"I brought dessert too," she told the group now, smiling. "But I didn't make it. Alison, who is Violet's new boss, makes the best pie ever." Lane took a pastry box out of the fridge and set it down on the kitchen island. She lifted the lid slowly, an expression that looked not unlike one she made when he kissed her neck crossing her face. "Lemon meringue. And it's going to be so good."

"My favorite." Cain stood and made his way over to the counter, plate in hand. "Are you going to learn how to do this, Violet?"

"If I do," she said, taking her plate over to the pie box too, "then I'm going to charge you the going rate. Whatever Alison pays me an hour, you're going to have to pay too."

"If you do that, I'm going to send you a bill for the expenses of raising you." Lane deposited a large slice of pie onto Cain's plate, and he went back to sit down.

Suddenly, Finn didn't feel much like eating pie. Mostly, he just wanted to watch her, and he couldn't quite pin down why. There was something about having her here. In his kitchen, where she had been a million times before. Just a few weeks ago her presence had made him mad. Because it felt like a window into something they didn't actually have, something that he had wanted to a degree.

This was starting to feel like it was more than want. It was starting to move into need. And he didn't want that. Didn't want to *need* anyone.

He liked her needing him. And maybe that was hypocritical, but he didn't see anything wrong with it. It meant that he was giving her something, after all.

She looked up, and her eyes met his. Then her cheeks turned pink, and she looked back down at the pie, serving up a piece for Liam, and another for Alex. She lifted her thumb to her lips, her tongue sliding over her skin, picking up a little bit of meringue.

Arousal hit him, low and swift in the gut. And that was a much more comfortable feeling than what he had been grappling with before.

He stole a quick glance at his brothers, annoyed at the thought that they had seen that too. That unconscious move that seemed completely sexual to him. They seemed oblivious to it.

Lane moved away from the pie to where he was. She lifted her hand and pressed her palm against his shoulder, sliding it to the middle of his back, then returning it to his shoulder. Very much a nonfriend kind of touch. Something that people in relationships did.

"Are you going to have pie?"

"Probably not," he said, extremely conscious of her hand still pressed against his shoulder.

"There's plenty."

"I have a feeling that Cain is going to finish it off."

She looked over at Cain, then back to Finn. "Well, he better not. Because I want some."

"Why don't you sit down?"

"Really?"

"Yes, Lane. Let me bring you pie."

She smiled at him, then went to sit at the table, at a spot with an empty chair next to her. He cut her a piece of pie, then set it in front of her, before taking that spot right beside her.

He let her talk. Let everyone else talk while they ate. Then, underneath the table, he felt light fingertips against his thigh. Everything in his body hardened, his arousal hot and uncontrolled. Like wildfire.

She moved her hand down to his knee, then back up again. It was strange, this kind of interaction with her. He was used to friendship. And now, being naked. But with her dropping touches against his skin as casually as she spoke, it was blending into something else. Bridging this gap between friends and lovers.

She moved her hand once more, and her fingertips

connected with his. She paused for a moment. Then laced her fingers through his. She squeezed him tight, drawing his hand over to her lap. She looked up at him, something bashful in her expression that made his stomach squeeze.

She looked almost more nervous to be holding hands than she had been to get naked in front of him. He felt like something jagged had hit him in the heart, slid right underneath his defenses and gone deep.

"Thank you," she said, her tone as muted as her expression. "For the pie."

"Sure," he said, "you worked hard all day too. You deserve to have somebody take care of you." He meant it. And that was what he wanted to do. It was one of the few things he didn't doubt at all.

"Who takes care of you?"

"You do," he said simply, squeezing her hand gently.

That seemed to satisfy her, at least to a degree.

Everyone insisted that Lane stay seated during cleanup. All the men helped with dishes and putting away the food, and then slowly, his brothers filtered into the living room, and Violet went back upstairs to her more comfortable solitude.

That left just Lane and himself in the kitchen. Finn rested his palms flat on the countertop, looking at Lane, who was still sitting at the table. She stood, making her way slowly across the room, placing her fingertips lightly over the tops of his hands and looking at him, a kind of dreamy smile on her face.

Suddenly, he was seized by the fierce desire to kiss her. To take them straight out of this gray area and into something a little bit hotter. A little bit more certain. So he did.

CHAPTER TWENTY-ONE

THERE WAS SOMETHING different about Finn's kiss. A desperation to it that Lane couldn't quantify. She wasn't sure she wanted to. She just wanted to be kissed. And kissed, and kissed, by the only man she could imagine wanting for the rest of her life.

He wrapped his arms around her waist, folding her into his embrace. This felt less like a claiming, and more like a coming together.

She thought back to that very first kiss that had happened in the Mercantile. How angry she had been. How she had felt like he had demolished all of the very necessary walls she had placed between them.

The little fictions she had erected in order to maintain their friendship.

This was different.

This was a kiss to rebuild. Each press of his lips. Each pass of his tongue worked to remake what had been destroyed. Or maybe that wasn't even it. Maybe this was building something new entirely.

She had felt it. From the moment she had walked into the house tonight. That this was the time. To make it different. To build a bridge between that time they spent talking and laughing, and the time they spent in bed.

It scared her. To realize that she didn't want to be friends and lovers. To realize she wanted to blend the two. To realize that she actually did want to change the friendship.

It was scary enough that it made her want to run away, even now. Even though she was the one who wanted it. She had been silly in the beginning. Thinking that they could have those two things, keep them separate. Keep them distinct.

As if they would be two separate people. Friends by day, in each other's pants by night. Life didn't work that way. It just didn't. Yes, they could have a friendship right along with everything else, but she wanted all of it, all the time.

Intimacy. Sharing space. Sharing bodies. Sharing trauma. Sharing good things and bad. Not being afraid to reach down deep and explore those dark, hidden scars. To scrape back the facade that they both showed the rest of the world. To trust each other with everything.

The difference between choosing people who helped reinforce your individual defenses against the world, she supposed, and finding that one person she wanted to hunker down with. That was what she wanted. To build a wall around them both, with nothing between them. For him to be the one that she clung to when life got hard. She wanted him to do the same to her.

"Finn," she said, her voice soft.

He ignored her, pressing his lips to hers again, tightening his hold.

She put her hand between them, bracing her fingertips against his chest. "Finn. I want to talk."

He drew back, the look of horror on his face almost comical. She supposed she was being the worst. And, if she were only his hookup, she might feel a little bit bad about it. But since she was also his friend, and she wanted to be more, she was going to go ahead and be the worst.

"Why?" she began, but her throat was dry, and she realized that she hadn't really framed the question all that well. "Why are you against getting married? Why don't you want kids? We had that discussion about me. We had this whole, symbolic letting go. And it was really good. It meant something. It changed something. And I feel… I feel closer to you. And a lot closer to where I need to be to be a sane, healthy person. I want that for you too."

He shook his head slowly, taking a step back. "Lane," he started, "I know that this is new and different for you. And I needed you to trust me in order for what we are doing here to work. Because it was a change for you. To start… To start sleeping with me. But like I've already said, it's not a change for me."

"So… You don't have anything else to tell me about yourself? We don't have anywhere to go?"

"What does that mean? Anywhere to go? We're friends. We always have been. I always wanted you— now I'm having you."

Frustration clawed at her, along with the nameless need that she didn't want to stop and examine right now. "You know what I mean. You can't…you can't sleep together and not have things change."

It was all in direct contradiction with everything they'd talked about before. But frankly, what was happening between them was in direct contradiction with that too. Like he'd said, she had to change. She had to drop her guard, give him parts of herself that she had held back before. So why didn't he have to? He could talk all he wanted about how his feelings hadn't changed, because he always wanted her, but their actions had changed and that had to count.

She'd had physical relationships that hadn't contained any real intimacy. But when it came to Finn, he couldn't go deep inside her body without going deep into her soul too. She couldn't have known that beforehand. And even if she could have, she might have ignored it. Might have ignored all the warnings and the potential consequences so that she could have what she wanted.

As a great many red-blooded women would have.

But she had reached that point. That point where she could no longer ignore the potential consequences. Where she could no longer ignore all the changes this new intimacy was effecting inside of her.

It was only now that she felt so close to him that she was conscious of the distance he kept between them. When she was hiding too, she hadn't fully realized that he was doing it. He had seemed like her dependable, easygoing friend, and she hadn't looked much deeper than that.

But now that she was stripped bare, now that she had told him everything. Now that she had laid it all on the table, brought herself closer to him, determined that she wanted all the empty spaces between them closed, that she wanted to be pressed up against him, as close as two people could be, she could see what was preventing that.

It was him.

"That's all?" she asked. "You're having me? That's the beginning and end of it? Am I supposed to be flattered by that characterization?"

"It was good enough for you last night."

She shook her head, furious. "No, it wasn't. But I assumed that all of the things that were changing in me were changing in you too."

"What things, Lane?" His blue eyes were sharp, dangerous.

She felt something weighing her down, pressure building in her chest. She didn't want to be in this conversation. Didn't want to be in this argument. Didn't want to have to dig deep enough to find an honest answer to his question. All of the feelings that were currently howling through her like wind in a storm were difficult for her to pin down. Difficult for her to identify. She didn't want to. She just wanted to feel them. And she wanted him to understand them.

"I don't want to be nothing to you," she said, knowing that she was being overdramatic.

"You're not nothing to me," he said. "You know that. You're very important to me. If you weren't, I would have kissed you the day I met you. Instead, I resisted for ten damn years, so don't talk to me like you believe that."

"Fine. Then maybe I just don't want to be on par with Mark. Except you make out with me."

He shifted, a muscle twitching in his jaw. "You know that you're not like Mark."

"Why?" she asked, feeling desperate now. "Because you're having sex with me? Because that feels like two different things. Two things that are on the opposite end of the spectrum with a massive gulf between them. Like we're friends over here, and doing it over here, and that doesn't work for me."

"You seemed fine with all of this not long ago."

"I know. But things are changing. I'm changing. That whole thing that happened down by the lake… And I realized when I poured all of that out to you how much I keep from everyone. How almost nobody that's in my life that I consider a friend knows me at all. And when

I got over thinking about myself, thinking about how all of that applied to me, I realized that it was true for you too. I don't know you, Finn."

"That is the second most ridiculous thing you've said. Along with saying that you don't matter to me."

"You're avoiding the question. Why don't you want to get married?"

"You know all this, Lane. You know why. My damned father went and made a new family rather than staying with me. At least that wasn't unique to me. He did it to Cain too. But you know, getting abandoned by one parent can be random. Getting abandoned by both at different times? That's a little harder to ignore. I just don't want anything to do with having a family in that way. My father never married my mother. They were both terrible parents. The thought of trying those types of relationships again—even on the parent side—just doesn't appeal to me at all."

She didn't really know what to say to that. Because part of her wanted to ask if he honestly believed that she would abandon him too. If a marriage and children would really be so bad, so toxic, as long as there were no bad and toxic people in it. But she didn't want to put that out there. Didn't want to put herself out there like that.

"Finn," she said, the words muted, "just because your parents left… I… It's not the way everyone will be. It's not the way everything will be. You can't let one thing… stop you from being happy."

"But you can?"

She bristled. "That's different."

"Maybe it would be best if you went home tonight," he said, the words falling heavy between them. She could still fix this. She could still say something. But there was always the chance that what she had to say would break things even more.

All that thinking about rebuilding. And now here she was. But then, it was entirely possible that this was new construction. That the old building, the one that housed their friendship, was condemned. Had nothing to do with what they had now. What they would have in the future.

Suddenly, it all seemed black, blank. She couldn't see back; she couldn't see forward. She was far too different from whom she'd been. And so was he. Well, no. He wasn't different. That was the problem.

He turned and walked out of the kitchen, leaving her standing there by herself. She stayed there for a moment, completely immobilized. Surprised by the turn that things had taken.

She shook her head, getting a grip on herself before striding out the way that Finn had just gone. He was halfway up the stairs, headed toward his room, she imagined. She frowned. She looked toward the front door, and then she looked back toward the stairs.

She thought about leaving. But then she asked herself when the hell Finn had ever made it easy for her. He had pushed and pushed and pushed when he had decided that he wanted her and he was going to do something about it. He hadn't listened when she told him she wasn't ready.

Why should she give him courtesy he hadn't offered her?

She made her way over to the stairs, taking them two at a time to try to catch up with him. By the time she got to his room, the door was closed firmly. She thought about knocking. But, in the grand spirit of not respecting his agency in the least, she figured she would just barge in.

She did. But he wasn't in the room. She heard the shower turn on in the bathroom. She didn't even have to think about what she did next. She stripped her shirt off, throwing it onto the floor. Followed by her bra, her jeans and her underwear. She kicked them both to the side and took a deep breath.

Finn had seen her naked more times than she could count now. Actually, if she thought about it she probably could count them. She remembered every time with him. Absolutely every time. Because each one was unique, each one had changed her in some way. Had stripped another bit of her defenses away.

And that was why it was so maddening to realize how much of his were still in place. Defenses he didn't even seem bothered by. He had demanded that she tell him everything. That she give him everything, and all the while he had not intended to do the same for her. He didn't even think he needed to.

She didn't want to make love to a brick wall. Not when she herself was so reduced.

Thankfully, she knew there was more behind it. Knew there was more to her friend. To her lover. To the man who could very well become everything.

She pushed the bathroom door open, and Finn was already in the shower. She paused, looking at the long, lean shape of him that was visible through the glass door. She couldn't see the details of his perfect, honed body. This was like an impressionistic rendering of Finn. And as gorgeous and artistic as it was it wasn't enough.

She padded over to the door and pulled it open. He

looked up, an expression of surprise on his handsome face. "Move over," she said.

She didn't wait for him to comply. Instead, she simply stepped inside, closing the door behind them, enveloping them both in warm steam.

"I told you that you should probably go," he said.

"And you're the only one who gets to break rules? I have to respect personal boundaries? Screw that, I say. You need to be pushed. So I'm pushing you."

His expression hardened, but that wasn't all that hardened. His body didn't mind that she had joined him in the shower, no matter what his lips might say.

"I'm not in the mood," he said.

She arched a brow. "Really? Because it doesn't look like you have a headache to me."

"Lane," he said, his tone a warning.

"No. That's not how this works. You're not in charge. You don't get to push at me, come into my store and kiss me. Take me down to the lake and strip me completely. Make me tell you all my secrets while you get to stay protected. It doesn't work that way, Finn. You have to give back. You have to."

Water sluiced over his shoulders, down his chest, trailing over the ridges and contours of his abdominal muscles, down those enticing lines that made an arrow that seemed to point to the most masculine part of him. It would be easy to forget exactly what her gripe was. Exactly why they were arguing. To simply reach out and touch him, and let them both get lost in the heat that seemed to explode between them now whenever they were alone.

"Or what?" he asked, his hard features blocked off. Shuttered.

"I'm not issuing ultimatums," she said. "That's a

game for the desperate and the controlling, and I don't consider myself either." She wondered for a moment if that was true at all. Because right now she felt pretty desperate. And she had spent a good portion of her life being pretty damned controlling.

But still, she wouldn't play games the way that her parents had. Wouldn't hold something hostage to try and get the outcome they wanted. Their love, their support, unless she chose to give the baby up for adoption. An ultimatum that had led to a lifetime of doubts. No, she wouldn't do that to Finn. Mostly because she didn't want to ever wonder if that was why she had gotten what she wanted. And she didn't want him to regret it.

"It would be a damn sight easier if you would." He reached out, curling his fingers around her wrist and backing her up against the shower wall. He pinned her hand there, his hard body radiating even more heat than the space around them. "Then I would at least know what you wanted. Instead, you're saying all this vague shit that doesn't mean a damn thing to me."

It was strange to argue with him naked. They had argued with each other a lot with clothes on. They had a long-standing friendship, so of course they'd had disagreements. But naked... Not so much.

She looked past him and noticed a shampoo bottle and a bar of soap. Next to that was a razor. They were simple things. Everyday things. Intimate things.

This was where he shaved. This was where he washed his hair and his body. Where he scrubbed away the evidence of a hard day's work.

And this, she realized, was part of that blending. Whether or not he would easily give up information, easily show her who he was, this was part of that space between friends and lovers. Arguing naked. Being in his shower.

Loving him.

What a strange realization to have, pressed against the wall with more than six feet of angry man glaring at her. Right now, with tension as high as it had ever been, with him more than a little bit pissed at her, she was realizing that she loved him.

It wasn't even a revelation. Not really.

That was what was so strange. It was like holding a rock in your hand for years and years, and then turning it over to discover that it was a thunder egg, and that there were multifaceted crystals where before all you had seen was that rough gray exterior.

She loved him. She had for years. But now, she was seeing the rest of that love. The depth of it. And all that it could be.

She took a deep breath, her breasts scraping against his chest hair, the slight friction sending little pinpricks of pleasure through her body. Then she rolled her hips forward, bringing the cleft between her thighs up against his hardened length.

His eyes flared with heat, his jaw tightening further. Clearly, he was determined not to enjoy this, even if he wanted it. Even if he was going to give in.

"But I don't want to," she said, her tone muted. "I don't need this to be perfect. But that doesn't mean I'm not going to ask for what I want. It doesn't mean that I'm not going to work toward what I do think is perfect."

"So you're going to try and badger me into giving you what you want?"

"Why not?" she asked. "You did that to me."

He really didn't like that. She could tell by the way that heat in his eyes sparked, just about caught fire.

Too bad.

"I'm not going to badger you. That's what I would have done when I was just your friend. I would have rambled at you until you would tell me anything I wanted to hear to get me to shut up. But I'm not your friend anymore," she said, the words coming out shaky, trembling. "At least, not only that. So I don't have to go about it that way. Not when I could just do this."

She stretched forward, kissing his lips. He growled, grabbing hold of her other wrist and drawing it up over her head and against the wall, just like the first. She arched against him, luxuriating in his dominant hold. She liked this. This very sexual facet of that rough, masculine part of him that she had seen play out in so many other ways over the years.

The way he worked the land, the way he rode a horse. The way he had dealt with a cranky and cantankerous grandfather, instituting changes at the ranch where he could, negotiating for what he wanted with unmatched skill.

Seeing it all focused like this, seeing what he could do with that when he had a naked woman at his disposal was intoxicating. And unsurprisingly, everything she had ever wanted. Even though she hadn't quite realized it.

She had known him for a long time. And she hadn't known anything about the way that he made love to a woman, but she had known the way he carried himself. The way he walked. Had seen the firm hand he used in his daily life.

Some part of her had known he applied those same things in the bedroom. Or the shower, as the case might be.

Rough language. Rough hands.

She didn't mind. She didn't mind at all.

She pulled against his hold, and he tightened his grip, pressing her more firmly against the tile, the edge of one of the squares biting into the back of her hand. "I'm not in charge—is that it?" he asked, his voice low, even. "I think I just might be, sweetheart."

"Who are you talking to?" she asked, suddenly seized with the desire for him to find this all as unique and different as she did.

"What?"

"Sweetheart. That could be any bimbo that you brought back to your place. I need to know that I'm the bimbo you're talking to."

"Possessive, Lane?"

"I've always been possessive of you," she admitted, fire burning in her chest. "Every woman you've dated has annoyed me. Just so you know."

"Good thing none of them lasted very long."

"Yes," she said, "good thing. But I want to know that I'm different. So when you talk to me like that, you better make sure that you're talking to me."

He released her wrist, lowering his hand to brush his thumb over her bottom lip. "You think I have any other sweethearts, Lane? I don't. I never have."

Her heart leaped in her chest, tumbled against her breastbone. It was so close to what she wanted. So close to perfect. But his expression was still impossible to read, and she could still feel this wall between them. But maybe it didn't matter. Maybe right now she would imagine that it didn't matter at all.

Maybe right now, she would just kiss him.

She did. She tasted him long, deep, and when he said *sweetheart* again, the word sounding tortured, it did something to her insides that hurt.

He wasn't holding on to her arm anymore, and she used the opportunity to plant her hands against his chest and drop slowly down to her knees. She let her fingertips trace along the paths the water drops had taken, down those perfectly delineated muscles.

She rested her palms against his thighs, looking up, eye level with his arousal.

He leaned forward, bracing his hands on the wall, looking down at her, a warning glint in his eye. But he didn't tell her to stop. It didn't matter if he did, she wasn't going to.

She reached out, testing him with her hand first before she leaned in, flicking her tongue against his straining erection.

A gasp of breath seemed to catch in his chest and he reached down, grabbing hold of her hair. She closed her eyes, leaning in more determinedly, sliding her tongue all the way up and down his length. He cursed, and she gloried in the lack of control.

"Sweetheart," he said, that rough voice of his so very Finn. Her best friend in the entire world. The man who held her heart in the palm of his hand, the man whose cock she held in the palm of hers. Oh, how she wished she had his heart. But if she didn't, she would take this. She would take this pretty damn happily.

"Lane," he said, and that word alone was enough to push her right up against the edge of climax, and he hadn't even touched her.

She rose up slightly on her knees, taking him deep inside her mouth, feeling his muscles tense in his thighs, in his stomach as she continued to pleasure him that way.

"I'm not going to last," he said.

I don't care. But she realized she hadn't managed

to say that out loud, because her mouth was busy. And she wasn't inclined to stop. Not at all. He tugged her hair even tighter, and that only spurred her on. Evidence of just how close to the edge he was. She craved that. Craved a crack in that wall. Some evidence that he didn't feel nothing. Evidence that this was more to him.

That someday, she might reach him. That she wouldn't feel like she was standing on the outside of Finn Donnelly, wondering who he was for the rest of her life.

Suddenly, frustration, anguish swamped her. This man she had known for a decade, this man she considered her best friend, felt like a stranger right now. A stranger she wanted to be closer to. A stranger who meant the world to her.

She was physically as close to him as it was possible to be, and she felt isolated.

He gripped her hair harder, urging her up, and she followed the motion, getting to her feet. When he took her mouth, it was fierce, rough. He opened the door to the shower, not bothering to turn the water off. They tangled together, and he walked her backward into the bedroom, laying her damp body down on the bed, rising over her, kissing her as he settled between her legs.

Then he hooked his arm around her waist, reversing their positions and bringing her down on top of him, his arousal pressed against the softest part of her. She rocked her hips, gasping when he came into contact with her.

At least there was this. And this made it feel simpler. Made it easy to forget. Made him feel like less of a stranger.

Even if it was fake, even if it was manufactured, a trick of the arousal coursing through her veins, she would take it. The other option was breaking apart, and she didn't really want to break apart. Not right now.

"Take me inside you," he said, his voice strained.

She lifted her hips, positioning herself over him and guiding him slowly inside of her. She clenched her teeth, letting her head fall back as he filled her inch by inch. She trembled, and she realized that if she had been hoping to avoid breaking apart, this was probably the worst way to go about it.

Because when he had filled her completely, when she braced her hands against his strong shoulders and looked down at his eyes, at the intensity in his expression, she felt like he could see all of her.

And she couldn't see anything of him. Nothing but need. But heat and desire.

She knew what he didn't want. And that was about it. It wasn't enough. And at the same time, his body, buried deep inside of hers, was too much.

"Ride me," he said, the command husky.

She rolled her hips, establishing a steady rhythm that was designed to torture them both. Rising up so that he was just barely inside of her, then teasing him there for a moment before taking him in deep. He gripped her hips, his blunt fingertips digging into her skin.

She couldn't think anymore. She was lost in this. Lost in him.

Her arousal built inside of her like storm clouds, rolling in over the ocean, getting darker and darker until there was no choice but for it all to break open and rain down. When she broke, she clung to him, crying out her release, not caring if anybody heard.

She could barely acknowledge that there was anyone else in the world, let alone anyone else in the house.

The only thing that mattered was the two of them. The only thing.

She was still shaking, shuddering when he turned her back over, settling between her thighs and thrusting deep, his rhythm wild, feral, as he chased his own pleasure. She was sure that she was done. That every last bit of pleasure had been wrung out of her. But she was wrong.

He froze against her, pressing right against that sensitized bundle of nerves as he pulsed deep within her, his release hitting hard and fast, and triggering another one for her.

She turned her head toward his neck, scraping that tendon there with her teeth, biting down hard. He groaned, his hips jerking forward, creating another spasm of pleasure deep inside her.

And if she'd had any doubts before, they were gone now. She loved him. And she needed to tell him.

CHAPTER TWENTY-TWO

W HEN THEY FINISHED , they were still breathing hard. And she didn't feel relaxed. Didn't feel satisfied. She felt needy. Like an endless, aching well of need.

She rolled over onto her side and looked at him. He had his eyes closed, his face turned toward the ceiling.

And she felt alone.

She reached out, pressing her fingertips against his chest. "Please," she said. "I need you to talk to me. To help me understand why you feel the way you do about…everything. Why you think you can't have children. Why you think you can't get married. Because I love you, Finn, and if I didn't then maybe I wouldn't need to know. But I do. And I need to feel like maybe you might love me too."

She had expected that he wouldn't immediately burst forth with declarations. What she hadn't expected was for him to roll away from her. The sudden movement was so shocking, left her so cold that she shivered.

"Lane…"

"It's not ridiculous. Actually, what's ridiculous is saying it like it's a revelation. I've always loved you, Finn."

He turned back to her, one dark brow raised. "Right. And that's what you mean. You love me, because I'm your friend."

She sat up, moving to the edge of the bed, putting

even more space between them. She picked at the top of the bedspread. "No. I just mean… I've always loved you. And over the past few weeks, it changed. I should have known that was a possibility. I think actually I always did. That's why I didn't want you to know anything about me. It's why I didn't share my past, why I never… Why everything was so strictly platonic. Because I knew. I knew what it could become. At least, somewhere deep down inside of me where I keep all of my excellent self-protective instincts. And trust me, I am excellent at self-protection."

"You're rambling," he said, his tone completely flat now.

"Well," she said, standing up and stomping her foot. "You probably aren't going to like what I have to say anyway, so maybe don't rush it. Maybe we can take a detour into something ridiculous like Robert the mouse."

"You have two options. You can stop talking, or you can finish." He stood too, crossing his arms over his broad, bare chest. "We are not going to draw it out like this."

"What do you mean?"

"If you're going to go, if that's going to be the bottom line of this little conversation, then I need you to hurry up and fucking go."

She felt like she'd been slapped. He was angry, that was obvious. And to a degree she had expected some pushback from him. After all, she had been enraged when he kissed her. When he had confessed his attraction to her. When he had pushed her into this space that she hadn't felt prepared for. That she had been hiding from.

So yes, she had expected something of the same from him. But not this. Not this outrage.

"You think I don't know what this is?" he asked, his expression drawn, angry. "You think I don't know what it looks like right before somebody walks away? I am an expert in abandonment, Lane Jensen. I know exactly what it looks like when someone gives up."

"Do you? So you recognize that that's what you're doing," she said, not caring that her tone was accusatory.

"You think I'm the one giving up? That's where you're wrong. You're changing the rules. Changing the rules so you don't have to play the game anymore. If that's what you want, because you're too scared to keep doing this…"

"You really do have your head so far up your own ass," she said. "I told you everything. I laid my pain out right in front of you, and you won't give me anything back. All you do is throw up defenses, throw up walls. Everything you've ever accused me of and more. And you do your very best to sidestep by turning it back around on me."

He looked stunned. Like she had hauled off and hit him. Well, it might just come to that.

"There's nothing to talk about."

"If there was nothing, then you would tell me what was going on."

"Why? We've managed to have a friendship for the past ten years without you knowing all the details of my childhood. If you want to trade, if that's what you need to feel okay about your own past, I guess I can see the point. But otherwise…"

"You're not an idiot, Finn. Regardless of the fact that you're doing a really great impression of one right now. It has nothing to do with me wanting to feel like I'm not alone in having a really crappy past. It's because… It costs me to let go. Because I'm trying. Because there's still this big ball of pain and fear in my chest, but I'm trying to move past it. I'm trying to make sure it at least doesn't control my life. That it doesn't control everything I do, that it doesn't dictate who I love, or what I can have. I lived that way for too long. With one foot in the past. Pretending that I was moving on while I did everything—absolutely everything—in deference to that pain. To coddle it, to keep it precious and safe, and in its own little place where I could go back to it, remind myself of why I needed to be safe, and not demand anything, not love anyone too much. I don't want you to do the same. I don't want the man I'm with to be stuck in that place I'm trying so desperately to get out of."

She pushed her hair back from her face, suddenly very aware of the fact that she still didn't have any clothes on. But she didn't make a move to collect them either.

"Do you think that a few moments of confession down by the lake healed everything inside of me?" she continued. "It was just a start. And this is me trying to continue. This is me trying to be healed."

"Right. So you think that knowing what happened to me is going to make me decide that I'm wrong about love and marriage?"

Something inside of her shrank down, died a little bit. Or at least, got really, really sick. "Well," she said, her voice small, "kind of. Because it certainly started working for me. I can be patient, Finn. I don't need you to say all the words today. I just want to know that we maybe could work toward that. That you could."

"I want you to move in with me," he said. "Be… what we are now. But in my house. That's what I want.

I want to have this, have you. I don't see why it needs to be anything else."

"Friends and sex," she said. "Friends who have sex. Friends who are roommates and have sex. That's it."

"It's good, Lane."

"No," she said.

"Why the hell not?"

"Because," she said, her tone desperate. "Because I know exactly what it's like to live with people who don't really love you. To feel isolated and alone with people who really should understand you. I know what kinds of decisions those people make on your behalf."

"Are you comparing me to your parents now? That seems a bit convenient."

"Well, aren't you comparing me to yours? Isn't that what's happening? You're talking about abandonment like you think I would leave. Finn, I'm not going to leave. I have been your best friend for ten years, and now I'm more. And you think I'm going to walk away from you? Why would you think that? And don't tell me it won't help to give me a reason. I need something. Because I'm standing here screaming at you bare ass naked with my whole heart and everything else just kind of wrenched out in the open for you and you're looking at me... I don't even know how you're looking at me. That's the problem. I can't read you. I don't know what you're thinking. I don't know what you want. And don't say to have me. Because that's not enough."

"I'm not enough for you," he said, "that's what you're telling me. And you're trying to make out like I'm the one that's being selfish?"

She growled, grabbed hold of one of the pillows on the bed and slung it back onto the floor. "I want you to try," she exploded. "That's what I want. I want you to do something other than stand there with a blank expression on your face. Tell me who you are, Finn."

"I am less lovable than my mother's abusive boyfriend," he said. "That's who I am. Is that what you want to hear, Lane?"

"What?" Her stomach plummeted.

"Yeah. That's the rest of that story. I walked in on the guy my mother was dating beating the ever-loving hell out of her, and I kicked his ass so good the cops got called. And you want to know what? My mother wanted to press charges against me. I stopped him from beating her up and she wanted to press charges on me." Finn's voice was vibrating with rage. With pain. And Lane felt it all echoing through her. "Of course, nothing stuck because it was clearly justified on my end. But she also wouldn't press charges on him. Right after that, they left. And I didn't want to end up in some foster home, so I took my ass down to Copper Ridge. To my grandfather's ranch, because it was the only place on Earth I had ever spent a decent summer." His lip curled, and he moved across the room to his dresser, taking out a pair of jeans.

"Then I spent almost twenty years breaking my back for this place, for that old man, and he left everything to my brothers. Split evenly between us like we were the same. Like that had to be fair, when nothing else in our lives was. Of course, wasn't fair to me. But that's how it works. You love people, you pour everything into them, you give them everything, and then they kick you in the balls. You want to know why I don't want to get married? Why I don't want kids? That's why. I'm not a masochist."

"But when you thought about getting married you

were thinking of a hypothetical woman." She crossed the room, put her hands on his chest. "This is me."

"Is that supposed to reassure me? The woman who hid her feelings even from herself for a decade is trying to tell me that I don't have to worry about things getting tough and her running away?"

She pulled away from him. "That was low."

"It was honest. But it's a dead end either way, Lane. It doesn't matter. Because I don't love you like that."

She felt like she'd been slapped. "You don't? You don't love me like that? You dreamed of having me for ten years, and you couldn't force yourself to not want me."

"You're underestimating just how extremely fucked-up I am. You've seen the way I treat my brothers, the way that I feel about my family. There's only so much I can give. Why can't you be happy with that?"

"Because I've been living with not enough for way too long. That's been every moment of every day since I left Massachusetts. Taking little bits here and there. Cherry-picking my friendships and what I shared in them. Keeping you close to me, obsessively so, because something in me knew that I needed you, but I didn't want you to be everything, God forbid, because then I might get hurt. So I shoved you to the side, and you're right. I made you my handyman because I was too afraid to make you my boyfriend. So I dated easy men, men that I knew wouldn't hurt me, but would give me just enough evidence that I was normal that I would never have to deal with all of the...bleh inside of me."

"Why would you want to change everything?" he asked, his voice rough, raw. "Just... Why can't this be enough?"

She shook her head, a sudden onslaught of tears

slamming against the back of her eyes. Because she realized that she was losing this. Losing him. That he wasn't going to back down. That he wasn't going to tell her someday maybe she would have his whole heart. All of him.

And she was tempted. Tempted to just say okay. That she would live with him. That she didn't need him to love her. That she could love him enough for both of them, and that maybe she would even be able to lie to herself when they made love and he held her at night, and tell herself that he loved her, even if he couldn't say it.

"I'm tired of walls," she said, her voice wobbly, thin and defeated. "Everything inside of me has been like a maze. And I just felt trapped in it. Lost in it. Claustrophobic. I want more than that. I want to be free of that. My ex-boyfriend got married—he had a family. He has the adoration of millions of people. I don't even want that. But I want to be something other than my past. I want to be made of something different. I realized that all this time I've pretty much been made of my love for you. Even though you were my friend and nothing more, even though I did everything in my power to pretend I didn't, I loved you. For you, I want to be open. I want to be free. I want to be everything. But I can't chain myself to somebody who won't do the same."

She felt her entire posture begin to fold forward, collapse. All of the hope, all of the strength drained out of her. It was hard to feel anything but lost while she watched this brief glimmer of an imagined future slip through her fingers.

His face was still hard, impassable. For the first time she wondered if there really was nothing beneath it. If he was as damaged as he said he was. If being abandoned by his father, then by his mother—his mother who he had been trying to protect, who had called the police on her own son—really couldn't feel things the way that other people could.

It was terrifying. Like suddenly realizing that the floor beneath her was quicksand and she was going to be swept right down in it. Nothing was certain in that moment. Nothing was stable.

"You know what I have on offer," he said, his tone flat. "If that's not enough... Then go now. Because I will be damned if I give you a place in my home and you leave me then. If I make room for you in my life and you take off like everybody else just because I'm not enough for you."

She knew there was genuine pain beneath his words. They were coming from a place of hurt. But she didn't really care. Because right now she was hurting. Because she was watching him ruin this thing between them, this thing he had pushed for, this thing he had wanted, because now he was being asked for something. Being asked to give everything she had.

And that just made her mad.

"You were the one that wanted this," she said, her voice low. "You were the one who pushed for this. And this is what you wanted? To hold us in some kind of weird limbo for all of eternity? Yeah, I get that we were both in pretty deep denial when this started, thinking that we could do that, but I don't think either of us actually believed it. Of course there were going to be feelings, Finn. But I'm ready to deal with them."

"I made my position clear." He took a step back.

"You're willing to let me walk away? For what? For pride?"

"You won't walk away," he said, his confidence staggering. "You never have. And I don't think you will now. You need me."

He said the words in a monotone, but they were vibrating with urgency. With emotion that betrayed the fact that he wasn't as unshakable as he was trying to appear.

"You're right," she said slowly. "I do need you. I need you for so many things, and I always have. But I need you to need me too, Finn. Anything less isn't going to work." Slowly, she walked over to where her clothes were and began to pull them on. They felt heavy, and her limbs felt like they were filled with lead.

She waited for him to say something. Waited for him to stop her, but he didn't. Instead, he let her get dressed all the way. Let her walk to the bedroom door.

She stopped, her throat tightening. She bit her lip to keep from crying right there in front of him. She had already broken down in front of him too many times. And yes, he'd held her. He'd braced her. Because he was a wall. And that was easy for a wall. But asking him to bend, asking him to soften, asking him to make himself vulnerable to her in any way… He wasn't going to give in.

And it reminded her too much of the life in her past. Of living with inflexible, distant people. Of feeling alone in a home that had an actual staff. Because if you could maintain that kind of detachment then you could easily send your own child off to have a baby on her own, to hide her pregnancy from the neighborhood, from the garden club.

Because your own self-preservation would always be more important.

Finn wasn't her parents. She knew that. But it was far too close. Far too close to everything she had run away from once already. To the things that had damaged and wounded her beyond repair—or so she'd thought.

As she opened the bedroom door and began to walk away, something broke inside of her, and she wondered if she was right back where she'd been as a seventeen-year-old girl driving into town the first time. If there was something in her that would take another decade to heal.

Then, as she made her way down the stairs and out the front door to her car, all the time hoping that he would come after her, she realized something. That it might take ten years for this pain to heal all the way, that it might never heal all the way. But that she would be able to live even with the pain there.

Because she was stronger now. Because she refused to hold on to it. Because she refused to be defined by all of the things she didn't have. By all of the second-guessing. By the life that someone else was living.

She was broken. She wasn't destroyed.

That was because of Finn. Ironic now that he was the one causing this destruction when he had been the one to heal so much of it before.

No less ironic, she supposed, than the fact that he was the one ending things when he was the one who had pushed for things to begin. That he was the one who was afraid now, when he had been as confident as a bulldozer in the beginning.

Tears slid down her cheeks as she drove down the winding highway toward her house. It was dark outside and her headlights bathed the road and the bottoms of the pine trees in a wedge of yellow. It was the only light in the darkness.

She laughed. She supposed since it was so dark she was going to have to make her own light.

She would. She would make her subscription boxes, she would laugh with her friends. And sometimes, only sometimes, she would cry.

Because she loved Finn Donnelly with all of herself. Without reservation. And he refused to let himself love her back.

CHAPTER TWENTY-THREE

HE HAD DAMN well expected her to fight for this a little bit harder. For their friendship. The one that she had elevated above everything else that first day he'd kissed her.

But no, the minute she wanted something he didn't, she walked away.

Typical.

Typical of every damn person in his life.

Finn took the bottle of his grandfather's favorite whiskey off the bar and didn't even bother to pour himself a glass. No, he just uncorked the top and took a long drink. He wiped his mouth, starting to feel the effects, since it wasn't the first drink he'd had in the last few hours.

He couldn't sleep. There was no point. She wasn't here. She was gone. As she felt was justified.

He ignored the voice inside of him that called him a raving hypocrite. The same voice that had been poking at him from the time down by the lake when he demanded that she give him her burdens.

But hell. He'd told her. He'd told her that his mother had called the police on him. That he had caught her being beaten bloody by some bastard, had done as much damage as a skinny sixteen-year-old could do, and she'd still left him.

That his grandfather had taken years' worth of work

out of him, and then whatever the reason, everything he'd done still hadn't been enough to prove that he could run the Laughing Irish on his own.

"What's that about?" he asked the empty room. "You old Irish jackass. I did everything you asked me to do. And you didn't love me more than any of the rest of them, did you? I was probably just cheap labor."

A searing pain went through him at the thought. One person had said she loved him. Lane Jensen. And he'd told her he couldn't love her back.

The truth was, he didn't want to. Even if he could.

"What's going on down here?"

Finn turned and saw Cain standing in the doorway of the kitchen. Inquisitive bastard. Finn missed his isolation. He wished his brother would go the hell back to Texas. And that Alex would go the hell back to the army. And that Liam would go back to wherever the hell he'd come from. Hell, most likely.

"You live in a house with about a million other people. You come down to check on every noise?" Finn asked, noticing that his words sounded a little bit soft, thanks to the liquor.

"I have a sixteen-year-old daughter. I assume every noise that happens in the night is her sneaking out or a boy sneaking in. Granted, it's less likely here, since she doesn't know anybody and there's no way she could walk to town, and she wouldn't be able to hot-wire my car, but my paranoia has served me well so far when it comes to parenting, so I go with it."

"No teen angst down here. Do you want to see some ID?" He turned back to the bar and picked up the bottle of whiskey again, tipping it back as he pressed it up against his lips.

"Do you want to talk about it?"

"No. Does any man on earth ever want to talk about it?"

"What do you want to do then?"

"I want to drink about it," Finn said, doing just that. "If you want to join me, you can do that. Otherwise, why don't you go back to bed."

"Wow. My cold, empty bed, or, stay here and get hammered. Tough choice. But, I'll have a tumbler of the Jack Daniel's."

Finn slid a glass across the bar, and then pointed to a bottle. "This is a no-service establishment. Help yourself."

"I take it," Cain said, taking the stopper out of the bottle, "that you had a fight with Lane."

A fight. He wished it had been a fight. A real fight. One where she stood her ground. One where she had pushed back. She had just left.

You let her.

Yeah, well. Enough people had walked away from him that he had learned not to go chasing after anyone. After a while it just started to look sad.

"Not really," he said, lifting the bottle to his lips again.

"Oh, come on," Cain said, grabbing hold of the bottle and wrenching it away from Finn. "Have some damn pride. Pour it in a glass. Don't get sloppy over a woman."

Cain poured a measure of the amber liquid into a glass and handed that to Finn.

Finn glared, but took it without argument. "Do you know of a better reason to get sloppy drunk?" Finn asked. "If you do, I'm happy to hear it."

"Teenagers," Cain said, lifting his own full glass. "But, since you don't have one, women I guess. But only women that mean something."

His chest ached. Of course Lane meant something.

She had always meant something. That wasn't up for debate.

It was all this other stuff, her asking for things, saying things. The kinds of things that a man like him had decided he never wanted to hear. And then she was saying them. Lane. If he had ever wanted to hear it from any woman, it was her. Except, it was bull. Because she had immediately walked away. That was the kind of love he was used to. And if that was all the love he could ever get? He would do without it. He would deal just fine.

"Well," Finn said, "she's my best friend."

"I have a buddy back in Dallas—we call him Slim, because it's Texas and they really do things like that. We had our disagreements. I've never gotten drunk over him. I just don't feel that strongly about him, even though he's great to go out skeet shooting with."

"Well, unless you're also sleeping with him, I guarantee that you don't have the same attachment to him that I have to Lane."

"No," Cain said, "we are not that close."

"Right."

"This looks like love stuff to me, I'm just saying."

"You can *just say* your way back to Dallas," Finn said, taking another drink. "I don't think I asked for brotherly advice from the brother that I didn't even grow up with."

"All you have are brothers you didn't grow up with," Cain responded. "Grandpa is dead, your best friend is mad at you, so, who else are you going to talk to?"

"No one is a good option."

"Yeah, that's an option. It's definitely the one I went with when my marriage was falling apart. It worked out well for me. I ended up without a wife, and my daughter ended up without a mother. I definitely endorse that."

"Lane isn't my wife," Finn said, "and she isn't going to be."

"Right. Not if you keep avoiding the problem. Not if you keep existing in deep denial."

"Did you see a therapist after your wife left you, or something?"

Cain shifted uncomfortably. "I took Violet to one. A family therapist. I was there too. I was worried about her. And I may have internalized some things."

Finn arched a brow. "Okay."

"My point is, you obviously want more. You're not letting yourself have more. Why is that?"

"She's all talk," Finn said, the alcohol and his anger warming his blood, making the words flow free and easy. "She says she loves me. But what does that mean? I wasn't ready to say it back to her and she walked out."

"Yeah, women don't like that."

"So, she changes what she wants," Finn went on as though Cain hadn't spoken. "And I'm supposed to change right along with her, on her schedule. She would have left anyway. Sometime, she would have left. The fact that she couldn't handle this proves that."

Silence settled between himself and Cain, and his brother's expression took on an uncharacteristically serious look.

"That's what you wanted to prove, though, isn't it?" Cain asked finally, his words quiet and steady.

"What are you talking about?"

"You were trying to prove that she would leave. You pushed her away. That's what you do to people, Finn, if you hadn't noticed. You were a mean son of a bitch to all of us from the moment we got here."

"Did it ever occur to you that I just don't want you here?" Finn asked. He lifted the glass to take another drink, and Cain wrenched it out of his hand, setting it down on the bar top with a loud click.

"No," Cain said, "it did not occur to me that you didn't want us here. You do want us here. You want a family, Finn. We all do. That's why we're here. If we can be honest for a second and just cut the bullshit I think we'd all have to admit that. This ranch means something. Grandpa meant something to us. We are all each other has. Collectively, our parents sucked. Dad is God knows where. My mother can't be bothered to leave the casino for two seconds to deal with me, let alone her granddaughter. I assume you don't even know where your mother is."

"You assume correctly."

"I made a family. I got married. That went to hell, so here I am. Alex was in the military. Clearly that didn't work out—he came here. Liam... Who the hell even knows. But he's here too. My point is you do want us here, just as much as we want to be here, but you can't admit that. Because you have to push. You have to push and push until people prove that they won't walk. I get it—I do. But there's a certain point where you make it impossible for people to do anything but disappoint you. You tell a woman you don't love her... She's gonna leave." Cain blinked, a muscle in his jaw working. "That's how it goes. You're a self-fulfilling prophecy, Finn. How does it feel?"

"You don't know what you're talking about. Your mother raised you, at least. She might not be mom of the year, but she was there. You know where she is. If you needed to go drag her out of a casino, you could."

Cain lifted a shoulder. "We all have a sob story. But

do you want to be the sob story or do you want to be a man?"

"You think it's that simple? Well, of course you do. Because in the end, this all worked out for you, didn't it? Did you ever think just how insulting it was to me that our grandfather left us equal shares in this ranch after I lived here for all this time, worked it, invested my time, my money. I took care of this place. I took care of the old man. And apparently, he thought I was about as useful as my parents did. Because he brought in all of you. Apparently, what I did didn't matter."

"Dumbass," Cain said. "That's the only thing you can figure it is?"

"You think you know," Finn said, snatching his glass of whiskey back. "You didn't even know him. Not really."

"From the sounds of it, neither did you."

"Great," Finn said, setting the glass down again before crossing his arms over his chest. "Tell me about it, Cain. Maybe when you're finished I won't want to punch you in the face."

Cain rocked back on his heels, and once again, Finn was conscious of the fact that the two of them were standing in exactly the same position. That they were brothers, even if they felt more like strangers.

"Did you ever think that he didn't want to leave you the whole burden to carry alone? Did you ever think that maybe, just maybe, he thought we needed each other?"

Cain's words hit Finn hard. "No," he said, "I didn't."

"Of course you didn't. Because you're lost in your own little world where nobody loves you and everybody leaves you."

"My own mother left me. My mother called the police on me, tried to get me arrested for dealing with her abuser." And there it was. He'd admitted it. To Lane, and to Cain. That his own mother hadn't even seen the point in sticking around with him. That she'd found life more worthwhile with an asshole who beat her than she'd found it with him.

"I'm not saying you didn't go through hard times. I'm not saying I'm not messed up too. I'm just saying, if you can be close enough to something that matters, *this close,* close enough that you're trying to drink away the pain, maybe you just deal with your issues instead."

"Right. Give me the number of your therapist."

Cain snorted. "Unfortunately for you, I'm the only therapist you have. Let me tell you, I can't be pushed away. I stayed with my wife even when our marriage sucked. Eventually, she had to leave because I just wouldn't. And now I'm staying with my daughter even though she kinda hates me, and I have to deal with her attitude all the time. I am not an easy man to scare away, Finn. I'm the wrong person to test. I might end up beating your ass, but I'm not going anywhere. Lane loves you. Any idiot can see that. But you have to give her something."

Everything inside Finn rebelled against that. Because hadn't he given her all of his support? Hadn't he listened to her as she'd told all of her secrets?

Except, Cain was pushing against exactly what Lane had just yelled at him about. About him keeping everything from her. Everything locked down inside. About her being the only one who was vulnerable.

Yeah, well, he wanted to be vulnerable about as much as he wanted a stick in the eye.

"Do you want to prove yourself right or do you want to be happy?" Cain asked. "You can only have one of those things. But you need to be honest with yourself. And you need to stop being such a dumb fuck."

"I don't think therapists say stuff like that."

"Older brothers do. And you have one. You could have a lot, actually. A lot of family. A lot of love. If you weren't so afraid of it."

Those words hit hard. Like an arrow right on target.

No man wanted to be told he was afraid. He wanted even less to find the words true.

"Fix it," Cain said.

Then he turned and walked out of the kitchen. Finn could hear his brother's heavy footsteps on the stairs. But he just stood there, his hand wrapped around the whiskey tumbler.

Then he tilted it back and took it all in one swallow.

He closed his eyes, and all he could see was Lane's face. All he could see was the pain he had caused her. He had pushed. He had pushed, and he had pushed.

His heart squeezed tight, like someone had punched a hole through his chest and grabbed it, yanked it out.

All he could do was picture the way he'd treated her before they slept together for the first time. That day he'd stormed into the Mercantile, yelled at her, taken her in his arms.

He had been pushing then. But she had stayed.

He had asked, he had taken, he had forced her out of her comfort zone. And she had proven that she was up to the challenge. The challenge that was him.

And tonight, when she had asked for something from him, he had done what he did best. He had done exactly what Cain had accused him of doing.

He had tried to make her run. To prove that he was right about himself. That there was nothing in him worth loving enough for anybody to stay.

He had decided, when she had walked away with all the hurt in her eyes, that it proved his point.

Right. He was an ass.

He braced his hands on the bar top, lowering his head. He closed his eyes, and images flashed through his mind. Lane, tonight, mixed together with that day his mother had left.

He didn't even have a real image of his mom walking away. He had made one up in his head. A kind of strange vision of her walking off into the sunset with a small suitcase that didn't even look like anything she'd actually had. And he was sure she hadn't walked anywhere. She had most definitely gone with her boyfriend. And they had taken a car. Still, that was the image that lived in his brain.

There was nothing real there. Everything about it was imagined. Because it had been much less dramatic than that. He had come home from school one day to find the house empty of all her things.

She hadn't taken the pictures. That was the most notable thing to him. All of the pictures of his childhood, the pictures of the two of them together, the life they had built after his father had left... She had well and truly left it behind. No reminders needed.

He swallowed hard, his throat aching, his limbs shaking.

He had tried to be everything for her. He had tried to protect her. He had gone to his grandfather's ranch to give her space, to give her time alone over the summer. He had done his very best to be good. To never intrude on her life.

Except, he hadn't been able to watch that man take his fists to her face.

But even then, she had found him wrong. Found him disappointing.

And it had been the final thing that pushed her away.

How would he ever know? How would he ever know what the last straw would be with anyone? His father had just left. There had been no warning. There was nothing to learn from. With his mother... He had tried. He had.

He had thought he was doing the right thing, and it had gone the worst possible way.

How would he ever know if that would happen again? Trust.

He imagined Lane again, pressing her hands against his chest, looking at him with earnestness in her brown eyes. She was right. This wasn't a hypothetical wife. Not a hypothetical love. It was her.

The woman he had damn well loved from the moment he first laid eyes on her more than ten years ago.

He felt like he'd been kicked in the chest by a horse. Following on the heels of feeling like he'd been punched clean through the chest, it was a very heavy feeling.

He did love her. He always had. And he was no better than she was. He was nothing but a coward.

He had told himself all those years he was protecting her, because she was vulnerable. That she wouldn't be able to handle him. That he would ruin the friendship.

But he had simply been afraid of the strength of his own feelings. And when he hadn't been able to control them anymore, he had taken a different approach. Had pushed the line to try and get what he wanted, while half expecting her to run the other way. And, deep down, part of him had figured that if she did run it might be a win anyway. Because he would know. Because it would be over. Because his heart wouldn't exist in this damned limbo where he was desperate to regain all control of it while Lane Jensen held on to it.

Control. All of these years he had tried to keep control.

He had found some of it on the ranch, and then when his grandfather had died he had lost even that semblance of it. And now, he could really feel it all being wrenched from his grasp. He had messed everything up. He had nothing of his own. He didn't even have his best friend.

Standing in this giant, beautiful ranch house, and outfitted with everything he could possibly want, everything he could possibly need, it seemed a little absurd to contemplate. But he had less now than he'd ever had at any moment in the past decade.

There was a freedom in that. A strange, exhilarating freedom. He had nothing left to lose. He was standing here in the middle of his worst fear. Lane had left him. He had succeeded in pushing her away.

But it didn't have to be over. Like Cain had said, he could be a sob story or he could be a man.

Finn Donnelly was a damn man.

CHAPTER TWENTY-FOUR

LANE WANTED BEREAVEMENT LEAVE. Or at least for someone to bring her bereavement food. She had made three casseroles, and she didn't even want to eat them. And now, she was manning the counter at her store knowing that she looked like a wraith and not particularly wanting to do anything about it.

By the time the third little old lady had told her she would be prettier if she smiled, she considered trying. But she only gave it the barest bit of consideration.

She was moping halfway through the day when Alison came in with a box of pie in her arms. "Cassie told me that you looked like you needed butter when she walked by earlier today." Alison frowned. "What's wrong?"

Lane reached down and grabbed a couple of receipts that were stacked on the counter. She threw them up in the air and made an explosion noise.

"Yeah," Alison said, "I don't speak sound effects. Words would be good."

Lane rested her elbows on the counter, and her cheeks in her hands. She knew that she looked pathetic, as pathetic as she felt. She didn't even care. In fact, she was somewhat satisfied by it. That her exterior so fully matched her interior.

"I have no words," she told her friend.

"That is deeply concerning," Alison said, setting

down the pie. "You always have words. An excess of words. I have never, not once, seen you without them."

Lane lifted her head and spread her hands. "None."

"Okay, drama queen. Find some."

Lane opened her mouth to say what was wrong, she really did, but then her throat got tight, and her eyes filled with tears. She really didn't want to cry in the store, because a real customer could come in at any moment and she didn't want to be some cliché weeping woman, blubbering at work over a guy.

But, she really felt like blubbering at work over a guy.

"Okay," Alison said. "Now you're really scaring me."

"It's Finn. He...he doesn't love me."

Alison's arms were around her before she could say anything else. "I will cut him," she said, "right in the junk."

"Thanks," Lane said, her voice muffled.

"I probably won't actually do that," Alison said. "I've worked hard to build a life for myself. I really don't need to end up in prison. Although, I bet if I talked to Sheriff Garrett he would make me a really good deal." She pulled away from Lane. "He would probably attest to my psychological issues and general rage at the male species."

"I really appreciate your willingness to go on psychiatric lockdown over my emotional trauma. But you don't need to do that. It's my fault." She sucked in a shaking breath. "We both said what we wanted... Or, what we didn't want at the beginning. I'm the one that changed. I decided that I wanted more. Because I decided to do this stupid emotional healing thing, where I let down all my walls and demanded to be loved. What a stupid idea. I should have stayed dysfunctional. Then I would have my friend, and I would have sex."

Alison nodded. "I see the appeal."

"What was I thinking?"

"Well, I imagine you were thinking that you couldn't limit yourself for a man. For anyone. Trust me, if you try to shrink yourself down for a relationship you'll end up disappearing. I've been there. I've done that."

"Yeah," Lane said. "But Finn isn't like Jared. He would never... He would never hurt me on purpose." Except, last night had felt both pointed and purposeful. "Physically," she amended.

"I feel like I'm the wrong person to have walked in on this crisis," Alison said. "I have nothing but a dim view of romantic relationships."

"I know."

"But I don't like to see you sad." She lifted a shoulder. "I also would be a little sad to be the last single one in the group, so I suppose there's a silver lining for me."

Lane snorted. "Good. I'm glad that your needs are being met."

"Hey," Alison said, popping the lid on the pie box, "I am seeing to your needs too."

"Thank you," she said, meaning it. "But I can't afford to go full food coma until after I close up shop."

Alison stood there for a moment. "I have to get back soon."

"Sure," Lane said.

"I'm training Violet. She's kind of delightful. I mean, if you can see past the snark. But I actually don't have to see past the snark to enjoy her. I kind of like it."

"Well, at least one of us has a working relationship."

Alison frowned. "This sucks," she said. "I wish it were me. You know, that I could take your place. Because I wouldn't care."

That made Lane laugh with sincerity. "Well, in that case, I wish you could be me too."

"What are you going to do?"

She took a deep breath. "What I was doing. I'm going to get the subscription boxes working. I'm going to use products from the Laughing Irish. I'm going to grow my business, just like I wanted to do. Honestly, if I learned anything from dealing with the reappearance of Cord McCaffrey in my life—even if it was just a virtual reappearance—it's that I can't afford to let pain from the past dictate my future. Even if it's really serious pain. Although, in this instance, I suppose I am letting pain from my past motivate me, but, that I think might be okay."

"You're a badass," Alison said, "and not nearly as pathetic as I was when I went through my divorce. You're going to rebound nicely."

Lane tried to smile. "Thank you. I'll try to cling to the rebound hope."

"I'll check in with you later. You want Rebecca to come over in about an hour? Then Cassie can come after her."

"You don't have to take tragedy shifts. I'm fine." She wasn't fine, but she kind of preferred to do her weeping in private.

"All right. But if you do, just let me know."

"I will."

She watched her friend exit the store, and then she looked over at the box of pie. She was… So profoundly grateful to have people to lean on if she needed it. People who knew the whole story. Of Finn, of everything that had come before him. She hadn't realized what she had been missing before.

That's why all of this was worth it. All of the pain. Telling him no. Telling him that she wanted everything.

Because Alison was right. She couldn't allow herself to stagnate. To stay back where he was. She had to move forward. Even if it sucked.

She made a moaning sound and laid her head down on the counter, resting her cheek on her forearms. Then she popped back up. She had to finish the day out. If she could just do that, then maybe she would survive tomorrow too.

Okay, that was thinking too far ahead.

She would just focus on breathing through the next hour. Then, maybe someday, she would breathe through two hours. Then six. Then twelve. Then maybe she would stretch it out to a whole day.

She heard a scraping sound, and turned just in time to see a little brown fluff ball scurry across the floor. She jumped back. "Hey," she scolded, "Robert, you have to stop scaring people."

She laughed helplessly. And a tear slipped down her cheek. "Also," she added, "you are officially my best friend. So do something about how creepy and gross you are."

She was talking to a mouse. A mouse she had named Robert. And there was only one person on earth she wanted to tell that story to. But she couldn't call him. She couldn't text him with her ridiculousness.

Suddenly, she felt isolated in a way that was terrifying. A way that transcended anything she had experienced before.

There was no way to fully understand the gaping hole losing Finn was going to leave in her life. Not immediately. Because he had filled so much of her existence for so long.

But it could never be the same again. No matter what, it could never be the same.

She took a breath. She just needed to keep breathing for an hour.

MOST MEN WOULD show up with a bouquet of flowers. Most men who had screwed up beyond reason would bring jewelry. Maybe chocolate.

Finn Donnelly had a big ass box of dairy products.

But the woman he loved owned a specialty food store and loved him almost as much for his cheese as she did for his body—if she still loved him at all.

He parked his truck against the curb and got out, grabbing hold of the box of hastily assembled items and heading toward the door, his heart pounding hard.

He had never done this before. He had never gone after somebody once they had left.

When he got to the front door, Lane was standing up against it, turning the lock. She stopped, her eyes meeting his through the window, round and filled with horror. Her expression would have almost been comical if not for the fact that he could see she was in pain, and it was a pain that matched his own.

He wanted to punch his own face in. For doing this to them.

"Let me in," he said.

"I reserve the right to refuse service to anyone," she said, leaning on the door. "I refuse."

"Dammit, Lane," he said. "Let me in."

"I have to wash my hair. I have to scrub my feet with my pumice stone."

"Lane," he said, "this box is heavy."

"I'm hanging out with Robert. We don't want you here."

"I don't care what the mouse wants," he said. "I care about what I want. And I want you, so let me in the damn door before I break it down."

Well, there went his romantic speech.

"You want… Me?" she asked, her voice muffled by the door.

"I'm not shouting at you on Main Street. People are staring."

"That," she said, "is no less than you deserve. But I'm going to let you in." He heard the lock jiggling, and then she tugged it open. "Don't make me sorry. Don't make me cry again."

He walked inside before she could change her mind. "I can't make any guarantees about that." He shifted his hold on the box. "I brought you some stuff."

"What stuff?"

"Samples. Of the kind of thing you can put in your subscription boxes. And some things you can stock here in the store. I worked all day on this stuff, so if you hate it, don't tell me. At least, don't tell me today. Or maybe do tell me today, because you probably owe me."

She put her hand on his, her expression unspeakably sad. "If you came here to try to pick up our friendship where it left off, you can't. And you need to go. The hardest thing for me to deal with over the past couple of days—even before you told me you didn't love me— was realizing that I couldn't be your friend. I mean, it's complicated. But I want something more. Friends and lovers aren't the same. I want a romance. I want you to be… Everything. And friendship is certainly included in that, but there's something else too. And that's what I need. That's scary. It's terrifying. I don't like it really. Except, I also found it exciting. To realize that we were on the verge of making something new. Something that was just us. We both have friends. But you're my only Finn. And I want to be your only Lane. And I want our relationship to be fully unique. Fully ours. So if you came here to banter with me about dairy, I need you to go."

He shook his head. "That's not why I came." He set the box down on the floor, his heart hammering. He hated this. Feeling nervous. He didn't do that. Ever. He wasn't afraid of much of anything. Except, apparently, his tiny little friend whom he loved with all of his heart and soul. "That's not why I spent all day on this. On low pasteurized milk and a list of cheeses and different soaps."

Her eyebrows shot up. "Soap?"

"Soap," he confirmed. "Don't think for one second I did all that because I wanted to be your friend. Because I wanted to pretend that nothing happened."

"Then stop talking about dairy and say the thing you came here to say."

"I'm a miserable bastard," he said, reaching out and taking her hands. "I'm a miserable bastard who expects everybody to walk away from me eventually, and so I try to push them. I do it to everyone. Not to you. Not at first. I met you at your brother's house, and you were so bright and beautiful, and so obviously sad. And I wanted to take all of that onto myself. I wanted to be everything for you. And I wanted you to be everything for me. For the first time since my mother left I wanted… I wanted more. But I thought if I could put you in a particular place, and tell myself I was protecting you, I wouldn't have to drive you away. Of course, when my grandfather died and my brothers showed up, everything started breaking apart. And that was when I started pushing. Because I couldn't control myself around you anymore. So I figured I would either have my way..."

"Or I would walk away. Which is exactly what you did to me last night, isn't it?"

The betrayal on her face cut him deep. "Yes," he said, his voice rough. "Not that I realized it then. It took my older brother to knock some sense into me. It turns out maybe I do need family. Which was a distressing revelation, Lane, make no mistake."

"Wow. I bet. Though not half as distressing as having the man you love look you in the eye and say he can't love you."

"I'm sorry," he said. "I'm so damned sorry. I held back all this time from letting myself have you because I knew I'd hurt you. But the ridiculous thing about that is it was just a self-fulfilling prophecy."

"Damn right it is, Finn Donnelly. You couldn't hear that from me? You had to go brood your way to a revelation?"

"I had to get my head out of my ass. And I had to... I had to deal with all my shit." He shook his head. "I've never been able to figure out the magic combination. The thing that makes people finally decide I'm not worth the effort. It scares me. It might seem silly to you, but I can't shake this feeling that one day I could wake up, and you would be gone."

Lane shook her head, her eyes filling with tears, then she closed the space between them, pressing her palm against his cheek. "I've walked away from enough. I'm done. I can't lose anyone else. And you know that's why I suppressed all of my feelings for you. Because I needed you. But I didn't want to do the work to become what you needed." She laughed suddenly. "You know

how they put people in medically induced comas when
they're really badly injured?"

He blinked, not quite sure where she was going with
this. But then, with Lane it was almost impossible to
know. That was part of what he loved about her. The
endless vibrancy, the constant surprises. The rambling.
Lord, but he loved that woman's rambling.

"Yeah," he said slowly.

"That was us. All of our feelings were in a medically
induced coma. Or maybe a trauma induced coma? Until
we could heal enough to handle it."

He laughed, taking her hands, holding both of them
and sliding his thumbs over her palms. "Unfortunately,
you healed a little faster than I did."

"I did. I'm not even going to give you a pass on that."

He looked at her, and a sensation filled his chest
until he could barely breathe around it. He thought it
might take him over completely. And he wasn't sure if
he minded. "I haven't said this…" He cleared his throat.
"When I came home from school and found that my
mom was gone. That she'd left me, for real. That she
chose her deadbeat boyfriend over me… I never wanted
to feel that way again." He paused for a moment, trying
to collect his emotions, to keep them from spilling out.

"She left all the pictures of us," he continued, "on the
walls, in the photo albums. I broke the picture frames.
And then I burned everything. So that I wouldn't be
tempted to ever look back at it."

"Finn… Oh Finn." She wrapped her arms around
him, held him close. He braced his hands on her hips,
rested his face in the crook of her neck.

"I never wanted to feel like that again," he repeated.
"I never wanted to be blindsided. I never wanted to need
somebody that much. I wanted… I wanted something I

could tame. Something I could control. That's why the ranch has been everything to me for so long. It made me feel like I could reach down and grab hold of the earth. And with you…it's not about control. The last thing I ever wanted was for you to become everything, Lane Jensen. I could only just barely handle you as a friend. I knew that losing you even if I never touched you would devastate me. That's scary. To give you this. To want you like this."

"You're kind of preaching to the choir," she said softly. "I've been dealing with a pretty significant amount of fear myself."

"I'm out of practice saying this," he said, drawing the moment out longer.

"That's okay."

"I love you," he said. "As a friend. As a lover. As everything in between. And I want… I do want you to be everything. I want to give you everything. I want you to know me, like nobody else does. I want exactly what you said we could be. That whole picture you painted. I want that."

"I love you too," she whispered.

"I love you," he said again. "I love you. I love you. I'm already feeling less out of practice."

Every time the words came out of his mouth they felt a little bit lighter, and so did he. And it helped that Lane held even tighter to him each and every time.

That with every press of her body she made a vow not to let him go.

"I never wanted to get married. And I never wanted to have children. But you're right. That was when I put a generic, faceless person in that place as my wife. As the mother of my kids. A woman who would only end up leaving me. But when I imagine you there? I want it all. And I know you'll stay. I know you will. Because I know you." He stared at her for a heartbeat, watched as a variety of emotions played across her face.

"I didn't think…" She cleared her throat. "I didn't think I would ever want that life. Mostly, I didn't think I deserved it, so I trained myself not to want it. But I think we both do. I think we deserve all of it. I think we deserve everything. But you're the only person I could have everything with, Finn." She clung to him more tightly still, pressing her cheek against his, and he felt a tear fall onto his face, dropping from her eye. "It's always been you. It really has been."

"For me too," he said, wrapping his arms around her, holding nothing back, pulling her against him completely, with nothing between them.

He held her like that for a long time, just listening to her breathe. Feeling the softness of her body, of her hair, inhaling that scent that was so uniquely Lane.

"So," he said. "Since I love you, do you think you might want to marry me? You were talking about that thing that was like a lover, and like a friend, but was more. And I think the word you might have been looking for was *wife*."

She tilted her head back, tears trailing down her cheeks. "Yes," she said. "I would really, really like that."

"Me too," he said, leaning in to kiss her.

"Maybe Robert can be our best man."

"No," he said, wrapping his arm around her waist. He was going to have a hard time letting go of her. Now that he had her back, he wanted to hang on forever. Wanted to touch her forever. "I draw a hard line at a best mouse."

He slid his thumb over her cheekbone. "You know my brothers will have to be in our wedding."

She laughed. "Oh really? You think they'll put on tuxes?"

"Wait. You think I will?"

"Hmm. I think you would if I asked you to, Finn. But I have to say there's some appeal in having you marry me in a white T-shirt and jeans. And your hat and boots, of course."

"Doesn't matter to me, as long as you marry me."

"Try and stop me. Hey, maybe Violet can be the flower girl."

"She'd probably want to wear black and throw dead flowers."

"That's super metal, but possibly not what I want for a wedding."

"Your brother has to be the best man," Finn said. "Since he did kind of introduce us."

"Wow. We get to tell Mark."

"Something tells me he'll be okay with it. Since all he's ever really wanted was for you to be happy."

"What a coincidence, that's what I want for me too." She kissed him. "That's what I want for us."

"I think we stand a pretty good chance at being happy."

"For how long?" she asked, a smile curving her lips.

"Forever."

It was funny to think that just a few weeks ago having his house full, having his brothers there, sharing the ranch, sharing his life had seemed like the end of everything he'd worked for.

Now it seemed like a beginning.

With Lane by his side, with his family around him, his life was full for the first time.

"Do you want another casserole?" Lane asked.

That snapped him out of his thoughts. "I thought that was sadness food."

"It is," she said. "I mean, usually. And I made it because I was sad. But now I'm happy and I have casserole. So, maybe we make a new tradition."

"I'm going to have anniversary casserole for the rest of my life, aren't I?"

She laughed. "Probably."

And he did.

EPILOGUE

IT WAS LANE'S favorite time of the month. Time to cu-
rate a new batch of The Best of Copper Ridge boxes.
She liked to prepare them three months at a time. And
of course, now that her subscription business had expanded to include other regions in the state of Oregon,
plus a Best of Oregon box, she was even busier.

Luckily, she had a crew of tiny taste-testers always
on hand to offer opinions. Though she had quickly
learned that her three-year-old son was an unreliable
authority on hazelnuts, since he deemed them "yucky."

She smiled to herself as she walked to the end of
the long driveway that led from the main house of the
Laughing Irish ranch down to the highway. She opened
the mailbox and took out the mail, leafing through it as
she wandered back up to the house.

There was a small white envelope in the middle of
the stack that made her heart stop. She tore it open while
she ran up to the house, her heart galloping.

She remembered that Finn was still out in the field,
and veered away from the house toward where she
guessed he might be.

She'd already read it all by the time she found Finn,
and tears were tracking down her cheeks. When he saw
her, his face contorted.

"What happened?" he asked. "Is everything okay?
Cade? Alana?"

"They're fine," she said. "I just… I just got this letter from the adoption agency. The one…the one."

She offered her husband the letter and he took it, holding it gently as he read the contents. She didn't know why, but for some reason it made her heart stop, watching for his response.

"He got into Harvard," Finn said softly.

"He did," Lane replied, a fresh tear falling down her cheek. "And he has a great family. He…he thanked me, Finn. For giving him up. I never thought… I mean I was afraid to hope…"

Finn reached out and pulled her into his arms, holding her tight. "I'm so happy for you, sweetheart," he said, his voice gruff. "Happy for us."

In the past six years their lives together had been wonderful. She loved her husband and her children, and she'd made peace with her past. But she'd still wondered about her firstborn. She thought of him often, especially when Cade was born.

But he'd written to her now, through the agency. To tell her he was well. That he was going to school. That he was grateful.

It was all she'd ever wanted to know. All she'd given up hope on ever knowing for sure.

She looked up at Finn, the love of her life, her best friend, and she felt complete. All the pieces of her heart were right here. Her family, this ranch, this town.

So many wonderful things, it didn't leave any room for fear.

"I love you, you know," she said.

"Me too. I pretty much always have. Ever since that time we watched a movie together and I saw you—really saw you—for the first time. But it's changed too. Every time I see you smile—" he dragged his thumb over her cheek "—every time you cry. When you first made love with me. When you married me. When you had our daughter, when you had our son. And I think…just in the last minute or so, seeing this, it changed again. Got deeper. I think that's how it always will be."

She felt another tear slip down her cheek, and she sniffed. "Same goes, Finn Donnelly. Same goes."

"That's good," he said. "Because if I didn't have you I'd probably have to room with Robert."

She laughed, a bubble of absurdity that welled up and escaped her lips. "Who?"

"The mouse. Your best friend. The one that you liked better than you liked me for a brief moment in time."

"Oh, Robert! Yeah, he left a while ago. I think he moved to the woods and met a mouse hottie and had babies. He doesn't want to room with you."

"Well, that settles it. You have to keep me."

"I think I can do that." She cleared her throat. "So, I have to ask, does your love for me get stronger every time we…" She trailed off, eyeing him suggestively

He grabbed her hand and started leading her out of the barn—quickly. "You know," he said, pausing for a moment to pull her against his chest and plant a kiss on her lips, "I think I might need to test that theory."

* * * * *

*The Donnelly brothers might be
putting down roots in Copper Ridge,
but the road to happily ever after
is hardly a smooth one.
Look for Cain's book,
DOWN HOME COWBOY,
from Maisey Yates
and HQN Books!
Read on for an exclusive sneak peek...*

CHAPTER ONE

Cᴀɪɴ Dᴏɴɴᴇʟʟʏ ᴡᴀs sick to death of being alone.

Or, more specifically, he was sick and tired of going to bed alone. It had been a long time since he'd touched a woman.

Four years.

Four years since Kathleen had walked out on him and Violet. And in that time, he had been consumed with trying to salvage what he could of his daughter's childhood. With trying to make a new life for them, with trying to build something that belonged to the two of them, and didn't have his ex-wife's ghost lingering in the shadows.

That was why they had come to Copper Ridge, Oregon, from Texas just a month earlier. The transition had been rocky so far.

He lifted his beer bottle to his lips and scanned the room. He didn't know how he had allowed his younger half brothers to talk him into going out. He had to admit that his daughter made a pretty convenient excuse for his hermitage. Of course, Violet was sixteen now, and she could stay alone for a while.

Though, if his brother Finn and his new girlfriend, Lane, weren't at home, he probably would have used the excuse of them being in a new place to avoid going out. Out in the middle of nowhere like the Laughing

Irish ranch was, Violet was likely to get scared. Or some other lie.

But Lane and Finn were at home, and Cain had found himself fresh out of excuses. So he was sitting in the local bar, Ace's or something. Which was the name of the guy who owned it, he'd been told.

The place was a strange collision of surf and turf. There were fishing nets, half a boat hung up on the wall and other little pieces of evidence that Copper Ridge was a coastal town before it was anything else. But there were also Western touches that could rival any honkytonk he had been to in Dallas.

Including a mechanical bull. Which he had to admit was providing a decent amount of entertainment.

"Are you going to watch that thing all night?"

Cain turned to look at his brother Alex, who had been eyeing a pack of blonde chicks in the corner and glanced at Cain just long enough to give him a baleful stare.

They were too young. All those girls, standing in the corner and scanning the room to see if they could catch the eye of some guy who might buy them another drink. He knew his brothers were up for it. Liam and Alex would happily jump right in the middle of them— in the next thirty seconds, most likely.

Cain felt too old for all of this. He was supposed to be done. That was the point of getting married. He had liked that. That routine. That certainty.

He had been so certain about the decision to marry Kathleen. She'd been pregnant, and he'd always known that if that happened, he'd be marrying the woman. In many ways he'd been thrilled. To have something in his life that he'd felt long denied.

Stability. A family.

He'd become a father at twenty-two, and it had been the proudest day of his life. And for a while, everything had been exactly like he wanted it.

Obviously it hadn't been what Kathleen had wanted.

And *this* wasn't what *he* wanted—this bar, this night. But he was just so damn sick of being alone. Being celibate. Yeah, it was the celibate thing. He didn't want another relationship. There was no point. Violet was sixteen, and bringing somebody else into their life when it was already hard enough just wasn't going to happen.

He had never felt right about bringing a woman home for sex with his daughter in the house. And he had really never felt right about spending the night out while he left her. Not when his wife had left the way she had.

So, here he was. Contemplating his celibacy in a bar. Looking at a mechanical bull rather than women. It was all depressing and mind-numbing enough to make him *reflect*.

On the slow breakdown of his marriage, the day Kathleen had packed up all her stuff and left without telling him what she was planning and where she was going.

The day she'd surrendered parental rights to their daughter, because she needed a clean break.

He looked away from the bull-riding spectacle and over toward the bar, where he saw something that most definitely caught his attention.

There was a petite redhead leaning up against the counter, her ass perfectly showcased by the tight jeans that she was wearing. She shifted, and her hair shimmered beneath the multicolored lights. Then she lifted her arm, brushing all that glossy beauty to one side. Cain was transfixed by the sight of that arm. Pale, freckled, slim. She looked soft.

Just for a moment, he could imagine touching her so vividly that he could feel that creamy soft skin beneath his hand.

More likely, it was a full-on hallucination. He wasn't even sure if he remembered what a woman's skin felt like.

Maybe she wouldn't be quite so pretty from the front. It was always possible. But he hoped that she was. He hoped that when she turned around she provided him with more fuel for the fires of his fantasies. Because hell, fantasy was all he had.

The beautiful redhead did not disappoint. And she was, in fact, beautiful from all angles. She turned, scanning the bar with a smile on her face. Damn, she was probably there with some other man. Not that he was in a position to do anything about it either way.

Still, it was nice to know that he could get excited about somebody.

"If you're going to sit there looking like you'd rather be anywhere else, maybe you should be somewhere else," Liam said, never quite as easygoing as Alex was.

Cain didn't welcome the interruption to his fantasies. "This is my happy face," he returned.

"You're scaring women away," Liam said.

"That would be *your* ugly face," he said.

Alex laughed. "I love bonding time."

Cain rolled his eyes and took another drink of his beer. Here he was, out on the town. On a Saturday night. And it just felt wrong. He preferred the life he'd had.

Bars, picking up women, he'd done all that in his early twenties. He was just so far past it now. He couldn't even remember what he'd found appealing about it.

"It's better than sitting at home," Alex said, clearly

looking for some kind of reaction that he just wasn't going to get.

"Okay," Cain relented, "it was nice to go and eat a hamburger?"

"And spend time with us," Alex added. "Because we're so charming."

"I work with you dumbasses all day, every damn day. I wasn't exactly hurting for quality time."

"That makes me feel sad, Cain," Alex said. "I really thought we were making progress with our brotherly bond."

Of the four of them, only Alex and Liam had grown up together. They were also the only two full-blood brothers. Cain had been the product of his father's first attempt at commitment, and then Finn had been the second. Both attempts had been short-lived and unsuccessful.

For the most part, Cain had been raised in Texas, while his brothers had spent their childhoods on the West Coast. All of them had spent sporadic summers at the Laughing Irish, their grandfather's ranch on the outskirts of Copper Ridge.

Last month, they'd all inherited an equal share in the place, and since then, it had been a labyrinth of trying to figure out how to navigate the new family dynamic. Mostly, he liked his brothers. Mostly, he didn't want to punch them all in the face every day. *Mostly.*

"For me," Cain said, "this is progress. Drinking in public instead of drinking alone."

"Well," Liam said, "you might look like you enjoy it more."

"Like you?"

Liam lifted a shoulder. "Women like the brooding thing."

"It's true," Alex said, "they do. I go with wounded war hero smiling bravely through my pain, and Liam... well, he does that. Hell if I know how it works, but something about looking angry at the world seems to draw them in. You could work that angle, Cain."

"I don't want an angle to work," he said, taking another drink, looking across the room to try and find the redhead again. She had sat down at a table with a couple of other women, and they were eating, laughing. Definitely having more fun than he was.

She laughed at something that must've been particularly funny, throwing her head back and making all that hair shimmer again.

He had to wonder if what he had just said to his brother was true.

"Planning on being alone forever?" Alex asked.

"I'm not alone. I have a daughter. You two don't know anything about that kind of responsibility. I'm not going to bring women in and out of her life just because I want to get laid. It's not responsible."

"Plenty of people have kids and relationships," Alex pointed out.

"Yeah, well, those people aren't parenting Violet. She's not happy with the move, you know that."

"She seems happier since she got her job at the bakery," Liam said.

"It's hard to tell with her." His stomach tightened slightly, thinking about his daughter and all of the things he seemed to get wrong with her.

"We've all got shit to handle," Alex said, taking a drink. "But that doesn't mean we can't have fun too."

"You don't know from having shit to handle," Cain growled. Then felt like a dick because for all that Alex played it down, he *was* a war hero, and given the fact that he never talked about it in a substantial way, Cain had a feeling Alex was pretty deeply affected by it.

It was the Donnelly way. The more it hurt, the more you laughed it off.

He forced his gaze resolutely away from the redhead. Because there was no point in fostering any fantasies. He had too much on his plate.

"So," Alex said, "are you just going to sit here all night?"

"I was planning on it."

"Okay. As long as we're clear that it's your choice, and we're not abandoning you." He stood up, clapping Cain on the back. "We're going to go be social." Alex picked up his cowboy hat from the table and placed it firmly on his head, then he and Liam headed over to the group of women they had pointed out earlier.

Cain shook his head, leaning back in his chair, his arms crossed. He wasn't envious of them. In his opinion, they really didn't understand what was important in life yet. They didn't have anything bigger to live for. Not like him. He had Violet.

And even when she was challenging, she was the reason he got up every morning. He didn't envy his brothers. Or their so-called freedom. It was empty as far as he was concerned.

He took one more look back at the redhead, ignoring the tightening in his gut, in his groin. Yeah, he didn't envy them at all. But, while he saw their freedom as empty, his bed was empty too. And right now, he was just damn sick of that.

TAKE ME, COWBOY

CHAPTER ONE

WHEN ANNA BROWN walked into Ace's bar, she was contemplating whether or not she could get away with murdering her older brothers.

That's really nice that the invitation includes a plus one. You know you can't bring your socket wrench.

She wanted to punch Daniel in his smug face for that one. She had been flattered when she'd received her invitation to the community charity event that the West family hosted every year. A lot less so when Daniel and Mark had gotten ahold of it and decided it was the funniest thing in the world to imagine her trying to get a date to the coveted fund-raiser.

Because apparently the idea of her having a date at all was the pinnacle of comedic genius.

I can get a date, jackasses.

You want to make a bet?

Sure. It's your money.

That exchange had seemed both enraging and empowering about an hour ago. Now she was feeling both humiliated and a little bit uncertain. The fact that she had bet on her dating prowess was...well, *embarrassing* didn't even begin to describe it. But on top of that, she was a little concerned that she had no prowess to speak of.

It had been longer than she wanted to admit since she'd actually had a date. In fact, it was entirely possible that she had never technically been on one. That quick roll in the literal hay with Corbin Martin hadn't exactly been a date per se.

And it hadn't led to anything, either. Since she had done a wonderful job of smashing his ego with a hammer the next day at school when she'd told her best friend, Chase, about Corbin's…limitations.

Yeah, her sexual debut had also been the final curtain.

But if men weren't such whiny babies, maybe that wouldn't have been the case. Also, maybe if Corbin had been able to prove to her that sex was worth the trouble, she would view it differently.

But he hadn't. So she didn't.

And now she needed a date.

She stalked across the room, heading toward the table that she and Chase, and often his brother, Sam, occupied on Friday nights. The lighting was dim, so she knew someone was sitting there but couldn't make out which McCormack brother it was.

She hoped it was Chase. Because as long as she'd known Sam, she still had a hard time making conversation with him.

Talking wasn't really his thing.

She moved closer, and the man at the table tilted his head up. Sam. Dammit. Drinking a beer and looking grumpy, which was pretty much par for the course with him. But Chase was nowhere to be seen.

"Hi," she said, plopping down in the chair beside him. "Bad day?"

"A day."

"Right." At least when it came to Sam, she knew the difficult-conversation thing had nothing to do with her. That was all him.

She tapped the top of her knee, looking around the bar, trying to decide if she was going to get up and order a drink or wait for someone to come to the table. She allowed her gaze to drift across the bar, and her attention was caught by the figure of a man in the corner, black cowboy hat on his head, his face shrouded by the dim light. A woman was standing in front of him looking up at his face like he was her every birthday wish come true.

For a moment the sight of the man standing there struck her completely dumb. Broad shoulders, broad chest, strong-looking hands. The kind of hands that made her wonder if she needed to investigate the potential fuss of sex again.

He leaned up against the wall, his forearm above his head. He said something and the little blonde he was talking to practically shimmered with excitement. Anna wondered what that was like. To be the focus of a man's attention like that. To have him look at you like a sex object instead of a drinking buddy.

For a moment she envied the woman standing there, who could absolutely get a date if she wanted one. Who would know what to wear and how to act if she were invited to a fancy gala whatever.

That woman would know what to do if the guy wanted to take her home after the date and get naked. She wouldn't be awkward and make jokes and laugh when he got naked because there were all these feelings that were so…so weird she didn't know how else to react.

With a man like that one…well, she doubted she would laugh. He would be all lean muscle and wicked smiles. He would look at her and she would… Okay, even in fantasy she didn't know. But she felt hot. Very, very hot.

But in a flash, that hot feeling turned into utter horror. Because the man shifted, pushing his hat back on his head and angling slightly toward Anna, a light from above catching his angular features and illuminating his face. He changed then, from a fantasy to flesh and blood. And she realized exactly who she had just been checking out.

Chase McCormack. Her best friend in the entire world. The man she had spent years training herself to never, ever have feelings below the belt for.

She blinked rapidly, squeezing her hands into fists and trying to calm the fluttering in her stomach. "I'm going to get a drink," she said, looking at Sam. *And talk to Ace about the damn lighting in here.* "Did you want something?"

He lifted his brow, and his bottle of beer. "I'm covered."

Her heart was still pounding a little heavier than usual when she reached the bar and signaled Ace, the establishment's owner, to ask for whatever pale ale he had on tap.

And her heart stopped altogether when she heard a deep voice from behind her.

"Why don't you make that two."

She whisked around and came face-to-chest with Chase. A man whose presence should be commonplace, and usually was. She was just in a weird place, thanks to high-pressure invitations and idiot brothers.

"Pale ale," she said, taking a step back and looking up at his face. A face that should also be commonplace. But it was just so very symmetrical. Square jaw, straight nose, strong brows and dark eyes that were so direct they bordered on obscene. Like they were looking straight through your clothes or something. Not that he would ever want to look through hers. Not that she would want him to. She was too smart for that.

"That's kind of an unusual order for you," she continued, more to remind herself of who he was than to actually make commentary on his beverage choices. To remind herself that she knew him better than she knew herself. To do whatever she could to put that temporary moment of insanity when she'd spotted him in the corner out of her mind.

"I'm feeling adventurous," he said, lifting one corner of his mouth, the lopsided grin disrupting the symmetry she had been admiring earlier and somehow making him look all the more compelling for it.

"Come on, McCormack. Adventurous is bungee jumping from Multnomah Falls. Adventurous is not trying a new beer."

"Says the expert in adventure?"

"I'm an expert in a couple of things. Beer and motor oil being at the top of the list."

"Then I won't challenge you."

"Probably for the best. I'm feeling a little bit bloodthirsty tonight." She pressed her hands onto the bar top and leaned forward, watching as Ace went to get their drinks. "So. Why aren't you still talking to short, blonde and stacked over there?"

He chuckled and it settled oddly inside her chest, rattling around before skittering down her spine. "Not really all that interested."

"You seemed interested to me."

"Well," he said, "I'm not."

"That's inconsistent," she said.

"Okay, I'll bite," he said, regarding her a little more closely than she would like. "Why are you in the mood to cause death and dismemberment?"

"Do I seem that feral?"

"Completely. Why?"

"The same reason I usually am," she said.

"Your brothers."

"You're fast, I like that."

Ace returned to their end of the bar and passed two pints toward them. "Do you want to open a tab?"

"Sure," she said. "On him." She gestured to Chase.

Ace smiled in return. "You look nice tonight, Anna."

"I look…the same as I always do," she said, glancing down at her worn gray T-shirt and no-fuss jeans.

He winked. "Exactly."

She looked up at Chase, who was staring at the bartender, his expression unreadable. Then she looked back at Ace.

Ace was pretty hot, really. In that bearded, flannel-wearing way. Lumbersexual, or so she had overheard some college girls saying the other night as they giggled over him. Maybe *he* would want to be her date. Of course, easy compliments and charm aside, he also had his pick of any woman who turned up in his bar. And Anna was never anyone's pick.

She let go of her fleeting Ace fantasy pretty quickly.

Chase grabbed the beer from the counter and handed one to her. She was careful not to let their fingers brush as she took it from him. That type of avoidance was second nature to her. Hazards of spending the years since adolescence feeling electricity when Chase got too close, and pretending she didn't.

"We should go back and sit with Sam," she suggested. "He looks lonely."

Chase laughed. "You and I both know he's no such thing. I think he would rather sit there alone."

"Well, if he wants to be alone, then he can stay at home and drink."

"He probably would if I didn't force him to come out. But if I didn't do that, he would fuse to the furniture and then I would have all of that to deal with."

They walked back over to the table, and gradually, her heart rate returned to normal. She was relieved that the initial weirdness she had felt upon his arrival was receding.

"Hi, Sam," Chase said, taking his seat beside his brother. Sam grunted in response. "We were just talking about the hazards of you turning into a hermit."

"Am I not a convincing hermit already?" he asked. "Do I need to make my disdain for mankind a little less subtle?"

"That might help," Chase said.

"I might just go play a game of darts instead. I'll catch up with you in a minute." Sam took a long drink of his beer and stood, leaving the bottle on the table as he made his way over to the dartboard across the bar.

Silence settled between Chase and herself. Why was this suddenly weird? Why was Anna suddenly conscious of the way his throat moved when he swallowed a sip of beer, of the shift in his forearms as he set the bottle back down on the table? Of just how masculine a sound he made when he cleared his throat?

She was suddenly even conscious of the way he breathed.

She leaned back in her chair, lifting her beer to her lips and surveying the scene around them.

It was Friday night, so most of the town of Copper Ridge, Oregon, was hanging out, drowning the last vestiges of the workweek in booze. It was not the end of the workweek for Anna. Farmers and ranchers didn't take time off, so neither did she. She had to be on hand to make repairs when necessary, especially right now, since she was just getting her own garage off the ground.

She'd just recently quit her job at Jake's in order to open her own shop specializing in heavy equipment, which really was how she found herself in the position she was in right now. Invited to the charity gala thing and embroiled in a bet on whether or not she could get a date.

"So why exactly do you want to kill your brothers today?" Chase asked, startling her out of her thoughts.

"Various reasons." She didn't know why, but something stopped her from wanting to tell him exactly what was going on. Maybe because it was humiliating. Yes, it was definitely humiliating.

"Sure. But that's every day. Why specifically do you want to kill them today?"

She took a deep breath, keeping her eyes fixed on the fishing boat that was mounted to the wall opposite her, and very determinedly not looking at Chase. "Because. They bet that I couldn't get a date to this thing I'm invited to and I bet them that I could." She thought about the woman he'd been talking to a moment ago. A woman so different from herself they might as well be different species. "And right about now I'm afraid they're right."

CHASE WAS DOING his best to process his best friend's statement. It was difficult, though. Daniel and Mark had solid asshole tendencies when it came to Anna—that much he knew—but this was pretty low even for them.

He studied Anna's profile, her dark hair pulled back into a braid, her gray T-shirt that was streaked with oil.

He watched as she raised her bottle of beer to her lips. She had oil on her hands, too. Beneath her fingernails. Anna wasn't the kind of girl who attracted a lot of male attention. But he kind of figured that was her choice.

She wasn't conventionally beautiful. Mostly because of the motor oil. But that didn't mean that getting a date should be impossible for her.

"Why don't you think you can get a date?"

She snorted, looking over at him, one dark brow raised. "Um." She waved a hand up and down, indicating her body. "Because of all of this."

He took a moment to look at *all of that*. Really look. Like he was a man and she was a woman. Which they were, but not in a conventional sense. Not to each other. He'd looked at her almost every day for the past fifteen years, so it was difficult to imagine seeing her for the first time. But just then, he tried.

She had a nice nose. And her lips were full, nicely shaped, her top lip a little fuller than her bottom lip, which was unique and sort of…not sexy, because it was Anna. But interesting.

"A little elbow grease and that cleans right off," he said. "Anyway, men are pretty simple."

She frowned. "What does that mean?"

"Exactly what it sounds like. You don't have to do much to get male attention if you want it. Give a guy what he's after…"

"Okay, that's just insulting. You're saying that I can get a guy because men just want to get laid? So it doesn't matter if I'm a wrench-toting troll?"

"You are not a wrench-toting troll. You're a wrench-toting woman who could easily bludgeon me to death, and I am aware of that. Which means I need to choose my next words a little more carefully."

Those full lips thinned into a dangerous line, her green eyes glittering dangerously. "Why don't you do that, Chase."

He cleared his throat. "I'm just saying, if you want a date, you can get one."

"By unzipping my coveralls down to my belly button?"

He tipped his beer bottle back, taking a larger swallow than he intended to, coughing as it went down wrong. He did not need to picture the visual she had just handed to him. But he was a man, so he did.

It was damned unsettling. His best friend, bare beneath a pair of coveralls unfastened so that a very generous wedge of skin was revealed all the way down…

And he was done with that. He didn't think of Anna that way. Not at all. They'd been friends since they were freshmen in high school and he'd navigated teenage boy hormones without lingering too long on thoughts of her breasts.

He was thirty years old, and he could have sex whenever he damn well pleased. Breasts were no longer mysterious to him. He wasn't going to go pondering the mysteries of *her* breasts now.

"It couldn't hurt, Anna," he said, his words containing a little more bite than he would like them to. But he was unsettled.

"Okay, I'll keep that in mind. But barring that, do you have any other suggestions? Because I think I'm going to be expected to wear something fancy, and I don't own anything fancy. And it's obvious that Mark and Daniel think I suck at being a girl."

"That's not true. And anyway, why do you care what they—or anyone else—think?"

"Because. I've got this new business…"

"And anyone who brings their heavy equipment to you for a tune-up won't care whether or not you can walk in high heels."

"But I don't want to show up at these things looking…" She sighed. "Chase, the bottom line is I've spent a long time not fitting in. And people here are nice to me. I mean, now that I'm not in school. People in school sucked. But I get that I don't fit. And I'm tired of it. Honestly, I wouldn't care about my brothers if there wasn't so much…truth to the teasing."

"They do suck. They're awful. So why does it matter what they think?"

"Because," she said. "It just does. I'm that poor Anna Brown with no mom to teach her the right way to do things and I'm just…tired of it. I don't want to be poor Anna Brown. I want to be Anna Brown, heavy equipment mechanic who can wear coveralls and walk in heels."

"Not at the same time, I wouldn't think."

She shot him a deadly glare. "I don't fail," she said, her eyes glinting in the dim bar light. "I won't fail at this."

"You're not in remote danger of failing. Now, what's the mystery event that has you thinking about high heels?" he asked.

Copper Ridge wasn't exactly a societal epicenter. Nestled between the evergreen mountains and a steel-gray sea on the Oregon Coast, there were probably more deer than people in the small town. There were only so many events in existence. And there was a good chance she was making a mountain out of a small-town molehill, and none of it would be that big of a deal.

"That charity thing that the West family has every

year," she mumbled. "Gala Under the Stars or whatever."

The West family's annual fund-raising event for schools. It was a weekend event, with the town's top earners coming to a small black-tie get-together on the West property.

The McCormacks had been founding members of the community of Copper Ridge back in the 1800s. Their forge had been used by everyone in town and in the neighboring communities. But as the economy had changed, so had the success of the business.

They'd been hanging on by their fingernails when Chase's parents had been killed in an accident when he was in high school. They'd still gotten an invitation to the gala. But Chase had thrown it on top of the never-ending pile of mail and bills that he couldn't bring himself to look through and forgotten about it.

Until some woman—probably an assistant to the West family—had called him one year when he hadn't bothered to RSVP. He had been…well, he'd been less than polite.

Dealing with a damned crisis here, so sorry I can't go to your party.

Unsurprisingly, he hadn't gotten any invitations after that. And he hadn't really thought much about it since.

Until now.

He and Sam had managed to keep the operation and properties afloat, but he wanted more. He needed it.

The ranch had animals, but that wasn't the source of their income. The forge was the heart of the ranch, where they did premium custom metal- and leatherwork. On top of that, there were outbuildings on the property they rented out—including the shop they leased to Anna. They had built things back up since their parents had died, but it still wasn't enough, not to Chase.

He had promised his father he would take an interest in the family legacy. That he would build for the Mc-Cormacks, not just for himself. Chase had promised he wouldn't let his dad down. He'd had to make those promises at a grave site because before the accident he'd been a hotheaded jackass who'd thought he was too big for the family legacy.

But even if his father never knew, Chase had sworn it. And so he'd see it done.

In order to expand McCormack Iron Works, the heart and soul of their ranch, to bring it back to what it had been, they needed interest. Investments.

Chase had always had a good business mind, and early on he'd imagined he would go to school away from Copper Ridge. Get a degree. Find work in the city. Then everything had changed. Then it hadn't been about Chase McCormack anymore. It had been about the McCormack legacy.

School had become out of the question. Leaving had been out of the question. But now he saw where he and Sam were failing, and he could see how to turn the tide.

He'd spent a lot of late nights figuring out exactly how to expand as the demand for handmade items had gone down. Finding ways to convince people that highly customized iron details for homes and businesses, and handmade leather bridles and saddles, were worth paying more for.

Finding ways to push harder, to innovate and modernize while staying true to the family name. While actively butting up against Sam and his refusal to go out and make that happen. Sam, who was so talented he didn't have to pound horseshoe nails if he didn't want

TAKE ME, COWBOY

to. Sam, who could forget gates and scrollwork on stair-
cases and be selling his artwork for a small fortune.
Sam, who resisted change like it was the black plague.

He would kill for an invitation to the Wests' event.
Well, not kill. But possibly engage in nefarious activities or the trading of sexual favors. And Anna had an
invitation.

"You get to bring a date?" he asked.

"That's what I've been saying," she said. "Of course,
it all depends on whether or not I can actually acquire
one."

Anna needed a date; he wanted to have a chance
to talk to Nathan West. In the grand tradition of their
friendship, they both filled the gaps in each other's
lives. This was—in his opinion—perfect.

"I'll be your date," he said.

She snorted. "Yeah, right. Daniel and Mark will
never believe that."

She had a point. The two of them had been friends
forever. And with a bet on the table her brothers would
never believe that he had suddenly decided to go out
with her because his feelings had randomly changed.

"Okay. Maybe that's true." That frown was back.
"Not because there's something wrong with you," he
continued, trying to dig himself out of the pit he'd just
thrown himself into, "but because it's a little too convenient."

"Okay, that's better."

"But what if we made it clear that things had changed
between us?"

"What do you mean?"

"I mean…what if…we built up the change? Showed
people that our relationship was evolving."

She gave him a fierce side-eye. "I'm not your type."

He thought back to the blonde he'd been talking to only twenty minutes earlier. Tight dress cut up to the tops of her thighs, long, wavy hair and the kind of smile that invited you right on in. Curves that had probably wrecked more men than windy Highway 101. She was his type.

And she wasn't Anna. Barefaced, scowling with a figure that was slightly more…subtle. He cleared his throat. "You could be. A little less grease, a little more lipstick."

Her top lip curled. "So the ninth circle of hell basically."

"What were you planning on wearing to the fund-raiser?"

She shifted uncomfortably in her seat. "I have black jeans. But…I mean, I guess I could go to the mall in Tolowa and get a dress."

"That isn't going to work."

"Why not?"

"What kind of dress would you buy?" he asked.

"Something floral? Kind of…down to the knee?"

He pinched the bridge of his nose. "You're not Scarlett O'Hara," he said, knowing that with her love of old movies, Anna would appreciate the reference. "You aren't going dressed in the drapes."

Anna scowled. "Why the hell do you know so much about women's clothes?"

"Because I spend a lot of time taking them off my dates."

That shut her up. Her pale cheeks flamed and she looked away from him, and that response stirred…well, it stirred something in his gut he wished would go the hell away.

"Why do *you* want to go anyway?" she asked, still not looking at him.

"I want to talk to Nathan West and the other businessmen there about investment opportunities. I want to prove that Sam and I are the kind of people that can move in their circles. The kind of people they want to do business with."

"And you have to put on a suit and hobnob at a gala to do that?"

"The fact is, I don't get chances like this very often, Anna. I didn't get an invitation. And I need one. Plus, if you take me, you'll win your bet."

"Unless Dan and Mark tell me you don't count."

"Loophole. If they never said you couldn't recruit a date, you're fine."

"It violates the spirit of the bet."

"It doesn't have to," he insisted. "Anyway, by the time I'm through with you, you'll be able to get any date you want."

She blinked. "Are you… Are you Henry Higgins-ing me?"

He had only a vague knowledge of the old movie *My Fair Lady*, but he was pretty sure that was the reference. A man who took a grubby flower girl and turned her into the talk of the town. "Yes," he said thoughtfully. "Yes, I am. Take me up on this, Anna Brown, and I will turn you into a woman."

CHAPTER TWO

ANNA JUST ABOUT laughed herself off her chair. "You're going to make me a…a…a woman?"

"Why is that funny?"

"What about it *isn't* funny?"

"I'm offering to help you."

"You're offering to help me be something that I am by birth. I mean, Chase, I get that women are kind of your thing, but that's pretty arrogant. Even with all things considered."

"Okay, obviously I'm not going to make you a woman." Something about the way he said the phrase this time hit her in an entirely different way. Made her think about *other* applications that phrase occasionally had. Things she needed to never, ever, ever, ever think about in connection with Chase.

If she valued her sanity and their friendship.

She cleared her throat, suddenly aware that it was dry and scratchy. "Obviously."

"I just meant that you need help getting a date, and I need to go to this party. And you said that you were concerned about your appearance in the community."

"Right." He wasn't wrong. The thing was, she knew that whether or not she could blend in at an event like this didn't matter at all to how well her business did. Nobody cared if their mechanic knew which shade of lipstick she should wear. But that wasn't the point.

She—her family collectively—was the town charity case. Living on the edge of the community in a run-down house, raised by a single father who was in over his head, who spent his days at the mill. Her older brothers had been in charge of taking care of her, and they had done so. But, of course, they were also older brothers. Which meant they had tormented her while feeding and clothing her. Anyway, she didn't exactly blame them.

It wasn't like the two of them had wanted to raise a sister when they would rather be out raising hell.

Especially a sister who was committed to driving them crazy.

She loved her brothers. But that didn't mean they always had an easy relationship. It didn't mean they didn't hurt her by accident when they teased her about things. She acted invulnerable, so they assumed that she was.

But now, beneath her coveralls and engine grease, she was starting to feel a little bit battered. It was difficult to walk around with a *screw you* attitude barely covering a raw wound. Because eventually that shield started to wear down. Especially when people were used to being able to lob pretty intense rocks at that shield.

That was her life. It was either pity or a kind of merciless camaraderie that had no softness to it. Her dad, her brothers, all the guy friends she had…

And she couldn't really blame them. She had never behaved in a way that would demonstrate she needed any softness. In fact, a few months ago, a few weeks ago even, the idea would have been unthinkable to her.

But there was something about this invitation. Something about imagining herself in yet another situation where she was forced to deflect good-natured comments about her appearance, about the fact that she was more like a guy than the roughest cowboys in town. Yeah, there was something about that thought that had made her want to curl into a ball and never unfurl.

Then, even if it was unintentional, her brothers had piled on. It had hurt her feelings. Which meant she had reacted in anger, naturally. So now she had a bet. A bet, and her best friend looking at her with laser focus after having just promised he would make her a woman.

"Why do you care?" He was pressing, and she wanted to hit him now.

Which kind of summed up why she was in this position in the first place.

She swallowed hard. "Maybe I just want to surprise people. Isn't that enough?"

"You came from nothing. You started your own business with no support from your father. You're a female mechanic. I would say that you're surprising as hell."

"Well, I want to add another dimension to that. Okay?"

"Okay," he said. "Multidimensional Anna. That seems like a good idea to me."

"Where do we start?"

"With you not falling off your chair laughing at me because I've offered to make you a woman."

A giggle rose in her throat again. Hysteria. She was verging on hysteria. Because this was uncomfortable and sincere. She hated both of those things. "I'm sorry. I can't. You can't say that to me and expect me not to choke."

He looked at her again, his dark eyes intense. "Is it a problem, Anna? The idea that I might make you a woman."

He purposefully made his voice deeper. Purposefully added a kind of provocative inflection to the words. She knew he was kidding. Still, it made her chest tighten. Made her heart flutter a little bit.

Wow. How *annoying*. She hadn't had a relapse of Chase Underpants Feelings this bad in a long time.

Apparently she still hadn't recovered from her earlier bit of mistaken identity. She really needed to recover. And he needed to stop being…Chase. If at all possible.

"Is it a problem for *you*?" she asked.

"What?"

"The idea that I might make you a soprano?"

He chuckled. "You probably want to hold off on threats of castration when you're at a fancy party."

"We aren't at one right now."

She was her own worst enemy. Everything that she had just been silently complaining about, she was doing right now. Throwing out barbs the moment she got uncomfortable, because it kept people from seeing what was actually happening inside of her.

Yes, but you really need to keep Chase from seeing that you fluttered internally over something he said.

Yes. Good point.

She noticed that he was looking past her now, and she followed his line of sight. He was looking at that blonde again. "Regrets, Chase?"

He winced, looking back at her. "No."

"So. I assume that to get a guy to come up and hit on me in a bar, I have to put on a dress that is essentially a red ACE bandage sprinkled with glitter?"

He hesitated. "It's more than that."

"What?"

"Well, for a start, there's not looking at a man like you want to dismember him."

She rolled her eyes. "I don't."

"You aren't exactly approachable, Anna."

"That isn't true." She liked to play darts, and hang out, and talk about sports. What wasn't approachable about that?

"I've seen men try to talk to you," Chase continued. "You shut them down pretty quick. For example—" he barreled on before she could interrupt him "—Ace Thompson paid you a compliment back at the bar."

"Ace Thompson compliments everything with boobs."

"And a couple of weeks ago there was a guy in here that tried to buy you a drink. You told him you could buy your own."

"I *can*," she said, "and he was a stranger."

"He was flirting with you."

She thought back on that night, that guy. *Damn*. He had been flirting. "Well, he should get better at it. I'm not going to reward mediocrity. If I can't tell you're flirting, you aren't doing a very good job."

"Part of the problem is you don't think male attention is being directed at you when it actually is."

She looked back over at the shimmery blonde. "Why would any male attention be directed at me when *that's* over there?"

Chase leaned in, his expression taking on a conspiratorial quality that did…things to her insides. "Here's the thing about a girl like that. She knows she looks good. She assumes that men are looking at her. She assumes that if a man talks to her, that means he wants her."

She took a breath, trying to ease the tightness in her chest. "And that's not…a turnoff?"

"No way." He smiled, a sort of lazy half smile. "Confidence is sexy."

He kind of proved that rule. The thought made her bristle.

"All right. So far with our lessons I've learned that

I should unzip my coveralls and as long as I'm confident it will be okay."

"You forgot not looking like you want to stab someone."

"Okay. Confident, nonstabby, showing my boobs."

Chase choked on his beer. "That's a good place to start," he said, setting the bottle down. "Do you want to go play darts? I want to go play darts."

"I thought we were having female lessons."

"Rain check," he said. "How about tomorrow I come by the shop and we get started. I think I'm going to need a lesson plan."

CHASE HADN'T EXACTLY excelled in school, unless it was at driving his teachers to drink. So why exactly he had decided he needed a lesson plan to teach Anna how to be a woman, he didn't know.

All he knew was that somewhere around the time they started discussing her boobs last night he had become unable to process thoughts normally. He didn't like that. He didn't like it at all. He did not like the fact that he had been forced to consider her breasts more than once in a single hour. He did not like the fact that he was facing down the possibility of thinking about them a few more times over the next few weeks.

But then, that was the game.

Not only was he teaching her how to blend in at a function like this, he was pretending to be her date.

So there was more than one level of hell to deal with. Perfect.

He cleared his throat, walking down the front porch of the farmhouse that he shared with his brother, making his way across the property toward the shop that Anna was renting and using as her business.

It was after five, so she should be knocking off by now. A good time for the two of them to meet.

He looked down at the piece of lined yellow paper in his hand. His lesson plan.

Then he pressed on, his boots crunching on the gravel as he made his way to the rustic wood building. He inhaled deeply, the last gasp of winter riding over the top of the spring air, mixing with the salt from the sea, giving it a crisp bite unique to Copper Ridge.

He relished this. The small moment of clarity before he dived right into the craziness that was his current situation.

Chase McCormack was many things, but he wasn't a coward. He was hardly going to get skittish over giving his best friend some seduction lessons.

He pushed the door open but didn't see Anna anywhere.

He looked around the room, and the dismembered tractors whose various parts weren't in any order that he could possibly define. Though he knew that it must make sense to Anna.

"Hello?"

"Just up here."

He turned, looked up and saw Anna leaning over what used to be a hayloft, looking down at him, a long dark braid hanging down.

"What exactly are you doing up there?"

"I stashed a tool up here, and now I need it. It's good storage. Of course, then I end up climbing the walls a little more often than I would like. Literally. Not figuratively."

"I figured you would be finished for the day by now."

"No. I have to get this tractor fixed for Connor Garrett. And it's been a bigger job than I thought." She disappeared from view for a moment. "But I would like a reputation as someone who makes miracles. So I better make miracles."

She planted her boot hard on the first rung of the ladder and began to climb down. She was covered from head to toe in motor oil and dust. Probably from crawling around in this space, and beneath tractors.

She jumped down past the last three rungs, brushing dirt off her thighs and leaving more behind, since her hands were coated, too. "You don't exactly look like a miracle," he said, looking her over.

She held up her hand, then displayed her middle finger. "Consider it a miracle that I don't punch you."

"Remember what we talked about? Not looking at a guy like you want to stab him? Much less threatening actual bodily harm."

"Hey, I don't think you would tell a woman that you actually wanted to hook up with that she didn't look like a miracle."

"Most women I want to hook up with aren't quite this disheveled. Before we start anyway."

Much to his surprise, color flooded her cheeks.

"Well," she said, her voice betraying nothing, "I'm not most women, Chase McCormack. I thought you would've known that by now."

Then she sauntered past him, wearing those ridiculous baggy coveralls, head held high like she was queen of the dust bowl.

"Oh, I'm well aware of that," he said. "That's part of the problem."

"And now it's your problem to fix."

"That's right. And I have the lesson plan. As promised."

She whipped around to face him, one dark brow lifted. "Oh, really?"

"Yes, really." He held up the lined notepaper.

"That's very professional."

"It's as professional as you're gonna get. Now, the first order of business is to plant the seed that we're more than friends."

She looked as though he had just suggested she eat a handful of bees. "Do we really need to do that?"

"Yeah, we *really* need to do that. You won't just have a date for the charity event. You're going to have a date every so often until then."

She looked skeptical. "That seems...excessive."

"You want people to believe this. You don't want people to think I'm going because of a bet. You don't want your brothers to think for one moment that they might be right."

"Well, they're going to think it for a few moments at least."

"True. I mean, they are going to be suspicious. But we can make this look real. It isn't going to be that hard. We already hang out most weekends."

"Sure," she said, "but you go home with other girls at the end of the night."

Those words struck him down. "Yes, I guess I do."

"You won't be able to do that now," she pointed out.

"Why not?" he asked.

"Because if I were with you and you went home with another woman, I would castrate you with nothing but my car keys and a bottle of whiskey."

He had no doubt about that. "At least you'd give me some whiskey."

"Hell no. The whiskey would be for me."

"But we're not really together," he said.

"Sure, Chase, but the entire town knows that if any man were to cheat on me, I would castrate him with my car keys, because I don't take crap from anyone. So if they're going to believe that we're together, you're going to have to look like you're being faithful to me."

"That's fine." It wasn't all that fine. He didn't do celibacy. Never had. Not from the moment he'd discovered that women were God's greatest invention.

"No booty calls," she said, her tone stern.

"Wait a second. I can't even call a woman to hook up in private?"

"No. You can't. Because then *she* would know. I have pride. I mean, right now, standing here in this garage taking lessons from you on how to conform to my own gender's beauty standards, it's definitely marginal, but I have it."

"It isn't like you really know any of the girls that I…"

"Neither do you," she said.

"This isn't about me. It's about you. Now, I got you some things. But I left them in the house. And you are going to have to…hose off before you put them on."

She blinked, her expression almost comical. "Did you buy me clothes?"

He'd taken a long lunch and gone down to Main Street, popping into one of the ridiculously expensive shops that—in his mind—were mostly for tourists, and had found her a dress he thought would work.

"Yeah, I bought you clothes. Because we both know you can't actually wear this out tonight."

"We're going out *tonight*?"

"Hell yeah. I'm taking you somewhere fancy."

"My fancy threshold is very low. If I have to go eat tiny food on a stick sometime next month, I'm going to need actual sustenance in every other meal until then."

He chuckled, trying to imagine Anna coping with miniature food. "Beaches. I'm taking you to Beaches."

She screwed up her face slightly. "We don't go there."

"No, we haven't gone there. We go to Ace's. We shoot pool, we order fried crap and we split the tab. Because we're friends. And that's what friends do. Friends don't go out to Beaches, not just the two of them. But lovers do."

She looked at him owlishly. "Right. I suppose they do."

"And when all this is finished, the entire town of Copper Ridge is going to think that we're lovers."

CHAPTER THREE

ANNA WAS REELING slightly by the time she walked up the front porch and into Chase's house. The entire town was going to think that they were...*lovers*. She had never had a lover. At least, she would never characterize the guy she'd slept with as a lover. He was an unfortunate incident. But fortunately, her hymen was the only casualty. Her heart had remained intact, and she was otherwise uninjured. Or pleasured.

Lovers.

That word sounded...well, like it came from some old movie or something. Which under normal circumstances she was a big fan of. In this circumstance, it just made her feel...like her insides were vibrating. She didn't like it.

Chase lived in the old family home on the property. It was a large, log cabin–style house with warm, honey-colored wood and a green metal roof designed to withstand all kinds of weather. Wrought-iron details on the porch and the door were a testament to his and Sam's craftsmanship. There were people who would pay millions for a home like this. But Sam and Chase had made it this beautiful on their own.

Chase always kept the home admirably clean considering he was a bachelor. She imagined that the other house on the property, the smaller one inhabited by Sam, wasn't quite as well kept. But she also imagined that Sam didn't have the same amount of guests over that Chase did. And by *guests*, she meant female companions. Which he would be cut off from for the next few weeks.

Some small, mean part of her took a little bit of joy in that.

Because you don't like the idea of other women touching him. It doesn't matter how long it's been going on, or how many women there are, you still don't like it.

She sniffed, cutting off that line of thinking. She was just a crabby bitch who was enjoying the idea of him being celibate and suffering a bit. That was all.

"Okay, where are my...girlie things?"

"You aren't even going to look at them until you scrub that grease off."

"And how am I supposed to do that? Are you going to hose me off?"

He clenched his jaw. "No. You can use my shower."

She took a deep breath, trying to dispel the slight fluttering in her stomach. She had never used Chase's shower before. She assumed countless women before her had. When he brought them up here, took their clothes off for them. And probably joined them.

She wasn't going to think about that.

"Okay."

She knew where his shower was, of course. Because she had been inside his bedroom casually, countless times. It had never mattered before. Before, she had never been about to get naked.

She banished that thought as she walked up the stairs and down the hall to his room. His room was...well, it was very well-appointed, but then again, obviously designed to house guests of the female variety. The bed was large and full of plush pillows. A soft-looking green throw was folded up at the foot of it. An over-stuffed chair was in the corner, another blanket draped over the back.

She doubted the explosion of comfort and cozy was for Chase's benefit.

She tamped that thought down, continuing on through the bathroom door, then locking it for good measure. Not that he would walk in. And he was the only person in the house.

Still, she felt insecure without the lock flipped. She took a deep breath, stripped off her coveralls, then the clothes she had on beneath them, and started the shower. Speaking of things that were designed to be shared...

It was enclosed in glass, and she had a feeling that with the door open it was right in the line of sight from the bed. Inside was red tile, and a bench seat that... She wasn't even going to think what that could be used for.

She turned and looked in the mirror. She was grubby. More than grubby. She had grease all over her face, all up under her fingernails.

Thankfully, Chase had some orange-and-pumice cleaner right there on his sink. So she was able to start scrubbing at her hands while the water warmed up.

Steam filled the air and she stepped inside the shower, letting the hot spray cascade over her skin.

It was a *massaging* showerhead. A nice one. She did not have a nice massaging showerhead in her little rental house down in town. Next on her list of Ways She Was Changing Her Life would be to get her own house. With one of these.

She rolled her shoulders beneath the spray and sighed. The water droplets almost felt like fingers moving over her tight muscles. And, suddenly, it was all too easy to imagine a man standing behind her, working at her muscles with his strong hands.

She closed her eyes, letting her head fall back, her mouth going slack. She didn't even have the strength to fight the fantasy, God help her. She'd been edgy and aroused for the past twenty-four hours, no denying it. So this little moment to let herself fantasize…she just needed it.

Then she realized exactly whose hands she was picturing.

Chase's. Tall and strong behind her, his hands moving over her skin, down lower to the slight dip in her spine, just above the curve of her behind…

She grabbed hold of the sponge hanging behind her and began to drag it ferociously over her skin, only belatedly realizing that this was probably what he used to wash himself.

"He uses it to wash his balls," she said into the space. Hoping that that would disgust her. It really should disgust her.

It did not disgust her.

She put the scrubber back, taking a little shower gel and squeezing it into the palm of her hand. Okay, so she would smell like a playboy for a day. It wasn't the end of the world. She started to rub the slick soap over her flesh, ignoring the images of Chase that were trying to intrude.

She was being a crazy person. She had showered at friends' houses before, and never imagined that they were in the shower stall with her.

But ever since last night in the bar, her equilibrium had been off where Chase was concerned. Her control was being sorely tested. She was decidedly unstoked about it.

She shut the water off and got out of the shower, grabbing a towel off the rack and drying her skin with more ferocity than was strictly necessary. Almost as though she was trying to punish her wicked, wicked skin for imagining what it might be like to be touched by her best friend.

But that would be crazy.

Except she felt a little crazy.

She looked around the room. And realized that her stupid friend, who had not wanted her to touch the nice clothing he had bought her, had left her without anything to wear. She couldn't put her sweaty, grease-covered clothes back on. That would negate the entire shower.

She let out an exasperated breath, not entirely certain what she should do.

"Chase?" she called.

She didn't hear anything.

"Chase?" She raised the volume this time.

Still no answer.

"Butthead," she muttered, walking over to the door and tapping the doorknob, trying to decide what her next move was.

She was being ridiculous. Just because she was having an increase of weird, borderline sexual thoughts about him, did not mean he was having them about her. She twisted the knob, undoing the lock as she did, and opened the door a crack. "Chase!"

The door to the bedroom swung open, and Chase walked in, carrying one of those plastic bags fancy dresses were stored in and a pair of shoes.

"I don't have clothes," she hissed through the crack in the door.

"Sorry," he said, looking stricken. At least, she thought he looked stricken.

She opened the door slightly wider, extending her arm outside. "Give them to me."

He crossed the room, walking over to the bathroom door. "You're going to have to open the door wider than that."

She already felt exposed. There was nothing between them. Nothing but some air and the towel she was clutching to her naked body. Well, and most of the door. But she still felt exposed.

Still, he was not going to fit that bag through the crack.

She opened the door slightly wider, then grabbed hold of the bag in his hand and jerked it back through. "I'll get the shoes later," she called through the door.

She dropped the towel and unzipped the bag, staring at the contents with no small amount of horror. There was…underwear inside of it. Underwear that Chase had purchased for her.

Which meant he had somehow managed to look at her breasts and evaluate their size. Not to mention her ass. And ass size.

She grabbed the pair of panties that were attached to a little hanger. Oh, they had no ass. So she supposed the size of hers didn't matter much.

She swallowed hard, taking hold of the soft material and rubbing her thumb over it. He would know exactly what she was wearing beneath the dress. Would know just how little that was.

He isn't going to think about it. Because he doesn't think about you that way.

He never had. He never would. And it was a damn

good thing. Because where would they be if either of them acted on an attraction between them?

Up shit creek without a paddle or a friendship.

No, thank you. She was never going to touch him. She'd made that decision a long time ago. For a lot of reasons that were as valid today as they had been the very first time he'd ever made her stomach jump when she looked at him.

She was never going to encourage or act on the attraction that she occasionally felt for Chase. But she would take his expertise in sexual politics and use it to her advantage.

Oh, but those panties.

The bra wasn't really any less unsettling. Though at least it wasn't missing large swathes of fabric.

Still, it was very thin. And she had a feeling that a cool ocean breeze would reveal the shape of her nipples to all and sundry.

Then again, maybe it was time all and sundry got a look at her nipples. Maybe if they had a better view, men would be a little more interested.

She scowled, wrenching the panties off the hanger and dragging them on as quickly as possible, followed closely by the bra. She was overthinking things. She was overthinking all of this. Had been from the moment Chase had walked into the barn. As evidenced by that lapse in the shower.

She had spent years honing her Chase Control. It was just this change in how they were interacting that was screwing with it. She was not letting this get inside her head, and she was not letting hot, unsettled feelings get inside her pants.

She pulled the garment bag away entirely, revealing

a tight red dress slightly too reminiscent of what the woman he had been flirting with last night was wearing.

"Clearly you have a type, Chase McCormack," she muttered, beginning to remove the slinky scrap of material from the hanger.

She tugged it up over her hips, having to do a pretty intense wiggle to get it up all the way before zipping it into place. She took a deep breath, turned around. She faced her reflection in the mirror full-on and felt nothing but deflated.

She looked…well, her hair was wet and straggly, and she looked half-drowned. She didn't look curvy, or shimmery, or delightful.

This was the problem with tight clothes. They only made her more aware of her curve deficit.

Where the blonde last night had filled her dress out admirably, and in all the right places, on Anna this dress kind of looked like a piece of fabric stretched over an ironing board. Not really all that sexy.

She sighed heavily, trying to ignore the sinking feeling in her stomach.

Chase really was going to have to be a miracle worker in order to pull this off.

She didn't really want to show him. Instead, she found the idea of putting the coveralls back on a lot less reprehensible. At least with the coveralls there would still be some mystery. He wouldn't be confronted with just how big a task lay before him.

"Buck up," she said to herself.

So what was one more moment of feeling inadequate? Honestly, in the broad tapestry of her life it would barely register. She was never quite what was expected. She never quite fit. So why'd she expect that she was going to put on a sexy dress and suddenly be transformed into the kind of sex kitten she didn't even want to be?

She gritted her teeth, throwing open the bedroom door and walking out into the room. "I hope you're happy," she said, flinging her arms wide. "You get what you get."

She caught a movement out of the corner of her eye and turned her head, then recoiled in horror. It was even worse out here. Out here, there was a full-length mirror. Out here, she had the chance to see that while her breasts remained stunningly average, her hips and behind had gotten rather wide. Which was easy to ignore when you wore loose attire most days. "I look like the woman symbol on the door of a public restroom."

She looked over at Chase, who had been completely silent upon her entry into the room, and remained so. She glared at him. He wasn't saying anything. He was only staring. "Well?"

"It's nice," he said.

His voice sounded rough, and kind of thin.

"You're a liar."

"I'm not a liar. Put the shoes on."

"Do you even know what size I wear?"

"You're a size ten, which I know because you complain about how your big feet make it impossible for you to find anything in your size. And you're better off buying men's work boots. So yes, I know."

His words made her feel suddenly exposed. Well, his words in combination with the dress, she imagined. They knew each other a little bit too well. That was the problem. How could you impress a guy when you had spent a healthy amount of time bitching to him about your big feet?

"Fine. I will put on the shoes." He held them up,

and her jaw dropped. "I thought you were taking me out to dinner."

"I am."

"Do I have to pay for it by working the pole at the Naughty Mermaid?"

"These are *nice* shoes."

"If you're a five-foot-two-inch Barbie like that chick you were talking to last night. I'm like…an Amazon in comparison."

"You're not an Amazon."

"I will be in those."

"Maybe that would bother some men. But you want a man who knows how to handle a woman. Any guy with half a brain is going to lose his mind checking out your legs. He's not going to care if you're a little taller than he is."

She tried her best to ignore the compliment about her legs. And tried even harder to keep from blushing.

"I care," she muttered, snatching the shoes from his hand and pondering whether or not there was any truth to her words as she did.

She didn't really date. So it was hard to say. But now that she was thinking about it, yeah. She was self-conscious about the fact that with pretty low heels she was eye level with half the men in town.

She finished putting the shoes on and straightened. It was like standing on a glittery pair of stilts. "Are you satisfied?" she asked.

"I guess you could say that." He was regarding her closely, his jaw tense, a muscle in his cheek ticking.

She noticed that he was still a couple of inches taller than her. Even with the shoes. "I guess you still meet the height requirement to be my dinner date."

"I didn't have any doubt."

"I don't know how to walk in these," she said.

"All right. Practice."

"Are you out of your mind? I have to *practice* walking?"

"You said yourself, you don't know how to walk in heels. So, go on. Walk the length of the room."

She felt completely awash in humiliation. She doubted there was another woman on the planet that Chase had ever had to instruct on walking.

"This is ridiculous."

"It's not," he said.

"All of women's fashion is ridiculous," she maintained. "Do you have to learn how to walk when you put on dress shoes? No, you do not. And yet, a full-scale lesson is required for me to go out if I want to wear something that's considered *feminine*."

"Yeah, it's sexist. And a real pain in the ass, I'm sure. It's also hot. Now walk."

She scowled at him, then took her first step, wobbling a bit. "I don't understand why women do this."

She took another step, then another, wobbling a little less each time. But the shoes did force her hips to sway, much more than they normally would. "Do you have any pointers?" she asked.

"I date women in heels, Anna. *I've* never walked in them."

"What happened to helping me be a woman?"

"You'll get the hang of it. It's like…I don't know, water-skiing maybe?"

"How is this like water-skiing?"

"You have to learn how to do it and there's a good likelihood you'll fall on your face?"

"Well, I take it all back," she said, deadpan. "These

shoes aren't silly at all." She took another step, then another. "I feel like a newborn baby deer."

"You look a little like one, too."

She snorted. "You really need to up your game, Chase. If you use these lines on all the women you take out, you're bound to start striking out sooner or later."

"I haven't struck out yet."

"Well, you're still young and pretty. Just wait. Just wait until time starts to claim your muscular forearms and chiseled jawline."

"I figure by then maybe I'll have gotten the ranch back to its former glory. At that point women will sleep with me for my money."

She rolled her eyes. "It's nice to have goals."

In her opinion, Chase should have better goals for himself. But then, who was she to talk? Her current goal was to show her brothers that they were idiots and she could too get a date. Hardly a lofty ambition.

"Yes, it is. And right now my goal is for us not to miss our reservation."

"You made a…reservation?"

"I did."

"It's not like it's Valentine's Day or something. The restaurant isn't going to be full."

"Of course it won't be. But I figured if I made a reservation for the two of us, we could start a rumor, too."

"A rumor?"

"Yeah, because Ellie Matthews works at Beaches, and I believe she has been known to *service* your brother Mark."

Anna winced at the terminology. "True."

"I thought the news of our dining experience might make it back to him. Like I said, the more we can make this look organic, the better."

"No one ever need know that our relationship is in fact grown in a lab. And in no way GMO free," she said.

"Exactly."

"I don't have any makeup on." She frowned. "I don't have any makeup. At all."

"Right," he said. "I didn't really think of that."

She reached out and smacked him on the shoulder. "You're supposed to be my coach. You're failing me."

He laughed, dodging her next blow. "You don't need makeup."

She let out an exasperated sigh. "You're just saying that."

"In fairness, you did threaten to castrate me with your car keys earlier."

"I did."

"And you hit me just now," he pointed out.

"It didn't hurt, you baby."

He took a deep breath, and suddenly his expression turned sharp. "Believe me when I tell you you don't need makeup." He reached out, gripping her chin with his thumb and forefinger. His touch was like a branding iron, hot, altering. "As long as you believe it, everyone else will, too. You have to believe in yourself, Anna."

He released his hold on her, straightening. "Now," he said, his tone getting a little bit rougher, "let's go to dinner."

CHASE FELT LIKE he had been tipped sideways and left walking on the walls from the moment that Anna had emerged from the bathroom at his house wearing that dress. Once she had put on those shoes, the feeling had only gotten worse.

But who knew that underneath those coveralls his best friend looked like that?

She had been eyeing herself critically, and his brain had barely been working at all. Because he didn't see anything to criticize. All he saw was the kind of figure that would make a man willingly submit to car key castration.

She was long and lean, toned from all the physical labor she did. Her breasts were small, but he imagined they would fit in a man's hand nicely. And her hips... well, using the same measurement used for her breasts, they would be about perfect for holding on to while a man...

Holy hell. He was losing his mind.

She was Anna. Anna Brown, his best friend in the entire world. The one woman he had never even considered going there with. He didn't want a relationship with the women he slept with. When your only criteria for being with a woman was orgasm, there were a lot of options available to you. For a little bit of satisfaction he could basically seek out any woman in the room.

Sex was easy. Connections were hard.

And so Anna had been placed firmly off-limits from day one. He'd had a vague awareness of her for most of his life. That was how growing up in a small town worked. You went to the same school from the beginning. But they had separate classes, plus at the time he'd been pretty convinced girls had cooties.

But that had changed their first year of high school. He'd ended up in metal shop with the prickly teen and had liked her right away. There weren't very many girls who cursed as much as the boys and had a more comprehensive understanding of the inner workings of engines than the teachers at the school. But Anna did.

She hadn't fit in with any of the girls, and so Chase and Sam had been quick to bring her into their group.

Over the years, people had rotated in and out, moved, gone their separate ways. But Chase and Anna had remained close.

In part because he had kept his dick out of the equation.

As they walked up the path toward Beaches, he considered putting his hand on her lower back. Really, he should. Except it was potentially problematic at the moment. Was he this shallow? Stick her in a tight-fitting dress and suddenly he couldn't control himself? It was a sobering realization, but not really all that surprising.

This was what happened when you spent a lot of time practicing no restraint when it came to sex.

He gritted his teeth, lifting his hand for a moment before placing it gently on her back. Because it was what he would do with any other date, so it was what he needed to do with Anna.

She went stiff beneath his touch. "Relax," he said, keeping his voice low. "This is supposed to look like a date, remember?"

"I should have worn a white tank top and a pair of jeans," she said.

"Why?"

"Because this looks… It looks like I'm trying too hard."

"No, it looks like you put on a nice outfit to please me."

She turned to face him, her brow furrowed. "Which is part of the problem. If I had to do this to please you, we both know that I would tell you to please yourself."

He laughed, the moment so classically Anna, so familiar, it was at odds with the other feelings that were buzzing through his blood. With how soft she felt beneath his touch. With just how much she was affecting him in this figure-hugging dress.

"I have no doubt you would."

They walked up the steps that led into the large white restaurant, and he opened the door, holding it for her. She looked at him like he'd just caught fire. He stared her down, and then she looked away from him, walking through the door.

He moved up next to her once they were inside. "You're going to have to seem a little more at ease with this change in our relationship."

"You're being weird."

"I'm not being weird. I'm treating you like a lady."

"What have you been treating me like for the past fifteen years?" she asked.

"A…bro."

She snorted, shaking her head and walking toward the front of the house where Ellie Matthews was standing, waiting for guests. "I believe we have a reservation," Anna said.

He let out a long-suffering sigh. "Yes," he confirmed. "Under my name."

Ellie's eyebrow shot upward. "Yes. You do."

"Under Chase McCormack and Anna Brown," Chase clarified.

"I know," she said.

Ellie needed to work on her people skills. "It was difficult for me to tell, since you look so surprised," Chase said.

"Well, I knew you were reserving the table for the two of you, but I didn't realize you were…reserving the table for *the two of you*." She was looking at Anna's dress, her expression meaningful.

"Well, I was," he said. "Did. So, is the table ready?"

She looked around the half-full dining area. "Yeah, I'm pretty sure we can seat you now."

Ellie walked them over to one of the tables by a

side window that looked out over the Skokomish River where it fed into the ocean. The sun was dipping low over the water, the rays sparkling off the still surface of the slow-moving river. There were people milling along the wooden boardwalk that was bordered by docks on one side and storefronts on the other, before being split by the highway and starting again, leading down to the beach.

He looked away from the scenery, back at Anna. They had shared countless meals together, but this was different. Normally, they didn't sit across from each other at a tiny table complete with a freaking candle in the middle. Mood lighting.

"Your server will be with you shortly," Ellie said as she walked away, leaving them there with menus and each other.

"I want a burger," Anna said, not looking at the menu at all.

"You could get something fancier."

"I'll get it with a cheese I can't pronounce."

"I'm getting salmon."

"Am I paying?" she asked, an impish smile playing around the corners of her lips. "Because if so, you better be putting out at the end of this."

Her words were like a punch in the gut. And he did his best to ignore them. He swallowed hard. "No, *I'm* paying."

"I'll pay you back after. You're doing me a favor."

"The favor's mutual. I want to go to the fund-raiser. It's important to me."

"You still aren't buying my dinner."

"I'm not taking your money."

"Then I'm going to overpay for rent on the shop next month," she said, her tone uncompromising.

"Half of that goes to Sam."

"Then he gets half of it. But I'm not going to let you buy my dinner."

"You're being stubborn."

She leaned back in her chair, crossing her arms and treating him to that hard glare of hers. "Yep."

A few moments later the waiter came over, and Anna ordered her hamburger, and the cheeses she wanted, by pointing at the menu.

"Which cheese did you get?" he asked, attempting to move on from their earlier standoff.

"I don't know." She shrugged. "I can't pronounce it."

They made about ten minutes of awkward conversation while they waited for their dinner to come. Which was weird, because conversation was never awkward with Anna. It was that dress. And those shoes. And his penis. That was part of the problem. Because, suddenly, it was actually interested in his best friend.

No, it is not. A moment of checking her out does not mean that you want to...do anything with her.

Exactly. It wasn't a big deal. It wasn't anything to get worked up about. Not at all.

When their dinner was placed in front of them, Anna attacked her sweet potato fries, probably using them as a displacement activity.

"Chase?"

Chase looked up and inwardly groaned when he saw Wendy Maxwell headed toward the table. They'd all gone to high school together. And he had, regrettably, slept with Wendy once or twice over the years after drinking too much at Ace's.

She was hot. But what she had in looks had been deducted from her personality. Which didn't matter when you were only having sex, but mattered later when you had to interact in public.

"Hi, Wendy," he said, taking a bite of his salmon.

Anna had gone very still across from him; she wasn't even eating her fries anymore.

"Are you… Are you on a date?" Wendy asked, tilting her head to the side, her expression incredulous.

Wendy wasn't very smart in addition to being not very nice. A really bad combination.

"Yes," he said, "I am."

"With Anna?"

"Yeah," Anna said, looking up. "The person sitting across from him. Like you do on a date."

"I'm just surprised."

He could see color mounting in Anna's cheeks, could see her losing her hold on her temper.

"Are you here by yourself?" Anna asked.

Wendy laughed, the sound like broken crystal being pushed beneath his skin. "No. Of course not. We're having a girls' night out." She eyed Chase. "Of course, that doesn't mean I'm going home with the girls."

Suddenly, Anna was standing, and he was a little bit afraid she was about to deck Wendy. Who deserved it. But he didn't really want to be at the center of a girl fight in the middle of Beaches.

That only worked in fantasies. Less so in real life.

But it wasn't Wendy whom Anna moved toward.

She took two steps, came to a stop in front of Chase and then leaned forward, grabbing hold of the back of his chair and resting her knee next to his thigh. Then she pressed her hand to his cheek and took a deep breath, making determined eye contact with him just before she let her lids flutter closed. Just before she closed the distance between them and kissed him.

CHAPTER FOUR

SHE WAS KISSING Chase McCormack. Beyond that, she had no idea what the flying F-bomb she was doing. If there was another person in the room, she didn't see them. If there was a reason she'd started this, she didn't remember it.

There was nothing. Nothing more than the hot press of Chase's lips against hers. Nothing more than still, leashed power beneath her touch. She could feel his tension, could feel his strength frozen beneath her.

It was…intoxicating. Empowering.

So damn *hot*.

Like she was about to melt the soles of her shoes hot. About to come without his hands ever touching her body hot.

And that was unheard-of for her.

She'd kissed a couple of guys, and slept with one, and orgasm had never been in the cards. When it came to climaxes, she was her own hero. But damn if Chase wasn't about to be her hero in under thirty seconds, and with nothing more than a little dry lip-to-lip contact.

Except it didn't stay dry.

Suddenly, he reached up, curling his fingers around the back of her head, angling his own and kissing her hard, deep. With tongue.

She whimpered, the leg that was supporting her body melting, only the firm hold he had on her face, and the support of his chair, keeping her from sliding onto the ground.

The slick glide of his tongue against hers was the single sexiest thing she'd ever experienced in her life. And just like that, every little white lie she'd ever told herself about her attraction to Chase was completely and fully revealed.

It wasn't just a momentary response to an attractive man. Not something any red-blooded female would feel. Not just a passing anomaly.

It was real.

It was deep.

She was so screwed.

Way too screwed to care that they were making out in a fancy restaurant in front of people, and that for him it was just a show, but for her it was a whole cataclysmic, near-orgasmic shift happening in the region of her panties.

Seconds had passed, but they felt like minutes. Hours. Whole days' worth of life-changing moments, all crammed into something that probably hadn't actually lasted longer than the blink of an eye.

Then it was over. She was the one who pulled away and she wasn't quite sure how she managed. But she did.

She wasn't breathing right. Her entire body was shaking, and she was sure her face was red. But still, she turned and faced Wendy, or whichever mean girl it was. There were a ton of them in her non-halcyon high school years and they all blended together. The who wasn't important. Only the what. The *what* being a kiss she'd just given to the hottest guy in town, right in front of someone who didn't think she was good enough. Pretty enough. Girlie enough.

"Yeah," she said, her voice a little less triumphant

and a lot more unsteady than she would like, "we're here on a date. And he's going home with me. So I'd suggest you wiggle on over to a different table if you want to score tonight."

Wendy's face was scrunched into a sour expression. "That's okay, honey, if you want my leftovers, you're welcome to them."

Then she flipped her blond hair and walked back to her table, essentially acting out the cliché of every snotty girl in a teen movie.

Which was not so cute when you were thirty and not fifteen.

But, of course, since Wendy was gone, they'd lost the buffer against the aftermath of the kiss, and the terrible awkwardness that was just sitting there, seething, growing.

"Well, I think that started some rumors," Anna said, sitting back down and shoving a fry into her mouth.

"I bet," Chase said, clearing his throat and turning back toward his plate.

"My mouth has never touched your mouth directly before," she said, then stuffed another fry straight into her mouth, wishing it wasn't too late to stifle those ridiculous words.

He choked on his beer. "Um. No."

"What I mean is, we've shared drinks before. I've taken bites off your sandwiches. Literally sandwiches, not— I mean, whatever. The point is, we've germ-shared before. We just never did it mouth-to-mouth."

"That wasn't CPR, babe."

She made a face, hoping the disgust in her expression would disguise the twist low and deep in her stomach. "Don't call me babe just because I kissed you."

"We're dating, remember?"

"No one is listening to us talk at the table," she insisted.

"You don't know that."

Her heart was thundering hard like a trapped bird in her chest and she didn't know if she could look at him for another minute without either scurrying from the room like a frightened animal or grabbing him and kissing him again.

She didn't like it. She didn't like any of it.

It all felt too real, too raw and too scary. It all came from a place too deep inside her.

So she decided to do what came easiest. Exactly what she did best.

"I expected better," she told him, before taking a bite of her burger.

"What?"

"You're like a legendary stud," she said, after swallowing her food. "The man who every man wants to be and who every woman wants to be with. Blah, blah." She picked up another sweet potato fry.

"It wasn't good for you?" he asked.

"Six point five from the German judge. Who is me, in this scenario." She was a liar. She was a liar and she was a jerk, and she wanted to punch her own face. But the alternative was to show that she was breaking apart inside. That she had been on the verge of the kind of ecstasy she'd only ever imagined, and that she wanted to kiss him forever, not just for thirty seconds. And that was…damaging. It wasn't something she could admit.

"Six point five."

"Sorry." She lifted her shoulder and shoved the fry into her mouth.

They finished the rest of the dinner in awkward silence, which made her mad because things weren't supposed to be awkward between them. They were friends, dammit. She was starting to think this whole thing was a mistake.

She could bring Chase as her plus one to the charity thing without her brothers buying into it. She could lose the bet. The whole town could suspect she'd brought a friend because she was undatable and who even cared?

If playing this game was going to screw with their friendship, it wasn't worth it.

Chase paid the tab—she was going to pay the bastard back whether he wanted her to or not—and then the two of them walked outside. And that was when she realized her truck was back at his place and he was going to have to give her a ride.

That sucked donkey balls. She needed to get some Chase space. And it wasn't going to happen.

She wanted to go home and put on soft pajamas and watch *Seven Brides for Seven Brothers*. She needed a safe, flannel-lined space and the fuzzy comfort of an old movie. A chance to breathe and be vulnerable for a second where no one would see.

She was afraid Chase might have seen already.

They still didn't talk—all the way back out of town and to the McCormack family ranch, they didn't talk.

"My dirty clothes are in your house," she said at last, when they pulled into the driveway. "You can take me to the house first instead of the shop."

"I can wash them with mine," he said.

Her underwear was in there. That was not happening.

"No, I left them folded in the corner of the bathroom. I'd rather come get them. And put my shoes on before I try to drive home actually. How do people drive in these?" She tapped the precarious shoes against the floor of the pickup.

Chase let out a harsh-sounding breath. "Fine," he said. He sounded aggrieved, but he drove on past the shop to the house. He stopped the truck abruptly, throwing it into Park and killing the engine. "Come on in."

Now he was mad at her. Great. It wasn't like he needed her to stroke his ego. He had countless women to do that. He had just one woman who listened to his bullshit and put up with all his nonsense, and in general stood by him no matter what. That was her. He could have endless praise for his bedroom skills from those other women. He only had friendship from *her*. So he could simmer down a little.

She got out of the truck, then wobbled when her foot hit a loose gravel patch. She clung tightly to the door, a very wussy-sounding squeak escaping her lips.

"You okay there, *babe*?" he asked, just to piss her off.

"Yeah, fine. Jerk," she retorted.

"What the hell, Anna?" he asked, his tone hard.

"Oh, come on, you're being weird. You can't pretend you aren't just because you're layering passivity over your aggression." She stalked past him as fast as her shoes would let her, walked up the porch and stood by the door, her arms crossed.

"It's not locked," he said, taking the stairs two at a time.

"Well, I wasn't going to go in without your permission. I have manners."

"Do you?" he asked.

"If I didn't, I probably would have punched you by now." She opened the door and stomped up the stairs, until her heel rolled inward slightly and she stumbled. Then she stopped stomping and started taking a little more consideration for her joints.

She was mad at him. She was mad at herself for

being mad at him, because the situation was mostly her fault. And she was mad at him for being mad at her for being mad at him.

Mad, mad, *mad*.

She walked into the bathroom and picked up her stack of clothes, careful not to hold the greasy articles against her dress. The dress that was the cause of so many of tonight's problems.

It's not the dress. It's the fact that you kissed him and now you can't deal.

Rationality was starting to creep in and she was nothing if not completely irritated about that. It was forcing her to confront the fact that she was actually the one being a jerk, not him. That she was the one who was overreacting, and his behavior was all a response to the fact that she'd gone full Anna-pine, with quills out ready to defend herself at all costs.

She took a deep breath and sat down on the edge of his bed, trading the high heels for her sneakers, then collecting her things again and walking back down the stairs, her feet tingling and aching as they got used to resting flat once more.

Chase wasn't inside.

She opened the front door and walked out onto the porch.

He was standing there, the porch light shining on him like a beacon. His broad shoulders, trim waist… oh, Lord, his ass. Wrangler butt was a gift from God in her opinion and Chase's was perfect. Something she'd noticed before, but right now it was physically painful to look at him and not close the space between them. To not touch him.

This was bad. This was why she hadn't ever touched him before. Why it would have been best if she never had.

She had needs. Fuzzy-blanket needs. She needed to get home.

She cleared her throat. "I'm ready," she said. "I just... If you could give me a lift down to the shop, that would be nice. So that I'm not cougar food."

He turned slowly, a strange expression on his face. "Yeah, I wouldn't want you to get eaten by any mangy predators."

"I appreciate that."

He headed down the steps and got back into the truck, and she followed, climbing into the cab beside him. He started the engine and maneuvered the truck onto the gravel road that ran through the property.

She rested her elbow on the armrest, staring outside at the inky-black shadows of the pine trees, and the white glitter of stars in the velvet-blue sky. It was a clear night, unusual for their little coastal town.

If only her head was as clear as the sky.

It was full. Full of regret and woe. She didn't like that. As soon as Chase pulled up to the shop, she scrambled out, not waiting for him to put the vehicle in Park. She was heading toward her own vehicle when she heard Chase behind her.

"What are you doing?" she asked, turning to face him.

But her words were cut off by what he did next. He took one step toward her, closing the distance between them as he wrapped his arm around her waist and drew her up against his chest. Then, before she could protest, before she could say anything, he was kissing her again.

This was different than the kiss at the restaurant. This was different than...well, than any kiss in the whole history of the world.

His kiss tasted of the familiarity of Chase and the

strangeness of his anger. Of heat and lust and rage all rolled into one.

She knew him better than she knew almost anyone. Knew the shape of his face, knew his scent, knew his voice. But his scent surrounding her like this, the feel of his face beneath her hands, the sound of that voice—transformed into a feral, passionate growl as he continued to ravish her—was an unknown. Was something else entirely.

Then, suddenly—just as suddenly as he had initiated it—the kiss was over. He released his hold on her, pushing her back. There was nothing but air between them now. Air and a whole lot of feelings. He was standing there, his hands planted on his lean hips, his chest rising and falling with each labored breath. "Six point five?" he asked, his tone challenging. "That sure as hell was no six point five, Anna Brown, and if you're honest with yourself, you have to admit that."

She sucked in a harsh, unsteady breath, trying to keep the shock from showing on her face. "I don't have to admit any such thing."

"You're a little liar."

"What does it matter?" she asked, scowling.

"How would you like it if I told you that you were only average compared to other women I've kissed?"

"I'd shut your head in the truck door."

"Exactly." He crossed his arms over his broad chest. "So don't think I'm going to let the same insults stand, honey."

"Don't *babe* me," she spat. "Don't *honey* me."

Triumph glittered in his dark eyes. The smugness so certain it was visible even in the moonlight. "Then don't kiss me again."

"You were the one who kissed me!" she shouted, throwing her arms wide.

"*This* time. But you started it. Don't do it again." He turned around, heading back toward his truck. All she could do was stand there and stare as he drove away.

Something had changed tonight. Something inside of her. She didn't think she liked it at all.

CHAPTER FIVE

"NOW, I DON'T want to be insensitive or hurt your feelings, princess, but why are you being such an asshole today?"

Chase looked over at Sam, who was staring at him from his position by the forge. The fire was going hot and they were pounding out iron, doing some repairs on equipment. By hand. Just the way both of them liked to work.

"I'm not," Chase said.

"Right. Look, there's only room for one of us to be a grumpy cuss, and I pretty much have that position filled. So I would appreciate it if you can get your act together."

"Sorry, Sam, are you unable to take what you dish out every day?"

"What's going on with you and Anna?"

Chase bristled at the mention of the woman he'd kissed last night. Then he winced when he remembered the kiss. Well, *remembered* was the wrong word. He'd never forgotten it. But right now he was mentally replaying it, moment by moment. "What did you hear?"

Sam laughed. An honest-to-God laugh. "Do I look like I'm on the gossip chain? I haven't talked to anybody. It's just that I saw her leaving your house last night wearing a red dress and sneakers, and then saw her this morning when she went into the shop. She was pissier than you are."

"Anna is always pissy." Sam treated his statement to a prolonged stare. "It's not a big deal. It's just that her brothers bet her that she couldn't get a date. I figured I would help her out with that."

"How?"

"Well…" he said, hesitating about telling his brother the whole story. Sam wasn't looking to change the business on the ranch. He didn't care about their family legacy. Not like Chase did. But Chase had made promises to tombstones and he wasn't about to break them.

It was one of their main sources of contention. So he wasn't exactly looking forward to having this conversation with his older brother.

But it wasn't like he could hide it forever. He'd just sort of been hoping he could hide it until he'd shown up with investment money.

"That's an awfully long pause," Sam said. "I'm willing to bet that whatever you're about to say, I'm not going to like it."

"You know me well. Anna got invited to go to the big community charity event that the West family hosts every year. Now I want to make sure that we can extend our contract with them. Plus…doing horseshoes and gates isn't cutting it. We can move into doing details on custom homes. To doing art pieces and selling our work across the country, not just locally. To do that we need investors. And the West fund-raiser's a great place to find them. Plus, if I only have to wear a suit once and can speak to everyone in town that might be interested in a single shot? Well, I can't beat that."

"Dammit, Chase, you know I don't want to commit to something like that."

"Right. You want to continue on the way we always have. You want to shoe horses when we can, pound metal when the opportunity presents itself, build gates, or whatever else might need doing, then go off and work on sculptures and things in your spare time. But that's not going to be enough. Less and less is done by hand, and people aren't willing to pay for handcrafted materials. Machines can build cheaper stuff than we can.

"But the thing is, you can make it look special. You can turn it into something amazing. Like you did with my house. It's the details that make a house expensive. We can have the sort of clients who don't want work off an assembly line. The kind who will pay for one-of-a-kind pieces. From art on down to the handles on their kitchen cabinets. We could get into some serious custom work. Vacation homes are starting to spring up around here, plus people are renovating to make rentals thanks to the tourism increase. But we need some investors if we're really going to get into this."

"You know I hate this. I don't like the idea of charging a ton of money for a…for a gate with an elk on it."

"You're an artist, Sam," he said, watching his brother wince as he said the words. "I know you hate that. But it's true."

"I hate that, too."

"You're talented."

"I hit metal with a hammer. Sometimes I shape it into something that looks nice. It's not really all that special."

"You do more than that and you know it. It's what people would be willing to pay for. If you would stop being such a nut job about it."

Sam rubbed the back of his neck, his expression shuttered. "You've gotten off topic," he said finally. "I asked you about Anna, not your schemes for exploiting my talents."

"Not really. The two are connected. I want to go to this thing to talk to the Wests. I want to talk about investment opportunities and expanding contracts with other people deemed worthy of an invite. In case you haven't noticed, we weren't on that list."

"Yeah, I get that. But why would the lately not-so-great McCormacks be invited?"

"That's the problem. This place hasn't been what it was for a couple of generations, and when we lost Mom and Dad…well, we were teenagers trying to keep up a whole industry, and now we work *for* these people, not with them. I aim to change that."

"You didn't think about talking to me?" Sam asked.

"Oh, I did. And I decided I didn't want to have to deal with you."

Sam shot him an evil glare. "So you're going as Anna's date. And helping her win her bet."

"Exactly."

"And you took her out last night, and she went back to your place, and now she's mad at you."

Chase held his hands up. "I don't know what you're getting at—"

"Yes, you do." Sam crossed his arms. "Did you bang her?"

Chase recoiled, trying to look horrified at the thought. He didn't *feel* horrified at the thought. Which actually made him feel kind of horrified. "I did not."

"Is that why you're mad? Because you didn't?"

His brother was way too perceptive for a guy who pounded heavy things with other heavy things for a living.

"No," he said. "Anna is my friend. She's just a friend.

We had a slight…altercation last night. But it's not that big a deal."

"Big enough that I'm worried with all your stomping around you're eventually going to fling the wrong thing and hit me with molten metal."

"Safety first," Chase said, "always."

"I bet you say that to your dates, too."

"You would, too, if you had any."

Sam flipped Chase the bird in response.

"Just forget about it," Chase said. "Forget about the stuff with the Wests, and let me deal with it. And forget about Anna."

When it came to that last directive, he was going to try to do the same.

ANNA WAS DREADING coming face-to-face with Chase again after last night. But she didn't really have a choice. They were still in this thing. Unless she called it off. But that would be tantamount to admitting that what had happened last night *bothered* her. And she didn't want to do that. More, she was almost incapable of doing it. She was pretty sure her pride would wither up and die if she did.

But Chase was coming by her shop again tonight, with some other kind of lesson in mind. Something he'd written down on that stupid legal pad of his. It was ridiculous. All of it was ridiculous.

Herself most of all.

She looked at the clock, gritting her teeth. Chase would be by any moment, and she was no closer to dealing with the feelings, needs and general restlessness that had hit her with the blunt force of a flying wrench than she had been last night.

Then, right on time, the door opened, and in walked

Chase. He was still dirty from work today, his face smudged with ash and soot, his shirt sticking to his muscular frame, showing off all those fine muscles underneath. Yeah, that didn't help.

"How was work?" he asked.

"Fine. Just dealing with putting a new cylinder head on a John Deere. You?"

"Working on a gate."

"Sounds…fun," she said, though she didn't really think it sounded like fun at all.

She liked solving the puzzle when it came to working on engines. Liked that she had the ability to get in there and figure things out. To diagnose the situation.

Standing in front of a hot fire forging metal didn't really sound like her kind of thing.

Though she couldn't deny it did pretty fantastic things for Chase's physique.

"Well, you know it would be fine if Sam wasn't such a pain in the ass."

"Sure," she said, feeling slightly cautious. After last night, she felt like dealing with Chase was like approaching a dog who'd bitten you once. Only, in this case he had kissed her, not bitten her, and he wasn't a dog. That was the problem. He was just much too *much* for his own good. Much too much for her own good.

"So," she said, "what's on the lesson plan for tonight?"

"I sort of thought we should talk about…well, talking."

"What do you mean?"

"There are ways that women talk to men they want to date. I thought I might walk you through flirting."

"You're going to show me how to flirt?"

"Somebody has to."

"I can probably figure it out," she said.

"You think?" he asked, crossing his arms over his chest and rocking back on his heels.

His clear skepticism stoked the flames of her temper, which was lurking very close to the surface after last night. That was kind of her default. Don't know how to handle something? Don't know *what* you feel? Get angry at it.

"Come on. Men and women have engaged in horizontal naked kickboxing for millennia. I'm pretty sure flirting is a natural instinct."

"You're a poet, Anna," he said, his tone deadpan.

"No, I'm a tractor mechanic," she said.

"Yeah, and you talk like one, too. If you want to get an actual date, and not just a quick tumble in the back of a guy's truck, you might want to refine your art of conversation a little."

"Who says I'm opposed to a quick rough tumble in the back of some guy's truck?"

"You're not?" he asked, his eyebrows shooting upward.

"Well, in all honesty I would probably prefer my truck, since it's clean. I know where it's been. But why the hell not? I have needs."

He scowled. "Right. Well, keep that kind of talk to yourself."

"Does it make you uncomfortable to hear about my *needs*, Chase?" she asked, not quite sure why she was poking at him. Maybe because she felt so unsettled. She was kind of enjoying the fact that he seemed to be, as well. Really, it wouldn't be fair if after last night he felt nothing at all. If he had been able to one-up her and then walk away as though nothing had happened.

"It doesn't make me uncomfortable. It's just unnecessary information. Now, talking about your needs is probably something you shouldn't do with a guy, either."

"Unless I want him to fulfill those needs."

"You said you wanted to date. You want the kind of date who can go to these functions with you, right?"

"It's moot. You're going with me."

"This time. But be honest, don't you want to be able to go out with guys who belong in places like that?"

"I don't know," she said, feeling uncomfortable.

Truth be told, she wasn't all that comfortable thinking about her needs. Emotional, physical. Frankly, if it went beyond her need for a cheeseburger, she didn't really know how to deal with it. She hadn't dated in years. And she had been fine with that. But the truth of the matter was the only reason Mark and Daniel had managed to get to her when they had made this bet was that she was beginning to feel dissatisfied with her life.

She was starting a new business. She was assuming a new position in the community. She didn't just want to be Anna Brown, the girl from the wrong side of the tracks. She didn't just want to be the tomboy mechanic for the rest of her life. She wanted…more. It had been fine, avoiding relationships all this time, but she was thirty now. She didn't really want to be by herself. She didn't want to be alone forever.

Dear Lord, she was having an existential crisis.

"Fine," she said, "it might be nice to have somebody to date."

Marriage, family—she had no idea how she felt when it came to those things. But a casual relationship… That might be nice. Yes. That might be nice.

Last night, she had gone home and gotten under a blanket and watched an old movie. Sometimes, Chase watched old movies with her, but he did not get under the blankets with her. It would be nice to have a guy to be under the blanket with. Somebody to go home to. Or at least someone to call to come over when she couldn't sleep. Someone she could talk to, make out with. Have sex with.

"Fine," she said. "I will submit to your flirting lessons."

"All the girls submit to me eventually," he said, winking.

Something about that made her stomach twist into a knot. "Talking about too much information…"

"There," he said, "that was almost flirting."

She wrinkled her nose. "Was it?"

"Yes. We had a little bit of back and forth. There was some innuendo."

"I didn't make innuendo on purpose," she said.

"No. That's the best kind. The kind you sort of walk into. It makes you feel a little dangerous. Like you might say the wrong thing. And if you go too far, they might walk away. But if you don't go far enough, they might not know that you want them."

She let out a long, frustrated growl. "Dating is complicated. I hate it. Is it too late for me to become a nun?"

"You would have to convert," he pointed out.

"That sounds like a lot of work, too."

"You can be pleasant, Anna. You're fun to talk to. So that's all you have to do."

"Natural to me is walking up to a hot guy and saying, 'Do you want to bone or what?'" As if she'd ever done that. As if she ever would. It was just…she didn't really know how to go about getting a guy to hook up with her any other way. She was a direct kind of girl. And nothing between men and women seemed direct.

"Fine. Let's try this," he said, grabbing a chair and pulling it up to her workbench before taking a seat.

She took hold of the back of the other folding chair

in the space and moved it across from his, positioning herself so that she was across from him.

"What are you drinking?" he asked.

She laughed. "A mai tai." She had never had one of those. She didn't even know what it was.

"Excellent. I'm having whiskey, straight up."

"That sounds like you."

"You don't know what sounds like me. You don't know me."

Suddenly, she got the game. "Right. Stranger," she said, then winced internally, because that sounded a little bit more Mae West in her head, and just kind of silly when it was out of her mouth.

"You here with anyone?"

"I could be?" she said, placing her elbow on the workbench and tilting her head to the side.

"You should try to toss your hair a little bit. I dated this girl Elizabeth who used to do that. It was cute."

"How does touching my hair accomplish anything?" she asked, feeling irritated that he had brought another woman up. Which was silly, because the only reason he was qualified to give her these lessons was that he had dated a metric ton of women.

So getting mad about the thing that was helping her right now was a little ridiculous. But she was pretty sure they had passed ridiculous a couple of days ago.

"I don't know. It's cute. It looks like you're trying to draw my attention to it. Like you want me to notice."

"Which…lets you know that I want you in my pants?"

He frowned. "I guess. I never broke it down like that before. But that stands to reason."

She reached up, sighing as she flicked a strand of her hair as best she could. It was tied up in a loose bun and had fallen partway thanks to the intensity of the day's physical labor. Still, she had a feeling she did not look alluring. She had a feeling she looked like she'd been caught in a wind turbine and spit out the other end.

"Are you new in town?"

"I'm old in town," she said, mentally kicking herself again for being lame on the return volley.

"That works, too," Chase said, not skipping a beat. Yeah, there was a reason the man had never struck out before.

She started to chew on her lip, trying to think of what to say next.

"Don't chew a hole through it," he said, smiling and reaching across the space, brushing his thumb over the place her teeth had just grazed.

And everything in her stopped dead. His touch ignited her nerve endings, sending a brush fire down her veins and all through her body.

She hadn't been this ridiculous over Chase since she was sixteen years old. Since then, she had mostly learned to manage it.

She pulled away slightly, her chair scraping against the floor. She laughed, a stilted, unnatural sound. "I won't," she said, her voice too loud.

"If you're going to chew on your lip," he said, "don't freak out when the guy calls attention to it or touches you. It looks like you're doing it on purpose, so you should expect a comment."

"Duh," she said, "I was. That was…normal."

She wanted to crawl under the chair.

"There was this girl Miranda that I—"

"Okay." She cut him off, growing more and more impatient with the comparisons. "I'm old in town, what about you?"

"I've been around."

"I bet you have been," she said.

"I'm not sure how I'm supposed to take that," he said, flashing her a lopsided grin.

"Right," she said, "because I don't know what I'm doing."

"Maybe this was a bad idea," he said. "I think you actually need to feel some chemistry with somebody if flirting's going to work."

His words were sharp, digging into her chest. *You actually had to feel some chemistry* to be able to flirt.

They had chemistry. She had felt it last night. So had he. This was his revenge for the six-point-five comment. At least, she hoped it was. The alternative was that he had really felt nothing when their lips attached. And that seemed…beyond unfair.

She had all this attraction for Chase that she had spent years tamping down, only to have it come roaring to the surface the moment she had begun to pretend there was more going on between them than just friendship. And then she had kissed him. And far from being a disappointment, he had superseded her every fantasy. The jackass. Then he had kissed her, kissed her because he was angry. Kissed her to get revenge. Kissed her in a way that had kept her awake all night long, aching, burning. And now he was saying he didn't have chemistry with her.

"It's just that usually when I'm with a girl it flows a little easier. The bar to the bedroom is a pretty natural extension. And all those little movements kind of lead into the other. The way they touch their hair, tilt their head, lean in for a kiss…"

Oh, that did it.

"The women that I usually hook up with tend to—"

"Right," she said, her tone hard. "I get it. They flip

their hair and scrunch their noses and twitch at all the appropriate times. They're like small woodland creatures who only emerge from their burrows to satisfy your every sexual whim."

"Don't get upset. I'm trying to help you."

She snorted. "I know." Just then, she had no idea what devil possessed her. Only that one most assuredly did. And once it had taken hold, she had no desire to cast it back out again.

She was mad. Mad like Chase had been last night. And she was determined to get her own back.

"Elizabeth was good at flipping her hair. Miranda gave you saucy interplay like so." She stood up, taking a step toward him, meeting his dark gaze with her own. "But how did they do this?" She reached down, placing her hand between his thighs and rubbing her palm over the bulge in his jeans.

Oh, sweet Lord, there was more to Chase McCormack than met the eye.

And she had a whole handful of him.

Her brain was starting to scream. Not words so much as a high-pitched, panicky whine. She had crossed the line. And there was no turning back.

But her brain wasn't running the show. Her body was on fire, her heart pounding so hard she was afraid it was going to rip a hole straight through the wall of her chest and flop out on the ground in front of him. Show him all its contents. Dammit, *she* didn't even want to see that.

But it was her anger that really pushed things forward. Her anger that truly propelled her on.

"And how," she asked, lowering herself slowly, scraping her fingernails across the line of his zipper, before dropping to her knees in front of him, "did they do this?"

CHAPTER SIX

For one blinding second, Chase thought that he was engaged in some sort of high-definition hallucination.

Because there was no way that Anna had just put her hand…there. There was no way that she was kneeling down in front of him, looking at him like she was a sultry-eyed seductress rather than his best friend, still dirty from the workday, clad in motor-oil-smudged coveralls.

He blinked. Then he shook his head. She was still there. And so was he.

But he was so hard he could probably pound iron with his dick right about now.

He knew what he should do. And just now he had enough sense left in his skull to do it. But he didn't want to. He knew he should. He knew that at the end of this road there was nothing good. Nothing good at all. But he shut all that down. He didn't think of the road ahead.

He just let his brain go blank. He just sat back and watched as she trailed her fingers up the line of his zipper, grabbing hold of his belt buckle and undoing it, her movements clumsy, speaking of an inexperience he didn't want to examine too closely.

He didn't want to examine any of this too closely, but he was powerless to do anything else.

Because everything around the moment went fuzzy as the present sharpened. Almost painfully.

His eyes were drawn to her fingers as she pulled his zipper down, to the short, no-nonsense fingernails, the specks of dirt embedded in her skin. That should... well, he had the vague idea it should turn him off. It didn't. Though he had a feeling that getting a bucket of water thrown on him while he sat in the middle of an iceberg naked wouldn't turn him off at this point. He was too far gone.

He was holding his breath. Every muscle in his body frozen. He couldn't believe that she would do what it appeared she might be doing. She would stop. She had to stop. He needed her to stop. He needed her to never stop. To keep going.

She pressed her palm flat against his ab muscles before pushing her hand down inside his jeans, reaching beneath his underwear and curling her fingers around him. His breath hissed through his teeth, a shudder racking his frame.

She looked up at him, green eyes glittering in the dim shop light. She had a smudge of dirt on her face that somehow only highlighted her sharp cheekbones, somehow emphasized her beauty in a way he hadn't truly noticed it before. Yes, last night in the red dress she had been beautiful, there was no doubt about that. But for some reason, her femininity was highlighted wrapped in these traditionally masculine things. By the backdrop of the mechanic shop, the evidence of a day's hard work on her soft skin.

She tilted her chin up, her expression one of absolute challenge. She was waiting for him to call it off. Waiting for him to push her away. But he wasn't going to. He reached out, forking his fingers through her hair and tightening them, grabbing ahold of the loose bun that sat high on her head. Her eyes widened, her lips going slack. He didn't pull her away. He didn't draw her closer. He just held on tight, keeping his gaze firmly focused on hers. Then he released her. And he waited.

She licked her lips slowly, an action that would have been almost comically obvious coming from nearly anyone else. Not Anna.

Then she squeezed him gently before drawing her hand back. He should be relieved. He was not.

But her next move was not one he anticipated. She grabbed hold of the waistband of his jeans and underwear, pulling them down slowly, exposing him. She let out a shaky, shuddering breath before leaning in and flicking her tongue over the head of his arousal.

"Hell." He wasn't sure at first if he had spoken it out loud, not until he heard it echoing around him. It was like cursing in a church somehow, wrong considering the beauty of the gift he was about to receive.

Still, he couldn't think of anything else as she drew the tip of her tongue all the way down to the base of his shaft before retracing her path. She shifted, and that was when he noticed her hands were shaking. Fair enough, since he was shaking, too.

She parted her lips, taking him into her mouth completely, her lips sliding over him, the wet, slick friction almost too much for him to handle. He didn't know what was wrong with him. If it was the shock of the moment, if it was just that he was this base. Or if there was some kind of sick, perverted part of him that took extra pleasure in the fact that this was wrong. That he should not be letting his best friend touch him like this.

Because he'd had more skilled blow jobs. There was no question about that. This didn't feel good because Anna was an expert in the art of fellatio. Far from it.

Still, his head was about to blow off. And he was about to lose all of his control. So there was something.

Maybe it was just her.

She tilted her head to the side as she took him in deep, giving him a good view of just what she was doing. And just who was doing it. He was so aware of the fact that it was Anna, and that most definitely added a kick of the forbidden. Because he knew this was bad. Knew it was wrong.

And not many things were off-limits to him. Not many things had an illicit quality to them. He had kind of allowed himself to take anything and everything that had ever seemed vaguely sexy to him.

Except for her.

He shoved that thought in the background. He didn't like to think of Anna that way, and in general he didn't.

Sure, in high school, there had been moments. But he was a guy. And he had spent a lot of time with Anna. Alone in her room, alone in his. He had a feeling that half the people who had known them had imagined they were getting it on behind the scenes. Friends with benefits, et cetera. In reality, the only benefit to their friendship had been the fact that they'd been there for each other. They had never been there for each other in this way.

Maybe that's what was wrong with him.

Of course, nothing felt wrong with him right now. Right now, pleasure was crackling close to the surface of his skin and it was shorting out his brain. All he could do was sit back and ride the high. Embrace the sensations that were boiling through his blood. The magic of her lips and tongue combined with a shocking scrape of her teeth against his delicate skin made him buck his hips against her even as he tried to rein himself in.

But he was reaching the end of his control, the end of himself. He reached down, cupping her cheek as she continued to pleasure him, as she continued to drive him wild, urging him closer to the edge of control he hadn't realized he possessed.

He felt like he lived life with the shackles off, but she was pushing him so much further than he'd been before that he knew he'd been lying to himself all this time.

He'd been in chains, and hadn't even realized it.

Maybe because of her. Maybe to keep himself from touching her.

She gripped him, squeezing as she tasted him, pushing him straight over the edge. He held on to her hair, harder than he should, as a wave of pleasure rode up inside of him. And when it crashed he didn't ride it into shore. Oh, hell no. When it crashed it drove him straight down to the bottom of the sea, the impact leaving him spinning, gasping for breath, battered on the rocks.

But dammit all, it was worth it. Right now, it was worth it.

He knew that any moment the feeling would fade and he would be faced with the stark horror of what he'd just done, of what he'd just allowed to happen. But for now, he was foggy, floating in the kind of mist that always blanketed the ocean on cold mornings in Copper Ridge.

And he would cling to it as long as possible.

OH, DEAR GOD. What had she done? This had gone so far beyond the kiss to prove they had chemistry. It had gone so far past the challenge that Chase had thrown down last night. It had gone straight into Crazy Town, next stop You Messed Up the Only Friendship You Hadville.

In combination with the swirling panic that was wrapping its claws around her and pulling her into a spiral was the fuzzy-headed lingering arousal. Her lips felt swollen, her body tingling, adrenaline still making her shake.

She regretted everything. She also regretted nothing.

The contradictions inside her were so extreme she felt like she was going to be pulled in two.

One thing her mind and body were united on was the desire to go hide underneath a blanket. This was definitely the kind of situation that necessitated hiding.

The problem was, she was still on her knees in front of Chase. Maybe she could hide under his chair.

What are you doing? Why are you falling apart? This isn't a big deal. He has probably literally had a thousand blow jobs.

This one didn't have to be that big a deal. Sure, it was the first one she had ever given. But he didn't have to know that, either.

If she didn't treat it like a big deal, it wouldn't be a big deal. They could forget anything had ever happened. They could forget that in a moment of total insanity she had allowed her anger to push her over the edge, had allowed her inability to back down from a challenge to bring them to this place. And that was all it was—the fact that she was absolutely unable to deal with that blow to her pride. It was nothing else. It couldn't be anything else.

She rocked back on her heels, planting her hands flat on the dusty ground before rising to her feet. She felt dizzy. She would go ahead and blame that on the speed at which she had stood up.

"I think it's safe to say we have a little bit more chemistry than you thought," she said, clearing her throat and brushing at the dirt on her pants.

He didn't say anything. He just kept sitting there,

looking rocked. And he was still exposed. She did her very best to look at the wall behind him. "I can still see your..."

He scrambled into action, standing and tugging his pants into place, doing up his belt as quickly as possible. "I think we're done for the day."

She nodded. "Yeah. Well, *you* are."

She could feel the distance widening between them. It was what she needed, what she wanted, ultimately. But for some reason, even as she forced the breach, she regretted it.

"I don't... What just happened?"

She laughed, crossing her arms and cocking her hip out to the side. "If you have to ask, maybe I didn't do a very good job." The bolder she got, the more she retreated inside. She could feel herself tearing in two, the soft vulnerable part of her scrambling to get behind the brash, bold outward version that would spare her from any embarrassment or pain.

"You're...okay?"

"Why wouldn't I be okay?"

"Because you just..."

She laughed. Hysterically. "Sure. But let's not be ridiculous about it. It isn't like you punched me in the face."

Chase looked stricken. "Of course not. I would never do that."

"I know. I'm just saying, don't act like you punched me in the face when all I did was—"

"There's no need to get descriptive. I was here. I remember."

She snorted. "You should remember." She turned away from him, clenching her hands into fists, hoping he didn't notice that they were shaking. "And I hope you remember it next time you go talking about us not having chemistry."

"Do you *want* us to have chemistry?"

She whirled around. "No. But I have some pride. You were comparing me to all these other women. Well, compare that."

"I…can't."

She planted her hands on her hips. "Damn straight."

"We can't… We can't do this again," he said, shaking his head and walking away.

For some reason, that made her feel awful. For some reason, it hurt. Stabbed like a rusty knife deep in her gut.

"I don't want to do it again. I mean, you're welcome, but I didn't exactly get anything out of it."

He stopped, turning to face her, his expression tense. "I didn't ask you to do anything."

"I'm aware." She shook her head. "I think we're done for tonight."

"Yeah. I already said that."

"Well," she said, feeling furious now, "now I'm saying it."

She was mad at herself. For taking it this far. For being upset, and raw, and wounded over something that she had chosen to do. Over his reaction, which was nothing more than the completely predictable response. He didn't want her. Not really.

And she knew that. This evening's events weren't going to change it. An orgasm on the floor of the shop she rented from him was hardly going to alter the course of fifteen years of friendship.

An orgasm. Oh, dear Lord, what had she done? She really had to get out of here. There was no amount of bravado left in her that would save her from the melt-down that was pending.

"I have to go."

SHE WAS GONE before he had a chance to protest. He should be glad she was gone. If she had stayed, there was no telling what he might have done. What other stupid bit of nonsense he might have committed.

He had limited brainpower at the moment. All of his blood was still somewhere south of his belt.

He turned, surveying the empty shop. Then, in a fit of rage, he kicked something metal that was just to the right of the chair. And hurt his foot. And probably broke the thing. He had no idea if it was important or not. He hoped it wasn't. Or maybe he hoped it was. She deserved to have some of her tractor shit get broken. What had she been thinking?

He hadn't been able to think. But it was a well-known fact that if a man's dick was in a woman's mouth, he was not doing much problem solving. Which meant Chase was completely absolved of any wrongdoing here.

Completely.

He gritted his teeth, closing his eyes and taking in a sharp breath. He was going to have to figure out how to get a handle on himself between now and the next time he saw Anna. Because there was no way things could continue on like this. There weren't a whole lot of people who stuck around in his world. There had never been a special woman. After the death of his and Sam's parents, relatives had passed through, but none of them had put down roots. And, well, their parents, they might not have chosen to leave, but they were gone all the same. He couldn't afford to lose anyone else. Sam and Anna were basically all he had.

Which meant when it came to Sam's moods and general crankiness, Chase just dealt with it. And when it came to Anna…no more touching. No more… No more of any of that.

For one second, he allowed himself to replay the moment when she had unzipped his pants. When she had leaned forward and tasted him. When that white-hot streak of release had undone him completely.

He blinked. Yeah, he knew what he had been thinking. That it felt good. Amazing. Too good to stop her. But physical pleasure was cheap. A friendship like theirs represented years of investment. One simply wasn't worth sacrificing the other for. And now that he was thinking clearly he realized that. So that meant no more. No more. Never.

Next time he saw her, he was going to make sure she knew that.

CHAPTER SEVEN

ANNA WAS BENEATH three blankets, and she was starting to swelter. If she hadn't been too lazy to sit up and grab hold of her ice-cream container, she might not be quite so sweaty.

The fact that she was something of a cliché of what it meant to be a woman behind closed doors was not lost on her. Blankets, old movies, Ben & Jerry's. But hey, she spent most of the day up to her elbows in engine grease, so she supposed she was entitled to a few stereotypes.

She reached her spoon out from beneath the blankets and scraped the top of the ice cream in the container, gathering up a modest amount.

"Oklahoma!" she sang, humming the rest of the line while taking the bite of marshmallow and chocolate ice cream and sighing as the sugar did its good work. Full-fat dairy products were the way to happiness. Or at least the best way she knew to stop from obsessing.

Her phone buzzed and she looked down, cringing when she saw Chase's name. She swiped open the lock screen and read the message.

In your driveway. Didn't want to give you a heart attack.

Why are you in my dr—

She didn't get a chance to finish the message before there was a knock on her front door.

She closed her eyes, groaning. She really didn't want to deal with him right now. In fact, he was the last person on earth she wanted to deal with. He was the reason she was currently baking beneath a stack of blankets, seeking solace in the bosom of old movies.

Still, she couldn't ignore him. That would make things weirder. He was still her best friend, even if she had— Well, she wasn't going to think about what she had. If she ignored him, it would only cater to the weirdness. It would make events from earlier today seem more important than they needed to be. They did not need to be treated as though they were important.

Sure, she had never exactly done *that* with a man. Sure, she hadn't even had sexual contact of any kind with a man for the past several years. And sure, she had never had that kind of contact with Chase. But that was no reason to go assigning meaning. People got ribbons and stickers for their first trips to the dentist. They did not get them for giving their first blow job.

She groaned. Then she rolled off the couch, pushing herself into a standing position before she padded through the small living area to the entryway. She jerked the door open, pushing her hair out of her face and trying to look casual.

Too late, she realized that she was wearing her pajamas. Which were perfectly decent, in that they covered every inch of her body. But they were also baggy, fuzzy and covered in porcupines.

All things considered, it just wasn't the most glorious of moments.

"Hello," she said, keeping her body firmly planted in the center of the doorway.

"Hi," he returned. Then he proceeded to study her pajamas.

"Porcupines," she informed him, just for something to say.

"Good choice. Not an obvious one."

"I guess not. Considering they aren't all that cuddly. But neither am I. So maybe it's a more obvious choice than it originally appears."

"Maybe. We'll have to debate animal-patterned pajama philosophy another time."

"I guess. What exactly did you come here to debate if not that?"

He stuffed his hands in his pockets. "Nothing. I just came to…check on you."

"Sound of body and mind."

"I see that. Except you're in your pajamas at seven o'clock."

"I'm preparing for an evening in," she said, planting her hand on her hip. "So pajamas are logical."

"Okay."

She frowned. "I'm fine."

"Can I come in?"

She was frozen for a moment, not quite sure what to say. If she let him come in…well, she didn't feel entirely comfortable with the idea of letting him in. But if she didn't let him in, then she would be admitting that she was uncomfortable letting him in. Which would betray the fact that she actually wasn't really all that okay. She didn't want to do that, either.

No wonder she had avoided sexual contact for so long. It introduced all manner of things that she really didn't want to deal with.

"Sure," she said finally, stepping to the side and allowing him entry.

He just stood there, filling up the entry. She had never really noticed that before. How large he was in the small space of her home. Because he was Chase, and his presence here shouldn't really be remarkable. It was now.

Because things had changed. She had changed them. She had kissed him the other day, and then…well, she had changed things.

"There. You are in," she said, moving away from him and heading back into the living room. She took a seat on the couch, picking up the remote control and muting the TV.

"Movie night?"

"Every night is movie night with enough popcorn and a can-do attitude."

"I admire your dedication. What's on?"

"Oklahoma!"

He raised his brows. "You haven't seen that enough times?"

"There is no such thing as seeing a musical too many times, Chase. Multiple viewings only enhance the experience."

"Do they?"

"Sing-alongs, of course."

"I should have known."

She smiled, putting a blanket back over her lap, thinking of it as a sort of flannel shield. "You should know these things about me. Really, you should know everything about me."

He cleared his throat, and the sudden awkwardness made her think of all the things he didn't know about her. And the things that he did know. It hit her then— of course, right then, as he was standing in front of her—just how revealing what had happened earlier was.

Giving a guy pleasure like that…well, a woman didn't do that unless she wanted him. It said a lot about how she felt. About how she had felt for an awfully long time. No matter that she had tried to quash it, the fact remained that she did feel attraction for him. Which he was obviously now completely aware of.

Silence fell like a boulder between them. Crushing, deadly.

"Anyway," she said, the transition as subtle as a landslide. "Why exactly are you here?"

"I told you."

"Right. Checking on me. I'm just not really sure why."

"You know why," he said, his tone muted.

"You check on every woman you have…encounters with?"

"You know I don't. But you're not every woman I have encounters with."

"Still. I'm an adult woman. I'm neither shocked nor injured."

She was probably both. Yes, she was definitely perilously close to being both.

He shifted, clearly uncomfortable. Which she hated, because they weren't uncomfortable with each other. Ever. Or they hadn't been before. "It would be rude of me not to make sure we aren't…okay."

She patted herself down. "Yes. Okay. Okay?"

"No," he said.

"No? What the hell, man? I said I'm fine. Do we have to stand around talking about it?"

"I think we might. Because I don't think you're fine."

"That's bullshit, McCormack," she said, rising from the couch and clutching her blanket to her chest. "Straight-up bullshit. Like you stepped in a big-ass pile somewhere out there and now you went and dragged it into my house."

"If you were fine, you wouldn't be acting like this."

"I'm sorry, how did you want me to act?"

"Like an adult, maybe?" he said, his dark brows locking together.

"Um, I am acting like an adult, Chase. I'm pretending that a really embarrassing mistake didn't happen, while I crush my regret and uncertainty beneath the weight of my caloric intake for the evening. What part of that isn't acting like an adult?"

"We're friends. This wasn't some random, forgettable hookup."

"It is so forgettable," she said, her voice taking on that brash, loud quality that hurt her own ears. That she was starting to despise. "I've already forgotten it."

"How?"

"It's a penis, Chase, not the Sistine Chapel. My life was hardly going to be changed by the sight of it."

He reached forward, grabbing hold of her arm and drawing her toward him. "Stop," he bit out, his words hard, his expression focused.

"What are you doing?" she asked, some of her bravado slipping.

"Calling you on *your* bullshit, Anna." He lowered his voice, his tone no less deadly. She'd never seen Chase like this. He didn't get like this. Chase was fun, and light. Well, except for last night when he'd kissed her. But even then, he hadn't been quite this serious. "I've known you for fifteen years. I know when your smile is hiding tears, little girl. I know when you're a whole mess of feelings behind that brick wall you put up to keep yourself separate from the world. And I sure as hell know when you aren't fine. So don't stand there and tell me that it didn't change anything, that it didn't mean anything. Even if you gave out BJs every day with lunch—and I know you don't—that would have still mattered because it's *us*. And we don't do that. It changed something, Anna, and don't you dare pretend it didn't."

No. *No*. Her brain was screaming again, but this time she knew for sure what it was saying. It was all denial. She didn't want him to look at her as if he was searching for something, didn't want him to touch her as if it was only the beginning of something more. Didn't want him to see her. To see how scared she was. To see how unnerved and affected she was. To see how very, very not brave she was beneath the shield she held up to keep the world out.

He already knows it's a shield. And you're already screwed ten ways, because you can't hide from him and you never could.

He'd let her believe she could. And now he'd changed his mind. For some reason it was all over now. Well, she knew why. It had started with a dress and high heels and ended with an orgasm in her shop. He was right. It had changed things.

And she had a terrible, horrible feeling more was going to change before they could go back to normal.

If they ever could.

"Well," she said, hearing her voice falter. Pretending she didn't. "I don't think anything needs to change."

"Enough," he said, his tone fierce.

Then, before she knew what was happening, he'd claimed her lips again in a kiss that ground every other kiss that had come before it into dust, before letting them blow away on the wind.

This was angry. Intense. Hot and hard. And it was

happening in her house, in spite of the fact that she was holding a blanket and *Oklahoma!* was on mute in the background. It was her safe space, with her safe friend, and it was being wholly, utterly invaded.

By him.

It was confronting and uncomfortable and scary as hell. So she responded the only way she could. She got mad, too.

She grabbed hold of the front of his shirt, clinging to him tightly as she kissed him back. As she forced her tongue between his lips, claiming him before he could stake his claim on her.

She shifted, scraping her teeth lightly over his bottom lip before biting down. Hard.

He growled, wrapping his arms around her waist. She never felt small. Ever. She was a tall girl with a broad frame, but she was engulfed by Chase right now. His scent, his strength. He was all hard muscle against her, his heart thundering beneath her hands, which were pinned between their bodies.

She didn't know what was happening, except that right now, kissing him might be safer than trying to talk to him.

It certainly felt better.

It let her be angry. Let her push back without saying anything. And more than that…he was an amazing kisser. He had taken her from zero to almost-there with one touch of his lips against hers.

He slid his hand down her back, cupping her butt and bringing her up even harder against him so she could feel him. All of him. And just how aroused he was.

He wanted her. Chase wanted her. Yes, he was pissed. Yes, he was…trying to prove a point with his tongue or whatever. But he couldn't fake a hard-on like that.

She was angry, but it was fading. Being blotted out by the arousal that was crackling in her veins like fireworks.

Suddenly, she found herself being lifted off the ground, before she was set down on the couch, Chase coming down over her, his expression hard, his eyes sharp as he looked down at her.

He pressed his hand over her stomach, pushing the hem of her shirt upward.

She should stop him. She didn't.

She watched as his strong, masculine hand pushed her shirt out of the way, revealing a wedge of skin. The contrast alone was enough to drive her crazy. Man, woman. Innocuous porcupine pajamas and sex.

Above all else, above anything else, there was Chase. Everything he made her feel. All of the things she had spent years trying *not* to feel. Years running from.

She couldn't run. Not now. Not only did she lack the strength, she lacked the desire. Because more than safety, more than sanity, she wanted him. Wanted him naked, over her, under her, *in* her.

He gripped the hem of her top and wrenched it over her head, the movement sudden, swift. As though he had reached the end of his patience and had no reserve to draw upon. That left her in nothing more than those ridiculous baggy pajama pants, resting low on her hips. She didn't have anything sexier underneath them, either.

But Chase didn't look at all disappointed. He didn't look away, either. Didn't have a faraway expression on his face. She wasn't sure why, but she had half expected to look up at him and be able to clearly identify that he was somewhere else in his mind, with someone else. But he was looking at her with a sharp focus, a kind of single-mindedness that no man, no *one*, had ever looked at her with before.

He knew. He knew who she was. And he was still hot for her. Still hard for her.

"You are so hot," he said, pressing his hand flat to her stomach and drawing it down slowly, his fingertips teasing the sensitive skin beneath the waistband. "And you don't even know it, do you?"

Part of her wanted to protest, wanted to fight back, because that was what she did. Instead, everything inside of her just kind of went limp. Melted into a puddle. "N-no."

"You should know," he said, his voice low, husky. A shot of whiskey that skated along her nerves, warming her, sending a kick of heat and adrenaline firing through her blood. "You should know how damn sexy you are. You're the kind of woman who could make a man lose his mind."

"I could?"

He laughed, but it wasn't full of humor. It sounded tortured. "I'm exhibit A."

He shifted his hips forward, his hard length pressing up against that very aroused part of her that wanted more of him. Needed more of him. She gasped. "Soon," he said, the promise in his words settling a heavy weight in her stomach. Anticipation, terror. Need.

He continued to tease her, his fingertips resting just above the line of her panties, before he began to trail his hand back upward. He rested his palm over her chest, reaching up and tracing her lower lip with his thumb.

She darted her tongue out, sliding the tip of it over his skin, tasting salt, tasting Chase. A flavor that was becoming familiar.

Then she angled her head, taking his thumb into

her mouth and sucking hard. His hips arched forward hard, his cock making firm contact, sending a shower of sparks through her body as he did.

"You're going to be the death of me," he said, every word raw, frayed.

"I might say the same about you," she said, her voice thick, unrecognizable. She didn't know who she was right now. This creature who was a complete and total slave to sexual sensation. Who was so lost in it, she could feel nothing else. No sense of self-preservation, no fear kicking into gear and letting her know that she needed to put her walls up. That she needed to go on the defense.

She was reduced. She had none of that. And she didn't even care.

"You're a miracle," he said, tracing the line of her collarbone with the tip of his tongue. "A damn *miracle*, do you know that?"

"What?"

"The other day I told you you didn't look like a miracle. I was a fool. And I was wrong. Every inch of you is a miracle, Anna Brown."

Those words were like being submerged in warm water, feeling it flow over every inch of her, a kind of deep, soul-satisfying comfort that she really, really didn't want. Or rather, she didn't *want* to want it. But she did, bad enough that she couldn't resist.

But it was all a little too heavy. All a little too much. Still, she didn't have the strength to turn him away.

"Kiss me."

She said that instead of *get the hell out of my house*, and instead of *we can't do this*, because it was all she had strength for. Because she needed that kiss. And maybe, just maybe, if they didn't talk, she could make it through.

Chase—gentleman that he was—obliged her.

He angled his head, reaching up to cup her breast as he did, his mouth crashing down on hers just as his palm skimmed her nipple. She gasped, arching up against him, the combination of sensations almost too much to handle.

Yeah, she did not remember sex being like this. Granted, it had been a million years, but she would have remembered if it had come anywhere close to this. And her conclusion most certainly wouldn't have been that it was vaguely boring and a little bit gross. Not if it had even been in the same ballpark as what she was feeling now.

There was no point in comparing. There was just flat out no comparison.

He kissed her, long, deep and hard; he kissed her until she couldn't breathe. Until she thought she was going to die for wanting more. He kissed her until she was dizzy. And when he abandoned her mouth, she nearly wept. Until he lowered his head and skimmed his tongue over one hardened bud, until he drew it between his lips and sucked hard, before scraping her sensitized flesh with his teeth.

She arched against him, desperate for more. Desperate for satisfaction. Satisfaction he seemed intent on withholding.

"I'm so close," she said, panting. "Just do it now." Then it would be over. Then she would have what she needed, and the howling, yawning ache inside of her would be satisfied.

"No," he said, his tone authoritative.

"What do you mean no?"

"Not yet. You're not allowed to come yet, Anna. I'm not done."

His words, the calm, quiet command, made everything inside of her go still. She wanted to fight him. Wanted to rail against that cruel denial of her needs, but she couldn't.

Not when this part of him was so compelling. Not when she wanted so badly to see where complying would lead.

"We're not done," he said, tracing her nipple with the tip of his tongue, "until I say we are." He lifted his head so that their eyes met, the prolonged contact touching something deep inside of her. Something that surpassed the physical.

He kissed her again, and as he did, he pulled his T-shirt over his head, exposing his incredible body to her.

Her mouth dried, and other parts of her got wet. Very, very wet.

"Oh, sweet Lord," she said, pressing her hand to his chest and drawing her fingertips down over his muscles, his chest hair tickling her skin as she did.

It was a surreal moment. So strange and fascinating. To touch her best friend like this. To see his body this way, to know that—right now—it wasn't off-limits to her. To know that she could lean forward and kiss that beautiful, perfect dip just next to his hip bone. Suddenly, she was seized with the desire to do just that. And she didn't have to fight it.

She pushed against him, bringing herself into a sitting position, lowering her head and pressing her lips to his heated skin.

"Oh, no, you don't," he said, his voice rough. He took hold of her wrist, drawing her up so that she was on her knees, eye to eye with him on the couch. "We're not finishing it like that," he said.

"Damn straight we aren't," she said. "But that doesn't mean I didn't want to get a little taste."

"You give way too much credit to my self-control, honey."

"You give too much credit to mine. I've never…" She stared at his chest instead of finishing her sentence. "It's like walking into a candy store and being told I can have whatever I want. Restraint is not on the menu."

"Good," he said, leaning in, kissing her, nipping her lower lip. "Restraint isn't what I want."

He wrapped his arm around her, drawing her up against him, her bare breasts pressing against his hard chest, the hair there abrading her nipples in the most fantastic, delicious way.

And then he was kissing her again, slow and deep as his hand trailed down beneath the waistband of her pants, cupping her ass, squeezing her tight. He pushed her pants down over her hips, taking her panties with them, leaving her completely naked in front of him.

He stood up, taking his time looking at her as he put his hands on his belt buckle.

Nerves, excitement, spread through her. She didn't know where to look. At the harsh, hungry look on his face, at the beautiful lines of muscle on his perfectly sculpted torso. At the clear and aggressive arousal visible through his jeans.

So she looked at all of him. Every last bit. And she didn't have time to feel embarrassed that she was sitting there naked as the day she was born, totally exposed to him for the first time.

She was too fascinated by him in this moment. Too fascinated to do anything but stare at him.

This was Chase McCormack. The man that women lost their minds—and their dignity—over on a regular basis. This was Chase McCormack, the sex god who could—and often did—have any woman he pleased.

She had known Chase McCormack, loyal friend and confidant, for a very long time. But she realized that up until now, she had never met *this* Chase McCormack. It was a strange, dizzying realization. Exhilarating.

And she was suddenly seized by the feeling that right now, he was hers. All hers. Because who else knew both sides of him? Did anyone?

She was about to.

"Get your pants off, McCormack," she said, impatience overriding common sense.

"You don't get to make demands here, Anna," he said.

"I just did."

"You want to try giving orders? You have to show me you can follow them." His eyes darkened, and her heart hammered harder, faster. "Spread your legs," he said, his words hard and uncompromising.

She swallowed. There was that embarrassment that she had just been so proud she had bypassed. But this was suddenly way outside her realm of experience. It was one thing to sit there in front of him naked. It was quite another to deliberately expose herself the way he was asking her to. She didn't move. She sat there, frozen.

"Spread your legs for me," he repeated, his voice heavy with that soft, commanding tone. "Or I put my clothes on and leave."

"You wouldn't," she said.

"You don't know what I'm capable of."

That was true. In this scenario, she really didn't know him. He was a stranger, except he wasn't.

Actually, if he had been a stranger, all of this would've been a lot easier. She could have spread her legs and she wouldn't have worried about how she looked. Wouldn't have worried about the consequences. If a stranger saw her do something like that, was somehow unsatisfied and then walked away, well, what did it matter? But this was Chase. And it mattered. It mattered so very much.

His hands paused on his belt buckle. "I'm warning you, Anna. You better do as you're told."

For some reason, that did not make her want to punch him. For some reason, she found herself sitting back on the couch, obeying his command, opening herself to him, as adrenaline skittered through her system.

"Good girl," he said, continuing his movements, pushing his jeans and underwear down his legs and exposing his entire body to her for the first time. And then, it didn't matter so much that she was sitting there with her thighs open for him. Because now she had all of him to look at.

The light in his eyes was intense, hungry, and he kept them trained on her as he reached down and squeezed himself hard. His jaw was tense, the only real sign of just how frayed his control was.

"Beautiful," he said, stroking himself slowly, leisurely, as he continued to gaze at her.

"Are you just going to look? Or are you going to touch?" She wasn't entirely comfortable with this. With him just staring. With this aching silence between them, and this deep, overwhelming connection that she felt.

There were no barriers left. There was no way to hide. She was vulnerable, in every way. And normally she hated it. She kind of hated it now. But that vulnerability was wrapped in arousal, in a sharp, desperate need unlike anything she had ever known. And so it was impossible to try to put distance between them, impossible to try to run away.

"I'm going to do a lot more than look," he said, dropping down to his knees, "and I'm going to do a hell of a lot more than touch." He reached out, sliding his hands around to her ass, drawing her forward, bringing her up toward his mouth.

"Chase," she said, the short, shocked protest about the only thing she managed before the slick heat of his tongue assaulted that sensitive bundle of nerves at the apex of her thighs. "You don't have to…"

He lifted his head, his dark eyes meeting her. "Oh, I know I don't have to. But you got to taste me, and I think turnabout is fair play."

"But that wasn't…"

"What?"

"It's just that men…"

"Expect a lot more than they give. At least some of them. Anyway, as much as I liked what you did for me—and don't get me wrong, I liked it a lot—you have no idea how much pleasure this gives me."

"How?"

He leaned in, resting his cheek on her thigh. "The smell of you." He leaned closer, drawing his tongue through her slick folds. "The taste of you," he said. "You."

And then she couldn't talk anymore. He buried his face between her legs, his tongue and fingers working black magic on her body, pushing her harder, higher, faster than she had imagined possible. Yeah, making out with Chase had been enough to nearly give her an orgasm. This was pushing her somewhere else entirely.

In her world, orgasm had always been a solo project. Surrendering the power to someone else, having her own pleasure not only in someone else's hands but in his complete and utter control, was something she had never even thought possible for her. But Chase was proving her wrong.

He slipped a finger deep inside of her as he continued to torture her with his wicked mouth, then a second, working them in and out of her slick channel while he teased her with the tip of his tongue.

A ball of tension grew in her stomach, expanded until she couldn't breathe. "It's too much," she gasped.

"Obviously it's not enough yet," he said, pushing her harder, higher.

And when the wave broke over her, she thought she was done for. Thought it was going to drag her straight out to sea and leave her to die. She couldn't catch her breath as pleasure assaulted her, going on and on, pounding through her like a merciless tide, battering her against the rocks, leaving her bruised, breathless.

And when it was over, Chase was looming over her, a condom in his hand.

She felt like a creature without its shell. Sensitive, completely unprotected. She wanted to hide from him, hide from this. But she couldn't. How could she? The simple truth was, they still weren't done. They had gone only part of the way. And if they didn't finish this, she would always wonder. He would, too.

She imagined that—whether or not he admitted it— was why he had come here tonight in the first place.

They had opened the lid on Pandora's box. And they couldn't close it until they had examined every last dirty, filthy sin inside of it.

Even though she thought it might kill her, she knew that they couldn't stop now.

He tore open the condom, positioning the protection over the blunt head of his arousal, rolling it down slowly.

She was transfixed. The sight of his own hand on his shaft so erotic she could hardly stand it.

She would pay good money to watch him shower, to watch his hands slide over all those gorgeous muscles. To watch him take himself in hand and lead himself to completion.

Oh, yeah. That was now her number one fantasy. Which was a problem, because it was a fantasy that would never be fulfilled.

Don't think about that now. Don't think about it ever.

He leaned in, kissing her, guiding her so that she was lying down on the couch, then he positioned himself between her legs, testing the entrance to her body before thrusting forward and filling her completely.

She closed her eyes tight, unable to handle the feeling of being invaded by him, both in body and in her soul.

"Look at me," he said.

And once more, she was completely helpless to do anything other than obey.

She opened her eyes, her gaze meeting his, touching her down deep, where his hands never could.

And then he kissed her, soft, gentle. That kind of tenderness that had been missing from her life for so long. The kind that she had always been too embarrassed to ask for from anyone. Too embarrassed to show that she needed. That she desperately craved.

But Chase knew. Because he was Chase. He just knew.

He flexed his hips again, his pelvis butting up against her, sending a shower of sparks through her body. There was no way she was ready to come again. Except he kept moving, creating new sensations inside of her, deeper than what had come before.

It shouldn't be possible for her to have another orgasm now. Not after the first one had stripped her so completely. But apparently tonight, nothing was impossible.

There was something different about this. About the two of them, working toward pleasure together. This wasn't just her giving it out to him, or him reciprocating. This was something they were sharing.

She focused on pieces of him. The intensity in his eyes. The way the tendons in his neck stood out, evidence of the control he was exerting. She looked at his hand, up by her head, grabbing hold of one of the blankets she had been using, clinging tightly to it, as though it were his lifeline.

She looked down at his throat, at the pulse beating there.

All these close, intimate snapshots of this man that she knew better than anyone else.

Her chest felt heavy, swollen, and then it began to expand. She was convinced that she was going to break apart. All of these feelings, all of this pleasure. It was just too much. She couldn't handle it.

"Please," she begged. "Please."

He released his grip on the blanket to grasp her hips, holding her steady as he pounded harder into her, as he pounded them both toward release. Toward salvation. It was too much. It needed to end. It was all she could think. She was begging him inside. *End it, Chase. Please, end it.*

Orgasm latched on to her throat like a wild beast, gripping her hard, violently, shaking her, pleasure exploding over her. Ugly. Completely and totally beyond control.

And then Chase let out a hoarse cry, freezing above her as he thrust inside her one last time, shivering, shaking as his own release took hold.

They were captive to it together. Powerless to do anything but wait until the savage beast was finished having its way. Until it was ready to move on.

And when it was over, only the two of them were left.

Just the two of them. Chase and Anna. No clothes, no shields.

She remembered the real reason she hadn't had sex since that first time. It had nothing to do with how good or bad it had felt. Nothing to do with what a jerk she'd been after.

It had been this. This feeling of being unable to hide. But with the other guy, it had been easy to regroup. Easy to pretend she felt nothing.

She couldn't do that with Chase. She was defenseless.

And for the first time in longer than she could remember, a tear slid down her cheek.

CHAPTER EIGHT

HE COULDN'T SWEAR creatively enough. He had just screwed his best friend's brains out on a couch in her living room. On top of what might be the world's friendliest, most nonsexual-looking blanket. With a Rodgers and Hammerstein musical on the TV in the background.

And then she had started crying. She had started crying, and she had wiggled out from beneath him and gone into the bathroom. Leaving him alone.

He had been sitting there by himself for a full thirty seconds attempting to reconcile all of these things.

And then he sprang into action.

He got up—still bare-ass naked—and walked down the hall. "Anna!" He didn't hear anything. And so he pounded on the bathroom door. "Anna!"

"I'm in the bathroom, dumbass!" came the terse, watery reply.

"I know. That's why I'm knocking on the bathroom door."

"Go away."

"No. I'm not going to go away. You need to talk to me."

"I don't want to talk."

"Anna, dammit, did I hurt you?"

He got nothing in return but silence. Then he heard the lock rattle, and the door opened a crack. One green eye looked up at him, accusing. "No."

"Why are you hiding?" He studied the eye more

closely. It was red-rimmed. Definitely still weeping a little bit.

"I don't know," she said.

"Well…you had me convinced that I… Anna, it happened really fast."

"Not *that* fast. Believe me, I've had faster."

"You wanted all of that…? I mean…"

She laughed. Actually laughed, pushing the door open a little bit wider. "After my emphatic… After all the *yes-ing*… You can honestly ask whether or not I wanted it?"

"I have a lot of sex," he said. "I don't see any point in beating around the bush there. And women have had a lot of reactions to the sex. But I can honestly say none of them have ever run away crying. So, yeah, I'm feeling a little bit shaky right now."

"You're shaky? I'm the one that's crying."

"And if I was alone in this…if I pushed you further than you wanted to go…I'm going to have to ask Sam to fire up the forge and prepare you a red-hot poker so you can have your way with me in an entirely different manner."

"I wanted it, Chase." Her tone was muted.

"Then why are you crying?"

"I'm not very experienced," she said.

"Well, I mean, I know you don't really hook up."

"I've had sex once. One other time."

He was stunned. Stunned enough that he was pretty sure Anna could have put her index finger on his chest, given a light push and knocked him flat on his ass. "Once."

"Sure. You remember Corbin. And that whole fiasco. Where I kind of made fun of his…lack of…attributes and staying power in the hall at school. And…basically ensured that no guy would ever touch me ever again."

"Right." He remembered that.

"Well, I didn't really get what the fuss was about."

"But you… I mean, you've had…"

"Orgasms? Yes. Almost every day of my life. Because I am industrious, and red-blooded, and self-sufficient."

He cleared his throat, trying to ignore the shot of heat that image sent straight through his blood. Anna. Touching herself.

What the hell was happening to him? Well, there was nothing happening. It had damn well *happened*. On the couch in Anna's living room.

He could never look at her again without seeing her there, obeying his orders. Spreading her thighs for him so that he could get a good look at her. Yeah, he could never unsee that. Wasn't sure if he wanted to. But where the hell did he go from here? Where did they go?

There were a lot of women he could have sex with, worry-free. Anna wasn't one of them. She was a rare, precious thing in his life. Someone who knew him. Who knew all about how affected he and Sam had been by the loss of their parents.

Someone he never had to explain it to because she'd been there.

He didn't like explaining all that. So the solution was keep the friends that were there when it happened, and make sure everyone else was temporary.

Which meant Anna couldn't be temporary. She was part of him. Part of his life. A load-bearing wall on the structure that was Chase McCormack. Remove her, and he would crumble.

That was why she had always stayed a friend. Why

he had never done anything like this with her before. It wasn't because of her coveralls, or her don't-step-on-the-grass demeanor. Or even because she'd neatly neutered the reputation of the guy she'd slept with in high school.

It was because he needed her friendship, not her body.

But the problem was now he knew what she looked like naked.

He couldn't get that image out of his head. And he didn't even want to.

Same with the image of all her self-administered, industrious climaxes.

Damn his dirty mind.

"Okay," he said, taking a step away from the door. "Why don't you come out?"

"I'm naked."

"So am I."

She looked down. "So you are."

"We need to talk."

"Isn't it women who are supposed to require conversation after basic things like sex?"

"I don't know. Because I never stick around long enough to find out. But this is different. This is you and me, Anna, and I will be damned if I let things get messed up over a couple of orgasms."

She chewed her lower lip. She looked...well, she looked young. And she didn't look too tough. It made him ache. "They were pretty good ones."

"Are you all right?"

"I'm fine. It's just that all of this is a little bit weird. And I'm not really experienced enough to pretend that it isn't."

"Right." The whole thing about her having been with

only one guy kind of freaked him out. Made him feel like he was responsible for some things. Big things, like what she would think of sex from this day forward. And then there was the bone-deep possessiveness. That he was the first one in all this time… He should hate it. It should scare him. It should not make him feel…triumph.

He was triumphant, dammit. "Why haven't you slept with anyone else?"

She lifted a shoulder. "I told you. I didn't really think my first experience was that great."

"So you just never…"

"I'm also emotionally dysfunctional, in case you hadn't noticed."

A shocked laugh escaped his lips. "Right. Same goes."

"I don't know. Sex kind of weirds me out. It's a lot of closeness."

"It doesn't have to be," he pointed out. It felt like a weird thing to say, though, because what they'd done just now had been the epitome of closeness.

"It just all feels…raw. And…it was good. But I think that's kind of why it bothered me."

"I don't want it to bother you."

"Well, the other thing is it was *you*. You and me, like you said. We don't do things like this. We hang out, we drink beer. We don't screw."

"Turns out we're pretty compatible when it comes to the screwing." He wasn't entirely sure this was the time to make light of what had just happened. But he was at sea here. So he had to figure out some way to talk to her. He figured he would make his best effort to treat her like he always did.

"Yeah," she said, finally pushing her way out of the

bathroom. "But I'm not really sure there's much we can do with that."

He felt like he was losing his grip on something, something essential, important. Like he was on a rope precariously strung across the canyon, trying to hang on and not fall to his doom. Not fall to *their* doom, since she was right there with him.

What she was saying should feel like safety. It didn't. It felt like the bottom of the damn canyon.

"I don't know if that's the way to handle it."

"You don't?" she asked, blinking.

Apparently. He hadn't thought that statement through before it had come out of his mouth. "Yeah. Look, you kissed me yesterday. You gave me...oral pleasure earlier. And now we've had sex. Obviously, this isn't going away. Obviously, there's some attraction between us that we've never really acknowledged before."

"Or," she said, "someone cast a spell on us. Yeah, we drank some kind of sex potion. Makes you horny for twenty-four hours and then goes away."

"Sex potion?"

"It's either that or years of repressed lust, Chase. Pick whichever one makes you most comfortable."

"I would go with sex potion if I thought such a thing existed." He took a deep breath. "You know there's a lot of people that think men and women can't just be friends. And I've always thought that was stupid. Maybe this is why. Maybe it's because eventually, something happens. Eventually, the connection can't just be platonic. Not when you've spent so long in each other's company. Not when you're both reasonably attractive and single."

She snorted. "*Reasonably* attractive. What happened to me being a *damn miracle*?"

"I was referring to myself when I said reasonably. I'd hate to sound egotistical."

"Honestly, Chase, after thirty years of accomplished egotism, why worry about it now?"

He looked down at her. She was stark naked, standing in front of him, and he felt like he was in front of the pastry display case at Pie in the Sky. He wanted to sample everything, and he didn't know where to start.

But he couldn't do anything about that now. He was trying to make amends. Dropping to his knees in front of her and burying his face between her legs probably wouldn't help with that.

He could feel his dick starting to wake up again. And since he was naked he might as well just go ahead and shout his intentions at her, because he wouldn't be able to hide them.

He couldn't look at her and not get hard, though. A new development in their relationship. But then, so was standing in front of each other without clothes.

"You're beautiful," he said, unable to help himself.

She wasn't as curvy as the women he usually gravitated toward. Her curves were restrained, her waist slim, with no dramatic sweep inward, just a slow build down to those wide, gorgeous hips that he now had fantasies about grabbing hold of while he pumped into her from behind. Her breasts were small but perfection in his mind. More would just be more.

He couldn't really imagine how he had ever looked at her face and found it plain. He had to kick his own ass mentally for that. He had been blind. Someone with unrefined, cheap taste. Who thought that if you stuck rhinestones and glitter on something, that meant it was prettier. But that wasn't Anna. She was simple, refined beauty. Something that only a connoisseur might appreciate. She was like a sunset over the ocean in comparison to a gaudy ballroom chandelier. Both had their strong points. But one was real, deep. Priceless instead of expensive.

That was Anna.

Something about those thoughts made a tightening sensation start in his gut and work its way up to his chest.

"Maybe what happened was just inevitable," he said, looking at her again.

"I can't really disprove that," she said, shifting uncomfortably. "You know, since it happened. I really need to put my clothes on."

"Do you have to?"

She frowned. "Yes. And you do, too. Because if we don't…"

"We'll have sex again."

The words stood between them, stark and far too true for either of their liking.

"Probably not," she said, sounding wholly unconvinced.

"Definitely yes."

She sighed heavily. "Chase, you can have sex with anyone you want. I'm definitely hard up. If you keep walking around flashing that thing, I'm probably going to hop on for a ride, I'll just be honest with you. But I understand if I'm not half as irresistible to you as you are to me."

Anger roared through him, suddenly, swiftly. And just like earlier, when she'd thrown her walls up and tried to drive a wedge between them, he found himself moving toward her. Moving to break through. He growled, backing her up against the wall, almost sighing in relief when his hardening cock met up with her soft skin, when her small breasts pressed against his chest. He grabbed hold of her hands, drawing them together and lifting them up over her head. "Let's get one thing straight, Anna," he said. "You are irresistible to me. If you weren't irresistible to me, I would still be at home. I never would have come here. I never would have kissed you. I never would have touched you. Don't you dare put yourself down. If this is because of your brothers, because of your dad…"

She closed her eyes, looking away from him. "Don't. It's not that."

"Then what is it? Why don't you think you can have this?"

"There's nothing to have. It's just sex. You mean the world to me. And just because I'm…suddenly unable to handle my hormones, I'm not going to compromise our friendship."

"It doesn't have to compromise it," he said, lowering his voice.

"What are you suggesting? We can't have a relationship with each other. We don't have those kinds of feelings for each other. A relationship is more than sex. It's romance and all kinds of stuff that I'm not even sure I want."

"I don't want it, either," he said. "But we're going to see each other. Pretty much every day. Not just because of the stupid bet. Not just because of the charity event. I'd call all that off right now if I thought it was going to ruin our friendship. But the horse has left the stable, Anna, well and truly. It's not going back in." He rolled his hips forward, and she gasped. "See what I mean? And if you were resistible? Then sure, I would tell you that we could just be done. We could pretend it didn't happen. But you're not. So I can't."

She opened her eyes again, looking up at him. "Then what are we doing?"

"You've heard of friends with benefits. Why can't we do that? I mean, I would never have set out to have that relationship. Because I don't think it's very smart. But…it's a little bit late for smart."

"Friends with benefits. As in…we stay friends by day and we screw each other senseless by night?"

Gah. That about sent him over the edge. "Yeah."

"Until what? Until…"

"Until you get that other date. Until the charity thing. As long as we're both single, why not? You're working toward the relationship stuff. You said you didn't want to be alone anymore. So, maybe this is good in the meantime. I know you're both industrious and red-blooded, and can get those orgasms all by yourself." He rolled his hips again and, much to his satisfaction, a small moan of pleasure escaped her lips. "But are they this good?"

"No," she said, her tone hushed.

"This is possibly the worst idea in the history of the world. But hell, you wanted to get some more experience… I'm offering to give it to you." The moment he said the words he wanted to bite his tongue off. The idea of giving Anna more experience just so she could go and do things with other men? That made him see red. Made him feel violent. Jealous. Things he never felt.

But what other option was there? He couldn't keep her. Not like this. But he couldn't let her go now.

He was messed up. *This* was messed up.

"I guess… I guess that makes sense. You know, until earlier today I'd never even given a guy a blow job."

"You're killing me," he said, closing his eyes.

"Well, I don't want you to die. You just offered me your penis for carnal usage. I want you alive."

"So that's it? My penis has now become the star of the show. Wow, how quickly our friendship has eroded."

"Our friendship is still solid. I think it just goes to prove how solid your dick is."

"With romantic praise like that, how are you still single?"

"I have no idea. I spout sonnets effortlessly."

He leaned forward, kissing her, a strange, warm sensation washing over him. He was kissing Anna. And it didn't feel quite as rushed and desperate as all the other times before it. A decision had been made. This wasn't a hasty race against sanity. This wasn't trying to get as much satisfaction as possible squeezed into a moment before reality kicked in. This was…well, in the new world order, it was sanctioned.

Instantly, he was rock hard again, ready to go, even though it'd been only a few minutes since his last orgasm. But there was one problem. "I don't have a condom," he said, cursing and pushing himself away from her. "I don't suppose the woman who has been celibate for the past thirteen years has one?"

"No," she said, sagging against the wall. "You only carry one on you?"

"Yeah. I'm not superhuman. I don't usually expect to get it on more than once in a couple of hours."

"But you were going to with me?"

He looked down at his very erect cock. "Does this answer your question?"

"Yeah."

"Well, then." He let out a heavy sigh.

"You could stay and watch…*Oklahoma!* with me."

He nodded slowly. He should stay and watch *Okla-*

homa! with her. If he didn't, it kind of made a mockery of the whole friends-with-benefits thing. Because, before the sex, he would have stayed with her to watch a movie, of course. To hang out, because she was one of his favorite people on earth to spend time with. Even if her taste in movies was deeply suspect.

Of course, he didn't particularly want to stay now, because she presented the temptation that he could not give in to.

"Unless you have to work early tomorrow."

"I really do," he said.

"Thank God."

His eyebrows shot up. "You want to get rid of me?"

"I don't really want to hang out with you when I know I can't have you."

"I felt the same way, but I didn't want to say it. I thought it seemed kind of offensive."

Strangely, she smiled. "I'm not offended. I'm not offended at all. I kind of like being irresistible."

Instead of leaving, he knew that he could drive down to the store and buy a box of condoms. And he seriously considered it. The problem with that was there had to be some boundaries. Some limits. He was pretty sure being so horny and desperate that you needed to buy condoms right away instead of just waiting until you had protection on hand probably didn't fit within the boundaries of friends with benefits.

"I'll see you tomorrow, then."

She nodded. "See you tomorrow."

CHAPTER NINE

BY THE TIME Anna swung by the grocery store in the afternoon, she was feeling very mature, and very proud of herself. She was having a no-strings sexual relationship with her friend. And she was going to buy milk, cheese and condoms. Because she was mature and adult and completely fine with the whole situation. Also, mature.

She grabbed a cart and began to slowly walk up and down the aisles. She was not making sure that no one she knew was around. Because, of course, she wasn't at all embarrassed to be in the store looking for milk, cheese and—incidentally—prophylactics. She was *thirty*. She was entitled to a little bit of sexual release. Anyway, no one was actually watching her.

She swallowed hard, trying to remember exactly which aisle the condoms were in. She had never bought any. Ever. In her entire life.

She had been extremely tempted to make a dash to the store last night when Chase had discovered he didn't have any more protection, but she had imagined that was just a little bit too desperate. She was going to be non-desperate about this. Very chill. And not like a woman who was a near virgin. Or like someone who was so desperate to jump her best friend's bones it might seem like there were deeper emotions at play. There were not.

The strong feelings she had were just...in her pants. Pants feelings. That's it.

Last night's breakdown had been purely because she was unaccustomed to sex. Just a little post-orgasmic release. That's all it was. The whole thing was a release. Post-orgasmic tears weren't really all that strange.

She felt bolstered by that thought.

She turned down the aisle labeled Family Planning and made her way toward the condoms. Lubricated. Extra-thin. Ribbed. There were options. She had to stand there and seriously ponder ribbed. She should have asked Chase what he had used last night. Because whatever that had been had been perfect.

"Anna." The masculine voice coming from her left startled her.

She turned and—to her utter horror—saw her brother Mark standing there.

"Hi," she said, taking two steps away from the condom shelf, as though that would make it less obvious why she was in the aisle. Whatever. They were adults. Neither of them were virgins and they were both aware of that.

Still, she needed some distance between herself and anything that said "ribbed for her pleasure" when she was standing there talking to her brother.

"Haven't seen you in a couple days."

"Well, you pissed me off last time I saw you."

He lifted a shoulder. "Sorry."

He probably was, too.

"Hey, whatever. I win your bet."

His brows shot up. "I heard a rumor about you and Chase McCormack kissing at Beaches, but I was pretty sure that…" His eyes drifted toward the condoms. *"Really?"*

Dying of embarrassment was a serious risk at the moment, but she was caught. Completely and totally caught. And as long as she was drowning in a sea of horror…well, she might as well ride the tide.

If he needed proof her date with Chase was real, she imagined proof of sex was about the best there was.

She took a fortifying breath. "Really," she said, crossing her arms beneath her breasts. "It's happening. I have a date. I have more than a date. I have a whole future full of dates because I have a relationship. With Chase. You lose."

"I'm supposed to believe that you and McCormack are suddenly—" his eyes drifted back to the condoms again "*—that.*"

"You don't have to believe it. It's true. He's also going to be my date to the charity gala that I'm invited to. I will take my payment in small or large bills. Thank you."

"I'm not convinced."

"You're not convinced?" She moved closer to the shelf and grabbed a box of condoms. "I am caught in the act."

"Convenient," he said, grabbing his own box.

She made a face. "It's not convenient. It happened."

"You're in love with him?"

The question felt like a punch to the stomach. She did not like it. She didn't like it at all. More than that, she had no idea what to say. *No* seemed…wrong. *Yes* seemed worse. And she wasn't really sure either answer was true.

You can't love Chase.

She couldn't not love him, either. He was her friend, after all. Of course she wasn't in love with him.

Her stomach twisted tight. No. She did not love him. She didn't do love. At all. Especially not with him. Because he would never…

"You look like you just got slapped with a fish,"

Mark said, and, to his credit, he looked somewhat concerned.

"I… Of course I love him," she said. That was a safe answer. It was also true. She did love him. As a friend. And…she loved his body. And everything about him as a human being. Except for the fact that he was a man slut who would never settle down with any woman, much less her.

Why not you?

No. She was not thinking about this. She wasn't thinking about any of this.

"Tell you what. If you're still together at the gala, you get your money."

"That isn't fair. That isn't what we agreed on."

He lifted a shoulder. "I know. But I also didn't expect you to grab your best friend and have him be your date. That still seems suspicious to me, regardless of… purchases."

"You didn't put any specifications on the bet, Mark. You can't change the rules now."

"We didn't put any specifications on it saying I couldn't."

"Why do you care?"

He snorted. "Why do you care?"

"I have pride, jackass."

"And I don't trust Chase McCormack. If you're still together at the gala, you get your money. And if he hurts you in any way, I will break his neck. After I pull his balls off and feed them to the sharks."

It wasn't very often that Mark's protective side was on display. Usually, he was too busy tormenting her. Their childhood had been rough. Their father didn't have any idea how to show affection to them, and as a result none of them were very good at it, either. Still,

she never doubted that—even when he was a jerk—
Mark cared about her.

"That's not necessary. Chase is my best friend. And
now…he's more. He isn't going to hurt me."

"Sounds to me like he has the potential to hurt you
worse than just about anybody."

His words settled heavily in the pit of her stomach. She should be able to brush them off. Because she
and Chase were in a relationship. She and Chase were
friends with benefits. And nothing about that would
hurt at all.

"I'll be fine."

"If you need anything, just let me know."

"I will."

He lifted the condom box. "We'll pretend this didn't
happen." Then he turned and started to walk away.

"Pretend what didn't happen?" She pulled her own
box of condoms up against her chest and held it tightly.
"See? I've already forgotten. Mostly because I can't
afford therapy. At least not until you pay me the big
bucks at the gala."

"We'll see," he said, walking out of sight.

She turned, chucking the box into her cart and
making her way quickly down to the milk aisle. Chase
wasn't going to hurt her, because Mark was wrong.
They were only friends, and she quashed the traitorous flame in her stomach that tried to grow, tried to
convince her otherwise.

She wasn't going to get hurt. She was just going to
have a few orgasms and then move on.

That was her story, and she was sticking to it.

"I'M TAKING YOU dancing tonight," Chase said as soon
as Anna picked up the phone.

"Did you bump your head on an anvil today?"

He supposed he shouldn't be that surprised to hear Anna's sarcasm. After last night—vulnerability, tears—he'd had a feeling that she wasn't going to be overly friendly today. In fact, he'd guessed that she would have transformed into one of the little porcupines that were on her pajamas. He had been right.

"No," he said. "I'm just following the lesson plan. I said I was taking you out, and so I am."

"You know," she said, her voice getting husky, "I'm curious about whether or not making me scream was anywhere on the lesson plan."

His body jolted, heat rushing through his veins. He looked over his shoulder at Sam, who was working steadily on something in the back of the shop. It was Anna's day off, so she wasn't on the property. But he and Sam were in the middle of a big custom job. A gate with a lot of intricate detail, with matching work for the deck and interior staircase of the home. Which meant they didn't get real time off right now.

"No," he returned, satisfied his brother wasn't paying attention, "that wasn't on the lesson plan. But I'm a big believer in improvisation."

"That was improvisation? In that case, it seems to be your strength."

The sarcasm he had expected. This innuendo, he had not. They'd both pulled away hard last night, no denying it. It would have been simple to go out and get more protection and neither of them had.

But damn, this new dynamic between them was a lot to get used to. Still, for all that it was kind of crazy, he knew what he wanted. "I'd like to show you more of my strengths tonight."

"You're welcome to improvise your way on over to

my bed anytime." There was a pause. "Was that flirting? Was that *good* flirting?"

He laughed, tension exiting his body in a big gust. He should have known. He wasn't sure how he felt about this being part of the lesson. Not when he had been on the verge of initiating phone sex in the middle of a workday with his brother looming in the background. But keeping it part of the lesson was for the best. He didn't need to lose his head. This was Anna, after all. He was walking a very fine line here.

On the one hand, he knew keeping a clear line drawn in the sand was the right thing to do. They weren't just going to be able to slide right back into their normal relationship. Not after what had happened. On the other hand, Anna was...Anna. She was essential to him. And she wasn't jaded when it came to sexual relationships. Wasn't experienced. That meant he needed to handle her with care. And it would benefit him to remember that he couldn't play with her the way he did women with a little more experience. Women who understood that this was sex and nothing more.

It could never be meaningless sex with Anna. He couldn't have a meaningless conversation with her. That meant that whatever happened between them physically would change things, build things, tear things down. That was a fact. A scary one. Taking control, trying to harness it, label it, was the only solution he had. Otherwise, things would keep happening when they weren't prepared. That would be worse.

Maybe.

He cleared his throat. "Very good flirting. You got me all excited."

"Excellent," she said, sounding cheerful. "Also, I bought condoms."

He choked. "Did you?"

"They aren't ribbed. I wasn't sure if the one you used last night was."

"No," he said, rubbing the back of his neck and casting a side eye at his brother. "It wasn't."

"Good. I was looking for a repeat performance. I didn't want to get the wrong thing. Though maybe sometime we should try ribbed."

Sometime. Because there would be more than once. More than last night. More than tonight. "We can try it if you want."

"I feel like we might as well try everything. I have a lot of catching up to do."

"Dancing," he said, trying to wage a battle with the heat that was threatening to take over his skull. "Do you want to go dancing tonight?"

"Not really. But I can see the benefit. Seeing as there will be dancing at the fund-raiser. And I bet I'm terrible at dancing."

"Great. I'm going to pick you up at seven. We're going to Ace's."

"Then I'll be ready."

He hung up the phone and suddenly realized he was at the center of Sam's keen focus. That bastard had been listening in the entire time. "Hot date tonight?" he asked.

"Dancing. With Anna," he said meaningfully. The meaning being *with Anna and not with you.*

"Well, then, you wouldn't mind if I tagged along." Jerkface was ignoring his meaning.

"I would mind."

"I thought this was just about some bet."

"It is," he lied.

"Uh-huh."

"You don't want to go out. You want to stay home and eat a TV dinner. You're just harassing me."

Sam shrugged. "I have to get my kicks somewhere."

"Get your own. Get laid."

"Nope."

"You're a weirdo."

"I'm selective."

Maybe Sam was, maybe he wasn't. Chase could honestly say that his brother's sex life was a mystery to him. Which was fine. Really, more than fine. Chase had a reputation, Sam...did not. Well, unless that reputation centered around being grumpy and antisocial.

"Right. Well, you enjoy that. I'm going to go out."

"Chase," Sam said, his tone taking on a note of steel. "Don't hurt her."

Those words poked him right in the temper. "Really?"

"She's the best thing you have," Sam said, his voice serious. "You find a woman like that, you keep her. In whatever capacity you can."

"She's my best friend. I'm not going to hurt her."

"Not on purpose."

"I don't think you're in any position to stand there and lecture me on interpersonal relationships, since you pretty much don't have any."

"I have you," Sam said.

"Right. I'm not sure that counts."

"I have Anna. But if you messed things up with her, I won't have her, either."

Chase frowned. "You don't have feelings for her, do you?" He would really hate to have to punch his brother in the face. But he would.

"No. Not like you mean. But I know her, and I care about her. And I know you."

"What does that mean?"

Sam pondered that for a second. "You're not her speed."

"I'm not trying to be." He was getting ready to punch his brother in the face anyway.

"I'm just saying."

"You're just saying," he muttered. "Go *just say* somewhere else. A guy whose only friends are his younger brother and that brother's friend maybe shouldn't stand there and make commentary on relationships."

"I'm quiet. I'm perceptive. As you mentioned, I am an artist."

"You can't pull that out when it suits you and put it away when it doesn't."

"Sure I can. Artists are temperamental."

"Stop beating around the bush. Say what you want to say."

Sam sighed. "If she offers you more than friendship, take it, dumbass."

"Why would you think that she would ever offer that? Why would you think that I want it?"

He felt defensive. And more than a little bit annoyed. "She will. I'm not blind. Actually, being antisocial has its benefits. It means that I get to sit back and watch other people interact. She likes you. She always has. And she's the kind of good… Chase, we don't get good like that. We don't deserve it."

"Gee. Thanks, Sam."

"I'm not trying to insult you. I'm just saying that she's better than either of us. Figure out how to make it work if she wants to."

Everything in Chase recoiled. "She doesn't want to. And neither do I." He turned away from Sam, heading toward the door.

"Are you sleeping with her yet?"

Chase froze. "That isn't any of your business."

"Right. You are."

"Still not your business."

"Chase, we both have a lot of crap to wade through. Which is pretty obvious. But if she's standing there willing to pull you out, I'm just saying you need to take her up on her offer."

"She has enough crap of her own that she's hip deep in, Sam. I don't need her taking on mine."

Sam rubbed his hand over his forehead. "Yeah, that's always the thing."

"Anyway, she doesn't want me. Not like that. I mean, not forever. This is just a...physical thing." Which was way more information than his brother deserved.

"Keep telling yourself that if it helps you sleep at night."

"I sleep like a baby, Sam." He continued out the door, heading toward his truck. He had to get back to the house and get showered and dressed so that he could pick up Anna. And he was not going to think about anything his brother had said.

Anna didn't want forever with him.

That thought immobilized him, forced him to imagine a future with Anna, stretching on and on into the distance. Holding her, kissing her. Sleeping beside her every night and waking up with her every morning.

Seeing her grow round with his child.

He shut it down immediately. That was a fantasy. One he didn't want. One he couldn't have.

He would have Anna as a friend forever, but the "benefits" portion of their relationship was finite.

So, he would just enjoy this while it lasted.

CHAPTER TEN

SHE LOOKED LIKE a cliché. A really slutty one. She wasn't sure she cared. But in her very short denim skirt and plaid shirt knotted above the waistline she painted quite the picture.

One of a woman looking to get lucky.

"Well," she said to her reflection—her made-up reflection, compliments of her trip to the store in Tolowa today, as was everything else. "You *are* looking to get lucky."

Fair. That was fair.

She heard the sound of a truck engine and tires on the gravel in her short little driveway. She was renting a house in an older neighborhood in town—not right in the armpit of town where she'd grown up, but still sort of on the fringe—and the yard was a little bit...rustic.

She wondered if Chase would honk. Or if he would come to the door.

Him coming to the door would feel much more like a date. A real date.

A *date* date.

Oh, Lord, what were they doing?

She had flirted with him on the phone, and she'd enjoyed it. Had wanted—very much—to push him even harder. Trading innuendo with him was...well, it was a lot more fun than she'd imagined.

There was a heavy knock on the door and she

squeaked, hopping a little bit before catching her breath. Then she grabbed her purse and started to walk to the entry, trying to calm her nerves. He'd come to the door. That felt like A Thing.

You're being crazy. Friends with benefits. Not boyfriend.

The word *boyfriend* made her stomach lurch, and she did her best to ignore it. She jerked the door open, watching his face intently for his response to her new look. And she was not disappointed.

"Damn," he said, leaning forward, resting his forearm on the doorjamb. "I didn't realize you would be showing up dressed as Country Girl from My Dirtiest Dreams."

She shouldn't feel flattered by that. But she positively glowed. "It seemed fair, since you're basically the centerfold of *Blacksmith Magazine*."

He laughed. "Really? How would that photo shoot go?"

"You posing strategically in front of the forge with a bellows over your junk."

"I am not getting my *junk* near the forge. The last thing I need is sensitive body parts going up in flames."

"I know I don't want them going up in flames." She cleared her throat, suddenly aware of a thick blanket of awkwardness settling over them. She didn't know what to do with him now. Did she...not touch him unless they were going to have sex? Did she kiss him if she wanted to or did she need permission?

She needed a friends-with-benefits handbook.

"Um," she began, rather unsuccessfully. "What exactly are my benefits?"

"Meaning?"

"My benefits additional to this friendship. Do I… kiss you when I see you? Or…"

"Do you want to kiss me?"

She looked up at him, all sexy and delicious looking in his tight black T-shirt, cowboy hat and late-in-the-day stubble. "Is that a trick question? Because the only answer to 'Do I want to kiss a very hot guy?' is yes. But not if you don't want to kiss me."

He wrapped his arm around her waist, drawing her up against him before bending down to kiss her slowly, thoroughly. "Does that help?"

She let out a long, slow breath, the tension that had been strangling her since he'd arrived at her house leaving her body slowly. "Yes," she said, sighing. "It does."

"All right," he said, extending his hand. "Let's go."

She took hold of his hand, the warmth of his touch flooding her, making her stomach flip. She let him lead her to the truck, open her door for her. All manner of date-type stuff. The additional benefits were getting bound up in the dating lessons and at the moment she wasn't sure what was for her and what was for the Making Her Datable mission.

Then she decided it didn't matter.

She just clung to the good feelings the whole drive to Ace's.

When they got there, she felt the true weight of the spectacle they were creating in the community. Beaches was one thing. Them being together there had certainly caused a ripple. But everyone in Copper Ridge hung out at Ace's.

Sierra West, whose family was a client of both her and Chase, was in the corner with some other friends who were involved with local rodeo events. Sheriff Eli

Garrett was over by the bar, along with his brother, Connor, and their wives, Sadie and Liss.

She looked the other direction and saw Holly and Ryan Masters sitting in the corner, looking ridiculously happy. Holly and Ryan had both grown up in foster care in Copper Ridge and so had been part of the town-charity-case section at school. Though Holly was younger and Ryan a little older, so she'd never been close friends with them. Behind them was Jonathan Bear, looking broody and unapproachable as usual.

She officially knew too many damn people.

"This town is the size of a postage stamp," she muttered as she followed Chase to a table where they could deposit their coats and her purse.

"That's good," he said. "Men are seeing you attached. It's all part of changing your reputation. That's what you want."

She grunted. "I guess." It didn't feel like what she wanted. She mostly just wanted to be alone with Chase now. No performance art required.

But she was currently a dancing monkey for all of Copper Ridge, so performance art was the order of the evening.

She also suddenly felt self-conscious about her wardrobe choice. Wearing this outfit for Chase hadn't seemed bad at all. Wearing it in front of everyone was a little much.

The jukebox was blaring, and Luke Bryan was demanding all the country girls shake it for him, so Anna figured—regardless of how comfortable she was feeling—it was as good a time as any for them to get out on the dance floor.

The music was fast, so people weren't touching. They were just sort of, well, *shaking it* near each other.

She was just standing there, looking at him and not shaking it, because she didn't know what to do next. It felt weird to be here in front of everyone in a skirt. It felt weird to be dancing with Chase. It felt weird to not touch him. But it would be weirder to touch him.

Hell if she knew what she was doing here.

Then he reached out, brushing his fingers down her arm. That touch, that connection, rooted her to the earth. To the moment. To him. Suddenly, it didn't matter so much what other people around them were doing. She moved in slightly, and he put his hand on her hip.

Then, before she was ready, the song ended, slowing things down. And now she really didn't know what to do. It seemed that Chase did, though. He wrapped his arm around her waist, drawing her in close, taking hold of her hand with his free one.

Her heart was pounding hard. And she was pretty sure her face was bright red. She looked up at Chase, his expression unreadable. He was not bright red. Of course he wasn't. Because even if this relationship was new for him, this kind of situation was not. He knew how to handle women. He knew how to handle sex feelings. Meanwhile, she was completely unsure of what to do. Like a buoy floating out in the middle of the ocean, just bobbing there on her own.

Her breathing got shorter, harder. Matching her heartbeat. She couldn't just dance with him like this. She needed to not be in front of people when she felt these things. She felt like her arousal was written all over her skin. Well, it was. She was blushing like a beacon. She could probably guide ships in from the sea.

She looked at Chase's face again. There was no way to tell what he was thinking. His dark gaze was shielded by the dim lighting, his jaw set, hard, his mouth in a firm line. That brief moment of connection that she'd felt was gone now. He was touching her still, but she had no idea what he was feeling.

She looked over to her left and noticed that people were staring. Of course they were. She and Chase were dancing and that was different. And, of course, a great many of the stares were coming from women. Women who probably felt like they should be in her position. Like she didn't belong there.

And they could all see how much she wanted it. That she wanted him more than he wanted her. That she was the one who was completely and totally out of control. Needing him so much she couldn't even hide it.

And they all knew she didn't deserve it.

She pulled away from him, looking around, breathing hard. "I think… I just need a break."

She crossed the room and went back to their table, grabbing her purse and making her way over to the bar.

Chase joined her only a few moments later. "What's up?"

She shook her head. "Nothing."

"We were dancing, and then you freaked out."

"I don't like everybody watching us."

"That's the point, though."

That simple statement stabbed her straight through the heart. "Yeah. I know." That was the problem. He was so conscious of why they were doing this. This whole thing. And she could so easily forget. Could so easily let down all the walls and shields that she had put in place to protect her heart. And just let herself want.

She hated that. Hated craving things she couldn't have. Affection she could never hope to earn.

Her mother had left. And no amount of wishing that she would come back, no amount of crying over that lost love, would do anything to fix it. No amount of hoping her father would drop that crusty exterior and give her a hug when she needed it would make it happen. So she just didn't want. Or at least, she never let people see how much she wanted.

"I know," she said, her tone a little bit stiffer than she would like.

She was bombing out here. Failing completely at remaining cool, calm and unaffected. She was standing here in public, hemorrhaging needs all over the place.

"What's wrong?"

"I need a drink."

"Why don't we leave?"

She blinked. "Just…leave?"

"If you aren't having fun, then there's no point. Let's go."

"Where are we going?"

He grabbed her hand and started to lead her through the bar. "Somewhere fun."

She followed him out into the night, laughing helplessly when they climbed into the truck. "People are going to talk. That was all a little weird."

"Let them talk. They need something to do."

He started the engine and backed out of the parking lot, turning sharply and heading down the road, out of town.

"Where are we going?"

"Somewhere I bet you've never been."

"You don't know my life, Chase McCormack. You don't know where I've been."

"I do know your life, Anna Brown."

She gritted her teeth, because, of course, he did. She said nothing as they continued to drive up the road. And still said nothing when he turned onto a dirt road that forked into a narrower dirt road as it went up the mountain.

"What are we doing?" she asked again.

Just then, they came to a flat, clear area. She couldn't see anything; there were no lights except for the headlights on the truck, illuminating nothing but the side of another mountain, thick with evergreens.

"I want to make out with you. This is where you go do that."

"We're adults," she said, ignoring the giddy fluttering in her stomach. "We have our own bedrooms. And beds. We don't need to go make out in a car."

"*Need* is not the operative word here. We're expanding experiences and stuff." He flicked the radio on, country music filling the cab of the truck. "Actually, I think before we make out—" he opened the driver's-side door "—we should dance."

Now there was nobody here. Which meant there was no excuse. Actually, this made her a lot more emotional. She did not like that. She didn't like the superpower that Chase seemed to have of reaching down inside of her, past all the defenses, and grabbing hold of tender, emotional things.

But she wasn't going to refuse, either.

It was dark out here. At least there was that.

Before she had a chance to move, Chase was at her side of the truck, opening her door. He extended his hand. "Dance with me?"

She was having a strange out-of-body experience. She wasn't sure who this woman was, up in the woods with only a gorgeous man for company. A man who wanted to dance with her. A man who wanted to make out with her.

She unbuckled, accepting his offered hand and pop-

ping out of the truck. He spun her over to the front of the
vehicle, the headlights serving as spotlights as the music
played over the radio. "I'm kind of a crappy dancer," he
said, pulling her in close.

"You don't seem like a crappy dancer to me."

"How many men have you danced with?"

She laughed. "Um, counting now?"

"Yeah."

"One."

He chuckled, his breath fanning over her cheekbone.
So intimate to share the air with him like this. Shocking. "Well, then, you don't have much to compare it to."

"I guess not. But I don't think I would compare either way."

"Oh, yeah? Why is that?"

"You're in a league of your own, Chase McCormack,
don't you know?"

"Hmm. I have heard that a time or two. When teachers told me I was a unique sort of devil, sent there to
make their lives miserable. Or all the times I used to
get into it with my old man."

"Well, you did raise a lot of hell."

"Yeah. I did. I continue to raise hell, in some fashion. But I need people to see a different side of me," he
said, drawing her even tighter up against him. "I need
for them to see that Sam and I can handle our business.
That we can make the McCormack name big again."

"Can you?" she asked, tilting her head up, her lips
brushing his chin. The stubble there was prickly, masculine. Irresistible. So she bit him. Just lightly. Scraping her teeth over his skin.

He gripped her hair, pulling her head back. The sudden rush of danger in the movements sending a shot
of adrenaline through her blood. This was so strange.

Being in his arms and feeling like she was home. Like he was everything comforting and familiar. A warm blanket, a hot chocolate and a musical she'd seen a hundred times.

Then things would shift, and he would become something else entirely. A stranger. Sex, sin and all the things she'd never taken the time to explore. She liked that, too.

She was starting to get addicted to both.

"Oh, I can handle myself just fine," he said, his tone hard.

"Can you handle me?" she asked.

He slid his hand down to cup her ass, his eyes never leaving hers as they swayed to the music. "I can handle you. However you want it."

"Hard," she said, her throat going dry, her words slightly unsteady. She wasn't sure what had possessed her to say that.

"You want it hard?" he asked, his words sounding strangled.

"Yes," she said.

"How else do you want it?" he asked, holding her against him, moving in time with the beat. She could feel his cock getting hard against her hip.

"Aren't you the one with the lesson plan?"

"You're the one in need of the education," he said.

"I don't want tonight to be about that," she said, and she was as sure about that as she'd been about wanting it hard and equally unsure about how she knew it.

"What do you want it to be about?"

"You," she said, tracing the sharp line of his jaw. "Me. That's about it."

"What do you want from me?" he asked.

Only everything. She shied away from that thought. "Show me what the fuss is about."

"I did that already."

Something hot and possessive spiked in her blood. Something she never could have anticipated, because she hadn't even realized that it lived inside of her. "No. Something you don't give other women, Chase. You're my friend. You're...more to me than one night and an orgasm. You're right. I could have gotten that from a lot of guys. Well, maybe not the orgasm. But sex for sure. My coveralls aren't that much of a turnoff. And you could have any woman. So give me you. And I'll give you me. Don't hold back."

"You're...not very experienced."

She stretched up on tiptoes, pressing her lips to his. "Did I ask for a gentleman? Or did I ask for hard?"

He tightened his grip on her hair, and this time when she looked up at his face, she didn't see a stranger. She saw Chase. The man. The whole man. Not divided up into parts. Not Her Friend Chase or Her Lover Chase, but just...Chase.

He was all of these things. Fun and laid-back, intense and deeply sexual. She wanted it all. She craved it all. As hard as he could. As much as he could. And still, it would never, ever be enough.

"Go ahead," she said, "take me, cowboy."

She didn't have to ask twice.

He propelled them both backward, pressing her up against the truck, kissing her deeply, a no-holds-barred possession of her mouth. She hadn't even realized kissing like this existed. She wasn't entirely sure what she had thought kissing was for. Affection. A prelude to sex. This was something else entirely. This was a language all its own. Words that didn't exist in English. Words that she knew Chase would never be able to say.

And her body knew that. Understood it. Responded. As surely as it would have if he had spoken.

She was drowning. In this, in him. She hadn't expected emotion to be this…fierce. She hadn't really expected emotion at all. She hadn't understood. She really had not understood.

But then she didn't have the time to think about it. Or the brainpower. He tugged on her hair, drawing her head to the side before he pressed his lips to her tender neck, his teeth scraping along the sensitive skin before he closed his lips around her and sucked hard.

"You want it hard?" he asked, his voice rough. "Then we're going to do it my way."

He grabbed hold of her hips, turning her so that she was facing the truck. "Scoot just a little bit." He guided her down to where the cab of the truck ended and the bed began. "Grab on." She curved her fingers around the cold metal, a shiver running down her spine. "You ever do it like this?" he asked.

She laughed, more because she was nervous than because she thought the question was funny. "Chase, before you I had never even given a guy a blow job. Do you think I've ever done this before?"

"Good," he said, his tone hard, very definitely him. "I like that. I'm a sick bastard. I like the fact that no other man has ever done this to you before. I should feel guilty." He reached around and undid the top button on her top. "But I'm just enjoying corrupting you."

He undid another button, then another. She wasn't wearing a bra underneath the top. Because, frankly, when you were as underendowed as she was, there really wasn't any point. Also, it made things a little bit more easy access. Though that wasn't something she had thought about until just now. Until Chase undid the last button and left her completely bare to the cool night air.

"I'm kind of enjoying being corrupted."

"I didn't tell you you could talk."

She shut her mouth, surprised at the commanding tone he was taking. Not entirely displeased about it. He cupped her breasts, squeezing them gently before moving his hands down her stomach, bringing them around her hips. Then he tugged her skirt down, leaving her in nothing but her boots and her underwear.

"We'll leave the boots on. I wouldn't want you to step on anything sharp."

She didn't say anything. She bit her lip, eagerly anticipating what he might do next. He slipped his hand down between her thighs, his fingertips edging beneath her panties. He stroked his fingers through her folds, a harsh growl escaping his lips. "You're wet for me," he said—not a question.

She nodded, closing her eyes, trying to keep from hurtling over the edge as soon as his fingertips brushed over her. But it was a pretty difficult battle she was waging. Just the thought of being with Chase again was enough to take her to the precipice. His touch nearly pushed her over immediately.

He gripped her tightly with his other hand, drawing her ass back up against his cock as he teased her between her legs with his clever fingers. He slipped one deep inside of her, continuing to toy with her with the edge of his thumb while he thrust in and out of her slowly. He added a second finger, then another. And she was shaking. Trembling with the effort of holding back her climax.

But she didn't want it to end like this. Didn't want it to end so quickly. Mostly, she just didn't want him to know that with one flick of his fingertip over her sensitized flesh he could make her come so hard she wouldn't be able to see straight. Because at the end of the day it didn't matter how much she wanted him; she still had her pride. She still rebelled against the idea of revealing herself quite so easily.

She probably already had. Here she was, mostly naked, out underneath the stars. Here she was, telling him she wanted just the two of them, that she wanted it hard. Probably there were no secrets left. Not really. There were all sorts of unspoken truths filling in the silences between them, but she felt like they were easy enough to read, if he wanted to look at them.

He might not. She didn't really want to. Yet it didn't make them go away.

But she could ignore them. She could focus on this. On his touch. On the dark magic he was working on her body, the spell that was taking her over completely.

He swept her hair to the side, pressing a hot kiss to the back of her neck. And then there was no holding back. Climax washed over her like a wave as she shuddered out her release.

"Good girl," he whispered, kissing her again before moving away for a moment. He pushed her panties down her legs, helping her step out of them, then he kissed her thigh before straightening.

She heard him moving behind her. But she didn't change her position. She stood there, gripping the back of the truck. Dimly, she was aware the radio was still on. That they had a sound track to this illicit encounter in the woods. It added to the surreal, out-of-body quality.

But then he was back with her, touching her, kissing her, and it didn't feel so surreal anymore. It was too raw. Too real. His voice, his scent, his touch. He was there. There was no denying it. This wasn't fantasy. Fantasy was gauzy, distant. This was sharp, so sharp she was afraid it would cut right into her. Dangerous. She wanted it. All of it. And she was afraid that in the end there would be nothing of her left. At least nothing that she recognized. That his friendship wouldn't be something that she recognized. But they'd gone too far to turn back, and she didn't even want to anymore. She wanted to see what was on the other side of this. Needed to see what was on the other side.

He reached up, bracing his hand on the back of her neck, holding her hip with the other as he positioned himself at the entrance to her body. He pressed the blunt head of his erection against her, sliding in easily, thrusting hard up inside her. She gasped as he went deeper than he had before. This was almost overwhelming. But she needed it. Embraced it.

His hold was possessive, all-encompassing. She felt like she was being consumed by him completely. By her desire for him. Warmth bloomed from where he held her, bled down beneath the surface of her skin, hemorrhaged in her chest.

"I fantasized about this," he said, the words seeming to scrape along his throat. Rough, raw. "Holding you like this. Holding on to your hips as I did this to you."

She couldn't respond. She couldn't say anything. His words had grabbed ahold of her, squeezing her throat tight, making it impossible for her to speak. He had fantasized about her. About this.

This position should feel less personal. More distant. But it didn't. That made it… It made it exactly what she had asked for. This was for her. And this was him. What he wanted, not just the next item on a list of things she needed to learn. Not just a set routine that he had with women he slept with.

He slid his hand down along the line of her spine, pressing firmly, the impression of his possession lingering on her skin. Then he held both of her hips tight, his blunt fingertips digging into her skin. He thrust harder into her, his skin slapping against hers, the sound echoing in the darkness. She gripped the truck hard, lowering her head, a moan escaping her lips.

"You wanted hard, baby," he ground out. "I'll give it to you hard."

"Yes," she whispered.

"Who are you saying yes to?" There was an edge to his words, a desperation she hadn't imagined he would feel, not with her. Not over this.

"Chase," she said, closing her eyes tight. "Yes, Chase. Please. I need this. I need you."

She needed all of him. And she suddenly realized why those thoughts about having someone to spend her nights with had seemed wrong. Because at the end of the day when she thought of sharing evenings with someone, when she thought of curling up under a blanket with someone, of watching *Oklahoma!* with someone for the hundredth time, it was Chase. It was always Chase. And that meant no other man had ever been able to get close enough to her. Because he was the fantasy. And as long as he was the fantasy, no one else had a place.

And now, now after this, she was ruined forever. Because she would never be able to do this with another man. Ever. It would always be Chase's hand she imagined on her skin. That firm grip of his that she craved.

He flexed his hips, going harder into her, then slipped his fingers around between her thighs again, stroking her as he continued to fill her. Then he leaned forward, biting her neck as he slammed into her one last time, sending them both over the edge. He growled, pulsing inside of her as he found his release. The pain from his teeth mingled with the all-consuming pleasure rolling through her in never-ending waves, pounding over her so hard she didn't think it would ever end. She didn't think she could survive it.

And when it passed, it was Chase who held her in his arms.

There was no denying it. No escaping it. And she was scraped raw. As stripped as she'd been after their first encounter, she was even more exposed now. Because she had read into all those empty, unspoken things. Because she had finally realized what everything meant.

Her asking him for help. Her kissing him. Her going down on him.

Her not having another man in her life in any capacity.

It was because she wanted Chase. All of Chase. It was why everything had come together for her tonight. Why she'd realized she couldn't compartmentalize him.

She wasn't ready to think the words yet, though. She couldn't. She did her very best to hold them at bay. To stop herself from thinking the things that would crumble her defenses once and for all.

Instead, she released her hold on the truck and turned to face him, looping her arms around his neck, pressing her bare body against his, luxuriating in him.

"That was quite the dance lesson," she said finally.

"A lot more fun than it would have been in Ace's." He slid his hand down to her butt, holding her casually. She loved that. So much more than she should.

"Yeah, we would have gotten thrown out for that."

"But can you imagine the rumors?"

"Are they really rumors if everyone has actually seen you screw?"

"Good question," he said, leaning forward and nipping her lower lip.

"You're bitey," she said.

"And you like to be bitten."

She couldn't deny it. "I guess I should... I mean, I have to work tomorrow."

"Me, too," he said, sounding regretful.

She wanted so badly to ask him to stay with her. But he wasn't bringing it up. And she didn't know if the almighty Chase McCormack actually *slept* with the women he was sleeping with.

So she didn't ask.

And when he dropped her off at her house, leaving her at her doorstep, she tried very, very hard not to regret that.

She didn't succeed.

CHAPTER ELEVEN

THE BEST THING about having her own shop was working alone. Some people might find it lonely; Anna found it a great opportunity to run through every musical number she knew. She had already gone through the entirety of *Oklahoma!* and was working her way through *Seven Brides for Seven Brothers*.

Admittedly, she wasn't the best singer in the world, but in her own shop she was the best singer around.

And if the music helped drown out all of the neuroses that were scampering around inside of her, asking her to deal with her Chase feelings, then so much the better. She didn't want to deal with Chase feelings.

"When you're in love, when you're in love, there is no way on earth to hide it," she sang operatically, the words echoing off the walls.

She snapped her mouth shut. That was a bad song. A very bad song for this moment. She was not... She just wasn't going to think about it.

She turned her focus back to the tractor engine she currently had in a million little pieces. At least an engine was concrete. A puzzle she could solve. It was tactile, and most of the time, if she could just get the right parts, find the source of the problem, she could fix it. That wasn't true with much of anything else in life. That was one reason she found a certain sort of calm in the garage.

Plus, it was something her father knew how to do. He was his own mechanic, and weekends were often spent laboring over his pickup truck, getting it in working order so that he could drive it to work Monday. So she had watched, she had helped. It was about the only way she had been able to connect with her gruff old man. It was still about the only way she could connect with him.

It certainly wasn't through musicals. It could never have been a desire to be seen differently by other kids at school. A need to look prettier for a boy that she liked.

So she had chosen carburetors.

"But it can't be carburetors forever." Well, it could be. In that she imagined she would do this sort of work for the rest of her life. She loved it. She was successful at it. She filled a niche in the community that needed to be filled. But…it couldn't be the only thing she was. She needed to do more than fill. She needed to…be filled.

And right now everything was all kind of turned on its head. Or bent over the back of a pickup truck. Her cheeks heated at the memory.

Yeah, Chase had definitely come by his reputation honestly. It wasn't difficult to see why women lost their ever-loving minds over him.

That made her frown. Because she didn't like to think that she was just one of the many women losing their minds over him because he had a hot ass and skilled hands. She had known about the hot ass for years. It hadn't made her lose her mind. In fact, she didn't really think she had lost her mind now. She knew exactly what she was doing. She frowned even more deeply.

Did she know what she was doing? They had stopped and had discussions, made conscious decisions to do this friends-with-benefits thing. Tricked themselves into thinking that they were in control of this. Or at least that's what she had been doing. But as she had been carried away on a wave of emotion last night, she had known for an absolute fact that she wasn't in control of any of this.

"Doesn't mean I'm going to stop."

That, at least, was the absolute truth. He would have to be the one to call it off.

Just the thought made her heart crumple up into a little ball.

"Quitting time yet?"

She turned to see Chase standing in the doorway. This was a routine she could get used to. She wanted to cross the space between them and kiss him. And why not? She wasn't hiding her attraction to him. They weren't hiding their association.

She dropped her ratchet, wiped her hands on her coveralls and took two quick steps, flinging herself into his arms and kissing him on the lips. She wasn't embarrassed until about midway through the kiss, when she realized she had been completely and totally enthusiastic and hadn't hidden any of it. But he was holding on to her, and he was kissing her back, so maybe it didn't matter. Maybe it was okay.

When they parted, he was smiling.

Her heart felt tender, exposed. But warm, like it was being bathed in sunlight. Something to do with that smile of his. With that easy acceptance of what she had offered. "I think it's about time to quit," she said.

"I like your look," he said, gesturing to her white tank top, completely smeared with grease and dirt, and her coveralls, which were unbuttoned and tied around her waist.

"Really?"

"Last night you were my dirty country girl fantasy and today you're a sexy mechanic fantasy. Do you take requests? Around Christmas you could go for Naughty Mrs. Claus."

She rolled her eyes, grabbing the end of her tank top and knotting it up just under her breasts. "Maybe more like this? Though I think I'm missing the breast implants."

His smile turned wicked. "Baby, you aren't missing a damn thing."

Her heart thundered harder, a rush of adrenaline flowing through her. "I didn't think this was your type. Remember? You had to give me a makeover."

"Yeah, that was stupid. I actually think I just needed to get knocked upside the head."

"Did I…knock you upside the head?"

"Yeah." He wrapped his arms around her bare waist, his fingertips playing over her skin. "You're pretty perfect the way you are. You never needed a dress or high heels. I mean, you're welcome to wear them if you want. I'm not going to complain about that outfit you wore last night. But all that stuff we talked about in the beginning, about you needing to change so that people would believe we were together… I guess everyone is just going to have to believe that I changed a little bit."

"Have you changed?" she asked, brushing her thumb over his lower lip. A little thrill skittered down her spine. That she could touch him like this. Be so close to him. Share this kind of intimacy with a man she had had a certain level of emotional intimacy with for years and years.

It was wonderful. It also made her ache. Made her feel like her insides were being broken apart with a chisel. And she was willingly submitting to it. She didn't know quite what was happening to her.

Are you sure you don't?

"Something did," he said, his dark eyes boring into hers.

"You know," she said, trying to tamp down the fluttering that was happening in her chest, "I think it's only fair that I give you a few lessons."

"What kind of lessons?" he asked, his gaze sharpening.

"I'm not sure you know your way around an engine quite the way you should," she said, smiling as she wiggled out of his hold.

"Oh, really?"

She nodded, grabbing hold of a rag and slinging it over her shoulder before picking up her ratchet again. "Really."

"Is this euphemistic engine talk?"

"Do you think I'm expressing dissatisfaction with the way you work under my hood?"

He chuckled. "You're really getting good at this flirting thing."

"I am. That was good. And dirty."

"I noticed." He moved behind her, sweeping her hair to the side and kissing her neck. "But if you're implying that I didn't do a very good job...I would have to clear my good name."

"I was talking about literal engines, Chase. But if you really want to try to up your game, I'm not going to stop you."

"What's that?" he asked, reaching past her and pointing to one of the parts that were spread out on the worktable in front of her.

"A cylinder head. I'm replacing that and the head

gasket on the engine. And I had to take a lot of things apart to get to it."

"When do you need to have it done?"

"Not until tomorrow."

"So you don't need me to play the part of lovely assistant while you finish up tonight?"

"I would like you to assist me with a few things," she said, planting her hand at the center of his chest and pushing him lightly. The backs of his knees butted up against the chair that was behind him and he sat down, looking up at her, a predatory smile curving his lips.

"Is this going to be a part of my lesson?"

"Yeah," she said, "I thought it might be."

Last night had been incredible. Last night, he had given her something that felt special. Personal. Now she wanted to give him something. To show him what was happening inside of her, because she could hardly bring herself to think it. She wanted… She just wanted. In ways that she hadn't allowed herself to want in a long time. More. Everything.

"What exactly are you going to teach me?"

"Well, I could teach you all the parts of the tractor engine. But we would be here all night. And it would just slow me down. Someday, we can trade. You can give me some welding secrets. Teach me how to pound steel."

"That sounds dirty, too."

"Lucky me," she said, stretching her arms up over her head, her shirt riding up a little higher. She knew what she wanted to do. But she also felt almost petrified. This was…well, this was the opposite of protecting herself. This was putting herself out there. Risking humiliation. Risking doing something wrong while revealing how desperately she wanted to get it right.

But she wanted to give him something. And honestly, there was no bigger gift she could give him than vulnerability. To show him just how much she wanted him.

She swayed her hips to the right, then moved them back toward the left in a slow circle. She watched his face, watched the tension in his jaw increase, the sharpness in his eyes get positively lethal. And that was all the encouragement she needed. She'd seen enough movies with lap dances that she had a vague idea of how this should go. Maybe her idea was the PG-13-rated version, but she could improvise.

He moved his hand over the outline of his erection, squeezing himself through the denim as she continued to move. Maybe it wasn't rhinestones and a miniskirt, but he didn't seem to mind her white tank top and coveralls. He was still watching her with avid interest as she untied the sleeves from around her waist and let the garment drop down around her feet. She kicked it off to the side, revealing her denim cutoff shorts underneath it.

"Come here," he said, his voice hard.

"I'm not taking orders from you. You have to be patient."

"I'm not feeling very patient, honey."

"What's my name?"

"Anna," he ground out. "Anna, I'm not feeling very patient."

"Not enough women have made you wait. You're getting spoiled."

She slid her hand up her midsection, her own fingertips combined with the electric look on Chase's face sending heat skittering along her veins. She let her fingers skim over her breast, gratified when his breath hissed through his teeth.

"Anna…"

"You know me pretty well, don't you? But you didn't know all this." She moved her hand back down, over her stomach, her belly button, sliding her fingers down beneath the waistband of her shorts, stroking herself where she was wet and aching for him. His fingers curled around the edge of the chair, his knuckles white, the cords on his neck standing out, the strength it was taking him to remain seated clear and incredibly compelling.

"Take them off," he said.

"Didn't I just tell you that you're not in charge?"

"Don't play games with me."

"Maybe patience is the lesson you need to learn."

"I damn well don't," he growled.

She turned around, facing away from him, taking a deep breath as she unsnapped her shorts and pushed them down her hips, revealing the other purchase she had made at the store yesterday. A black, lacy thong, quite unlike any other pair of underwear she had ever owned. And she had slipped it on this morning hoping that this would be the end of her day.

"Holy hell," he said.

She knew that she was not the first woman to take her clothes off for him. Much less the first woman to reveal sexy underwear. But that only made his appreciation for hers that much sweeter. She swayed her hips back and forth before dropping down low, and sweeping back up. It felt so cheesy, and at the same time she was pretty proud of herself for pulling it off.

When she turned to face him, his expression was positively feral.

Her shirt was still knotted beneath her breasts, and now she was wearing work boots, a thong and the top.

If Chase thought the outfit was a little bit silly, he certainly didn't show it.

She moved over to the chair, straddling him, leaning in and kissing him on the lips. "I want you," she said.

She had said it before. But this was more. Deeper. This was the truth. Her truth, the truest thing inside of her. She wanted Chase. In every way. Forever. She swallowed hard, grabbing hold of his T-shirt and tugging it up over his head. She licked her lips, looking at his body, at his chest, speckled with just the right amount of dark hair, at his abs, so perfectly defined and tempting.

She reached between them, undoing his belt and jerking it through the loops, before tugging his pants and underwear down low on his hips. He put his hand on her backside, holding her steady as she maneuvered herself so that she was over him, rubbing up against his arousal. "I would never have considered doing something like this before last week. Not with anyone. It's just you," she said, leaning in and kissing his lips lightly. "You do this to me."

He shuddered beneath her, her words having the exact effect she hoped they would. He liked feeling special, too.

He took hold of her hand, drawing it between them, curving her fingers around him. "And you do this to me. You make me so hard, it hurts. I've never wanted a woman like this before. Ever."

She flexed her hips, squeezed him tighter, trapping him between her palm and the apex of her thighs. "Why? Why do you want me like this?"

It was important to know. Essential.

"Because it's you, Anna. There's this idea that having sex with a stranger is supposed to be exciting. Because it's dirty. Because it's wrong. Maybe because it's unknown? But I've done that. And this is… You're right. I know you. Knowing you like this… Your face is so familiar to me, your voice. Knowing what it looks like when I make you come, how you sound when I push you over the edge, baby, there's nothing hotter than that."

His words washed over her, everything she had never known she needed. This full, complete acceptance of who she was. Right here in her garage. The mechanic, the woman. The friend, the lover. He wanted her. And everything that meant.

She didn't even try to keep herself from feeling it now. Didn't try to keep herself from thinking it.

She loved him. So much. Every part of him, with every part of her. Her friend. The only man she really wanted. The only person she could imagine sharing her days and nights and blankets and musicals with.

And that realization didn't even make her want to pull away from him. Didn't make her want to hide. Instead, she wanted to finish this. She wanted to feel connected to him. Now that she was in, she was in all the way. Ready to expose herself completely, scrape herself raw, all for him.

She rose up so that she was on her knees, tugged her panties down her hips and maneuvered herself so that she was able to dispense with them completely before settling over him, grabbing hold of his broad shoulders as she sank down onto his hardened length.

He swore, the harsh word echoing in the empty space. "Anna, I need to get a condom."

She pulled away from him quickly, hovering over him as he lifted his hips, grabbing his wallet and pulling out a condom with shaking hands, taking care of the practicalities quickly. She was trembling, both with the adrenaline rush that accompanied the stupidity of her mistake and with need. With regret because she wished that he was still inside of her even though it wouldn't be responsible at all.

Soon, he was guiding her back onto him, having protected them both. Thankfully, he was a little more with it than she was.

He gripped her tightly, guiding her movements at first, helping her establish a rhythm that worked for them both.

He moved his hands around, brushing his fingertips along the seam of her ass before teasing her right where their bodies were joined. She gasped, grabbing hold of the back of the chair, flexing her hips, chasing her own release as he continued to touch her. To push her higher.

She slid her hands up, cupping his face, holding him steady. She met his gaze, a thrill shooting down her spine. "Anna," he rasped, the words skating over her skin like a caress, touching her everywhere.

Pleasure gripped her, low and tight, sending her over the edge. She held his face as she shuddered out her orgasm and chanted his name, endlessly. Over and over again. And when it was over, he held her to him, kissing her lips, whispering words against her mouth that she could barely understand. She didn't need to. The only words she understood were the ones she most needed to hear.

"Stay with me tonight."

CHAPTER TWELVE

THEY DRESSED AND drove across the property in Chase's truck. His heart was still hammering like crazy, and he had no idea what the hell he was doing. But then, it was Anna. She wasn't some random hookup. He wanted her again, and having her spend the night seemed like the best way to accomplish that.

He ignored the little terror claws that wrapped themselves around his heart and squeezed, and focused instead on the heavy sensation in his gut. In his dick. He wanted her, and dammit, he was going to have her.

The image of her dancing in front of him in the shop…that would haunt him forever. And it was his goal to collect a few more images that would make his life miserable when their physical relationship ended.

That was normal.

He parked the truck, then got out, following Anna mutely up the steps. When they got to the door, Anna paused.

"I don't…have anything with me. No porcupine pajamas."

Some of the tension in his chest eased. "You won't need pajamas in my bed," he said, his voice low, almost unrecognizable even to himself.

Which was fair enough, since this whole damn situation was unrecognizable. Saying this kind of stuff to Anna. Seeing her like this. Wanting her like this.

She was a constant. She was stability. And he felt shaky as hell right now.

"I've never spent the night with anyone," she blurted.

The words hit him hard in the chest. Along with the realization that this was a first for him, too. He knew it, logically. But for some reason it hadn't seemed momentous when he'd issued the invitation. Because it was Anna and sleeping with her had seemed like the most natural thing on earth. He liked talking to her, liked kissing her, liked having sex with her, and he didn't want her to leave. So the obvious choice was to ask her to stay the night.

Now it was hitting him, though. What that usually meant. Why he didn't do it.

But it was too late to take the invitation back, and anyway, he didn't know if he wanted to.

"I haven't, either," he said.

She blinked. "You...haven't? I mean, I had a ten-minute roll in the hay—literally—with a loser in high school, so I know why I've never spent the night with anyone. But you...you do this a lot."

"Are you calling me a slut?"

"Yes," she said, deadpan. "No judgment, but yeah, you're kind of slutty."

"Well, you don't have to spend the night with someone when you're done with them. I guess that's why I haven't. Because I am kind of slutty, and it has nothing to do with liking the person I'm with. Just..."

Oblivion. The easiest, most painless connection on earth with no risk involved whatsoever.

But he wasn't going to say that.

Anna wasn't oblivion. Being with her was like... being inside his own skin, really in it, and feeling it, for the first time since he was sixteen.

Like driving eighty miles per hour on the same winding road that had killed his parents, daring it to come for him, too. He'd felt alive then. Alive and pushing up against the edge of mortality as hard as he could.

Then he'd backed way off the gas. And he'd backed way off ever since.

This was the closest thing to tasting that surge of adrenaline, that rush he'd felt since the day he'd basically begged the road to take him, too.

You're a head case.

Yes, he was. But he'd always known that. Anna hadn't, though.

"Just?" she asked, eyebrows shooting up. She wasn't going to let that go, apparently.

"It's just sex."

"And what is this?" she asked, gesturing between the two of them.

"Friendship," he said honestly. "With some more to it."

"Those benefits."

"Yeah," he said. "Those."

He shoved his hands in his pockets, feeling like he'd just failed at something, and he couldn't quite figure out what. But his words were flat in the evening air. Just sort of dull and resting between them, wrong and weird, but he didn't know what to do about it.

Because he didn't know what else to say, either.

"Want to come inside?" he asked finally.

"That is where your bed is," she said.

"It is."

They made their way to the bedroom, and somehow it all felt different. He could easily remember when she'd been up here just last week, walking in those heels and that dress. When he'd been overwhelmed with the need to touch her, but wouldn't allow himself to do so.

He could also remember being in here with her plenty of times before. Innocuous as sharing the space with any friend.

How? How had they ever existed in silences that weren't loaded? In moments that weren't wrapped in tension. In isolation that didn't present the very tempting possibility of chasing pleasure together. Again and again.

This wasn't friendship plus benefits. That implied the friendship remained untouched and the benefits were an add-on. Easy to stick there, easy to remove. But that wasn't the case.

Everything was different. The air around them had changed. How the hell could he pretend the friendship was the same?

"I'm just—" She smiled sheepishly and pulled her shirt up over her head. "Sorry." Then she unhooked her bra, tossing it onto the floor. He hadn't had a chance to look at her breasts the last time they'd had sex. She'd kept them covered. Something that had added nicely to the tease back in the shop. But he was ready to drop to his knees and give thanks for their perfection now.

"Why are you apologizing for flashing me?"

"Because. In the absence of pajamas I need to get comfortable now." She stripped her shorts off, and her underwear—those shocking black panties that he simply hadn't seen coming, much like the rest of her—and then she flopped down onto his bed. He didn't often bring women back here.

Sometimes, depending on the circumstances, but if they had a hotel room, or their own place available, that was his preference. So it was a pretty unusual sight in general. A naked woman in his room. Anna, in this familiar place—naked and warm and about as inviting as anything had ever been—was enough to make his head explode.

His head, and other places.

"You never have to apologize for being naked." He stripped his shirt off, then continued to follow her lead, until he was wearing nothing.

He lay down beside her, not touching her, just looking at her. This was hella weird. If a woman was naked, he was usually having sex with her, bottom line. He didn't lie next to one, simply looking at her. Right now, Anna was something like art and he just wanted to admire her. Well, that wasn't *all* he wanted. But it was what he wanted right now. To watch the soft lamplight cast a warm glow over her curves, to examine every dip and hollow on the map of her figure. To memorize the rosy color of her nipples, the dark hair at the apex of her thighs. The sweet flare of her hips and the slight roundness of her stomach. She was incredible. She was Anna. Right now, she was his.

That thought made his stomach tighten. How long had it been since something was his?

This place would always be McCormack, through and through. The foundation of the forge and the business…it was built on his great-grandfather's back, carried down by his grandfather, handed to their father.

And he and Sam carried it now.

This ranch would always be something they were bound to by blood, not by choice. Even if given the choice, he could probably never leave. Their family… It didn't feel like their family anymore. It hadn't for a lot of years.

It was two of them, him and Sam. Two of them trying so damn hard to push this legacy back to where it had been. To make their family extend beyond these walls, beyond these borders. To fulfill all of the promises he'd made to his dad, even though the old man had never actually heard them.

Even though Chase had made them too late.

And so there was something about that. Anna, this moment, being for him. Something that he chose, instead of something that he'd inherited.

"I like when you look at me like that," she said, her voice hushed.

"I like when you take control like you did back in the shop. I like seeing you realize how beautiful you are," he said. It was true. He was glad that she knew now. And pissed that she was going to take that knowledge and work her magic on some other man with her new-found power. He wanted to kill that man.

But he could never hope to take his place, so he wouldn't.

"You're the first person who has made me feel like it all fit. And maybe it's because you're my friend. Maybe it's because you know me," she said.

"I don't follow."

"I had to be tough," she said, her tone demonstrating just that. "All my life I've had to be tough. My brothers raised me, and they did a damn good job, and I know you think they're jerks, and honestly a lot of the time they are. But they were young boys who were put in charge of taking care of their kid sister. So they took care of me, but they tortured me in that way only brothers can. Probably because I tortured them in ways that most little sisters could never dream. They didn't go out in high school. They had to make sure I was taken care of. They didn't trust my dad to do it. He wasn't stable enough. He would go out to the bar and get drunk, and he would call needing a ride home. They handled things so that I didn't have to. And I never felt like I could make their lives more difficult by showing how hard it was for me."

She shifted, sighing heavily before she continued. "And then there was my dad. He didn't know what to do with a daughter. As pissed as he was that his wife left, I think in some ways he was relieved, because he didn't have to figure out how to fit a woman into his life anymore. But then I kind of started becoming a woman. And he really didn't know what to do. So I learned how to work on cars. I learned how to talk about sports. I learned how to fit. Even though it pushed me right out of fitting when it came to school. When it came to making friends."

He knew these things about Anna. Knew them because he'd absorbed them by being in her house, being near her, for fifteen years. But he'd never heard her say them. There was something different about that.

"You've always fit with me, Anna," he said, his voice rough.

"I know. And even though we've never talked about this, I'm pretty sure somehow you knew all of it. You always have. Because you know me. And you accept me. Not very many people know about the musicals. Because it always embarrassed me. Kind of a girlie thing."

"I guess so," he said, the words feeling inadequate.

"Also, it was my thing. And…I never like anyone to know how much I care about things. I… My mom loved old musicals," she said, her voice soft. "Sometimes I wonder what it would be like to watch them with her."

"Anna…"

"I remember sneaking out of my room at night, seeing the TV flickering in the living room. She would be watching *The Sound of Music* or *Cinderella. Oklahoma!* of course. And I would just hang there in the hall. But I didn't want to interrupt. Because by the end of the day she was always out of patience, and I knew she didn't want any of the kids to talk to her. But it was kind of like watching them with her." Anna's eyes filled with tears. "But now I just wish I had. I wish I had gone in and sat next to her. I wish I had risked her being upset with me. I never got the chance. She left, and that was it. So, maybe she would've been mad at me, or maybe she wouldn't have let me watch them with her. But at least I would've had the answer. Now I just wonder. I just remember that space between us. Me hiding in the hall, and her sitting on the couch. She never knew I was there. Maybe if I'd done a better job of connecting with her, she wouldn't have left."

"That's not true, Anna."

"She didn't have anyone to watch the movies with, Chase. And my dad was so… I doubt he ever gave her a damn scrap of tenderness. But maybe I could have. I think… I think that's what I was always trying to do with my dad. To make up for that. It was too late to make her stay, but I thought maybe I could hang on to him."

Chase tried to breathe past the tightness in his chest, but it was nearly impossible. "Anna," he said, "any parent that chooses to leave their child…the issue is with them. It was your parents' marriage. It was your mom. I don't know. But it was never you. It wasn't you not watching a movie with her, or irritating her or making her angry. There was never anything you could do."

She nodded, a tear tracking down her pale cheek. "I do know that."

"But you still beat yourself up for it."

"Of course I do."

He didn't have a response to that. She said it so matter-of-factly, as though there was nothing else but to blame herself, even if it made no sense. He had no response because he understood. Because he knew what it was like to twist a tragedy in a thousand different ways to figure out how you could take it on yourself. He knew what it was like to live your life with a gaping hole where someone you loved should be. To try to figure out how you could have stopped the loss from happening.

In the years since his parents' accident he had moved beyond blame. Not because he was stronger than Anna, just because you could only twist death in so many different directions. It was final. And it didn't ask you. It just was. Blaming himself would have been a step too far into martyrdom.

Still, he knew about lingering scars and responses to those scars that didn't make much sense.

But he didn't know what it was like to have a parent choose to leave you. God knew his parents never would have chosen to abandon their sons.

As if she'd read his mind, Anna continued. "She's still out there. I mean, as far as I know. She could have come back. Anytime. I just feel like if I had given her even a small thing…well, then, maybe she would have missed me enough at some point. If she'd had anything back here waiting for her, she could have called. Just once."

"You were you," he said. "If that wasn't enough for her…fuck her."

She laughed and wiped another tear from her face. Then she shifted, moving closer to him. "I appreciate that." She paused for a moment, kissing his shoulder, then she continued. "It's amazing. I've never told you that before. I've never told anyone that before. It's just kind of crazy that we could know each other for so long and…there's still more we don't know."

He wanted to tell her then. About the day his parents died. About the complete and total hole it had torn in his life. She knew to a degree. They had been friends when it happened. He had been sixteen, and Sam had been eighteen, and the loss of everything they knew had hit so hard and fast that it had taken them out at the knees.

He wanted to tell her about his nightmares. Wanted to tell her about the last conversation he'd had with his dad.

But he didn't.

"Amazing" was all he said instead.

Then he leaned over and kissed her, because he couldn't think of anything else to do, couldn't think of anything else to say.

Liar.

A thousand things he wanted to tell her swirled around inside of him. A thousand different things she didn't know. That he had never told anybody. But he didn't want to open himself up like that. He just… He just couldn't.

So instead, he kissed her, because that he could do. Because of all the changes that existed between them, that was the one he was most comfortable with. Holding her, touching her. Everything else was too big, too unknown to unpack. He couldn't do it. Didn't want to do it.

But he wanted to kiss her. Wanted to run his hands over her bare curves. So he did.

He touched her, tasted her, made her scream. Because of all the things that were happening in his life, that felt right.

This was…well, it was a detour. The best one he'd ever taken, but a detour all the same. He was building the family business, like he had promised his dad he would do. Or like he should have promised him when he'd had the chance. He might never have been able to tell the old man to his face, but he'd promised it to his grave. A hundred times, a thousand times since he'd died.

That was what he had to do. That was on the other side of making love with Anna. Going to that benefit with her all dressed up, trying to help her get the kind of reputation she wanted. To send her off with all her new-found skills so that she could be with another man after.

To knuckle down and take the McCormack family ranch back to where it had been. Beyond. To make sure that Sam used his talents, to make sure that the forge and all the work their father had done to build the business didn't go to waste.

To prove that the fight he'd had with his father right before he died was all angry words and teenage bluster. That what he'd said to his old man wasn't real.

He didn't hate the ranch. He didn't hate the business. He didn't hate their name. He was their name, and damn him for being too young and stupid to see it then.

He was proving it now by pouring all of his blood, all of his sweat, all of his tears into it. By taking the little bit of business acumen he had once imagined might get him out of Copper Ridge and applying it to this place. To try to make it something bigger, something better. To honor all the work their parents had invested all those years.

To finish what they'd started.

He might not have ever made a commitment to a woman, but this ranch, McCormack Iron Works…was his life. That was forever.

It was the only forever he would ever have.

He closed those thoughts out, shut them down completely and focused on Anna. On the sweet scent of her as he lowered his head between her thighs and lapped at her, on the feel of her tight channel pulsing around his fingers as he stroked them in and out. And finally, on the tight, wet clasp of her around him as he slid home.

Home. That's really what it was.

In a way that nowhere else had ever been. The ranch was a memorial to people long dead. A monument that he would spend the rest of his life building.

But she was home. She was his.

If he let her, she could become everything.

No.

That denial echoed in his mind, pushed against him as he continued to pound into her, hard, deep, seeking the oblivion that he had always associated with sex before her. But it wasn't there. Instead, it was like a veil had been torn away and he could see all of his life, spreading out before him. Like he was standing on a ridge high in the mountains, able to survey everything. The past, the present, the future. So clear, so sharp it almost didn't seem real.

Anna was in all of it. A part of everything.

And if she was ever taken away…

He closed his eyes, shutting out that thought, a wave of pleasure rolling over him, drowning out everything. He threw himself in. Harder than he ever had. Grateful as hell that Anna had found her own release, because he'd been too wrapped up in himself to consider her first.

Then he wrapped his arms around her, wrapped her up against him. Wrapped himself up in her. And he pushed every thought out of his mind and focused on the feeling of her body against his, the scent of her skin. Feminine and sweet with a faint trace of hay and engine grease.

No other woman smelled like Anna.

He pressed his face against her breasts and she sighed, a sound he didn't think he'd ever get tired of. He let everything go blank. Because there was nothing in his past, or his future, that was as good as this.

CHAPTER THIRTEEN

CHASE WOKE IN a cold sweat, his heart pounding so heavily he thought it would burst through his bone and flesh and straight out into the open. His bed was empty. He sat up, rubbing his hand over his face, then forking his fingers through his hair.

It felt wrong to have the bed empty. After spending only one night wrapped around Anna, it already felt wrong. Not having her... Waking up in the morning to find that she wasn't there was... He hated it. It was unsettling. It reminded him of the holes that people left behind, of how devastating it was when you lost someone unexpectedly.

He banished the thought. She might still be here. But then, she didn't have any clean clothes or anything, so if she had gone home, he couldn't necessarily blame her. He went straight into the bathroom, took a shower, took care of all other morning practicalities. He resisted the urge to look at his phone, to call Anna's phone or to go downstairs and see if maybe she was still around. He was going to get through all this, dammit, and he was not going to behave as though he were affected.

As though the past night had changed something fundamental, not just between them, but in him.

He scowled, throwing open the bedroom door and heading down the stairs.

He stopped dead when he saw her standing there in

the kitchen. She was wearing his T-shirt, her long, slim legs bare. And he wondered if she was bare all the way up. His mouth dried, his heart squeezing tight.

She wasn't missing. She wasn't gone. She was cooking him breakfast. Like she belonged here. Like she belonged in his life. In his house. In his bed.

For one second it made him feel like he belonged. Like she'd been the missing piece to making this his, to making it more than McCormack.

He felt like he was standing in the middle of a dream. Standing there looking at somebody else's life. At some wild, potential scenario that in reality he would never get to have.

Right in front of him was everything. And in the same moment he saw that, he imagined the hole that would be left behind if it was ever taken away. If he ever believed in this, fully, completely. If he reached out and embraced her now, there would be no words for how empty his arms would feel if he ever lost her.

"Don't you have work?" he asked, leaning against the doorjamb.

She turned around and smiled, the kind of smile that lit him up inside, from his head, down his toes. He did his very best not to return the gesture. Did his best not to encourage it in any way.

And he cursed himself when the glow leached out of her face. "Good morning to you, too," she said.

"You didn't need to make breakfast."

"*Au contraire.* I was hungry. So breakfast was needed."

"You could've gone home."

"Yes, Grumpy-Pants, I could have. But I decided to stay here and make you food. Which seemed like an adequate thank-you for the multiple orgasms I received yesterday."

"Bacon? You're trying to pay for your orgasms with bacon?"

"It seemed like a good idea at the time." She crossed her arms beneath her breasts and revealed that she did not, in fact, have anything on beneath the shirt. "Bacon is a borderline orgasmic experience."

"I have work. I don't have time to eat breakfast."

"Maybe if you had gotten up at a decent hour."

"I don't need you to lecture me on my sleeping habits," he bit out. "Is there coffee?"

"It's like you don't know me at all." She crossed the room and lifted a thermos off the counter. "I didn't want to leave it sitting on the burner. That makes it taste gross."

"I don't really care how it tastes. That's not the point."

She rested her hand on the counter, then rapped her knuckles against the surface. "What's going on?"

"Nothing."

"Stop it, Chase. Maybe you can BS the other bimbos that you sleep with, but you can't do it to me. I know you too well. This has nothing to do with waking up late."

"This is a bad idea," he said.

"What's a bad idea? Eating bacon and drinking coffee with one of your oldest friends?"

"Sleeping with one of my oldest friends. It was stupid. We never should've done it."

She just stood there, her expression growing waxen, and as the color drained from her face, he felt something even more critical being scraped from his chest, like he was being hollowed out.

"It's a little late for that," she pointed out.

"Well, it isn't too late to start over."

"Chase…"

"It was fun. But, honestly, we accomplished everything we needed to. There's no reason to get dramatic about it. We agreed that we weren't going to let it affect our friendship. And it…it just isn't working for me."

"It was working fine for you last night."

"Well, that was last night, Anna. Don't be so needy."

She drew back as though she had been slapped and he wanted to punch his own face for saying such a thing. For hitting her where he knew it would hurt. And he waited. Waited for her to grow prickly. For her to retreat behind the walls. For her to get angry and start insulting him. For her to end all of this in fire and brimstone as she scorched the earth in an attempt to disguise the naked pain that was radiating from her right now.

He knew she would. Because that was how it went. If he pushed far enough, then she would retreat.

She closed the distance between them, cupping his face, meeting his eyes directly. And he waited for the blow. "But I feel needy. So what am I going to do about that?"

He couldn't have been more shocked than if she had reached up and slapped him. "What?"

"I'm needy. Or maybe…wanty? I'm both." She took a deep breath. "Yes, I'm both. I want more. Not less. And this is… This is the moment where we make decisions, right? Well, I've decided that I want to move forward with this. I don't want to go back. I can't go back."

"Anna," he said, her name scraping his throat raw.

"Chase," she said, her own voice a whisper in response.

"We can't do this," he said.

He needed the Anna he knew to come to his rescue now. To laugh it all off. To break this tension. To say that it didn't matter. To wave her hand and say it was all whatever and they could forget it. But she wasn't doing that. She was looking at him, her green eyes completely earnest, vulnerability radiating from her face. "We need to do this. Because I love you."

ANNA COULD TELL that her words had completely stunned Chase. Fair enough, they had shocked her just as much. She didn't know where all of this was coming from. This strength. This bravery.

Except that last night's conversation kept echoing in her mind. When she had told him about her mother. When she had told him about how she always regretted not closing the distance between them. Always regretted not taking the chance.

That was the story of her entire life. She had, from the time she was a child, refused to make herself vulnerable. Refused to open herself up to injury. To pain. So she pretended she didn't care. She pretended nothing mattered. She did that every time her father ignored her, every time he forgot an important milestone in her life. She had done it the first time she'd ever had sex with a guy and it had made her feel something. Rather than copping to that, rather than dealing with it, she had mocked him.

All of her inner workings were a series of walls and shields, carefully designed to keep the world from hitting the terrible, needy things inside of her. Designed to keep herself from realizing they were there. But she couldn't do it anymore. She didn't want to do it anymore. Not with Chase. She didn't want to look back and wonder what could have been.

She wanted more. She needed more. Pride be damned.

"I do," she said, nodding. "I love you."

"You can't."

"I'm pretty sure I can. Since I do."

"No," he said, the word almost desperate.

"No, Chase, I really do. I mean, I have loved you since I was fifteen years old. And intermittently thought you were hot. But mostly, I just loved you. You've been my friend, my best friend. I needed you. You've been my emotional support for a long time. We do that for each other. But things changed in the past few days. You're my…everything." Her voice broke on that last word. "This isn't sex and friendship, it isn't two different things, this is all the things, combined together to make something so big that it fills me completely. And I don't have room inside my chest for shields and protection anymore. Not when all that I am just loves you."

"I can't do this," he bit out, stepping away from her.

"I didn't ask if you could do this. This isn't about you, not right now. Yes, I would like you to love me, too, but right now this is just about me saying that I love you. Telling you. Because I don't ever want to look back and think that maybe you didn't know. That maybe if I had said something, it could have been different." She swallowed hard, battling tears. "I don't know what's wrong with me. Unless it's a movie, I almost never cry, but you're making me cry a lot lately."

"I'm only going to make you cry more," he said. "Because I don't know how to do this. I don't know how to love somebody."

"Bull. You've loved me perfectly, just the way I needed you to for fifteen years. The way that you take care of this place, the way that you care for Sam… Don't tell me that you can't love."

"Not this kind. Not this… Not this."

"I'm closing the gap," she said, pressing on, even though she could see that this was a losing battle. She was charging in anyway, sword held high, chest exposed. She was giving it her all, fighting even though she knew she wasn't going to walk away unscathed. "I'm not going to wonder what would've happened if I'd just been brave enough to do it. I would rather cut myself open and bleed out. I would rather risk my heart than wonder. So I'm just going to say it. Stop being such a coward and love me."

He took another step back from her and she felt that gap she was so desperate to close widening. Watched as her greatest fear started to play out right before her eyes. "I just... I don't."

"You don't or you won't?"

"At the end of the day, the distinction doesn't really matter. The result is the same."

She felt like she was having an out-of-body experience. Like she was floating up above, watching herself get rejected. There was nothing she could do. She couldn't stop it. Couldn't change it. Couldn't shield herself.

It was...horrible. Gut-wrenching. Destructive. Freeing.

Like watching a tsunami racing to shore and deciding to surrender to the wave rather than fight it. Yeah, it would hurt like hell. But it was a strange, quiet space. Past fear, past hope. All she could hear was the sound of her heart beating.

"I'm going to go," she said, turning away from him. "You can have the bacon."

She had been willing to risk herself, but she wouldn't stand there and fall apart in front of him. She would fall apart, but dammit, it would be on her own time.

"Stay and eat," he said.

She shook her head. "No. I can't stay."

"Are we going to… Are we going to go to the gala together still?"

"No!" She nearly shouted the word. "We are not going to go together. I need to… I need to think. I need to figure this out. But I don't think things can be the same anymore."

It was his turn to close the distance between them. He grabbed hold of her arms, drawing her toward him, his expression fierce. "That was not part of the deal. It was friends plus benefits, remember? And then in the end we could just stop with the benefits and go back to the friendship."

"We can't," she said, tears falling down her cheeks. "I'm sorry. But we can't."

"What the hell?" he ground out.

"We can't because I'm all in. I'm not going to sit back and pretend that it didn't really matter. I'm not going to go and hide these feelings. I'm not going to shrug and say it doesn't really matter if you love me or not. Because it does. It's everything. I have spent so many years not wanting. Not trying. Hiding how much I wanted to be accepted, hiding how desperately I wanted to try to look beautiful, how badly I wanted to be able to be both a mechanic and a woman. Hiding how afraid I was of ending up alone. Hiding under a blanket and watching old movies. Well, I'm done. I'm not hiding any of it anymore. And you know what? Nothing's going to hurt after this." She jerked out of his hold and started to walk toward the front door.

"You're not leaving in that."

She'd forgotten she wasn't exactly dressed. "Sure I am. I'm just going to drive straight home. Anyway, it's not your concern. Because I'm not your concern anymore."

The terror that she felt screaming through her chest was reflected on his face. Good. He should be afraid. This was the most terrifying experience of her life. She knew how horrible it was to lose a person you cared for. Knew what kind of void that left. And she knew that after years it didn't heal. She knew, too, you always felt the absence. She knew that she would always feel his. But she needed more. And she wasn't afraid to put it all on the line. Not now. Not after everything they had been through. Not after everything she had learned about herself. Chase was the one who had told her she needed more confidence.

Well, she had found it. But there was a cost.

Or maybe this was just the cost of loving. Of caring, deeply and with everything she had, for the first time in so many years.

She strode across the property, not caring that she was wearing nothing more than his T-shirt, rage pouring through her. And when she arrived back at the shop she grabbed her purse and her keys, making her way to the truck. When she got there, Chase was standing against the driver's-side door. "Don't leave like this."

"Do you love me yet?"

He looked stricken. "What do you want me to say?"

"You know what I want you to say."

"You want me to lie?"

She felt like he had taken a knife and stabbed her directly through the heart. She could barely breathe. Could barely stand straight. This was… This was her worst fear come true. To open herself up so completely, to make herself so entirely vulnerable and to have it all thrown back in her face.

But in that moment, she recognized that she was untouchable from here on out. Because there was nothing that could ever, ever come close to this pain. Nothing that could ever come close to this risk.

How had she missed this before? How had she missed that failure could be such a beautiful, terrible, freeing experience?

It was the worst. Absolutely the worst. But it also broke chains that had been binding her for years. Because if someone had asked her what she was so afraid of, this would have been the answer. And she was in it. Living it. Surviving it.

"I love you," she repeated. "This is your chance. Listen to me, Chase McCormack, I am giving you a chance. I'm giving you a chance to stop being so afraid. A chance to walk out of the darkness. We've walked through it together for a long time. So I'm asking you now to walk out of it with me. Please."

He backed away from the truck, his jaw tense, a muscle there twitching.

"Coward," she spat as he turned and walked away from her. Walked away from them. Walked back into the damned darkness.

And she got in her truck and started the engine, driving away from him, driving away from the things she wanted most in the entire world.

She didn't cry until she got home. But then, once she did, she was afraid she wouldn't stop.

CHAPTER FOURTEEN

SHE WAS GOING to lose the bet. That was the safest
thought in Anna's head as she stood in her bedroom
the night of the charity event staring at the dress that
was laid across her bed.

She was going to have to go there by herself. And
thanks to the elaborate community theater production
of their relationship everyone would know that they
had broken up, since Chase wouldn't be with her. She
almost laughed.

She was facing her fears all over the place, whether
she wanted to or not.

Facing fears and making choices.

She wasn't going to be with Chase at the gala tonight.
Wasn't going to win her money. But she had bought an
incredibly slinky dress, and some more makeup. Including red lipstick. She had done all of that for him.
Though in many ways it was for her, too. She had
wanted that experience. To go, to prove that she was
grown-up. To prove that she had transcended her up-
bringing and all of that.

She frowned. Was she really considering dressing
differently just because she wasn't going to be with
Chase?

Screw that. He might have filleted her heart and
cooked it like those hideous charred Brussels sprouts
cafés tries to pass off as a fancy appetizer, but he *wasn't*

going to take his lessons from her. She had learned confidence. She had learned that she was stronger than she thought. She had learned that she was beautiful. And how to care. Like everything inside her had been opened up, for better or for worse. But she would never go back. No matter how bad it hurt, she wouldn't go back.

So she wouldn't go back now, either.

As she slipped the black dress over her curves, laboring over the makeup on her face and experimenting with the hairstyle she had seen online, she could only think how much harder it was to care about things. All of these things. It had been so much easier to embrace little pieces of herself. To play the part of another son for her father and throw herself into activities that made him proud, ignoring her femininity so that she never made him uncomfortable.

All of these moments of effort came at a cost. Each minute invested revealing more and more of her needs. To be seen. To be approved of.

But there were so many other reasons she had avoided this. Because this—she couldn't help but think as she looked in the mirror—looked a lot like trying. It looked a lot like caring. That was scary. It was hard.

Being rejected when you had given your best effort was so much worse than being rejected when you hadn't tried at all.

This whole being-a-woman thing—a whole woman who wanted to be with a man, who loved a man—it was hard. And it hurt.

She looked at her reflection, her eyes widening. Thanks to the smoky eye shadow her green eyes glowed, her lips looking extra pouty with the dark red color on them. She looked like one of the old screen legends she loved so much. Very Elizabeth Taylor, really.

This was her best effort. And yes, it was only a dress, and this was just looks, but it was symbolic.

She was going to lay it all on the line, and maybe people would laugh. Because the tractor mechanic in a ball gown was too ridiculous for words. But she would take the risk. And she would take it alone.

She picked up the little clutch purse that was sitting on her table. The kind of purse she'd always thought was impractical, because who wanted a bag you had to hold in your hand all night? But the salesperson at the department store had told her it went with her dress, and that altogether she looked flawless, and Anna had been in desperate need of flattery. So here she was with a clutch.

It *was* impractical. But she *did* look great.

Of course, Chase wouldn't be there to see it. She felt her eyes starting to fill with tears and she blinked, doing her best to hold it all back. She was not going to smear her makeup. She had already put it all out there for him. She would be damned if she undid all this hard work for him, too.

With that in mind, Anna got into her truck and drove herself to the ball.

"HEY, JACKASS," SAM shouted from across the shop. "Are you going to finish with work anytime today?"

Okay, so maybe Chase had thrown himself into work with a little more vehemence than was strictly necessary since Anna had walked out of his life.

Anna. Anna had walked out of his life. Over something as stupid as love.

If love was so stupid, it wouldn't make your insides tremble like you were staring down a black bear.

He ignored his snarky internal monologue. He had been doing a lot of that lately. So many arguments with himself as he pounded iron at the forge. That was, when he wasn't arguing with Sam. Who was getting a little bit tired of him, all things considered.

"Do I look like I'm finished?" he shouted back.

"It's nine o'clock at night."

"That's amazing. When did you learn to tell time?"

"I counted on my fingers," Sam said, wandering deeper into the room. "So, are we just going to pretend that Anna didn't run out of your house wearing only a T-shirt the other morning?"

"I'm going to pretend that my older brother doesn't Peeping Tom everything that happens in my house."

"We live on the same property. It's bound to happen. I was on my way here when I saw her leaving. And you chasing after her. So I'm assuming you did the stupid thing."

"I told her that I couldn't be in a relationship with her." That was a lie. He had done so much more than that. He had torn both of their hearts out and stomped them into the ground. Because Sam was right, he was an idiot. But he had made a concerted effort to be a safe idiot.

How's that working for you?

"Right. Why exactly?"

"Look, the sage hermit thing is a little bit tired. You don't have a social life, I don't see you with a wife and children, so maybe you don't hang out and lecture me."

"Isn't tonight that thing?" Sam seemed undeterred by Chase's rudeness.

"What thing?"

"The charity thing that you were so intent on using to get investors. Because the two of us growing our family business and restoring the former glory of our hallowed ancestors is so important to you. And exploiting my artistic ability for your financial gain."

"Change of plans." He grunted, moving a big slab of iron that would eventually be a gate to the side. "I'm just going to keep working. We'll figure this out without schmoozing."

"Who are you and what have you done with my brother?"

"Just shut up. If you can't do anything other than stand there looking vaguely amused at the fact that I'm going through a personal crisis, then you can go straight to hell without passing Go or collecting two hundred dollars."

"I'm not going to be able to afford Park Place anyway, because you aren't out there getting new investors."

"I'm serious, Sam," Chase shouted, throwing his hammer down on the ground. "It's all fine for you because you hold everyone at a distance."

Sam laughed. The bastard. "*I* hold everyone at a distance. What do you think you do? What do you think your endless string of one-night stands is?"

"You think I don't know? You think I don't know that it's an easy way to get some without ever having to have a conversation? I'm well aware. But I don't need you standing over there so entertained by the fact that…"

"That you actually got your heart broken?"

Chase didn't have anything to say to that. Every single word in his head evaporated like water against molten metal. He had nothing to say to that because his heart was broken. But Anna wasn't responsible. It was his own fault.

And the only reason his heart was broken was because he...

"Do you know what I said to Dad the day that he died?"

Sam froze. "No."

No, he didn't. Because they had never talked about it. "The last thing I ever said to him was that I couldn't wait to get away from here. I told him I wasn't going to pound iron for the rest of my life. I was going to get away and go to college. Make something real out of myself. Like this wasn't real."

"I didn't realize."

"No. Because I didn't tell you. Because I never told anybody. But that's why I needed to fix this. It's why I wanted to expand this place."

"So it isn't really to harness my incredible talent?"

"I don't even know what it's for anymore. To what? To make up for what I said to a dead man. And for promises that I made at his grave... He can't hear me. That's the worst thing."

Sam stuffed his hands in his pockets. "Is that the only reason you're still here?"

"No. I love it here. I really do. I had to get older. I had to put some of my own sweat into this place. But now...I get it. I do. And I care about it because I care about it, not just because they cared about it. Not just because it's a legacy, but because it's worth saving. But..."

"I still remember that day. I mean, I don't just remember it," Sam said, "it's like it just happened yesterday. That feeling... The whole world changing. Everything falling right down around us. That's as strong in my head now as it was then."

"How many times can you lose everything?" Chase asked, making eye contact with his brother. "Anna is everything. Or she could be. It was easy when she was just a friend. But…I saw her in my house the other morning cooking me breakfast, wearing my T-shirt. For a second she made me feel like…like that house was our house, and she could be my…my everything."

"I wouldn't even know what that looked like for me, Chase. If you find that…grab it."

"And if I lose it?"

"You'll have no one to blame but yourself."

Chase thought back to the day his parents died. That was a kind of pain he hadn't even known existed. But, as guilty as he had felt, as many promises as he had made at his father's grave site, he couldn't blame himself for their death. It had been an accident. That was the simple truth.

But if he lost Anna now… Pushing her away hadn't been an accident. It was in his control. Fully and absolutely. And if he lost her, then it was on him.

He thought of her face as she had turned away from him, as she had gotten into her truck.

She had trusted him. His prickly Anna had trusted him with her feelings. Her vulnerability. A gift that he had never known her to give to anybody. And he had rejected it. He was no better than he had been as an angry sixteen-year-old, hurtling around the curves of the road that had destroyed his family, daring it to take him, too.

Anna, who had already endured the rejection of a mother, the silent rejection of who she was from her father, had dared to look him in the face and risk his rejection, too.

"I'll do it," Sam said, his voice rough.

"What?"

"I'm going to start...pursuing the art thing to a greater degree. I want to help. You missed this party tonight and I know it mattered to you..."

"But you hate change," Chase reminded him.

"Yeah," Sam said. "But I hate a lot of things. I have to do them anyway."

"We're still going to have to meet with investors."

"Yeah," Sam replied, stuffing his hands in his pockets. "I can help with that. You're right. This is why you're the brains and I'm the talent."

"You're a glorified blacksmith, Sam," Chase said, trying to keep the tone light because if he went too deep now he might just fall apart.

"With talent. Beyond measure," Sam said. "At least my brother has been telling me that for years."

"Your brother is smart." Though he currently felt anything but.

Sam shrugged. "Eh. Sometimes." He cleared his throat. "You discovered you cared about this place too late to ever let Dad know. That's sad. But at least Dad knew you cared about him. You know he never doubted that," Sam said. "But, damn, bro, don't leave it too late to let Anna know you care about her."

Chase looked at his brother, who was usually more cynical than he was wise, and couldn't ignore the truth ringing in his words.

Anna was the best he'd ever had. And had been for the past fifteen years of his life. Losing her...well, that was just a stupid thing to allow.

But the thing that scared him most right now was that it might already be too late. That he might have broken things beyond repair.

"And if it is too late?" he asked.

"Chase, you of all people know that when something

is forged in fire it comes out the other side that much stronger." His brother's expression was hard, his dark eyes dead serious. "This is your fire. You're in it now. If you let it cool, you lose your chance. So I suggest you get your ass to wherever Anna is right now and you work at fixing this. It's either that or spend your life as a cold, useless hunk of metal that never became a damn thing."

IT HAD NOT gone as badly as she'd feared. It hadn't gone perfectly, of course, but she had survived. The lowest point had been when Wendy Maxwell, who was still angry with Anna over the whole Chase thing, had wandered over to her and made disparaging comments about last season's colors and cuts, all the while implying that Anna's dress was somehow below the height of fashion. Which, whatever. She had gotten the dress on clearance, so it probably was. Anna might care about looking nice, but she didn't give a rat's ass about fashion.

She gave a couple of rat's asses about what had happened next.

Where's Chase?

Her newfound commitment to honesty and emotions had compelled her to answer honestly.

We broke up. I'm pretty upset about it.

The other woman had been in no way sympathetic and had in fact proceeded to smug all over the rest of the conversation. But she wasn't going to focus on the low.

The highs had included talking to several people whom she was going to be working with in the future. And getting two different phone numbers. She had made conversation. She had felt…like she belonged. And she didn't really think it had anything to do with the dress. Just with her. When you had already put everything out there and had it rejected, what was there to fear beyond that?

She sighed as she pulled into her driveway, straightening when she saw that there was a truck already there.

Chase's truck.

She put her own into Park, killing the engine and getting out. "What are you doing here, McCormack?" She was furious now. She was all dressed up, wearing her gorgeous dress, and she had just weathered that party on her own, and now he was here. She was going to punch his face.

Chase was sitting on her porch, wearing well-worn jeans and a tight black T-shirt, his cowboy hat firmly in place. He stood up, and as he began to walk toward her, Anna felt a raindrop fall from the sky. Because of course. He was here to kick her while she was down, almost certainly, and it was going to rain.

Thanks, Oregon.

"I came to see you." He stopped, looking her over, his jaw slightly slack. "I'm really glad that I did."

"Stop checking me out. You don't get to look at me like that. I did not put this dress on for you."

"I know."

"No, you don't know. I put this dress on for me. Because I wanted to look beautiful. Because I didn't care if anybody thought I was pretty enough, or if I'm not fashionable enough for Wendy the mule-faced ex-cheerleader. I did it because I cared. I do that now. I care. For me. Not for you."

She started to storm past him, the raindrops beginning to fall harder, thicker. He grabbed her arm and stopped her, twirling her toward him. "Don't walk away. Please."

"Give me a reason to stop walking."

"I've been doing a lot of thinking. And hammering."

"Real hammering, or is this some kind of a euphemism to let me know you're lonely?"

"Actual hammering. I didn't feel like I deserved anything else. Not after what happened."

"You don't. You don't deserve to masturbate ever again."

"Anna…"

"No," she said. "I can't do this. I can't just have a little taste of you. Not when I know what we can have. We can be everything. At first it was like you were my friend, but also we were sleeping together. And I looked at you as two different men. Chase, my friend. And Chase, the guy who was really good with his hands. And his mouth, and his tongue. You get the idea." She swallowed hard, her throat getting tight. "But at some point…it all blended together. And I can't separate it anymore. I just can't. I can't pull the love that I feel for you out of my chest and keep the friendship. Because they're all wrapped up in each other. And they've become the same thing."

"It's all or nothing," he said, his voice rough.

"Exactly."

He sighed heavily. "That's what I was afraid of."

"I'm sorry if you came over for a musical and a look at my porcupine pajamas. But I can't do it."

He tightened his hold on her, pulling her closer. "I knew it was going to be all or nothing."

"I can even understand why you think that might not be fair—"

"No. When you told me you loved me, I knew it was everything. Or nothing. That was what scared me so much. I have known… For a lot of years, I've realized that you were one of the main supports of my entire life. I knew you were one of the things that kept me together after my parents died. One of the only things. And I knew that if I ever lost you…it might finish me off completely."

"I'm sorry. But I can't live my life as your support."

"I know. I'm not suggesting that you do. It's just… when we started sleeping together, I had the same realization. That we weren't going to be able to separate the physical from the emotional, from our friendship. That it wasn't as simple as we pretended it could be. When I came downstairs and saw you in my kitchen…I saw the potential for something I never thought I could have."

"Why didn't you think you could have that?"

"I was too afraid. Tragedy happens to other people, Anna. Until it happens to you. And then it's like… the safety net is just gone. And everything you never thought you could be touched by is suddenly around every corner. You realize you aren't special. You aren't safe. If I could lose both my parents like that…I could lose anybody."

"You can't live that way," she said, her heart crumpling. "How in the world can you live that way?"

"You live halfway," he said. "You let yourself have a little bit of things, and not all of them. You pour your commitment into a place. Your passion into a job, into a goal of restoring a family name when your family is already gone. So you can't disappoint them even if you do fail." He took a deep breath. "You keep the best woman you know as a friend, because if she ever became more, your feelings for her could consume you. Anna… If I lost you…I would lose everything."

She could only stand there, looking at him, feeling

like the earth was breaking to pieces beneath her feet. "Why did you—"

"I wanted to at least see it coming." He lowered his head, shaking it slowly. "I was such an idiot. For a long time. And afraid. I think it's impossible to go through tragedy like I did, like we did, and not have it change you. I'm not sure it's even possible to escape it doing so much as defining you. But you can choose how. It was so easy for me to see how you protected yourself. How you shielded yourself. But I didn't see that I was doing the same thing."

"I didn't know," she said, feeling stupid. Feeling blind.

"Because I didn't tell you." He reached up, drawing his thumb over her cheekbone, his expression so empty, so sad. Another side of Chase she hadn't seen very often. But it was there. It had always been there, she realized that now. "But I'm telling you now. I'm scared. I've been scared for a long time. And I've made a lot of promises to ghosts to try to atone for stupid things I said when my parents were alive. But I've been too afraid to make promises to the people that are actually still in my life. Too afraid to love the people that are still here. It's easier to make promises to ghosts, Anna. I'm done with that.

"You are here," he said, cupping her face now, holding her steady. "You're with me. And I can have you as long as I'm not too big an idiot. As long as you still want to have me. You put yourself out there for me, and I rejected you. I'm so sorry. I know what that cost you, Anna, because I know you. And please understand I didn't reject you because it wasn't enough. Because you weren't enough. It's because you were too much, and I wasn't enough. But I'm going to do my best to be enough for you now. Now and forever."

She could hardly believe what she was hearing, could hardly believe that Chase was standing there making declarations to her. The kind that sounded an awful lot like love. The kind that sounded an awful lot like exactly what she wanted to hear. "Is this because I'm wearing a dress?"

"No." He chuckled. "You could be wearing coveralls. You could be wearing nothing. Actually, I think I like you best in nothing. But whatever you're wearing, it wouldn't change this. It wouldn't change how I feel. Because I love you in every possible way. As my friend, as my lover. I love you in whatever you wear, a ball gown or engine grease. I love you working on tractors and trying to explain to me how an engine works and watching musicals."

"But do you love my porcupine pajamas?" she asked, her voice breaking.

"I'm pretty ambivalent about your porcupine pajamas, I'm not going to lie. But if they're a nonnegotiable part of the deal, then I can adjust."

She shook her head. "They aren't nonnegotiable. But I probably will irritate you with them." Then she sobbed, unable to hold her emotions back any longer. She wrapped her arms around his neck, burying her face in his skin, breathing his scent in. "Chase, I love you so much. Look what we were protecting ourselves from."

He laughed. "When you put it that way, it seems like we were being pretty stupid."

"Fear is stupid. And it's strong."

He tightened his hold on her. "It isn't stronger than this."

Not stronger than fifteen years of friendship, than holding each other through grief and pleasure, laughter and pain.

When she had pulled up and seen his truck here, Anna Brown had murder on her mind. And now, everything was different.

"Remember when you promised you were going to make me a woman?" she asked.

"Right. I do. You laughed at me."

"Yes, I did." She stretched up on her toes and kissed his lips. "Chase McCormack, I'm pretty sure you did make me a woman. Maybe not in the way you meant. But you made me feel...like a whole person. Like I could finally put together all the parts of me and just be me. Not hide any of it anymore."

He closed his eyes, pressing his forehead against hers. "I'm glad, Anna. Because you sure as hell made me a man. The man that I want to be, the man that I need to be. I can't change the past, and I can't live in it anymore, either."

"Good. Then I think we should go ahead and make ourselves a future."

"Works for me." He smiled. "I love you. You're everything."

"I love you, too." It felt so good to say that. To say it and not be afraid. To show her whole heart and not hold anything back.

"I bet that I can make you say you love me at least a hundred more times tonight. I bet I can get you to say it every day for the rest of our lives."

She smiled, taking his hand and walking toward the house, not caring about the rain. "I bet you can."

He led her inside, leaving a trail of clothes in the hall

behind them, leaving her beautiful dress on the floor. She didn't care at all.

"And I bet—" he wrapped his arm around her waist, then laid her down on the bed "—tonight I can make you scream."

"I'll take that bet," she said, wrapping her legs around his hips.

And that was a bet they both won.

* * * * *

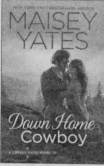
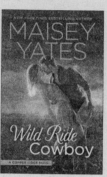

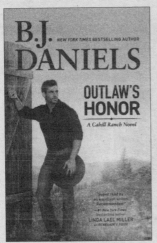

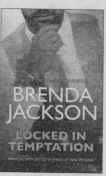

Get 2 Free Books,
Plus 2 Free Gifts –

just for trying the Reader Service!